# THAT NIGHT ON THISTLE LANE

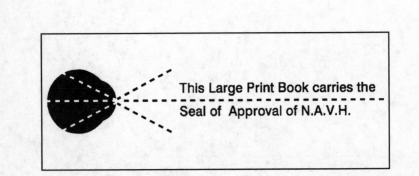

This Large Print Book carries the
Seal of Approval of N.A.V.H.

# THAT NIGHT ON THISTLE LANE

## CARLA NEGGERS

**THORNDIKE PRESS**
*A part of Gale, Cengage Learning*

GALE
CENGAGE Learning·

Detroit • New York • San Francisco • New Haven, Conn • Waterville, Maine • London

02/13

Copyright © 2013 by Carla Neggers.
Thorndike Press, a part of Gale, Cengage Learning.

Thorndike Press® Large Print Basic.
The text of this Large Print edition is unabridged.
Other aspects of the book may vary from the original edition.
Set in 16 pt. Plantin.

**LIBRARY OF CONGRESS CIP DATA ON FILE.
CATALOGUING IN PUBLICATION DATA FOR THIS BOOK
IS AVAILABLE FROM THE LIBRARY OF CONGRESS**

ISBN-13: 978-1-4104-5541-3 (hardcover)
ISBN-10: 1-4104-5541-6 (hardcover)

Published in 2013 by arrangement with Harlequin Books S.A.

Printed in the United States of America
1 2 3 4 5 6 7 17 16 15 14 13

To my three sisters, Bonnie,
Hilda and Gretchen —
nothing like jumping into a cold brook
on a hot summer day!

# ONE

Bumblebees hummed in the frothy catmint on the edge of the stone terrace, the only sound to disturb the hot New England summer afternoon. Phoebe O'Dunn watched a solo bee hover above a purple blossom, as if debating what to do, then dart past the green-painted bench where she was seated and disappear across the herb and flower gardens. None of its fellow bumblebees followed.

Phoebe had met on the terrace with her sister Maggie and her friend Olivia Frost to discuss the upcoming vintage fashion show at their small-town library, but inevitably talk had turned to the charity masquerade ball tomorrow night in Boston, two hours away. Maggie and Olivia were going. Phoebe wasn't, but she just might be able to help with costumes.

*The dresses would be perfect.*

If she'd had any doubts, they'd been

dispelled when Maggie and Olivia sank into their chairs at the round, natural-wood table across the terrace and said they were stumped. With just twenty-four hours before they had to leave Knights Bridge for Boston, they had no idea what to wear.

Phoebe did. She'd already had the dresses cleaned and now they were hanging in the back room at her little house on Thistle Lane, just off the Knights Bridge common. She hadn't mentioned them yet because — well, she didn't know why, except that she couldn't help feeling as if she were handling someone else's secrets. She'd discovered the dresses two weeks ago in a mysterious hidden room in the library attic. So far she hadn't told anyone about them or the room.

"We should have figured this out sooner," Maggie said from the shaded table. Like Phoebe, Maggie had wild strawberry-blond hair, hers a tone darker and four inches shorter. And they had freckles. Lots of freckles, Maggie especially.

"Dylan didn't give us much notice," Olivia said without a hint of criticism. Her fiancé, Dylan McCaffrey, had purchased tickets to the masquerade ball to support the cause, a neonatal intensive care unit at a Boston hospital. He'd handed them to Olivia just before he and several friends took off to the

White Mountains for a few days of hiking. She added with a sigh, "I've never been to a masquerade."

"Neither have I," Maggie said. "We must know someone in Boston who can help with costumes."

Phoebe listened to the bumblebees hard at work in the catmint. She and Maggie had been friends with Olivia since preschool. They were gathered in Olivia's backyard. Fair-haired and pretty, she'd returned to Knights Bridge in the spring to convert her classic 1803 center-chimney house into The Farm at Carriage Hill. In the process, she'd met and fallen in love with Dylan, a former hockey player, now a wealthy San Diego businessman. His arrival in Knights Bridge had turned the out-of-the-way rural Massachusetts town on its head.

Pushing back stray curls, Phoebe got to her feet. She and Maggie both wore sundresses and sandals, but Olivia had on shorts and an old T-shirt after spending the morning in her gardens. When she'd left Boston, she'd put her graphic design skills and boundless energy to work in transforming her historic house into an idyllic spot for showers, meetings, girlfriend weekends and the occasional wedding — including her sister's upcoming wedding in September and her own in December.

"You've been awfully quiet, Phoebe," Olivia said. "Any ideas what we could wear?"

"I was just thinking . . ." Phoebe tried to sound casual. "What if you two dressed up as Audrey Hepburn and Grace Kelly?"

Olivia pushed back her chair and eyed Phoebe with obvious interest. "How would we pull off Audrey Hepburn and Grace Kelly? Do you have something in mind?"

Maggie, a caterer with two young sons, stood with her iced tea, the sprig of peppermint and wedge of lemon that she'd artfully hooked onto the glass now floating among the ice cubes. She cast Phoebe an amused look. "Do you see me as Audrey Hepburn or Grace Kelly? Either one?"

Phoebe smiled at her sister. "Sure, why not?"

"You really do have an imagination," Maggie said. "What are they, dresses that came in for the vintage fashion show?"

Phoebe hesitated, framing her explanation. As director of the Knights Bridge Free Public Library, the vintage fashion show was her brainchild, an end-of-the-summer event that would involve the entire community. It would showcase clothing from 1900 to 1975. The various library reading

10

groups were focusing on twentieth-century books, the historical society was helping out, local businesses were donating food and staging materials — it was an all-consuming project that now, finally, was well in hand.

Phoebe had discovered the tiny hidden room while looking through the library attic for anything she could use for the show. It was as if she'd stepped into a time capsule, a secret hideaway. The room was filled with reproductions of dresses from movies up through the 1960s and from different historical periods — Medieval, Regency, Victorian, Edwardian, Roaring Twenties.

Who could have predicted such a thing?

She wanted to know more before she told anyone. Who had set up the room? Who had worked there, left everything behind? *Why?*

Did anyone else know about it?

She'd started volunteering at the library as a teenager and working there in college, and she'd never heard a word about a hidden attic room.

Finally she said, "Everyone's been going through trunks and boxes in closets and attics for the fashion show. It's been loads of fun so far."

Olivia nodded. "I helped Gran load up her car trunk with old clothes from her and her friends. They're all getting a kick out of the idea."

"I can think of several dresses that would be perfect for a costume ball," Phoebe said. "Two in particular. I'm not positive about sizes, but we can alter them if we need to."

"Easier to take in a seam than let one out," Maggie muttered.

"If we need to let out seams, we could add a strip of similar or contrasting fabric," Olivia said. "It's a costume ball. No one's going to kick us out if our costumes are a little quirky."

"You'll be wearing masks, too," Phoebe said.

"Ah, yes. Plausible deniability." Olivia grinned, obviously liking that idea. "No one else has to know it's me trying to pass myself off as Audrey Hepburn."

"Not as Audrey Hepburn herself," Phoebe amended. "As one of the characters she played."

Olivia laughed. "Well, that just makes all the difference, doesn't it? Hey, if one of these outfits works, I'm all for it."

"Me, too," Maggie said, with somewhat less confidence. "You're sure it's all right? We won't be stepping on anyone's toes borrowing a couple of the dresses?"

"It'll be fine," Phoebe said, leaving it at that. "Why don't you come by my cottage

12

later? We can open a bottle of wine and you can see if the dresses work for you."

"What about you, Phoebe?" Olivia asked. "You have to come with us now. We can't go off to the ball like the wicked stepsisters and leave you sweeping the ashes out of the fireplace. Dylan left a half-dozen tickets. No one will use them if we don't."

Whenever Olivia mentioned Dylan, Phoebe could see how very much her friend was in love with him.

*A happy ending.*

Phoebe's favorite books and movies were ones with happy endings, and she welcomed a real-life romantic happy ending, as rare as it could be.

She waved off a bee that had found its way to her. "It's very generous of Dylan. A neonatal ICU is a great cause, and it'll be a wonderful night for everyone, I'm sure, but I can't go."

"Why not?" Maggie asked, obviously skeptical.

"I have things to do." Phoebe glanced at her watch and winced. It really was later than she expected. "I have to get back to the library. I have story hour, but I'll be home by six if you want to come by then."

"We'll be there," Olivia said, then turned

to Maggie. "I guess I shouldn't speak for you."

"Wouldn't miss it," Maggie said. "I want to see these dresses and I need a costume."

Aware of her sister's eyes on her, Phoebe offered to help clear the table of the iced-tea glasses and plates of tarts they had sampled for possible addition to the Carriage Hill catering menu, but Olivia shooed her away. "You need to get to story hour. The kids will get restless if you're late."

"An understatement," Phoebe said with a smile as she snatched a tiny apple-pear tart. "This one's my favorite, but they're all fabulous. I'm off. I'll see you later."

Instead of going back through the house and disturbing Olivia's dog, Buster, asleep in the mudroom, Phoebe followed a bark-mulch path through basil, oregano and dill plants soaking up the summer sun, then crossed a patch of shaded lawn and went around the side of the house to the front yard.

She had the door open to her Subaru, which she'd owned since she'd started commuting to the University of Massachusetts in nearby Amherst, when her sister burst out from the kitchen ell, a later addition to Olivia's old house. Phoebe didn't have a chance to get into the car before Maggie flew down the front walk and caught up with her.

"Phoebe, what on earth is wrong with you?"

She knew exactly what her sister was getting at. "I pay my own way, Maggie. You know that."

"It's not as if Dylan offered to pay off your mortgage for you. The tickets are his donation to a worthy cause. It looks good if the ball is well attended. It's great publicity for the neonatal ICU and what it does, and it gets other people thinking about giving. Everyone wins." Maggie sighed at her older sister. "We can't be grinds all the time."

"I'm not a grind," Phoebe said. "I love what I do. I have fun —"

"And you live within your means and never take a false step," Maggie finished for her, then winced. "Sorry. That came out wrong."

"It's okay. It's just . . ." Phoebe stared at the tiny tart in her hand, suddenly wishing she had left it on the table. "It's a slippery slope, wanting more than you can have, but I take lots of false steps. We all do. I'm not being morally superior."

"Oh, Phoebe, I know. You're the kindest person in Knights Bridge. Probably in all of New England." Maggie's rich turquoise eyes shone with emotion. "I just don't want you to miss out on a good time."

"Dressing you and Olivia for a masquerade will be a *great* time," Phoebe said, smiling at her sister. "I have to go. Those boys of yours will be tearing up the library."

Maggie groaned. "They'll be full of energy after spending the day with Mom. She lets them do whatever they want. When I picked them up yesterday, they were helping her muck out the goat barn. Knee-deep in you-know-what. I wouldn't care except they didn't have a change of clothes. I'll never get the smell out of my van."

"It'll wear off in time but you probably don't want catering clients to get a whiff."

"No kidding."

Phoebe commiserated even as she was amused at the image of her mother and her young nephews. "I'll see you in a little while. I hope I wasn't rude to Olivia —"

"You weren't, and she'd understand if you were. Don't worry. She's trying to figure out things herself. This is new territory for her. For Dylan, too. He never pictured himself living in a little town like Knights Bridge until he met Olivia. He obviously still loves San Diego, too." Maggie stepped back from Phoebe's car and waved a hand. "They'll figure it out. I should have such

16

problems."

"What would you do with a fortune like Dylan has?"

Her eyes flashed with humor. "Get someone to paint my house. I hate ladders."

Phoebe laughed as she climbed into her car, but she also felt a pang of uncertainty about what was next for Dylan and his millions, and what it would mean for quiet, picturesque Knights Bridge.

She left her car windows open and drove back toward town. She could smell the clean, cool water of a stream that ran along the edge of the narrow road. Carriage Hill was the last house on the dead-end road, two miles from the Knights Bridge village center. The road hadn't always been a dead end. Once it had wound into the heart of the picturesque Swift River Valley. That was before four small valley towns were depopulated in the 1930s and deliberately flooded to create Quabbin Reservoir. The reservoir now provided pure drinking water for metropolitan Boston.

*Boston must have seemed so far away back then.*

It seemed far enough away now. Barely two hours, but so different from her life in Knights Bridge. She'd never lived anywhere else. Olivia and Maggie had both lived in

Boston for a few years before returning to their hometown, Olivia in March, Maggie last fall. Phoebe's biggest move had been from her mother's house — or madhouse, as she and her sisters would say fondly — to her own place on Thistle Lane. It was a cottage, really. Perfect for just her. She could even walk to her job at the library.

Phoebe appreciated the peaceful back road as she pulled her thoughts together. Story hours were a favorite part of her job, but her visit with Maggie and Olivia had left her feeling edgy and frayed.

Questioning, wanting . . . dreaming.

*I like my life,* she reminded herself as she came into Knights Bridge center, known as one of the prettiest villages in New England with its shaded town common surrounded by classic houses, a town hall, library, church and country store.

Phoebe parked in front of the library, a solid, rambling brick building filled with endless nooks and crannies. Persistent stories said the library was haunted, to the point that the producers of a television series about ghosts had considered it for a show before choosing another supposedly haunted New England library. Phoebe often heard creaks, groans, moans, whistles and — once — what she would have sworn were whispers. But she'd never considered she might encounter an actual ghost.

Specifically, George Sanderson, founder of the library in 1872.

Upon his death in 1904, he left the library his extensive collection of books and archives, a Steinway baby grand piano and a dozen straw hats made at one of the small mills he'd owned in the valley. The last Sanderson had vacated Knights Bridge during the Depression, when the family mills were demolished ahead of the damming of the Swift River for Quabbin. Homes, businesses, barns, fences, trees — everything in the valley went. Even graves were moved to a new cemetery on the southern end of the reservoir.

Old George's portrait still hung above the fireplace in the library's main room. He was handsome and stern-looking, not exactly the sort Phoebe imagined would encourage story hours for small children. As she headed up the sunlit brick walk, she heard squeals of laughter through the open front window, where the children's section was located.

Her five-year-old nephew, Aidan, Maggie's younger son, pressed his face against the window screen. "Hey, Aunt Phoebe!"

"Aidan Sloan, do *not* poke that screen,"

19

she said firmly, picking up her pace.

He giggled and disappeared from sight.

Phoebe ran up the steps and went inside, welcoming the cool, solid wood-paneled interior, hardly changed since the library was built to George Sanderson's specifications. The main room included a small stage, the piano tucked on one end. Before Phoebe's arrival as director, the library had seldom used the stage and the trustees had complained about the "wasted space." With careful planning, she'd gained their support and found the money to launch a modest concert series, with musicians who didn't expect more than a few dozen in the audience, and opened up the stage for art and garden shows. It was where the library would hold its vintage fashion show in less than two weeks.

*We make use of all that we have.*

That was Phoebe's motto for the library as well as her own life. Why moan about what she didn't have when so much was right within her grasp?

Her older nephew, Tyler, almost seven, was sitting cross-legged on the hardwood floor in front of the stage with a book about raptors in his lap. "Aunt Phoebe, did you know that raptors have three eyelids?"

"In fact, I did, Tyler." She laughed. "You'd

be surprised at what a librarian knows. Would you like to see a raptor's eyelids sometime?"

He nodded eagerly.

"We'll have to figure that out, then. Right now, though, let's go in with the other kids."

"I want to stay here."

Tyler — as redheaded as his mother — preferred to read a book on his own than to be read to, especially with his squirming younger brother. Phoebe put out a hand, but he ignored it and stood up on his own. He shuffled past her into the children's section, his head down, shoulders slumped, as if she'd asked him to walk the plank.

He and Aidan would be tired after spending most of the day with Elly O'Dunn, their energetic maternal grandmother. She'd taken the afternoon off from her job at the town offices to look after the boys while Maggie catered a lunch and then met with Olivia at Carriage Hill. Phoebe, her mother and her two youngest sisters were doing what they could to help Maggie as she managed two young boys and a catering business on her own, without Brandon Sloan, her adrenaline-junkie carpenter husband. Phoebe didn't have all the details, but she knew Brandon's construction work in Boston had been on-and-off at best the past year or so. It had to have put a strain on his marriage. He had a tendency to take off into the mountains or up the coast when things got tough, instead of talking.

Brandon was the third of six Sloan siblings — five brothers and a sister. His family owned a successful construction business in Knights Bridge and would welcome him back, but returning to his hometown would signal defeat in his eyes. Phoebe had known him since nursery school. He'd wanted out of Knights Bridge at ten. Then he and Maggie fell for each other as teenagers and married in college. Almost no one in town had believed their marriage would last. Phoebe had hoped it would, because they were so much in love.

She sighed. She could be *such* an idiotic romantic. Hadn't she learned by now?

She gathered the dozen boys and girls onto a round, dark red rug. They came quickly to order, even her nephews. They were reading Beatrix Potter and had just started *The Tale of Peter Rabbit,* their last book of the summer, and they couldn't wait to find out what happened next.

With Peter Rabbit and Knights Bridge's little ones safely back with their families, Phoebe locked up the library and walked across South Main Street and through the common to Main Street and the Swift River Country Store, a town fixture for the past hundred years. It sold everything from galoshes to canned goods and fresh vegetables to a decent selection of wine. The afternoon heat had eased but it was still warm when she headed back to the library with two bottles of pinot grigio, already chilled. Olivia would bring a bottle of some kind of red from a California winery owned by Noah Kendrick, Dylan's best friend and founder of NAK, Inc., the high-tech entertainment business that had made them both fortunes. The only thing Phoebe knew for sure was that her choice of white wine wouldn't be nearly as pricey as whatever red Olivia brought.

Having a friend fall for a wealthy Californian had its unexpected advantages.

Normally she'd have walked home but her visit with Maggie and Olivia meant she had her car. She got in, set her wine on the front seat next to her and shut her eyes a moment, listening to the rustle of leaves as a gentle breeze floated through the shade trees on the wide library lawn.

Finally she started her Subaru and turned off South Main onto Thistle Lane. The library stood on the corner. Thistle Lane

23

led away from the common, connecting to a back road with views of the reservoir in the distance. On her trips to the library as a girl, Phoebe had dreamed of living on the quiet, tree-lined street, away from the chaotic life she had out in the country with her parents and younger sisters. Thistle Lane represented order, independence and, at least to a degree, prosperity.

In less than five minutes, she turned into her short paved driveway. An old American elm graced the corner of the yard next to hers, holding on against the ravages of Dutch elm disease, in part due to intervention by the town. It was a beautiful tree, a symbol of the past and yet very much part of her everyday world. When she bought her house eighteen months ago, she'd thought she was being practical, never mind that she was the only one to make an offer. The house was built in 1912 by one of the early directors of the library, then sold to a series of owners, until, finally, the town was forced to take possession when the heir to the last owner couldn't be located and property taxes went into arrears.

Phoebe rolled up her car windows, shut off the engine and collected her wine bottles as she stepped out into the shade. With its new roof, furnace, windows, wiring and plumbing, the house was no longer a notch above a tear-down. It still needed a new kitchen and bathroom, but she had to save up before she tackled any more big projects. Right now, she was concentrating on some of the fun cosmetic work — paint, wallpaper, gardens and restoring flea-market and yard-sale finds.

With her painting skills and eye for color, Olivia had been a huge help, but The Farm at Carriage Hill and her new life with Dylan were creating uncertainties for her. Phoebe had welcomed having Maggie and then Olivia move back to Knights Bridge, but that didn't mean more changes weren't coming. Change was inevitable, Phoebe thought. Her own life was more settled than the lives of her sisters and most of her friends. Her job at the library was secure. She had no plans to move, go into business for herself or get involved with a man.

Five years from now, her life would likely look more or less as it did now.

"Just without an avocado-green refrigerator in my kitchen," she muttered happily as she headed down the curving stone walk with her wine.

The narrow clapboards of her small house were painted classic white. At Olivia's suggestion, Phoebe had chosen a warm, welcoming green for the front door. It was framed by pink roses that she'd pruned and trained to climb up the white-painted trellis by the porch steps. When she'd moved in, the yard was an overgrown mess. She didn't have Olivia's green thumb, but she'd none-theless managed to save many of the shrubs and perennials that had come with the prop-erty.

As she started up the steps to the small, covered porch, she saw that her twin sisters had arrived ahead of her. They were seated on wicker chairs that Phoebe had reclaimed and painted white, adding cushions in a mix of pink, blue and white flowers. Ava and Ruby, at twenty-three the youngest of the O'Dunn sisters, were fraternal twins, but they were so much alike that people often assumed they were identical. In both ap-pearance and temperament, they took after their late father, Patrick O'Dunn, an auburn-haired, green-eyed, gorgeous-looking dreamer, as hopelessly impractical as the widow he'd left behind almost ten years ago.

"Thanks for coming," Phoebe said as she unlocked the front door. "Olivia and Mag-gie will be here any minute."

"This is going to be so much fun," Ruby said, tucking a pink rose blossom behind her ear. She had on a long black skirt and a white tank top, her short, wavy hair dyed a purple-black that made her skin seem even paler, more translucent. "We brought all our goodies. Makeup, wigs, hairpieces, curling iron, needles and thread. We've already done up a half-dozen masks. Three are simple. You'd be able to recognize whoever's wearing them. Three are more elaborate. It'd be tougher to recognize who's wearing them."

Ava smiled. "We will not fail you." She twirled a rose stem in her fingertips. Her hair was its natural reddish brown, trailing down her back in a loose ponytail. Her skirt, which came to just above her knees, was a deep, warm red that worked surprisingly well with her turquoise lace top. "A masquerade ball in Boston. It doesn't get much fancier than that."

Phoebe pushed open the door. "Dylan has extra tickets if you want to go."

"I wish," Ava said wistfully, tossing her rose over the porch rail into the grass. "We have to work, and classes start again next week."

"Otherwise we'd go in a heartbeat," Ruby added.

No doubt they would, Phoebe thought. "It does sound grand," she said as she led them inside. "Maggie and Olivia are count-

27

ing on your theatrical flair. What do you think of Maggie in the blue gown Grace Kelly wore in *To Catch a Thief* and Olivia in Audrey Hepburn's black dress from *Breakfast at Tiffany's*?"

Ava turned, intrigued. "Do you have the dresses?"

Phoebe nodded. "I have the dresses."

"Oh, wow. Excellent. Ruby?"

"Grace's icy-blue chiffon gown? Audrey's little black dress?" Ruby laughed. "That's fantastic."

"I even have pearls and a cigarette holder," Phoebe said.

"Where did you get them?" Ava asked.

"I'm thinking of including them in our vintage fashion show," Phoebe said evasively. Her sisters followed her into the kitchen, where she put the wine in the refrigerator, a relic that, somehow, still worked.

Ava leaned against the counter, a cheap wood that Phoebe had painted creamy white, her first renovation when she'd moved in. "So, Phoebe," Ava said, crossing her arms on her chest. "Have you decided what you're wearing?"

Phoebe got out wineglasses and set them on the cracked Formica counter, sidestepping her sister's question. The twins were in graduate school — Ava in New York, Ruby in Boston — but they were spending the summer in Knights Bridge, living at home to save money. They had student loans that would take years if not decades to pay off, and big dreams that might never pay off, but Phoebe hoped everything would work out for them, believed in them. She knew they felt the same way about her but suspected they had their doubts about her choices. Not her library work. Her solitary life — or what to her sisters seemed like a solitary life. Meaning she didn't have a man.

She'd had one, once. She'd been on the road to marriage and a happy ending of her own, but it hadn't worked out that way.

Everyone in town knew her story — Phoebe O'Dunn, jilted at twenty, within forty-eight hours of finding her father dead from a tree-trimming accident. She'd shielded her mother and sisters from the depth of her pain, but the shock had taken its toll. Broken hearts healed but that didn't mean life was ever the same. Phoebe had deliberately shut the door on romance, at least for herself.

But it was fine, all fine, because she was fine. She loved her work, her family, her friends, her town. She couldn't be more content than she was right now.

Ava looked out the window over the sink at the backyard flower garden, dominated now, in mid-August, by hollyhocks that ranged from soft white through three shades of pink to deep maroon. "You're not going to the ball, are you, Phoebe?"

Phoebe changed her mind and decided to pour the wine now. She grabbed the pinot grigio out of the refrigerator and set it on the counter. "No, I'm not going," she said matter-of-factly as she rummaged in the utensil drawer for a corkscrew. "Do you both want wine?"

Ruby plopped her tote bag onto a chair at the table. "Phoebe, you know you'd have a great time. You never go anywhere —"

"I have so much to do here. I'm taking vacation days before the end of the summer. I'll go someplace then."

"Where?"

"I don't know. Someplace." Phoebe held up a glass. "Wine?"

"Sure," Ruby said with a sigh. "Just don't think I've given up."

"Me, either," Ava said. "You should go to this ball tomorrow, Phoebe. Maybe you'll change your mind when you see the masks Ruby and I made. Anyway, wine for me, too. I'll get our goodies out of the car."

"Hang on, I'll help." Ruby withdrew a

square of golden-colored soap from her tote bag and tossed it to Phoebe. "Check it out while we're setting up. It's a new soap Mom, Olivia and Maggie are trying out. Mom wants your opinion."

Olivia and Maggie were experimenting with making their own artisan goat's milk soaps to sell at The Farm at Carriage Hill. If it worked, Elly O'Dunn's goats could go from being an expensive and impractical hobby to earning their own keep. Phoebe was happy to do what she could to help and knew Ava and Ruby were, too, although Ava in particular wasn't crazy about their mother's goats — especially when she had to clean up after them. They all appreciated the mildness and purity of the soaps.

Phoebe took in the gentle lavender scent of the bar Ruby had tossed her. "It really is lovely, isn't it?"

"Olivia's already designed the labels," Ruby said. "Dreams do come true, Phoebe. Olivia's are."

"I know. I want yours to come true, too."

Ava stopped in the hall doorway. "What about your dreams?"

"My dream," Phoebe said lightly, abandoning the soap for her wine, "is to see Maggie and Olivia all set for their charity ball. Go grab your stuff. I'll get the dresses."

Three hours, two and a half bottles of wine, a pot of vegetable curry and much laughter later, Phoebe was again alone in her kitchen. Olivia and Maggie had precise instructions, beautiful handmade masks and everything else they needed to transform themselves into their own versions of Audrey Hepburn and Grace Kelly.

The dresses had worked out even better than Phoebe had imagined.

*The dresses.*

Ava had recognized them first. "Phoebe, these aren't *like* the dresses Audrey and Grace wore in *Breakfast at Tiffany's* and *To Catch a Thief.* They *are* the dresses."

"Close copies," Phoebe had said, then again deflected questions about where she'd gotten them.

She turned out the light in the kitchen and walked down a short hall to a small back room. For most of the past eighteen months, she'd used it to store paint supplies, tools and junk she'd collected from the rest of the house but wasn't sure what to do with. Then, on a rainy night earlier that summer, she'd cleaned everything out, wiped down the walls, mopped the floor and considered the possibilities. A guestroom? A study? A spa bathroom?

In another life, it would have made a great baby's room.

She felt the same pang of regret she'd felt that night, but it was ridiculous. If her father hadn't died and her steady college boyfriend hadn't given her an impossible ultimatum, she wouldn't have ended up on Thistle Lane at all, with or without babies.

*Florida.*

She'd have ended up in Florida.

She tore off the dry-cleaning plastic to a third dress she'd had cleaned along with the Grace Kelly and Audrey Hepburn dresses. It hung on a hook in the back room.

She stepped back, marveling at the creativity and the workmanship of the gown. It was Edwardian, one of the period pieces in the hidden room. Its creator had chosen a warm, rich brown silk satin, decorated it with sparkling beads, lace and embroidery, all in a matching brown. It had an empire waist, a deep square neckline and loose, belled lacy sleeves.

And there was a matching hat.

It was as romantic and beautiful a dress as any Phoebe had ever seen.

*A gown for a princess.*

She tried to shake off the thought. She'd

had too much wine. Just two glasses, but she felt . . . well, a little reckless.

*And why not?*

After all, what could be more perfect for a masquerade ball than a gorgeous, mysterious dress from a secret attic room?

# Two

"I could pass for a swashbuckler right now," Noah Kendrick said as he stretched out on an expanse of granite near the base of Mount Washington, the tallest peak in the White Mountains of northern New England. "If I don't shave or shower before tonight, I'll be all set."

Dylan McCaffrey shrugged off his pack and sat on another boulder. Noah saw no sign that four days of hiking had had any effect on his friend beyond sweat, stubble and a certain grubbiness. Two of Dylan's hockey player friends had joined them but had split off that morning for several more days of tramping in the mountains. It was Dylan's and Noah's first time hiking in the White Mountains. They were in good shape, but Mount Washington was a hell of a climb, their last summit before heading back to civilization.

And a charity ball.

*Great,* Noah thought without enthusiasm.

He doubted that anyone at NAK, Inc., had needed to reach him in the past three nights and four days. He was the founder of the high-tech entertainment company that bore his initials — NAK, for Noah Andrew Kendrick. The convergence of technology and entertainment had fascinated him for as long as he could remember, and he'd managed to turn it into a profitable business. NAK was just four years old but had gone public last fall, a grueling process that had consumed him and his senior managers.

He'd stepped down as CEO in June. His idea.

One of his smarter moves had been to get Dylan, fresh out of the NHL and looking for something new to do, to help with NAK. He'd eased back from day-to-day involvement now, too.

NAK would have gone bust within months without Dylan's help. Dylan knew how to read people. He knew how to fight in a way Noah didn't.

They were both keenly aware that a central challenge for a newly public company was to figure out what to do with the founder. Sometimes the best thing for the company was for the founder to stay on as CEO, or

"You don't *like* math. There's a difference. And your idea of 'math' is arithmetic. Adding fractions."

"I can add fractions. It's multiplying them that does me in."

Noah glanced at Dylan but couldn't tell if he was serious.

"We shouldn't sit too long," Dylan said. "We don't have much farther to go, but we want to make it down the mountain in time to get to Boston and turn into swashbucklers."

For a split second, Noah imagined himself lying back on the boulder and taking a nap. They'd encountered high winds, fog and temperatures in the low fifties on the last thousand feet or so to the summit. He appreciated the clear, quiet weather and relative warmth lower on the mountain. It was even sunny. By the time they reached the trailhead at Pinkham Notch, it would be in the seventies. He'd peeled off his jacket on the descent and continued in his special moisture-wicking Patagonia T-shirt and hiking pants. Dylan, who was built like a bull, was in Carhartt. Noah was fair and lean, more one for sessions in the gym or dojo than treks in the wilderness. Dylan had decided a few days in the White Mountains would be good for Noah.

Same with the masquerade ball tonight.
Good for him.

Noah had gone along. Why not? It wasn't
as if he had a whole lot else to do. Not like
even just a couple of months ago. A year,
two years, ten years ago, he'd navigated a
hectic schedule that would have flattened
most people he knew. So had Dylan.

"You couldn't sign me up for a simple
black-tie ball," Noah said, sitting up straight
on the New England granite. "No. No way.
My best friend since first grade has to sign
me up for a masquerade. I have to wear a
costume."

"More or less. It's not like Halloween."
Dylan was clearly unmoved by Noah's
complaints. "All in the name of fun and a
good cause."

"Right." Noah drank some water from his
water bottle, relieved that he didn't see any
mosquitoes. "I've agreed to dress up in
whatever swashbuckler outfit you've managed to find for me, but I'm skipping the
long-haired wig and funny beard."

"Just not the sword," Dylan said.

Noah grinned. "Never the sword."

"A reenactment musketeer rapier is waiting for you in Boston. No one needs to
know it's you behind the black mask. I
understand you don't want your photo

turning up on some gossip website asking if the most eligible bachelor in San Diego has lost his mind."

"Dylan, why do I have the feeling you aren't taking my concerns seriously?"

"Because I'm not. You'd have even more women flocking to you if they could see you in your sword-fighting duds."

*Sword-fighting duds.* Noah shook his head. Expecting Dylan to appreciate proper fencing terminology was a waste of time. No doubt he felt the same when it came to Noah and the nuances of hockey.

"The costume has a cape, too," Dylan added.

"There's no hope for you, my friend."

Dylan shrugged as he drank some of his own water.

"You used to be the most eligible bachelor in San Diego," Noah said.

"Best-looking. You were always more eligible. You just have a habit of choosing the wrong women."

Noah tucked his water bottle into the side mesh pocket on his pack and got to his feet, lifting the pack onto one shoulder. "What wrong women?"

"Hollywood babes for starters," Dylan said, standing with his pack.

"Only recently. I haven't been the same

since I got dumped by that computation engineer my senior year at MIT. She was brilliant, cute —"

"Not that cute. I remember her." Dylan jumped onto the trail. He didn't seem to consider that he might slip and hit his head, twist an ankle or fall off the damn mountain. Of course, he landed lightly on his feet. "She wasn't as cute as your latest actress."

"Her show just got canceled, and she's not cute. She's gorgeous."

"Smart?"

"Yes, I guess so. We didn't get that far before we went our separate ways."

"Not many people are smart compared to you. It's a relative term."

Also one Noah seldom considered, but he had learned through hard experience that not everyone thought the way he did. And what did he know about relationships? His latest "relationship," with the cute/gorgeous actress of the canceled Sunday-night show, had lasted three weeks and ended that spring. He'd known from the start it wasn't an until-death-do-us-part match, but he'd thought it would last at least through the summer.

He was the one who had ended it. Just had to be done. Expensive dinners, gifts and such were one thing. Manipulating him to bankroll a movie she could star in was another.

"It's good you had this time to enjoy nature," Dylan said without any evidence of sarcasm.

"Right. Sure. I didn't even bring a cell phone."

Waving off a mosquito that seemed to have singled him out, Noah joined Dylan in heading down the mountain. In a few minutes, they were in dappled shade, and he could hear water tumbling down a rock-strewn stream. Several hikers passed them, ascending the rugged, steep trail. There were no guaranteed safe trails up Mount Washington, but thousands climbed it without incident every year. Preparation and the right equipment were key, but so was the right mindset — a clear understanding of one's abilities and a willingness to turn back if conditions warranted. A foolish risk on Mount Washington could prove dangerous, even deadly.

When he'd decided to start his own business, Noah had assessed his situation with the same clarity and objectivity as he had when he agreed to join Dylan and his hockey friends hiking in the White Mountains. He'd realized within weeks of forming NAK that he needed Dylan McCaffrey on his team. They'd grown up together in suburban Los Angeles, but Noah had gone on to MIT and Dylan into the NHL. After a series of injuries ended Dylan's hockey career, he had blown most of his money and was sleeping in his car when Noah knocked on his window asking for his friend's help.

Dylan's instincts and no-nonsense view of people and business helped Noah get NAK going and keep it going. Its success had exceeded their dreams. Now Dylan was marrying a woman from a small New England town and reinventing his life.

Noah had no idea what he was doing beyond taking a hot shower when he was back in civilization.

More mosquitoes descended on him when he rounded the next bend in the trail, but by then he didn't care. He could hear cars. After three nights sleeping in a tent, he was ready to check into a five-star Boston hotel, even if a B-movie swashbuckler costume was waiting for him.

Dylan had booked a room at the sprawling Mount Washington Hotel, a National Historic Landmark that opened in Bretton Woods in 1902. Noah would have happily stayed there for several days and enjoyed the resort amenities and the spectacular views of the surrounding mountains, but he and Dylan had to get to Boston.

They took turns in the shower and changed into fresh clothes.

Noah didn't shave. Dylan grinned at him. "Four days' beard growth is essential for a swashbuckler, I take it."

Noah shrugged. "I'm just hoping it will help keep anyone from recognizing me."

He slipped into a black sport coat, which he wore over a silky black T-shirt and black trousers — the uniform he'd adopted after graduating from MIT. He didn't remember why, except it had seemed like a good idea at the time. Dylan insisted it was because he wanted to appear older. Maybe it had been. Whatever the reason, now people expected him to show up head-to-toe in black.

He cupped his iPhone in one hand and started out into the hall.

"How many messages did you have?" Dylan asked as they left the room.

"What makes you think I looked?" At his friend's roll of the eyes, Noah answered with an exaggeration. "Ten thousand."

"You mean ten, and one you answered."

It was close. That was Dylan. He could read people.

They headed down wide, elegant stairs to

the main lobby, then outside onto a sweeping porch overlooking expansive lawns and the stunning mountains where they'd spent the past four days and three nights.

As they walked to Dylan's car, he frowned at Noah. "Everything okay?"

"I got bit by mosquitoes. Do you worry about West Nile virus?"

"No, and you don't, either. What's up?"

Noah shook his head as he climbed into the passenger seat of Dylan's Audi. He'd bought the car for his Knights Bridge residence now that he was spending most of his time on the East Coast. Noah didn't offer to drive.

He needed to think.

In fact, he'd had one call from San Diego that made him uneasy. He would have to return it once they arrived in Boston. He had no choice.

He could see that Dylan was on alert. He would help in a heartbeat if Noah was in trouble. NAK trouble, personal trouble. It didn't matter.

This time, Noah didn't want Dylan to get involved.

The San Diego call was his problem.

Dylan seemed to guess that asking more questions would get him nowhere. His years on the ice, practicing, playing with a team,

46

had honed his natural instincts about when to make a move, when to hold back. Noah had always been more of a solo operator.

As he started the car, Dylan took a breath, obviously reining in an urge to interrogate Noah. Finally he said, "Olivia's done a lot of work on her house since you were there in April."

"That's good," Noah said neutrally. Olivia's house had needed a lot of work.

"We're tearing down my place," Dylan added.

"Ah."

As far as Noah was concerned, it was the only sensible option. He'd been to Knights Bridge just that one time, in early spring, not long after Dylan had received a handwritten note from Olivia Frost demanding he clean up his property, an eyesore for potential visitors to the getaway she was opening down the road from him.

Except her note was the first Dylan had heard of her, Knights Bridge or his ownership of a house there. He'd had no idea his treasure-hunter father had bought the house and left it to him upon his death two years ago. It was built in the 1840s but wasn't the architectural gem that Olivia's home was. In fact, it was a rundown wreck.

Dylan hadn't expected to discover that he

had roots of his own in the out-of-the-way Swift River Valley, and he certainly hadn't expected to fall in love with Olivia Frost.

Despite the miles he had hiked over the past few days, Noah felt restless, frustrated with his situation, even trapped, but at least he didn't have to keep the players straight in Knights Bridge, Massachusetts. He stuck out enough in Southern California but he enjoyed relative anonymity there compared to what he would endure in a small town straight out of Norman Rockwell. Dylan had tried to explain to him that, despite appearances to the contrary, time hadn't stopped in Knights Bridge.

Maybe it hadn't, but it was still small.

Really small.

Noah stared out the window as the mountains and woodlands of northern New England gave way to the suburbs of metropolitan Boston. Dylan drove with occasional suspicious glances at him, but Noah didn't budge. He wasn't talking.

When the Boston skyline came into view and traffic picked up, he sat up straight, wide-awake.

This was familiar territory.

Dylan valet-parked at the same five-star hotel in Copley Square where the charity event was being held and they each had booked a suite for the night. Their costumes for the evening would be delivered to their rooms.

"Noah," Dylan said as he climbed out of the car.

Noah knew there was no point denying there was a problem. He shook his head. "Later."

"Anytime. You know that."

"I do. Thanks."

When he reached his suite, Noah dug out his iPhone and stood in the window over-looking the familiar city streets as he dialed Loretta Wrentham's number in San Diego. Loretta was Dylan's personal lawyer and friend, a striking woman in her early fifties who recently admitted she'd been his fa-ther's lover, at least briefly. According to Loretta, Duncan McCaffrey had never told her why he'd bought a house in Knights Bridge, either, but it had changed his son's life.

That was Duncan, Noah thought. He'd been a restless soul, divorcing Dylan's mother, traveling the world, having adven-tures. Fifteen years ago, he'd turned up in Boston when Noah was a freshman at MIT. Noah had been homesick, feeling like a misfit even among people just as dedicated to math and science as he was. Duncan Mc-

Caffrey had suggested Noah take up a martial art. *"Karate, tae kwon do, tai chi, fencing. Something."* Noah had signed up for his first fencing lesson that week. Duncan had already gone off on some expedition.

Noah had known Loretta since she'd started working with Dylan during his early years with the NHL and considered her a friend.

She answered on the first ring. She must have pounced on the phone. "I haven't found out a thing," she said. "Not. A. Thing."

That wasn't good. Loretta was a hound. One sniff, and she pinned her nose to the trail straight to the end. This one had her stumped.

A few days before Noah flew to Boston for his hike in the White Mountains, he'd spotted a mystery man on his tail in San Diego. Or what he thought was a mystery man on his tail. He'd first noticed the man outside a waterfront restaurant, then at his fencing studio and finally outside the NAK offices in downtown San Diego.

On that third sighting, Noah had raced outside but got there too late. The man was gone. Loretta was on her way into the lobby of NAK's stylish high-rise. Noah asked her if she'd seen anyone. She said she hadn't, but offered to find out what she could. As a friend.

"It could just be my imagination that this guy's following me," Noah said, as he had a little over a week ago when he'd explained the situation to Loretta in San Diego.

"Do you have an imagination?" She caught her breath. "That didn't come out right. I don't mean it as an insult. You're just so . . . evidence-oriented. I'm a lawyer. I can relate."

Noah had learned not to dwell on people's stereotypes about him but he was tempted to tell Loretta that if he didn't have an imagination, there would be no NAK, Inc.

Nor would there be a fortune for anyone to scheme and fight over.

*If* that was what was happening.

He didn't know if the man's reasons for tailing him were personal, professional or money related — or even involved him.

"This guy could be a reporter," she said.

"I suppose," Noah said, unconvinced. So far, most journalistic interest in him since NAK had taken off had been legitimate, professional. No sneaking around, no following him.

"I wish you'd gotten a better look at him. Tall, gray hair, trim, wearing a dark gray

51

suit. That's not much. You're sure you'd recognize him again if you saw him?"

"Yes."

Loretta sighed. "Maybe he's looking into one of your Hollywood ex-girlfriends. A paparazzi type."

Noah grimaced as he watched a young couple run across Boylston Street hand in hand. "All I need is some idiot with a camera popping up out of nowhere and snapping shots of me dressed as a swashbuckler."

"A swashbuckler?" Loretta gave a soft chuckle on the other end of the line. "That I'd like to see. Dylan says you're damn good with a sword. Master fencer, right?"

"Something like that," Noah said. The couple disappeared from his sight. He drew back from the window. "I should get ready for this thing tonight. I really appreciate your help with this situation, Loretta."

"Happy to do what I can. I dealt with a few crazy stalker fans back in Dylan's hockey days. I'm not saying that's what's going on here, but you might send me a list of your ex-girlfriends."

It would be quite a list. "I'm not going that far, Loretta. Not without more to go on."

"See? I said you were evidence-oriented.

I'll pick at a few more possible leads, but I'm not optimistic. Keep your eyes open. If this thing gets serious and I think you have a real threat on your hands, I'll take additional steps."

"Such as?"

"Calling the police. Recommending a bodyguard."

Noah shook his head as if she were in the room with him. "No bodyguard. Not without an actual threat."

"Have you told Dylan about this guy?" Loretta asked.

"No. I don't want to distract him. He's moving on from NAK, as he should."

"He's still your friend. What if your mystery man is on your tail because of Dylan? Have you considered that?"

He had. "Now we're speculating. First things first. If there's a reason, I'll talk to Dylan. Right now there isn't."

"All right. Fair enough. How was your hike?"

"There were mosquitoes," Noah said with a smile, then assured Loretta he'd keep his eyes open and let her know if there were any new developments.

After they disconnected, he did a series of stretches. In addition to a master fencer, he was a brown belt in karate. He'd concentrate on advancing to black belt once he got over the nonstop work and pressure of taking NAK public — and the loss of his best friend and closest business ally to New England.

And to pretty, talented Olivia Frost.

She was the love of Dylan's life. And he of hers.

No question.

Noah centered his mind, focused on his movements, the rhythm, the technique. Everything else — doubts, questions, fears, noise — fell away as he did his basic *shorin ryu* karate warm-up routine of calisthenics, blocks, punches and kicks, then eased into a series of simple katas.

When he finished, he was sweating and loose, and he felt grounded, aware, in the moment.

His costume arrived. He laid it on the bed as if it were a dead musketeer and took another shower. He debated tripling his donation to the neonatal ICU and bowing out of tonight's festivities. He could stay in his room and watch movies.

No point. Dylan would just hunt him down. Might as well get on with it.

Still damp from his shower, Noah donned the all-black costume, including the cape and the fake sword. He winced at his reflection. It wasn't so much that he looked bad or foolish. He just didn't look like himself.

At least there was a mask. It, too, was black, but fortunately it covered most of his face.

In San Diego, someone might recognize him even with the mask. In Boston?

Unlikely.

"Good," he muttered, and headed down to the ballroom.

# THREE

Phoebe couldn't take her eyes off the man coming toward her as if they were the only two people in the crowded, glittering ballroom. As if nothing could stop him and he was determined to reach her.

She was standing by a pillar, next to a table of empty champagne glasses. She'd arrived twenty minutes ago, wanting just to watch the festivities with a glass of champagne. Olivia had left one of Dylan's extra tickets behind in case Phoebe decided to go after all, but she'd been so adamant about not going that now she didn't want to have to explain why she'd changed her mind. Because she was captivated by a dress, by the fantasy of an elegant masquerade ball?

Best just to be the proverbial fly on the wall, then go back home with no one being the wiser. Let Olivia and Maggie enjoy their evening without worrying about her.

She adjusted her mask. Of the half-dozen

56

masks Ava and Ruby had made for tonight, this one provided the most coverage. Her eyes and the line of her jaw were all that anyone could see of her face.

*Perfect.*

With this swordfighter gliding toward her, Phoebe appreciated the anonymity.

And he really was gliding. He moved with such smoothness, such an air of masculine purpose and self-control. He didn't pull away to the bar or meet up with another woman. His mask covered most of his face, as hers did, and he was tall and lean, wearing a black cape over sleek black trousers and shirt, with a sheathed costume sword at his side. He looked as if he could handle the sword, fake or not.

His eyes locked with hers.

Phoebe started to duck away, but she was transfixed.

*Why not stay?*

There was a lull in the live music provided by a small, eclectic band near the separate dance floor. Her sword-fighter continued toward her, his eyes still on her. She stared right back at him, ignoring the quickening of her heartbeat, the rush of self-consciousness.

*Do I know him?*

She shook her head. *Impossible.*

So far she'd managed to avoid running into Maggie and Olivia. It definitely helped that she knew what they were wearing. Even so, she'd almost turned back several times before arriving at her pillar. First, when she'd started onto Storrow Drive into the heart of Boston. Then when she'd eased her car into a tight space in the parking garage. Finally on the escalator up to the ballroom. She'd glanced down at the hotel lobby, full of giant urns of fresh flowers and artfully arranged sofas and chairs. Above her, she could hear people gathering outside the ballroom.

If she hadn't been on an escalator, she'd have bolted then, for sure.

Once she reached the ballroom, she got caught up in the crowd, the music, the lights, the laughter and especially the costumes. Her mysterious Edwardian dress passed muster — she'd known it would — striking just the right note of elegance and daring.

The swashbuckler stopped a few yards from her. His eyes were a clear, striking blue, sexy and captivating. It wasn't just the contrast with his black mask or the glow of the chandeliers or even her few sips of champagne at work. They were great eyes. Fantastic eyes.

She held her glass motionless in one hand as a couple passed in front of her, blocking her swashbuckler from her view. When they were gone, he was right in front of her.

Phoebe didn't breathe.

*I don't belong here.*

Then she remembered she was alone, anonymous and dressed as an Edwardian princess. Why not play the part? Why not be a little bold, even a little reckless?

With a deliberate smile, she raised her champagne glass in a flirtatious toast, hoping the man couldn't tell that her heart was hammering in her chest.

Next thing she knew, he was at her side, an arm around her waist. "Dance with me," he said, his voice low, deep and impossibly sexy.

Phoebe nodded without saying a word. He took her glass and set it on the table, then swept her onto the dance floor. His movements were sure, fluid and strong. He'd obviously known what he'd do the second he reached her.

She stifled a jolt of panic. A real princess would know how to dance better than she did. At least she had on strappy sandals that had seen her through several weddings and library events, and she managed not to stumble.

"Just follow my lead," he whispered into her ear.

She licked her lips. "All right."

Somehow he got her arm in position on his shoulder before she realized she had moved. She felt the ripple of lean muscle under his black cape and noticed the stubble of tawny beard around the edges of his mask. She had no idea who he was and expected it was the same for him with her. She'd followed the instructions her younger sisters had given to Olivia and Maggie in applying her makeup, but she'd had to figure out her hat and wig on her own. They felt secure, and she refused to consider what would happen if they flew off, revealing her pinned-up strawberry-blond curls.

The room spun as her dance partner whirled her among the hundreds of guests in costumes and masks in various shapes and colors. The feel of his palm on her lower back, the way he held her right arm — the way he moved with her — made dancing easy. He was confident, physical and strong, and Phoebe let herself pretend that he really could fight off bandits and scoundrels.

"Do you know how to use that sword?" she asked.

"I do, but it's a fake."

"You're a fencer?"

He smiled but didn't answer. The music switched to a faster tune. Phoebe barely paid attention to the actual music as her swashbuckler spun her across the dance floor. She was glad her dress was a good fit. If not, she'd have been bursting buttons and hooks-and-eyes. As it was, the dress revealed more cleavage than was her custom.

She felt sexy, lithe, wanted.

Not herself at all.

When the music ended, Phoebe realized they were on the opposite side of the ballroom. She gave her hat and mask a quick, subtle check to make sure they weren't about to fall off while her dance partner accepted two fresh glasses of champagne from a passing waiter, handing one to her.

"Nice dancing with you, Princess," he said, clicking his glass against hers.

"That was wonderful. Thank you. You're quite a dancer."

He laughed. "I watch a lot of movies. You're not so bad yourself."

"That's kind of you to say. What should I call you? D'Artagnan? Are you a king's musketeer?"

"That works for me."

Phoebe sipped her champagne, wondering if their dancing had loosened a strawberry curl or two from under her wig. Would her musketeer care that she didn't really have raven-black hair?

*What does it matter? None of this is real.*

She shut her eyes a moment, bringing herself back to reality. This was her secret night out on the town. She would be Phoebe O'Dunn again before dawn. Probably before the stroke of midnight.

"What brought you here tonight?" her swashbuckler asked.

Phoebe quickly reminded herself she was playing a part. Flirtatious, confident, rich. An Edwardian princess could afford to pay her own way to a charity masquerade ball and wouldn't feel bad if she hadn't. "It's a great cause," she said, settling on a vague answer.

"That it is."

"And you? What brings you here?"

He shrugged. "I owed a friend a favor." His so-blue eyes narrowed on her as he drank some of his champagne. "And it's a good cause."

The music started again, a slow, romantic song. He took her champagne glass from her and set it and his glass on a small table, then drew her into his arms and back onto the dance floor.

Phoebe laughed, feeling light-headed and free. She didn't want the night to end and yet she knew it would. Her swordfighter would go back to being whatever he was — a pediatrician, a hospital administrator, a lawyer, a Boston businessman, a professor at one of the local colleges. She would go back to Knights Bridge. They lived in the real world. He wasn't a musketeer and she wasn't a princess.

*Just for tonight . . .*

His hand eased lower, subtly, over the curve of her hip. "Close your eyes," he whispered. "Trust me."

Phoebe did as he asked as he held her even closer. She had one arm around his middle and one on his shoulder, could feel the warmth of his skin through the black fabric of his costume. He wasn't a man she'd conjured up on a lazy, hot, quiet afternoon at the library. He wasn't a figment of her imagination.

As they danced, she heard only the music, felt as if they were floating together, as one. When the music finally stopped, he kept her close as she caught her breath and opened her eyes. "That was amazing," she said with a smile.

His lips brushed hers. "You're amazing, Princess."

Phoebe started to tell him that she was no princess, but the words stuck in her throat.

She didn't want the fantasy to end. For a while longer she wanted to be a princess. She lowered her hand from his shoulder and opened her palm on his chest. Who was he, really? Did she even want to know?

Then she saw Dylan, dressed as a cross between Zorro and the Scarlet Pimpernel, standing with Olivia in her Audrey Hepburn dress. They gave no indication they recognized her or even were moving toward her. Phoebe glanced around for Maggie but didn't see her.

Her swashbuckler released her and stood back a few inches, the muscles in his jaw visibly tensed as his eyes narrowed on something — or someone — behind Phoebe. "Excuse me, I have something I need to do," he said, shifting back to her. He was enigmatic, decisive. "Will you wait for me?"

"I will. Yes, of course."

"Do you have friends with you?"

"I'll be fine. Please, do what you have to do."

He touched a fingertip to her lips, then was gone in an instant. Phoebe watched him as he headed quickly through the crowd, his black cape flowing, his movements smooth and controlled.

She hoped he would come back but wasn't

at all sure what she would do if he did.

She dipped out of Dylan and Olivia's line of sight and stopped at an hors d'oeuvres table. Out of the corner of her eye, she spotted her sister at the far end of the table in her gorgeous Grace Kelly gown. As a professional caterer, Maggie always liked to check out the food offerings at an event. Before Phoebe could decide what to do, her sister abruptly abandoned the hors d'oeuvres and whirled back toward Olivia and Dylan. At first Phoebe had no idea why. Then she saw a man dressed as a rogue of a pirate and she knew.

Brandon.

Phoebe immediately recognized her brother-in-law — Maggie's soon-to-be-ex husband — as he stopped at a tray piled high with miniature brownies. She tried not to react to his unexpected presence or call attention to herself in any way, but she was too late. His eyes met hers and then he grinned that grin that Phoebe had first seen in nursery school and her sister had fallen for at fifteen.

She groaned inwardly. It just figured Brandon Sloan would turn up as a pirate and that he would have no trouble recognizing her in her Edwardian costume.

Phoebe didn't dare bolt. That would only

draw more attention to her. Instead, pretending to be casual, she helped herself to a bit of apple and cheese and moved down the table to him.

"Oh, this is too good," Brandon said. "Phoebe O'Dunn in sequins and a feathered hat."

"Maggie and Olivia don't know I'm here," Phoebe said through her clenched teeth.

"Dylan?"

"No."

Brandon polished off a tiny brownie in one bite. "I didn't think you were the type to sneak into a charity ball. I'm proud of you, Phoebe."

"Do not make fun of me, Brandon."

His dark eyes softened behind his mask. "Okay, I won't. You're shaking. Is everything all right? I saw you dancing —"

"I don't want to talk about it."

"All right. We won't talk about it. Why are you here on the sly?"

"Just because."

"You've been doing too many kids' story hours. You sound like Aidan and Tyler."

Phoebe ignored his teasing her and peered into the crowd. She didn't see her swashbuckler. Everything she hadn't noticed while she was dancing she noticed now. A cluster of people here. Another one there. A

woman shrieking with laughter. A man spilling a drink down his front.

Clinking glasses.

Waiters with trays of drinks and hors d'oeuvres.

Reading materials and displays about the neonatal ICU.

*What was I thinking, coming here tonight?*

How had she let herself get caught up in dancing with a perfect stranger?

They were both playing a role.

"Phoebe?" Brandon took her by the elbow. "You look wobbly. Do you need to get out of here?"

She nodded. "Yes."

"How are you getting home?"

"I have my car."

He grinned. "You drove? Good for you."

She glared at him. "Brandon —"

"I'm not patronizing you. I meant it. Driving in Boston is no picnic even for someone used to it. Do you have your cell phone on you? Call me if you need help. Got that? Maggie would kill me if I knew you were sneaking out of here alone and didn't look after you."

"I don't need looking after. Really. I'll be fine. Thank you." Phoebe started to leave, but stopped and turned back to him. "Brandon, if you see the man I danced with . . ."

Was she completely mad? "Never mind."

She spun into the crowd before he could respond. As she came to the large exit doors, she scanned a knot of people gathered there but didn't see her swashbuckler. When she reached the relative quiet of the ballroom lobby, she hesitated instead of plunging straight onto the escalators. Maybe she should go back to the ballroom and find him. Olivia and Maggie would understand that the only way she could have come tonight was exactly the way she had — on her own, without telling anyone.

If she hadn't been on her own, hadn't been anonymous, she never would have danced with her swashbuckler. He might never have noticed her — or she him — if she'd been hanging out with Maggie, Olivia and Dylan.

Suddenly her head itched under the raven-colored wig, her makeup felt like paste and her feet hurt in her strappy sandals. She turned away from the escalator. She'd freshen up, get her bearings, before heading to her car.

As she started down a carpeted corridor to the restrooms, she heard a man's voice and realized it was coming from a coatroom. "He's here," the man said. "I saw him with my own eyes. He's dressed head to toe in black as a swordfighter or some damn thing."

Phoebe held her breath. *Was he talking about* her *swordfighter?* She edged to the wide-open doorway and peeked into the coatroom. A man was there, alone, his back to her as he spoke into a cell phone. He had short, dark hair with gray streaks and wore a black suit. He wasn't wearing a mask and he wasn't in costume.

"The bastard spotted me," he said. "He's looking for me now. We don't have enough time to take action. We need more."

Phoebe stiffened but didn't move from her position by the door.

*Who's* we? *What kind of action?*

"You should have seen him dancing. The guy can move. He was with some woman dressed up like she was about to board the *Titanic.*" Another pause, then a sigh. "No, I don't know who she is. I'll find out. It shouldn't be hard."

He snapped his phone shut.

Phoebe bolted down the hall and into the ladies' room, the door still swinging behind her as she ducked into a stall. She let out a breath. Should she try to find her swash-buckler and tell him what she'd just over-heard?

What *had* she just overheard?

She wasn't used to this kind of night. The crowds, the glitter, the elegance. She was out of her element. How could she judge the snippet of one-sided conversation with any clarity? For all she knew, her swashbuckler was in the middle of a divorce and tonight was his night to cut loose with a perfect stranger.

In which case it really was time to get back to Knights Bridge.

Phoebe left the stall and washed her hands at the sink, avoiding her reflection in the mirror, grateful she was alone in the ladies' room. Should she peel off as much of her costume as possible before venturing back into the corridor?

*No.*

She didn't have another outfit to change into, and if the man she'd eavesdropped on saw her, he could recognize her dress, snap a picture of her with his phone and there she'd be, strawberry curls, freckles and all. He'd have her name and address in a heartbeat.

Best just to make her exit now.

She'd planned to drive home tonight, anyway. She'd only had a few sips of champagne and was wide-awake. Dylan and Olivia were staying at the hotel, Maggie at Olivia's small apartment in town. Phoebe could join her sister, but that would mean telling her what she'd done.

*What I've done is gone completely mad.*

Easier just to stick to her plan and stay anonymous.

The dress had come with a tiny matching purse that hooked onto the waist. She pulled out the bright red lipstick that she had chosen from Ava and Ruby's theatrical makeup kit and reapplied it, noticing that her hand was shaking. *What a night.* She could be home with a nice cup of lemon-chamomile tea and a good book, or tucked on her couch watching a summer rerun of a favorite television show. Instead she was in Boston, dodging a stranger, her friends, her own sister.

Dancing with another stranger.

*A sexy stranger at that.*

Had he spotted the man in the coatroom? Was that why he'd left her so abruptly?

What was he hiding?

Phoebe tucked her lipstick back in her purse and pulled out her car keys as she finally took in her reflection. Her cheeks *were* flushed. Brandon hadn't been lying about that.

The dress and the hat and the elegant mask really were amazing.

She had no regrets, she realized. Even if

someone recognized her now, as she made her exit, the night was worth any possible embarrassment. So what if her friends and sister discovered she was the one who'd danced with the swashbuckler?

She'd had a blast.

Phoebe returned to the corridor and made it to the escalators without running into the man in the black suit, or anyone else.

As she stepped off the escalator, she glanced around the hotel lobby, half wishing that her dance partner would appear and sweep her into his arms again.

Maybe more than half wishing.

She kept putting one foot in front of the other until she was in the parking garage unlocking her car door. She kicked off her sandals and threw them in the back. She'd tossed gym socks and a pair of sneakers onto the passenger seat. She slipped them on, feeling more normal as she settled behind the wheel and pulled off her wig. It wouldn't fool anyone now, anyway. At this point, if the man she'd overheard spotted her, he had only to jot down her license plate to find out who she was.

The same with her swordfighter.

Her car started without any trouble. She'd visited Maggie, and even Olivia, often enough during their time in Boston that she

had no trouble finding her way back to Storrow Drive. When she reached Route 2, she
finally let out a long, cathartic breath.

*She'd done it.*

Now her coach could turn back into a
pumpkin and she could get back to her life
in Knights Bridge.

# FOUR

Maggie would have sworn the woman who had danced with Noah Kendrick was her sister Phoebe, but that just wasn't possible. It was wishful O'Dunn thinking at its craziest.

Even crazier was thinking the pirate sauntering through the crowd was her husband.

She gulped more champagne than she should have. She was letting herself get upset over nothing. No way would any Sloan, and especially Brandon Sloan, show up for a masquerade ball.

Of course, if Brandon did show up, it would be dressed as a pirate. She needed to get a better look at him.

"It can't be Brandon," Maggie said under her breath. "It just can't be."

Olivia eased next to her. "The pirate, you mean?"

She was stunning in her black Audrey Hepburn dress, complete with a revealing slit up one leg and multi-strand pearls. Maggie didn't feel nearly as elegant in her blue chiffon Grace Kelly dress.

"He reminds me of Brandon." She tried to sound dismissive. "I must have had too much champagne."

"Ah."

Maggie gave her friend a sharp look. "Olivia? *Is* it Brandon?"

"I don't know but I had the same thought when I saw the pirate. Dylan gave away so many tickets but he didn't mention Brandon. Several of his hockey buddies are here. Maybe the pirate's one of them."

"That must be it. He's one of Dylan's NHL friends."

"Do you want me to find out?" Olivia asked.

"No! Not when I'm dressed up as Grace Kelly. Brandon would suck all the fun out of the experience." Maggie polished off the last of her champagne. It wasn't the reason her head was spinning. That pirate was. She forced herself to smile at Olivia. "Several people have recognized my dress. I'm enjoying the fantasy, personally. The whole evening has been perfect."

"I'm glad. You deserve this break, Maggie."

"I do, don't I?" She laughed, but she was

on the verge of tears again. She had to put Brandon out of her mind. "But I wouldn't change a thing about my life right now. I love my work, and the boys are the best — I'd walk on hot coals for them. You're happy being back in our little hometown, aren't you?"

"I don't miss Boston as much as I thought I might," Olivia said.

"Having Dylan up the road helps. Where is he, by the way, and when do I get to meet Noah? I'm glad you pointed him out to me. I've seen pictures of him but I'd never have recognized him in his costume."

"It's a great costume, isn't it? Dylan's with a couple of his NHL friends. I haven't seen Noah but I want to introduce you to him."

Given her relationship with Dylan, Olivia was naturally more attuned to the other attendees at the ball. Masks or not, most people had obviously recognized Dylan and were intensely curious about her. Maggie liked being able to enjoy the festivities with a measure of anonymity.

"Are you going to see Brandon while you're in town?" Olivia asked.

"No," Maggie said without hesitation. "I'm heading back home first thing in the morning and I'm Grace Kelly tonight. I'm not Mrs. Brandon Sloan. I won't be for much longer, anyway. Might as well get used to it."

"Maggie . . ."

"I'm sorry. I don't know why I brought him up."

Olivia hesitated, then smiled. "Would you like more champagne? And have you tried the mini frittatas? They're great."

Maggie frowned at her friend. They'd known each other since they were tots and Olivia was clearly not telling her something. They'd driven to Boston together, taking Maggie's car. They'd dropped off Maggie's things at the small apartment Olivia still had from her days with a Boston design studio and then walked over to the hotel. Dylan was already there, in costume, with Noah and his NHL friends.

Olivia drank some of her champagne. Her behavior was definitely awkward, Maggie thought. "Olivia? What's going on?"

"I wouldn't bet good money that Brandon's at a sports bar watching the Red Sox tonight."

"What? Olivia — is the pirate Brandon?"

"I told you I don't know for sure." Olivia again hesitated. "I think Brandon may have been in touch with Dylan."

Maggie felt her mouth drop open but she quickly snapped it shut again. "In touch how? Why?"

"I don't know. The Sloans are working on Dylan's place. Maybe Brandon stopped by."

"He doesn't live in Knights Bridge. That's my life."

"His family's there. The boys."

"Believe me, I know."

Maggie heard the bitterness in her own voice and regretted it. *Don't do this tonight,* she told herself. Let Brandon live his own life. That was what he wanted, wasn't it? She shook off her confusion, her sense of violation — as if he had deliberately inserted himself into the new life she was building for herself, without him. She took in a deep breath. She prided herself on staying calm amid the chaos that her life sometimes threw at her as she juggled the multiple demands of her busy catering schedule, her two young sons, her three sisters, her widowed mother.

Her estranged husband.

She looked into the crowd to see if she could spot the pirate. It had to be Brandon.

She forced another smile at her friend. "We'll sort everything out later. We're Grace Kelly and Audrey Hepburn tonight, right?"

Olivia looked visibly relieved at Maggie's cheerful tone. "Come on. Let's go find Dylan. Noah's around here somewhere, too.

You'll have to meet him."

Maggie spotted Dylan alone by the doors out to the ballroom lobby. "He's on his way over here now. Why don't you two dance?"

"I'm not going to abandon you if you're upset about Brandon —"

"Nothing I'm not used to. Don't worry about me. If Brandon is the pirate, he had his chance to annoy me and resisted. I'm fine, honestly. Go."

When Olivia turned, Dylan was already in front of her. He took her in his arms and whisked her onto the dance floor. He moved like a hockey player on ice, Maggie thought, smiling as her friend snuggled close to her fiancé. Olivia had reinvented her life, too. She was doing well, and Maggie was glad to see her so happy.

A thick arm went around her waist. "No wallflowers allowed," the pirate whispered into her ear.

*Brandon.*

Maggie recognized his deep voice, his touch, but she pretended not to know it was him as she put a hand on his shoulder and let him spin her onto the dance floor. She'd be Grace Kelly in her flowing blue dress. Cool, calm, controlled, as if she were dancing with Cary Grant. But why was Brandon here? She let her questions die on her lips as he pulled her close to him. Did he know he was dancing with her — with his wife, the mother of his children?

Of course he knew.

He settled a hand on the curve of her hip. "Shh. Let's just dance."

It was what she wanted, too. Just to dance. To pretend he was about to lift her into his arms and carry her off as he had so many times in the past.

How long had it been since he had held her like this?

There had been only one man in her life. Brandon Sloan. They had been so right together . . . and then so wrong. Money, pride, dreams, the busyness of life. They'd let them all erode what they'd had together.

She had so many questions. So much she wanted to say to him.

"Do you know Dylan McCaffrey?"

Brandon didn't hear her, or pretended not to as he held her close.

Maggie almost didn't notice when the music stopped. He released her and smiled that rogue's smile of his. "You're beautiful, Maggie O'Dunn Sloan."

Then he was gone, and by the time Maggie pulled herself together, she was standing alone on the edge of the dance floor, wondering if she'd imagined him. Tears burned in her eyes but she hoped, with the mask, that no one would notice.

Suddenly she felt hot in her Grace Kelly dress, ridiculous.

Noah Kendrick eased in next to her in his swashbuckler costume and slipped off his mask. "Maggie, I'm Noah Kendrick. Dylan's friend. Can I get you a glass of water?"

"I'm all right, thanks. Just . . . just hot."

"The costumes have their drawbacks."

"They get us thinking about fantasies, don't they?" Maggie appreciated his diplomacy. As Phoebe had said yesterday, it was a slippery slope to want what you knew you couldn't have. Maggie cleared her throat, straightened her shoulders, wondering if it really could have been her sister who had danced with the California billionaire. Dylan's friend, and now Olivia's friend. "It's a pleasure to meet you, Noah."

He gave a mock bow. "A pleasure to meet you, too, Maggie."

"Have you enjoyed your evening? Who was that you were dancing with?"

He frowned. "I never got her name. Did you see where she went?"

Maggie shook her head. "Sorry, no."

His eyes settled on her. "Do you know her?"

"I never talked to her," she answered carefully. What if it *was* Phoebe who had danced with Noah? Had she realized who he was? Would she want Maggie blabbing her identity to him?

She gave herself a mental shake. She was being crazy. It wasn't Phoebe.

"I was just impressed with how you two danced together," Maggie said.

"I was distracted for a moment." He seemed to want to go on but sighed. "Well, it's nothing for you to worry about. You and Olivia look lovely. Great costumes."

"Thanks. They're fun. My sisters helped. I should call it an evening. My mother has my sons for the night, and I want to check in. They're live wires as it is, and she tends to —" Maggie broke off. She wasn't going to criticize her mother in front of a man she barely knew. "They always have a great time together."

"You're feeling better, then?"

She nodded. "It was just one of those things. I've learned to have my moments and move on. Are Dylan and Olivia still dancing?"

"They're good together," Noah said simply.

"Yes, they are," Maggie said without hesitation. "I hope you enjoyed your hike in the White Mountains."

"It was an experience," he said with a smile.

Noah was quiet, but he radiated a confidence that Maggie hadn't noticed at first, probably due more to her preset ideas about him than anything else. She hadn't expected a high-tech genius, a hard-driving entrepreneur, to be so self-possessed. "A good swordfight more to your taste than mountain climbing?"

"Than staying a step ahead of a cloud of mosquitoes, for sure."

Maggie laughed, feeling more herself again. "Brandon and I climbed Mount Washington before the boys came along. What an experience. The views stay with you forever, don't they?"

"I liked the hot dogs at the top," Noah said with a wink.

Dylan and Olivia joined them, and Maggie pulled off her mask. The evening was winding down and she wanted to change back into her regular clothes, forget any wild fantasies she'd had. She glanced around for her pirate husband, but he had disappeared. She expected to feel relief but she had to acknowledge a pang of disappointment, too.

And of loneliness, she thought. For so long, she and Brandon had been at each other's sides. Lovers, best friends, parents to their two little boys.

How had they let that get away from them?

Maggie pasted a smile on her face. She wasn't going to think about what had gone wrong between her and Brandon right now. She turned down Olivia and Dylan's offer to walk with her back to Olivia's apartment and instead headed out alone.

The night was warm and still, Copley Square filled with people. Maggie told herself she needed this time on her own. She'd loved living in Boston, but she didn't miss city life as much as she thought she would when she'd packed up herself and the boys and returned to Knights Bridge. Her hometown had plenty to offer, and it was a great place for Tyler and Aidan. They'd made new friends, loved being close to family. It was the same for Maggie. Even her work was better in Knights Bridge. In Boston, she'd worked part-time for different caterers. Now she had her own catering business, and it was getting off the ground faster than she'd anticipated or even had hoped it would.

She cut down to Commonwealth Avenue and continued on to attractive, residential Marlborough Street. She'd always wanted to live in Back Bay, but she and Brandon had rented a series of apartments in less expensive parts of the city. It wasn't just a question of finances, she'd finally realized. It was what he wanted, where he was comfortable. Back Bay wouldn't suit him.

She used Olivia's keys to get into the apartment. Olivia planned to give it up, but it definitely came in handy tonight. Maggie wouldn't have wanted to drive home after her evening as Grace Kelly.

She caught her reflection in the entry mirror. She'd managed to avoid mirrors all evening and was a little shocked at how she looked. Sexy, a little devil-may-care. Leave it to Ava and Ruby to get creative and theatrical. Phoebe's discovery of the look-alike dress from *To Catch a Thief* was perfect, but the twins were responsible for the subtle Grace Kelly makeup, the push-up bra, the blond wig and the glittery mask.

Maggie pulled off the wig, then unpinned her hair and let it fall to her shoulders.

Already she looked and felt more like Maggie O'Dunn, mom to two young boys, second of four sisters, caterer to showers, weddings, meetings, reunions, fundraisers and even the occasional wake.

If not always the most practical person, she was at least able to manage on her own.

Did she look and feel like the wife of Brandon Sloan anymore?

Had he left the hotel and found his way to a sports bar?

Everyone liked Brandon. He was easy to like since he didn't have to deal with the details of paying bills, raising their sons, figuring out their future. When faced with unemployment, he'd taken off for the mountains with a backpack and his dreams. He'd never meant to be a carpenter forever. He was good at it, he even liked it — but he thought he should be doing something else. Maggie didn't even know what anymore. She doubted he did, either.

She put him out of her mind and dialed her mother's house. Tyler picked up. "Gran's making hot chocolate."

"Hey, Tyler. Why are you still up?"

"The bat woke us up."

"I see." Bats weren't unheard of at her mother's farmhouse, especially in summer. "Where's the bat now?"

"Gran shooed it outside with a broom. I helped."

"Good for you. What about your brother?"

"He hid under his blanket. He's having hot chocolate, too."

"All right. Well, you two be good and help Gran. Tell her I called, okay?"

"I will, Mom. When are you coming home?"

"Tomorrow."

"Did you see Dad?"

She couldn't lie to her son. "I did, but just for a few minutes."

"He's taking me and Aidan camping."

Maggie heard the questioning note in Tyler's voice and responded without hesitation. "Yes, absolutely, he's taking you and Aidan camping." That was one thing she knew for certain: Brandon would keep his promise to his sons. "Go enjoy your hot chocolate. I'll see you tomorrow."

When she disconnected, she threw her phone onto the entry table and sank onto the sofa. It opened out into a bed. She would sleep there.

She kicked off her shoes and noticed a side seam in her flowing dress had split an inch, probably from dancing with her husband.

"Why aren't you here with me, Brandon?"

She hugged her arms around herself and burst into tears.

Phoebe could hear the pitter-pat of rain on the library roof as she sat cross-legged on the wood floor of the hidden attic room. Too wired to sleep after the masquerade ball and the drive back to Knights Bridge, she'd changed into yoga pants and a lightweight fleece tunic, intending to do a few stretches on the living room floor, but she'd ended up grabbing a flashlight and heading out into what was then a light drizzle. As she'd breathed in the damp night air, she imagined her swashbuckler's arms around her.

What a night it had been.

She'd walked down Thistle Lane to the library, letting herself in through the side door. Putting aside thoughts of ghosts, she'd debated a moment before starting up the back stairs. A more formal set of stairs in the main room led just to the second floor. In her five years with the library, she'd seldom ventured up to the attic. One of those rare times was two weeks ago, and it had resulted in the discovery of the dresses that she, Olivia and Maggie had worn tonight.

It was pouring rain now, pitch-dark outside. Phoebe had never been up to the attic at night. She half expected a bat to fly out from its dark recesses, crowded with cast-off library furnishings, archives, books and everything her waste-not, want-not predecessors over the past century-plus had thought might come in handy someday.

She'd come upon the hidden room accidentally, when she'd lifted a small paper bag sitting on top of an old filing cabinet and a dozen antique marbles broke out of the bottom. They dropped onto the floor, rolling every which way. Several rolled under two tin closets standing side by side, filled with more junk and treasures. She'd edged between the closets, determined to collect the marbles.

As she'd bent down to retrieve a colorful swirled boulder, she noticed a door behind the free-standing closets. She'd had no idea it was there. Madly curious, she'd tucked the marble in her dress pocket and shoved the closets back just enough to give her room to get at the door. It was unlocked but obviously hadn't been opened in a while. It hadn't given way easily.

She'd expected to find that it was a closet, probably stuffed with more of the mishmash of materials in the rest of the attic. Instead the door opened into a small room that she hadn't even realized existed. It was lined with shelves and cupboards neatly arranged with fabric, patterns, buttons, zippers, needles, thread, notions, buttons — everything an avid seamstress might need.

A secret sewing room.

It felt like a hideaway, a tiny retreat where someone could sit and work in peace and quiet. Another door opened onto a remote corner of the sprawling attic, by a small window that overlooked the town common. A dusty sewing table was positioned so that a seamstress could work with a pleasant view and a bit of natural light.

The only thing that seemed to be missing for a fully equipped sewing room was an actual sewing machine.

Phoebe had done a quick survey of the contents of the room and discovered the Hollywood-inspired and period dresses in two matching cedar-lined trunks and several hanging garment bags. Leaving everything undisturbed, she'd replaced the tin closets in front of the door and decided to keep the room her secret for the time being.

A few days later, she'd gone back and picked out the three dresses to be cleaned.

Now, tired, a little spooked with the dark night and rain, she raised the lid on a sewing basket. Given the conditions, she was ever-watchful for mice and spiders but the sewing kit yielded only pins, needles, thread, embroidery floss, a tracing wheel, cards of zigzag and seam binding.

Who had sewn up here? Why leave so much behind?

Phoebe took a sharp breath. Had the sewer of all these clothes died? Was that why the incredible dresses were still here?

*I have to know.*

She pulled all the notions and other items out of the sewing kit and laid them on the floor, looking for any clues that would help identify who had sewn the dresses she, Maggie and Olivia had worn to Boston tonight.

Her Edwardian gown had attracted her swashbuckler and hidden her from the scrutiny of the mystery man in the coatroom.

*A night of mysteries,* she thought, untangling several zippers.

A browned sheet of paper was matted to the bottom of the sewing basket. Phoebe carefully peeled it off and saw that it was a practice sheet of the conjugation of the French verb *to be* in a neat, feminine handwriting: *Je suis, tu es, il/elle est, nous sommes, vous êtes, ils/elles sont.*

Phoebe had taken French in high school and college but she was rusty and wasn't sure she could have managed to conjugate even a simple verb. Had the seamstress gone to high school in Knights Bridge? Had she been a student when she'd set up this room?

*So many questions.*

Phoebe returned the sheet of French verbs to the sewing kit and carefully replaced all the supplies. She stood, finally feeling the effects of her long day. She grabbed her flashlight and shut the door, moved the closets back into place, then headed back down the steep, dark stairs. The creaks and groans of the old building normally didn't faze her, but the hidden room had her thinking about ghosts as she locked up.

It was still raining when she started back down Thistle Lane. She'd gone out without a raincoat or umbrella, but it was a warm, gentle rain, as if to remind her what was real and what wasn't real.

Pretending to be a princess and dancing with a mysterious swashbuckler at a Boston charity ball had been a fleeting fantasy, a peek into another kind of life.

Someone else's life. Not hers.

# FIVE

Noah slept fitfully and awoke wishing he had sent a check for the neonatal ICU instead of attending the masquerade ball. He could have gone straight back to California after hiking in the White Mountains or stayed in California altogether. Either way, he'd have spared himself meeting the potential love of his life and letting her slip through his fingers.

It was his own fault. He never should have left his princess and chased after his mystery man, if, indeed, that was who he'd spotted.

There had to be a way to find her.

He decided he didn't want to deal with email and voice mail and "accidentally" dropped his iPhone in the water-filled bathroom sink.

The people who truly needed to reach him would figure it out.

He got dressed, appreciating his normal black trousers and black shirt. No more hiking clothes, no more swashbuckler cape. He went down for breakfast and tried to act as if he'd had a good night.

Once he had coffee, he decided he probably shouldn't have tossed his phone into the sink.

He'd run into people last night from his MIT days. Rumors were circulating about what was next for him now that NAK had gone public. One account had him staying on as CEO, another shifting into research and development. Focusing on his Central Coast winery. Getting deeper into venture capital, starting a new business, devoting himself to philanthropy, moving into academia.

None of the rumors were true, if only because Noah had no idea what was next for him beyond whole-wheat pancakes and warm Vermont maple syrup for breakfast.

He'd finished his pancakes when Dylan and Olivia wandered into the restaurant and joined him at his table. Waiters quickly brought out fresh place settings. Olivia had on lightweight jeans and a green linen top that matched her eyes. Dylan was in jeans and a hiking shirt, as if he hadn't thought about being at the Boston hotel this morning. Noah hadn't, either. He just generally wore the same thing.

honed his natural instincts about people, their motives and character. He'd turned down a larger role with NAK, but he'd been indispensable in transforming Noah's ideas and technical skills into a viable — and ultimately highly successful — company.

"Did you talk to this man you saw?" Noah asked.

Dylan shook his head. "He was watching you dance with your princess. Was she with him?"

"Why would you think that?"

"She left the ballroom right after he did. I tried to follow her but she disappeared before I could catch up with her. I didn't see the older gentleman."

"Did you recognize him?"

"No," Dylan said without hesitation, then turned to Olivia. "What about you? Did you see this man?"

She set down her coffee cup. "I spoke with him briefly. I think he's the one you're talking about. He asked what I knew about the woman Noah was dancing with."

"How did you respond?" Noah asked, keeping his tone neutral.

"I didn't, really. I just said I was there to enjoy the evening. I had the feeling he knew you, Noah. I didn't think anything of it. We spoke for less than a minute. Then he moved on. Is he a problem?"

"He's an unknown." Noah poured himself more coffee from a small silver pot. "He might not be a problem at all. I spotted him a few times in San Diego."

"How many is a 'few'?" Dylan asked.

"Three. At a restaurant where I was enjoying a nice fish dinner with a friend."

"One of your actresses?"

Noah ignored him. "Then at the fencing studio. Third time was outside our offices. I ran into Loretta and we agreed she'd see if she could find out who he is and what he wants."

"Why not use one of your own people?"

"Who are my people nowadays, Dylan?"

Dylan tapped his fingers on the white tablecloth. "Noah, is there any reason this guy would bird-dog you? Personal, professional — anything?"

Noah pushed away his untouched coffee refill. "Not everyone needs a reason."

"What does Loretta say?"

"She's stumped. I hoped it'd turn out to be a case of too much time on my hands. Then I saw this strange man again last night. It's too big a coincidence for me to spot him in San Diego and then in Boston."

Dylan sat back. "I'll talk to Loretta and take care of this."

Noah shook his head. "No, Dylan. Thank you, but Loretta and I are handling this on our own."

"Any ideas who he is, what he wants?" Dylan asked.

"No."

"Is he stalking you or what?"

"I wouldn't say stalking."

Dylan took in a sharp breath. "Maybe you should involve NAK security. You're worth a lot of money. Your company recently went public. You've made a few enemies in the process."

"I don't think this is about money, enemies or power. It feels different."

"Personal?"

"Maybe."

"An ex-girlfriend's father?" Olivia asked. "Something like that?"

Noah smiled at her. "You're assuming I have an ex-girlfriend."

"More like a legion of them," Dylan muttered. When Olivia raised her eyebrows, he added, "Noah's high-profile. A lot of women want to have a night on the town with him, at his expense. Deep down, though, he's still the high school geek who was better at math than most of his teachers. I wasn't, in case you were wondering."

"In other words," Noah said, his eyes on

Olivia, "I have a low threshold of trust where women are concerned." He sat back, wishing now he'd waited longer to have his pancakes. "I also get dumped a lot."

"Because you don't like being used," Dylan said. "Maybe you flipped the switch of one of your actress's crazy uncles, or someone is seizing the moment to see what they can get off you. We can speculate all morning. It won't get us anywhere."

"And it's not a problem until it's a problem," Noah said.

"This man hasn't made direct contact with you?"

"Not yet, no."

"Maybe he sent you one of the emails you didn't want to read this morning."

"I'm not worried, Dylan," Noah said truthfully. "If he wanted to physically harm me, he's had several chances."

"He could know you're a master fencer and a brown belt in karate."

"I hope he does."

"What if he's looking up dirt on you so that he can harm NAK?" Olivia asked. "What if he wants to harm you — your reputation?"

"Let him try. I have no skeletons in the closet." Noah gave her a slight smile. "I'm not that interesting, Olivia. More than likely this man is just angling for money."

Dylan eyed Noah. "Any chance there's a connection to me?"

"I have no reason to think so, or that there's a connection to Knights Bridge."

"Knights Bridge?" Olivia sat forward. "Why would there be a connection to Knights Bridge?"

Noah regretted his offhand comment and tried to reassure her. "I'm sure there isn't one." He decided to change the subject. "Unless my princess is hiding there. Are you positive you two didn't recognize her? She had quite arresting eyes. Almost turquoise. They reminded me of your friend Maggie's eyes but the color was deeper."

Olivia reached suddenly for the cream pitcher. "Really? I wonder who she could be."

She greeted the waiter a little too cheerfully when he arrived with her and Dylan's breakfasts. Noah glanced at Dylan and saw that he noticed her reaction, too.

The description of his dance partner had obviously struck a nerve with Olivia.

Noah smiled. His princess might not be so lost, after all.

Knights Bridge was even prettier than Noah remembered from his visit in early April.

101

Having leaves on the trees helped. He sat up front with Dylan while Olivia pointed out various landmarks from the backseat. She explained that the building of the Quabbin Reservoir and the subsequent flooding of much of the Swift River Valley had changed the development of the town, putting it off the beaten track and giving it a "time has stopped here" feel that was, both Olivia and Dylan again insisted, deceptive.

Maybe so, Noah thought, but that didn't mean he wanted to do more than float in and out again. He had a chartered jet scheduled to meet him at a nearby private airport that evening.

Of course, his princess could change everything. He'd hang out for a day or two in Knights Bridge and brave mosquitoes and its one restaurant if there was a chance he'd find out more about her.

Dylan turned onto a back road that wound toward Quabbin, his ease with the twists and turns suggesting a familiarity that reminded Noah that his best friend was, without a doubt, moving on from NAK. Less certain was whether he and Olivia planned to keep a home in San Diego. Noah would. Four New England winters during his years at MIT were enough for him.

Not that he had any reason to move to Knights Bridge or anywhere else in New England.

The Farm at Carriage Hill was located in a picturesque mix of meadows, woods and stone walls. Its hand-painted sign, decorated with a cluster of chives, worked with the 1803 house with its cream-colored clapboards and rich blue front door. As he followed Olivia through her kitchen out to the stone terrace, Noah could see that she was turning her vision for her historic house into a reality. Even subtle changes were infused with her sense of color and design, and her love for her hometown. According to Dylan, she'd always planned on returning to Knights Bridge to open her own version of a bed-and-breakfast, even if her departure from Boston hadn't been entirely on her terms.

"Dylan and I will make lunch," she said. "You can wait out here and familiarize yourself with New England herbs and flowers."

"You're assuming I want to know New England herbs and flowers."

She laughed. "Yes, I am."

She went back inside, and Noah sat at the round table and observed the backyard. It really was attractive. Small-town life suited

Olivia. He hadn't known her when she lived in Boston and worked at a prestigious design studio, but he knew from Dylan that she'd lost a major client in an underhanded way to a friend whose career Olivia had helped revive. The experience had served as a catalyst for her to transform her life.

One could only move forward from where one was standing, Noah thought as he stretched out his legs and tried to relax. Pretending otherwise was a fast way into trouble. He knew from hard experience that where he was standing at any given moment wasn't always where he wanted to be, or should be. That was just life. Not everything was under his control. Mistakes, incompetence, good intentions, bad intentions, good luck, bad luck, human nature — lots of things beyond his control played a role.

Of course, a lot under his control played a role in determining where he was, too. His own screwups, his own limitations, his own lack of vision and purpose.

Were they what had this mystery man on his tail?

Noah sank back in his chair, appreciating the quiet surroundings. Olivia certainly did have a knack with flowers and herbs. She came through the back door with a tray of sandwiches, her big, ugly dog trailing behind her.

He looked up at her as the dog, a German shepherd with a healthy mix of black Lab and probably several other breeds, promptly flopped down under the table, his big black-and-brown head on Noah's feet. "What's his name again?"

"Buster," Olivia said, placing the tray on the table. "He adopted me when I first moved back here."

Dylan followed her onto the terrace, carrying two glasses of iced tea. He set one in front of Noah. "Maybe you should get a dog, Noah."

He eased his foot out from under the dog's head. "Does Buster have a brother?"

"I hope not," Dylan said with a mock shudder.

Olivia grinned at him. "I thought you and Buster had bonded."

"We have, but one Buster is enough." He winked at her as he handed her the second glass of tea and sat across from Noah. "All the world needs."

Buster gave a deep, satisfied sigh from under the table. The dog was visibly calmer than when Noah had met him in April. A few months in Olivia's care no doubt had helped. Buster had clearly endeared himself to Dylan, despite an inauspicious meeting.

Now here they all were — Olivia Frost, Dylan McCaffrey and Buster.

Noah smiled at what a great family they made. He'd never seen Dylan happier, and Olivia was fast becoming a friend herself. Noah helped himself to a chicken salad sandwich. It had some kind of herb in it. Fresh tarragon, he thought. If his princess was in Knights Bridge, was she into herbs, too?

"Who'll be minding Buster while you two are in San Diego?" he asked casually.

"Maggie will be in every day," Olivia said. "She and I are basically business partners. We're thinking about doing the paperwork to make it official. We work so well together."

"And she lives in Knights Bridge and likes herbs," Noah said.

"She also likes her mother's goats," Dylan added, his tone neutral. As he'd explained to Noah, the bonds between the people of Knights Bridge were sometimes tricky to navigate. The Frosts had been in the Swift River Valley and surrounding hills for generations. Despite Dylan's newly discovered roots in the region, he was still an outsider.

"Maggie *loves* herbs and goat's milk," Olivia said with a laugh. "I don't know that much about goats, but the milk is perfect for the artisan soaps Maggie and I are making."

Noah tried to keep any reaction to himself as it sank in that he was talking goats and soap at a two-hundred-year-old house on a dead-end road, surrounded by meadows, shade trees, green grass and a lot of flowers and herbs. It was a first.

The goats, he'd learned, belonged to Maggie's widowed mother and were a source of both tension and enjoyment within the O'Dunn family.

Obviously in a happy mood, Olivia sat between him and Dylan. "I'll give you some samples of our goat's milk soap. We're still tinkering before we test-market it here. Maggie's on top of all the regulations."

"Complicated?"

"Not too bad unless we make actual medicinal claims."

"Which you won't?"

She shook her head. Noah saw that his interest surprised her, but she was the love of his best friend's life and he wanted to know about her and what she enjoyed. With Carriage Hill getting off the ground and the betrayal of her friend over stealing a client behind her, Olivia's natural optimism had clearly returned.

Falling in love didn't hurt, either.

Noah thought of his princess. He could feel the curve of her hip, see the warmth in her eyes, the soft swell of her creamy breasts. Why had he left her? Why hadn't he let the mystery man come to him?

Because he hadn't wanted his life in San Diego — who he really was — to intrude on the moment. The fantasy they both were enjoying.

Either that, or he hadn't known what the hell he was thinking.

He wasn't thinking she'd disappear, that was for sure.

"Noah?" Dylan asked with a frown.

He sighed. "Mind drifting. Thinking about hiking in the mountains, then playing a swashbuckler at a ball — I've got mental whiplash."

"Not a chance," his friend said without hesitation. "You never have mental whiplash, whatever that is."

"It's a big change to go from waking up in a sleeping bag on a mountain to dancing at a charity ball that night."

Dylan was still obviously unconvinced. "You knew the deal. There were no surprises." He shifted, then smiled. "Except for your princess. I guess she could have you whiplashed in a number of ways."

"Funny, Dylan," Noah said.

He grinned. "I thought so."

As they finished their simple lunch, Noah noticed a woman come out of a small shed at the far end of the yard. She had a cobalt-blue scarf tied around her head and long, dark strawberry curls trailing down her back. She started up a bark-mulch path, and Noah saw she wore a deep red top that accentuated her breasts and shorts that shaped slim hips. Her sport sandals, though, looked as if they'd gone up and down Mt. Washington a time or two.

When she reached the terrace, she stayed on the path and motioned toward a raised flower bed as she addressed Olivia. "The slugs got to the miniature dahlias, Liv. They're so gross. I put out slug bait and trimmed back the worst of the damage." She shuddered, then smiled brightly. "I was admiring the gardens and couldn't resist going on slug patrol when I saw the carnage."

"Yuck," Olivia said. "I hate slugs. Only thing worse are ticks."

Noah glanced at Dylan. Slugs? Ticks? What had happened to bucolic small-town New England?

Dylan seemed to read his mind, with obvious amusement. "Ticks suck blood and can

109

be hard to see," he explained, not that an explanation was necessary or desired.

"Oh, sorry," Olivia said. "Noah, this is my friend Phoebe O'Dunn. Maggie's sister. Phoebe, this is —"

"Noah. Noah Kendrick." He got to his feet and put out a hand. "A pleasure, Phoebe."

She wiped a palm on her hip and smiled as she shook his hand, her skin warm, soft, her fingers long and slender. "I wore garden gloves when I took on the slugs, but you never know. It's nice to meet you, Noah. I hope you're enjoying Knights Bridge."

"Hard not to on such a beautiful day, despite images of slugs and ticks."

"Sorry about that," she said, the twinkle in her eyes belying her words. "Are you here for long?"

"That's not the plan."

Noah saw that her eyes were a similar turquoise to her sister's but shook off any comparison with his princess from last night. The false eyelashes, the heavy makeup — how would he be able to tell for sure? He doubted he'd recognize her voice. He wasn't good at that sort of thing.

Now if he could touch her hips . . .

He shook off that thought, too. Whatever Olivia knew about his dance partner and

110

wasn't saying, it didn't involve this attractive slug-hunter in scarf and muddy clothes.

*Definitely* not the same turquoise eyes.

With one smooth movement, Phoebe pulled off her scarf and gave her curls a shake once they were free. She seemed natural, unselfconscious. In her element, he thought.

"Well, if you do decide to stay on," she said, "we'll make sure you're not bored."

Noah felt his eyebrows go up and heard Dylan give a little cough behind him.

"Phoebe's the town librarian," Olivia added quickly.

"She can keep me in reading material, then." Noah smiled at Knights Bridge's redheaded librarian. "Nothing like a good book."

"That's right. I love to read. I meant to tie a hammock to two shade trees in my backyard this summer but I haven't gotten to it. Reading a good book in a hammock in the shade — doesn't that sound like the perfect summer afternoon?"

"Provided the hammock is tick- and slug-free," Noah said mildly.

Phoebe laughed. "Definitely." Her gaze steadied on him, her face angled so that the sunlight brought out the gold highlights in her hair and the spray of freckles on her nose and cheeks. "Were you at the masquerade ball last night?"

"Yes, I was. Were you?"

She waved a hand. "My youngest sisters and I helped Olivia and Maggie with their costumes."

"More O'Dunn sisters?" Noah asked.

"There are four of us. Ava and Ruby are twins. They're home for the summer but they're in graduate school. They're studying theater. They'd have gone last night if they'd had the time."

"Maggie seemed to enjoy herself," Olivia said.

Phoebe smiled. "Oh, good. She'll be back home soon. I can't wait to hear how her night on the town went. I'm sure it was a fantastic evening."

Noah sat back on his chair. *There.* He could rule out Phoebe O'Dunn and her turquoise eyes. Not that he'd seriously considered her, given her penchant for gardening and hammocks and her willingness to take on slugs. That didn't fit with his princess.

So what did Olivia know that she wasn't saying?

Noah ground his teeth. What was he doing? The woman he'd danced with and then abandoned last night was as much a fantasy

for him as her swashbuckler was for her.

He was no swashbuckler.

Right now he was just bored. After the months of tension and the grueling pace of taking his company public, he finally had time to come up for air. He'd even looked forward to a few days hiking in the White Mountains.

His princess was a mirage, and maybe so was his mystery man.

He needed to head back to San Diego before he conjured up real trouble.

Except he didn't want to go back.

He felt his spine stiffen at the thought of staying in Knights Bridge. On the one hand, it felt like the right thing to do. A fun distraction. On the other hand . . . it was totally insane. The only person he really knew there was Dylan, and Dylan and Olivia were joining him on the flight back to San Diego tonight. She wanted to see NAK and her fiancé's home.

Noah watched Phoebe O'Dunn kick a chunk of dried mud off one sandal and found that he wouldn't mind getting to know Knights Bridge's slug-hunting librarian.

Three nights in the White Mountains must have affected his brain cells.

When he tuned back into the conversa-

tion, Olivia and Phoebe had started to cross the terrace, chatting as they disappeared through the screen door into the kitchen.

Noah frowned at Dylan. "What did I miss?"

Dylan sighed. "Phoebe rode her bike here. That's why we didn't see her car."

"Ah."

"This is why you study fencing and karate. They force you to stay focused. If your mind wanders, you get stabbed or punched."

"It's not that simple."

"Nothing is with you," Dylan said without any hint of criticism.

Noah stood. Except for a few holes in their waxy-green leaves, the flowers where Phoebe O'Dunn had done her slug work appeared fine to him. He wasn't sure he'd ever seen a slug. He stepped off the terrace onto the soft grass. Buster rolled out from under the table and followed him, then settled onto his stomach in the shade.

"I could always watch Buster while you and Olivia are in San Diego," Noah said.

Dylan scratched the side of his mouth. "Dog sit? You're kidding, right? You've never even owned a dog."

"What difference does that make? How hard could it be to keep an eye on Buster

here? Feed him, water him, walk him. Done."

Dylan didn't bother to hide his skepticism. "What are you thinking, Noah?"

He didn't really know what he was thinking. Sometimes he came up with a solution before he had fully, consciously grasped the problem. Buster yawned, then stretched as he relaxed completely. "What if I told you I want to make sure our mystery man isn't here?" Noah asked.

"In Knights Bridge, you mean?"

"Correct."

"Is that a hunch, or do you have evidence he could be here?"

"It's not even good enough to be a hunch."

Dylan didn't respond for a moment. They'd had similar conversations many times over their long friendship. "Is there any possibility this guy is connected to my father?"

"For all I know he's connected to the man on the moon." Noah reined in his frustration. "I have zero to go on. I only know what I've told you."

"It's not enough."

"No, it's not."

Olivia came out the back door. "Phoebe just left. Did you guys say anything to her?"

115

Dylan shook his head. "I didn't. Noah?"

"We talked slugs," Noah said. "Why?"

"She just seemed quieter than usual. I'm sure it's nothing. Noah, did I hear you say you want to dog sit?"

"Sure." He realized he was at least semi-serious. He squatted down and patted Buster. "Your pup and I have bonded."

"But you're . . ." Olivia looked at Dylan, then back at Noah as if she hadn't heard him right. "Of course you're welcome to stay here, but Maggie can look after Buster. I mean . . ." She seemed at a loss for words.

"You mean you don't understand why a billionaire would offer to dog sit," Noah finished for her, matter-of-factly.

She blushed. "I guess that's what I mean."

He suspected Olivia was eager to change the subject. "Your friend Phoebe seems very nice. I hope I wasn't rude."

"Not at all. Phoebe's cool. She doesn't ruffle easily. Maggie's like that, too, at least when she's working. She can be hotheaded otherwise. I wish Phoebe had come with us last night but she wouldn't. Long story." Olivia glanced back at the kitchen, then shifted again to Noah. "If you're not ready to go back to San Diego, Dylan and I can stay here with you. We're flexible. I want to see Southern California, but it's not going

116

anywhere."

Noah stood up. "Are you nervous about flying?"

"Nothing I can't handle." She spoke half under her breath, as if reminding herself that she had her fear of flying under control and wouldn't let it stop her from doing what she wanted to do. "If you really do want to stay, you're welcome to use one of the guestrooms here."

"Complete with vintage linens, from what Dylan has told me." Noah considered the graceful center-chimney house and surrounding acreage that comprised The Farm at Carriage Hill. "It sounds perfect, Olivia. I actually could use some time just to hang out on my own."

Dylan grunted. "No one would look for you here, dog sitting, that's for damn sure."

"The plane's gassed up and ready," Noah said. "Go on. I'll join you as soon as I've had enough of country life."

"Before we've reached altitude, then," Dylan joked. His good humor evaporated quickly and he narrowed his eyes again on Noah. "I don't like the idea of leaving you here alone with this guy on your tail."

"I won't be alone. I'll have Buster."

"There'll be guys working up the road at my place, too. The Sloans. Maggie's in-laws.

They're handling the construction." Dylan grimaced, shook his head. "I still don't like it."

"Amazingly, Dylan, my friend, I have managed not just whole hours and days but whole weeks and now even months without you down the hall from me. I'll be fine."

Buster roused himself and stood by Olivia. He seemed aware on some level that she was about to leave him with a stranger who knew next to nothing about dogs. She scratched his big head. "Staying here won't be what you're used to, Noah. Not that I know what you're used to, but I'm not . . ." She made a face but smiled through her discomfort. "Do people often get tongue-tied when they try to talk to you?"

Dylan answered before Noah could. "Only until they learn he got perfect scores on his SATs and graduated a year early from MIT. Then it gets interesting. A billion in the bank's nothing compared to being good at math."

Noah smiled at Olivia. "Ignore him. He's been like that since kindergarten."

"This place is coming together," she said, "but it's not done yet. There's so much more to do. So many possibilities."

"You love it here," Noah said.

"I do. As I mentioned, Maggie will be in

and out, if you don't mind."

"It's your house."

"She can help you with anything you need. Phoebe can, too. She's always willing to help people, and she knows at least as much about what's going on in town as her mother does. Elly works at the town offices. She's a ball of fire, if you run into her. She'll tell you anything you want to know about goats and then some."

"Good to know," Noah said with a sideways glance at Dylan. Goats. They were discussing goats again.

"Sure you want to stay?" Dylan asked with a grin.

Olivia ignored them both. "Noah, if you want to keep your presence here a secret, Maggie and Phoebe won't say anything. People in town are aware of who you are, because of my relationship with Dylan, but they'll assume you're in San Diego. They won't recognize you. For one thing, they'd expect you to have an entourage."

Noah was amused. "An entourage," he said.

"You know." Olivia shrugged. "People. Bodyguards and chauffeurs and valets. That sort of thing."

He'd had a chauffeur and a bodyguard from time to time, but never a valet. He'd always managed to get himself dressed. He might have danced with a woman pretending to be a princess, but he wasn't a prince.

"The women he dates have entourages," Dylan said. "Noah's just a guy with a lot of zeroes in his net worth."

Noah rolled his eyes but addressed Olivia. "Your fiancé is dangerous when he starts talking numbers."

She laughed. "I can see how you two were a good pair at NAK and have stayed friends for so long. I need to run into town. I want to see Maggie before we leave for the airport. Noah, you can hang out with Buster and see how it goes. There's still time to change your mind."

As she went back through the kitchen, Noah stepped back onto the terrace and sat at the table. He heard bumblebees buzzing in purple flowers behind a green-painted bench. They weren't chives. Some kind of mint, he thought. If he stayed in Knights Bridge for more than forty-eight hours, he probably would learn all about New England flowers and herbs.

"Do you think Olivia will fall in love with San Diego?" he asked.

Dylan's eyes darkened. "I hope so, but Knights Bridge is where she belongs. It's home for her. It always was, even when she was in Boston."

"You belong here, too," Noah said. "You know there's ice here in the winter, right? Also in the fall and spring, and probably at times in the dead of summer, too."

"You're a riot, Noah," Dylan said.

"Think Buster needs a walk?" Noah asked.

"You're the dog sitter. You tell me."

Noah frowned at the big dog. Hell if he could tell. "Think I've bitten off more than I can chew?"

"Way more."

"Well. *I* need a walk, and I'll bet I can talk Buster into coming along. What about you?"

Dylan shook his head in bemusement. "I'll get Buster's leash."

# SIX

Phoebe had her gorgeous brown silk gown zipped into a garment bag and hung in a closet before Maggie, wearing a black sundress that drained what color there was in her face, arrived with the outfits she and Olivia had worn.

"Olivia's getting cold feet about going to San Diego," Maggie said as she entered Phoebe's small living room. "I told her she has to go so she can bring the boys stuffed giraffes from the zoo."

"She'll go," Phoebe said. "It's just preflight jitters."

"I hope so. The ball was incredible last night. You'd have loved the costumes."

Maggie laid the Audrey Hepburn and Grace Kelly dresses on a loveseat angled against the front windows, the afternoon summer sun streaming through filmy curtains.

"Then you and Olivia had a good time?"

Phoebe asked.

"Olivia especially did. She's so much more comfortable in her own skin than she was when she moved back to town. Your dresses were a hit." Maggie gave her Grace Kelly gown a lingering look, as if she was thinking about last night and what might have been. She smiled stiffly at Phoebe. "What have you been up to?"

"I just came from Olivia's. The basil needs to be picked. She won't have time before she goes to San Diego. I thought maybe you and I could make pesto or something."

"Sure. That'd be great."

"She and Dylan arrived with Noah Kendrick," Phoebe said, wanting to do something — say something — to penetrate her sister's pensive mood. "Did you meet him last night? He's not what I expected."

"In what way?"

"I don't know. I guess I thought he'd be fidgety but he's not. He's . . ." She thought a moment. "Calm, I suppose."

"He and Dylan went straight from hiking in the White Mountains to the masquerade last night. He's probably tired, but it wouldn't matter. He strikes me as calm, too. Centered. I expected such a genius tech type to be a little weird, but he doesn't come across that way." Maggie smoothed a few wrinkles in the dress with her fingertips then stood back, marginally more cheerful. "I should go. I promised the boys I'd ride bikes with them. I missed them last night."

Phoebe followed her out to the porch, the afternoon still and warm. "Maggie, are you okay?"

"Just tired. I'm not used to nights on the town. What are you doing the rest of the day?"

"I'll stop at Mom's later. Right now I'm going to put my feet up in the shade and read a book. Maybe a good swashbuckler tale."

Maggie seemed to pull herself out of her own private thoughts and focus more on the conversation. "There were swashbucklers at the ball last night."

"I'm sure there were," Phoebe said. She didn't want to lie outright but skirting the truth seemed just as duplicitous. She changed the subject. "I'll have the dresses cleaned. We're going to use them in the fashion show. Maybe you and Olivia can model them."

"Only if you insist," Maggie said with a welcome laugh. "Olivia and I will pay for the cleaning. We just didn't want to do anything without checking with you first. It was quite an experience last night. You'll get the Edwardian gown cleaned at the same time?"

Phoebe felt her heartbeat quicken. "What Edwardian gown?"

Her sister paused on the top porch step and turned to her. "The deep brown sequined Edwardian gown you wore last night. It was you, wasn't it?" When Phoebe didn't respond, Maggie nearly choked. "Phoebe! It *was* you! I was just testing. I wasn't really serious."

Phoebe groaned. "Maggie . . ."

"I didn't know you could dance like that."

"I can't. The man I danced with can. I have no idea who he is. Please don't say anything, Maggie. I decided to go at the last minute. I know I could have called you and Olivia but if I had, I'd have chickened out and stayed here, or turned around halfway to Boston." Phoebe took a breath, trying to control the tumble of words, the feeling that she'd just been caught doing something embarrassing and dumb. "I'd have been too self-conscious if you two knew. I'd never have gone through with it."

"Why? You were gorgeous. Really. People couldn't take their eyes off you."

"That's kind of you to say —"

"It's true. I saw you and wondered if it was you. Then you disappeared, and I was

125

distracted."

Probably by Brandon, Phoebe thought. "You can't tell anyone I was there last night. I'd just die if anyone knew, and sneaking in like that just makes it worse. I wasn't myself." Phoebe looked at the pink roses trailing up her white-painted trellis. *This is my life.* She got her breathing and heartbeat under control and turned back to her sister. "There is one thing you could do for me. I'd like to get a message to the man I danced with. I wonder if Dylan might know him."

Maggie frowned. "What kind of message, Phoebe?"

"As I was leaving, I overheard another man talking on the phone about him. Not by name but by his description . . ." She paused, removing a folded piece of paper from her dress pocket. "After I got home last night, I typed up everything the man said." Except, she thought, what he'd said about finding out who her swashbuckler's dance partner was. She didn't want any reason for anyone — Dylan, Olivia, her sister — to worry about her. She thrust the note at Maggie. "I was going to give it to Dylan when he got back from Boston, but I chickened out."

"Because you don't want him to know you

were there last night," Maggie said with some sympathy.

Phoebe nodded. "I didn't tell Olivia, either. I got so carried away dancing. If I'd just slipped in, had a few hors d'oeuvres, checked out the costumes and left, that'd be one thing. But I didn't."

"You had a good time, Phoebe. You didn't make a spectacle of yourself, if that's what you're thinking."

It was exactly what she was thinking. "I just don't want to have to explain. It was a moment, and it's over." She smiled. "I'm back home where I belong."

"Right. I understand, Phoebe." Maggie held up the folded paper, a spark in her eyes now. "What's in the note? Anything juicy?"

"I only heard one end of the conversation so I don't have the context for what was said. It struck me as provocative. Like this guy had an ax to grind with my swashbuckler. He'd already disappeared on me, so I just got out of there. Then I thought about it and realized I probably should have found him and told him what I overheard. I hadn't wanted to chase him down if he didn't want . . . you know."

"You mean you didn't want to go find him if he'd ditched you," her sister said.

Phoebe felt her cheeks flame. "That's

what I mean, yes."

Maggie sighed. "I can't say I blame you."

"When I got home I decided I should write everything down."

"Was there an implied or direct threat in what you overheard? Were you afraid? We can always talk to Eric."

Eric Sloan was Brandon's eldest brother, a town police officer. "I'd have grabbed a security guard if I'd felt threatened. It wasn't anything that overt. Really, for all I know my swashbuckler was stepping out on his wife last night and she sicced this guy on him." Phoebe gave a small, thin laugh. "That'd be right up my alley, wouldn't it? Not that I'll ever see him again."

"Phoebe —"

She held up a hand, stopping her sister. "No, don't. Don't tell me anything you know, anything you suspect. I want to forget last night. I've assuaged my conscience by writing the note and giving it to you to give to Dylan. Let him think someone tucked it in your dress and you only just found it."

"You mean I lie to him instead of you lying to him?" Maggie grinned suddenly, tucking the note in her pocket. "I'm proud of you, Phoebe. I didn't think you had it in you to be a little devious."

"I just don't want this to become a thing.

You can read the note. If you think I'm overreacting and it's not worth giving to Dylan, just toss it out your window."

"And risk having some big gossip in town find it? No way. Did you include a description of this man you overheard?"

"I did, yes."

"You're a regular James Bond."

Phoebe was relieved to see Maggie more animated, even if it was at her own expense. "Whatever is going on, it has nothing to do with me. I was just a curiosity."

"Because of that killer dress, not to mention a couple of dips you took while dancing —"

"Maggie, please. Don't."

Her sister tilted her head back, studying Phoebe in the late-afternoon light. "This swashbuckler of yours really got to you, didn't he?"

"We had a moment and now it's over, as well it should be. It wasn't real. For me, or for him."

Maggie nodded. "Okay. If you say so. Meet you at Mom's in a bit?"

"Sure. Maggie, last night —"

"It was a strange night for both of us, Phoebe. Let's just leave it at that."

*Brandon,* Phoebe thought, but she said nothing as Maggie trotted down the porch steps and back out to her car, at least in a better mood than when she'd arrived. Brandon had to have been the reason for her melancholy. Phoebe tensed, wishing she could pick up the phone and give her brother-in-law a piece of her mind. She might not always speak up for herself — she wasn't by nature a bold person — but she would defend her sisters.

Only Maggie had told Phoebe, Ava, Ruby and their mother to stay out of the problems between her and Brandon, and she was totally right to do so. They'd never really discussed the details of what had driven Maggie back to Knights Bridge without her husband.

Phoebe sat on a wicker chair and breathed in the warm summer air, scented with roses. Why hadn't she wanted Maggie to tell her what she might know — any suspicions she might have — about her dance partner?

Maybe, Phoebe thought, it wasn't just that she was worried that, unmasked, she'd be a disappointment in real life. Maybe she was worried he would be, too.

She liked the fantasy of last night, she realized.

She didn't want it to end.

Maggie was close to hyperventilating as she

arrived at Carriage Hill, all but screeching to a stop on the side of the narrow back road.

What was she going to do? That was *Phoebe* last night. With *Noah Kendrick.*

"My sister," she said aloud.

She had to calm down. It was one night. That was all there was to it. There was no budding relationship between her sister and Noah Kendrick.

Maggie pushed open her van door with a groan. There'd been sparks between them, though.

*A lot of sparks.*

She jumped out and headed for the kitchen ell, a newer addition to the pretty antique house. She peered through the screen door but didn't see anyone and let herself in. Her breathing more or less back under control, she went through the mudroom out to the terrace.

Noah Kendrick sat alone at the round table. He was as still as a statue, dressed head-to-toe in black.

"Where's Olivia?" Maggie asked before he could say a word.

"Upstairs packing, I believe." He turned to her with an enigmatic smile. "Hello, Maggie."

"Hello. Sorry. I'm in a whirlwind."

"You enjoyed your night out in Boston?"

"I did, yes." She didn't dare ask him if he'd enjoyed his. He was smart, rich, experienced. He'd see right through her. "Olivia's packed for San Diego? She and Dylan are going back with you? She hasn't bailed on you, has she?"

"They're flying to San Diego together. I'm staying here." Noah's expression didn't change. "I'm dog sitting."

Maggie gulped in air. Dog sitting? Was he serious? She really was going to pass out if her family and friends kept throwing curveballs at her. Did Noah know about Phoebe? Was that why he was staying? Had to be, Maggie thought. Why else would a billionaire dog sit in little Knights Bridge, especially with his best friend in San Diego?

She gave herself a mental shake. Maybe Noah was staying because of the mystery man Phoebe had overheard. Of course Maggie had read the note. Phoebe had typed up her transcript and printed it, probably so no one could recognize her handwriting. She was thorough like that. Maggie would have thought of such a cover-up only after the fact.

"You're staying here alone?" she asked Noah.

"I'll have Buster for company."

Buster was a great dog but he didn't qualify as company for a billionaire. But what did she know about billionaires? "Do you think Olivia will love it in San Diego?"

Noah seemed surprised by her question, as if it would never occur to him to ask. "Dylan's place on Coronado is very nice. It's a great location. You can see the Pacific from almost every window."

"Sounds lovely. Brandon and I went to California right after we got married. He's always loved to travel. Well, I can't stay long. I promised the boys I'd ride bikes with them. We live in the village." Why couldn't she calm down? Noah was already looking suspicious, as if he could read her mind and knew she wasn't being entirely straight with him. Not straight at all, in fact. "I should go find Olivia."

"She said you'd be working here some of the time."

"That's right. Do you like herbs, Noah? I'm thinking about trying some new recipes."

His gaze, already steady, leveled on her. "Just be sure no slugs end up in the pot with them. I met your sister earlier. She'd been on slug patrol."

"My sister? I have three sisters —"

"Phoebe."

He gave no hint of recognition but he struck Maggie as a man of supreme self-control. She tried not to choke. "Phoebe loves to dig in the dirt. When she's not reading a book in the shade, that is. I'll . . . um . . ." She cleared her throat, wondering if she was purple from not breathing properly. "I'll watch for slugs. See you soon."

She welcomed the cooler air inside the house and ran through the living room to the stairs that led to the second floor. She paused to catch her breath and look where she was going. She tripped up Olivia's narrow, steep stairs half the time, even on a good day.

Did Phoebe have any idea that it was Noah last night? Noah clearly had no idea it had been her. Maggie got that. Phoebe in shorts and a T-shirt, poking around for slugs. Not exactly the image she'd presented at the masquerade. He'd be hoping for . . . well, not for Phoebe O'Dunn. Maggie felt a surge of resentment that anyone could reject her older sister, but she also had to admit that Phoebe at home in Knights Bridge wasn't at all like the woman in the Edwardian gown last night.

Brandon Sloan as a pirate, however — *that* matched who he really was.

Maggie mounted the stairs carefully, using the handrail. She'd gotten caught up in the fantasy of the charity ball herself. She'd danced with Brandon, pretended that all the frustration and pain of the past year didn't exist. It was a moment, no more real and lasting than what Phoebe had experienced.

She found Olivia zipping up her suitcase in her bedroom at the front of the house. "We have to talk," Maggie said in a low voice.

Olivia stood, pushing her fair hair out of her face. Maggie shut the door behind her. "It was Phoebe last night," she said without further preamble.

"In the Edwardian dress?"

"The woman who danced with Noah Kendrick, Olivia. It was *Phoebe.*"

Olivia sank onto the edge of her bed. "I was afraid of that."

"We can't tell anyone. I'm only telling you because Phoebe doesn't know it was Noah and Noah doesn't know it was Phoebe, and I'm not going to be the one to spill the beans, accidentally or on purpose. So you have to give Noah the note."

"What note?"

Leave it to Olivia to cut through everything else and focus on the crux of the matter at hand. Maggie pulled the note out of

135

her dress pocket and handed it over. "You can read it but I wouldn't if I were you. It's the transcript of one end of a phone call of some guy talking about Noah."

Olivia winced. "Middle-aged? No costume?"

"Yeah. He had on an expensive suit. Why?"

"Noah spotted him a few times in San Diego and now he seems to have followed him east. Maggie, he and Dylan will want to know who wrote this note."

Maggie stiffened. "I don't know who wrote it."

"You do, too," Olivia said, as if they were seven again. "It was Phoebe, wasn't it?"

"I didn't say that. I just said it's a transcript." Maggie waved a hand. "Tell Noah and Dylan I found the note on the ballroom floor, or someone tucked it in my pocket while I was sipping champagne. I don't care. Just don't mention Phoebe."

"But, Maggie —"

"Olivia. I mean it. You have to promise. I talked to Phoebe. She doesn't know anything."

Olivia sighed, clearly pained. "I can't keep things from Dylan."

"You're not keeping anything from Dylan. I'm telling you right now that I don't know who wrote that note." Unlike her eldest sister, Maggie had no compunctions about a strategic white lie. "You just can't say that Phoebe was Noah's princess. That shouldn't be hard. It's not as if Dylan would ask or it would make any difference in finding this guy tailing Noah."

Olivia leaned back on her elbows, frowning, obviously contemplating the knotty situation into which Maggie had just thrust her. "You, Phoebe and I are smart. We've slayed our share of dragons. But Dylan and Noah . . ."

"I know. They're in a different league when it comes to dragon-slaying. If they think we're hiding something about this guy, they have a right to be annoyed. But we're really not."

"I'm not saying they'll be annoyed. I'm saying they'll find out who wrote that note."

Maggie suspected her friend had a point and wished Phoebe had danced with someone else last night, or simply hadn't overheard the man in the coatroom.

She stood by a window, its simple curtain billowing slightly in the afternoon breeze. "Olivia, do you think Noah would hire someone to find out the identity of his princess from last night?"

"Hire someone? Who?"

"I don't know. A private investigator or

something."

Olivia sat up straight. "Now you're getting carried away. I guess we both are. It's probably because we didn't expect . . ." She sighed, shaking her head, then fastened her green eyes on Maggie. "It really was Phoebe last night?"

"It really was." Maggie glanced out the window, down at the shaded front yard and quiet back road. "Why do you think Noah is staying here? It's not to dog sit. Do you think he suspects his princess is in Knights Bridge?"

Olivia eased up off the bed and stood her suitcase on end on the polished wide-board pine floor.

Maggie narrowed her eyes on her friend. "Olivia?"

"I think I may have given him the impression that she's here. He mentioned that his princess's eyes reminded him of the color of your eyes. Not that he thought it was you he danced with. I don't think he assumes she was related to you. Just that I know more than I've let on, which now I do, for sure. I thought maybe it was Ava or Ruby, only because Phoebe was so adamant about not going to the ball."

"She prides herself on paying her own way," Maggie said.

Olivia nodded. "I can appreciate that."

"Phoebe feels she always has to be the sensible one. It's because the rest of us are all nuts. My mother and the twins and me. We're dreamers. We always have a bunch of different things going on at once. We've never been good with money. It's bad enough that I'm like that, but then I married a guy who's like that, too."

"You've done right by yourself and the boys," Olivia said. "That's what matters."

"I'm always afraid I'll go just that one step too far in my catering business, and it'll all come crashing down on my head. I tell myself that I'd work it out if I did make a mess of things." Maggie forced a smile. "We'd just move in with my mother and the goats."

Olivia groaned, but her mood was noticeably lighter. She fingered the handle of her suitcase. "I can postpone this trip to San Diego."

"No, that would only look suspicious, and you need to get out there and see where Dylan's from, what his life before he met you was like. You'll love it. I remember Brandon and I had piña coladas at the Hotel del Coronado. We didn't stay there. Too expensive. Noah said Dylan's house is just up the street."

"Dylan warned me it has no color. Everything in it is white, cream or cappuccino." Olivia laughed, only a slight strain in her voice as she continued, "I'm sure it's grand, but Knights Bridge has its charms."

"You two can always have a bicoastal life if you want to. You'll figure it out. No angsting, okay? Just go and enjoy yourself."

"I will. Promise. You'll keep an eye on Noah and Phoebe?"

"There is no Noah and Phoebe, Olivia."

"You know what I mean."

Maggie blew out a breath, calmer if no more certain of what was going on. "Noah must have all kinds of help in San Diego. Think he'll manage here on his own?"

"He's a genius. He'll manage." With a welcome smile, Olivia added, "Besides he'll have Buster."

"Maybe he can keep that mutt of yours from digging in the garden." Maggie wasn't one of Buster's big fans, but she noticed Olivia's smile fade and knew she was thinking about the long flight across the country. "Liv, come on. You flew to England and back with Dylan not that long ago. That went fine. This will, too."

"I know it will but I still . . ." Olivia didn't finish, just stared at her suitcase.

"I know. It's okay."

"Yeah." She looked up, smiled. "Noah already thinks I'm hiding something. I don't want to end up drawing attention to Phoebe by suddenly bailing on the trip. Does she regret last night?"

Maggie thought a moment, then shook her head. "No, I don't think she regrets it one little bit. She just doesn't want to get caught."

"If she knew it was Noah Kendrick —"

"I'm not telling her and neither are you, because you, my friend, are going to be in San Diego. Bring me back two stuffed giraffes from the zoo." She grinned at her longtime friend. "Not life-size ones."

They chatted a few more minutes, deciding on a plan of action to deal with Phoebe's note, and when Maggie headed back downstairs, she noticed that Dylan had joined Noah on the terrace. They seemed relaxed. She left them to their drinks in the shade and went back to her van.

She rolled down the windows and listened to the water flowing over rocks in the brook across the road, the twitter of birds hidden in the trees. Was she focusing on Phoebe's situation with Noah as a distraction from thinking about Brandon, or did she have good reason to worry about her sister?

"Time will tell," she muttered, starting

her van.

She felt only mildly guilty for not mentioning her encounter with Brandon last night. Olivia would want to know but she was just getting a handle on her anxiety over flying, and she didn't need more excuses to keep her from making this trip to San Diego.

So it was good, Maggie decided, that she'd kept quiet about that dance with her pirate of a husband.

After all, what were friends for?

She sniffled, suddenly wanting nothing more than to go bike-riding with her sons, listen to their tales of their overnight with their maternal grandmother. When Maggie had checked in that morning, her mother had them picking tomatoes for fresh home-made sauce. Nothing like the prospect of spaghetti for supper to motivate them.

Aidan had found a spider. Tyler was looking for snakes.

They were having the time of their lives, all that saved Maggie from wishing she'd done anything last night besides dance with their father, as sexy and irresistible as ever.

# SEVEN

"Dog sitting, Noah?" Dylan sat at the round terrace table with a glass of spiced iced tea, complete with an orange wedge and cinnamon stick. "Are you sure about this?"

Noah, seated on a green-painted bench, ran a palm over the minty-looking plants with the purple flowers. He wondered if they had slugs. He noticed the bumblebees were back and withdrew his hand. "It'll be easier on everyone if I stay," he said, although he wasn't precisely sure what he meant.

Obviously neither was Dylan, who gave Noah a skeptical look. "Having you here on your own will be easier on everyone? How?"

"I can tend to the gardens, as well as Buster."

"Have you ever done any gardening?"

In fact, Noah had not. Even as a kid, he'd never done more than water the flowerpots on the deck of his parents' townhouse in suburban Los Angeles, under his mother's supervision.

He stood up with his own iced tea. Plain. No spiced tea for him. "It'll be fine. Olivia will leave instructions. Remember, I recognized the chives on her note card when she wrote to you about your house. You thought they were clover. Anyway, you don't need me underfoot while you're showing her San Diego."

"I'm not buying it, Noah," Dylan said, shaking his head. "You're not staying here because you've suddenly turned into Farmer Kendrick. It's that note Olivia gave you."

Suddenly restless, Noah walked over to the table but didn't sit down. The afternoon had turned hazy and humid. Olivia and Dylan would be on their way to the airport soon. Noah wouldn't be going with them. He'd come close to changing his mind about staying. Then Olivia had handed him the note, telling him that he wasn't to ask where she got it.

*"It was given to me in confidence,"* she'd said.

Mostly likely that meant her friend Maggie O'Dunn had given the note to her. But where had Maggie gotten it? Had she written it herself? Based on the contents, Noah doubted it. Maggie would simply have pulled him aside and told him what she'd overheard.

The mysteries of little Knights Bridge.

The note sealed his decision to stay on at least for a few days. He had no intention of pushing Olivia to break a confidence or telling her what he suspected. Nor would he involve Dylan, given that he was engaged to Olivia.

"I read the note, Noah," Dylan said.

Noah sighed. "When I was walking Buster up the road, testing whether he and I would get along for a few days?"

"That's right. I figured you didn't want to hand the note to me outright but you wanted me to read it."

"Actually, I was just focused on keeping Buster from slobbering on me and didn't think about the note. I didn't want to involve you."

Dylan set his iced tea on the table. "Noah, *Olivia* gave you that note. I am involved."

"That doesn't change anything," Noah said.

"The note was printed off a computer. Whoever wrote it didn't want you to see his or her handwriting."

"Could it have been Brandon Sloan?"

"No," Dylan said without hesitation. "He'd just have told you on the spot."

Noah agreed. He sank onto a chair at the table, half wishing he were back in the White Mountains with nothing more pressing on his mind than survival. This was much more complicated. He looked over at his friend. "You know it would take two seconds to find out what Olivia and Maggie have been up to," he said.

Dylan grimaced as he nodded. "What makes you think Maggie's involved?"

"She's always involved, isn't she?"

"True. She and Olivia go back at least as far as you and I do." Dylan picked the cinnamon stick out of his tea and flicked it into the grass. "I'm not going to spend a lot of energy guessing. The note says what it says. The person who overheard the man in question provided a thorough account and description. There's nothing more to add."

"What about my princess?" Noah asked, his tone more serious than he'd intended.

"You mean is she a bystander? A potential victim? A potential accomplice?"

"The note doesn't mention her, and yet this man described my presence at the ball in detail. If that had been you, don't you think you'd have mentioned my dance partner in the Queen Victoria dress?"

"It was Edwardian," Olivia said, coming out from the kitchen. *"Titanic, Downton Ab-*

bey." She swallowed as if she might have gone too far. "I noticed her dress. It was gorgeous." She added quickly, "There were a lot of gorgeous dresses there last night."

As tempted as he was, Noah reminded himself that he wasn't going to grill his best friend's fiancée about what she was holding back.

Dylan watched her walk past them into her gardens, mumbling about dealing with the basil before it went to seed. He glanced at Noah. "Not a word."

"Nope. Not me." Noah put his feet up on another chair and settled back in the late-afternoon warmth. "I don't know which I want more — the identity of this stalker or of my princess. Wouldn't you have said that was a Victorian dress?"

"I'd have said it was a dark blue dress."

"It was dark brown, Dylan."

He shrugged. "I'm not big on colors."

"And you're engaged to a graphic designer who loves color?"

"A case of opposites attracting, at least on that one. We have other things in common." His gaze was fixed on Olivia, kneeling in a sunny herb patch, checking what Noah assumed was basil. Finally Dylan added, "Olivia and I are good together, Noah."

"No question about it. I'm happy for you."

"So, do you think she knows who your princess is?"

Noah debated answering, then said, "Yes, I think she does."

Dylan sighed. "I'm betting she does, too."

"A friend from Boston, maybe?"

He shifted his gaze to Noah. "I doubt it."

"Then a friend from Knights Bridge?"

"It doesn't have to be a friend. She knows everyone in town."

Noah looked up at the sky and contemplated the cloud formations. "If my princess is from Knights Bridge, and Olivia and Maggie don't want to tell me —"

"Then you need to forget about her," Dylan said.

"Meaning they'll never give her up and they'll never forgive me if I find her and she doesn't want to be found." Noah dropped his feet onto the stone terrace and sat up straight. "She wrote the note."

"Who? Olivia?"

"My princess."

Dylan got to his feet. He looked pensive, tight.

"I'm not speculating, Dylan. I'm as certain about this as I was about starting my own company — about knocking on your window when you were sleeping in your car. She wrote that note and got it to you because she thought you might know who her swashbuckler was and could get it to him."

"If that's the case, she took great pains to conceal her identity."

"Otherwise she would have just handed you the note herself, or Maggie and Olivia would have told you who she is."

"Maybe she doesn't want her swashbuckler to know who she is."

Noah ignored the amusement in Dylan's voice. "Olivia and Maggie know it was me dressed up like a musketeer last night. I don't think they've told her. Olivia said she was to give you the note because you might know the identity of the swashbuckler mentioned in the conversation. You invited a fair number of the guests, after all."

"She wasn't asked to get it specifically to Noah Kendrick. You, in other words."

"Right. No name."

Olivia moved to another cluster of herbs. Noah didn't think she could hear the discussion between him and Dylan but suspected she had a fair idea of what was on their minds. He was rarely confident of his ability to read body language with any accuracy. He really didn't know what Olivia was thinking, or even his best friend of nearly thirty years. In contentious board meetings, dealing with the occasional backstabber, the ever-present sharks in the water, Dylan was better at getting at what was going on beneath the surface. Noah tended to focus on what he wanted. For the past four years, what he wanted had centered on business.

Not right now. Right now, what he wanted was his princess.

He got to his feet and stood next to Dylan. "My princess last night doesn't know it was me behind the mask."

"Do you think she'd be disappointed to find out she danced with the founder of NAK?"

Dylan spoke as if disappointment was unimaginable. Noah remembered the persona he'd adopted last night. "I'm no D'Artagnan," he said.

"You're as good with a sword as any musketeer."

"That's different. Anyway, if this woman has information on my mystery man, then it could help that I'm just . . . you know. Me."

"Your average, garden-variety California billionaire," Dylan said with some humor.

"All right, maybe it won't help."

His friend groaned suddenly. "Are you confused at all? A mystery woman, a mystery stalker, small-town loyalties . . ." He held up a hand before Noah could answer.

150

"Never mind. I know you're not confused."

"Do you have a short list of possibilities of who my Edwardian princess might be?"

Dylan looked uncomfortable. "Noah . . ."

"Ah. A very short list. You don't have to tell me. I won't compromise you with your new friends here. I like a good challenge."

"Then you still plan to stay?"

Noah hadn't changed his mind. Not even close. "It'll be fine. Nobody knows me in Knights Bridge except Maggie and her sister."

"But you're determined to find out who your princess is," Dylan said.

"As much as ever. I'll just keep it to myself when I do. Relax, Dylan. Think of me as taking a few days to enjoy the bucolic surroundings."

"You don't like bucolic surroundings."

"I do. I just don't like mosquitoes. I'll wear bug spray."

Dylan was still obviously skeptical. "You're sure you're not just bored?"

"I was bored. I'm not now."

Olivia started up a path toward the terrace. Dylan kept his eyes on her as he continued, "Are you avoiding San Diego? It's an adjustment, going from controlling everything to do with NAK to —"

"Controlling nothing?" Noah gave a small

151

smile. "No one's going to feel sorry for me, Dylan, and I don't feel sorry for myself. You and I are both moving on. We made our choices about how we'd take NAK public. We still have a strong interest in the company, but we wanted fresh blood. The last thing the new people need is the founders skulking around."

"Founder," Dylan corrected. "Singular."

Noah didn't argue with him. They'd had this argument countless times in the past four years. "We're both pivoting to what's next for us. I just didn't expect you to fall for someone from a little town on the other side of the country."

Olivia joined them on the terrace and smiled at Noah as if she'd told him all she knew about the identity of his princess. "I love it here but you'll be roughing it by your standards."

Noah returned her smile. "Like I just told Dylan. I'll wear bug spray."

On his first evening alone in Knights Bridge, Noah listened to an owl in the woods behind the house and chased a mosquito out of the kitchen. He'd have killed it if he'd had the opportunity but it followed him outside when he walked Buster.

He had no problem killing mosquitoes.

His assistant in San Diego had arranged for a messenger to deliver a new phone to Carriage Hill. Noah scanned his messages. Loretta Wrentham had called seven times. When he called her back, she was annoyed with him for not responding sooner but she had no news.

He sat down at Olivia's white-painted kitchen table. "If you don't know anything, why did you call me seven times?"

"Because you didn't return my first two calls."

"That makes no sense, Loretta."

"It makes perfect sense to me. I hate being ignored."

"I wasn't ignoring you."

"What were you doing?" she asked.

"I didn't have a phone."

A half-beat's silence. "You didn't have a phone? Really?"

He heard the skepticism in her voice. "Really," he said. "I only got your voice mails just now."

"Don't you have an assistant who checks your messages?"

"Not one who checks my private number."

"So are you and Dylan about to head back out here?"

"Dylan is already en route," Noah said.

"Noah . . ." Loretta took in an audible

breath. "Where are you?"

"Knights Bridge. I'm staying at Olivia's place. I'm dog sitting."

Silence on the other end of the connection.

"I almost wish it were cool enough tonight for a fire," Noah added. "I like Olivia's fireplace. Fireplaces, actually. There are five or six. They all share one chimney. It's in the center of the house."

"Dear God."

He smiled into the phone. "Have you ever been to New England, Loretta?"

"Boston. Knights Bridge isn't Boston."

"Not even close." But he didn't mind that, he realized. At least for now. In another few days, it might make all the difference in the world. "Dylan and Olivia will be arriving in San Diego soon. Don't let him get involved in this thing. He needs to show Olivia around town, take her to the zoo. Stuff like that."

"You're a romantic at heart," Loretta said.

Noah laughed. "Yeah, right."

"Are you sure it's wise to stay out there by yourself? You have a higher profile right now with NAK going public. You need to take your safety seriously. You've had corporate security training and you know fencing and karate, but if this guy's actually stalking you —"

"I'm not worried, Loretta. I don't want you to worry, either. Let's just identify this man and figure out what he wants."

"That high-IQ mind of yours is working the problem. I can feel it all the way out here on the other side of the continent."

"The problem has gotten a bit more complicated since we last talked."

She sighed. "Of course it has. Tell me."

Noah explained about his princess and the note Olivia had handed him. "I'm positive my princess overheard our guy and wrote that note but I can't prove it."

"She doesn't know who you are and you don't know who she is," Loretta said.

"But Olivia and her friend Maggie know both — who I am and who she is."

"I get it, I get it. You want to find this woman and your stalker, and you think staying in Knights Bridge will help. How, I don't know, but you're the genius. What are you doing tonight, since it's too warm for a fire?"

"I'm listening to an owl right now."

Muttering, Loretta disconnected.

Noah got up from the table and stepped past a slumbering Buster onto the terrace, the early-evening air still and warm, fragrant with flowers and herbs. He looked out at the stone walls, fields and hills silhouetted against the darkening summer sky. He'd never been to this part of Massachusetts during his college days. On breaks, he'd gravitated to the beaches or gone home to Los Angeles. Not ever — not once — had he considered that Dylan might end up in a small New England town. He'd discovered that he had roots in the Swift River Valley — a grandmother he'd never known, a woman now in her nineties who'd given up his father at birth.

Hence Duncan McCaffrey's purchase of the house up the road and Dylan's presence in Knights Bridge.

As much as Dylan appreciated the answers he'd discovered last spring, Noah knew they weren't why his friend was still here. Dylan was in Knights Bridge because of Olivia Frost. If she fell in love with San Diego and wanted to live there part-time, he would do that. He had the freedom to make whatever came next for him work for her, too.

The Farm at Carriage Hill was charming and sophisticated, and Olivia had every reason to be proud of what she'd accomplished in such a short time. It wasn't a traditional bed-and-breakfast that took in the odd overnight guest, and there were no events scheduled during his stay. Maggie

O'Dunn would stop by during the day but for the most part Noah would have the place to himself.

Well, he and Buster would.

Olivia had lined up several painting projects in case he got bored.

She had a sense of humor. Noah did a lot of things but he didn't paint.

He headed upstairs to choose a bedroom for his New England sojourn. Only one, a small bedroom overlooking the side yard, didn't involve antique lace.

That was the one he chose.

# EIGHT

Phoebe took the call from Maggie in her back garden. They'd planned to head over to Carriage Hill and deal with Olivia's basil — make a nice Sunday afternoon of it — but Maggie couldn't. "Ava and Ruby got their wires crossed and neither one will be around today," Maggie said. "Mom needs help with the goats, although, of course, she insists she doesn't. The boys and I will go over there and do what we can."

"Nineteen goats are too many for her," Phoebe said.

"One goat is too many," Maggie added in exasperation, then sighed. "I know she loves the goats. She's never asked for any of us to help take care of them, but you know she'd never manage without us."

Phoebe didn't disagree. "Getting into goat's milk soaps could make a difference."

"She says she's looking into selling a few of the goats. She knows she has to. We don't need nineteen, even if the soaps do well."

"Let me know if I can do anything to help," Phoebe said.

"Oh, we'll manage. The boys are still young enough to think mucking out the stalls is fun. Enjoy your quiet afternoon. We'll make the pesto later this week."

"I have all the ingredients. I can head over to Olivia's and see how much I can get done on my own this afternoon."

Her younger sister took in a sharp breath. "Phoebe . . ."

"It'll be okay, Maggie. I can follow a recipe. If I screw up the pesto, there'll be more basil."

"What about Buster?"

"He and I get along just fine."

Maggie started to say something else, but Phoebe assured her she'd manage the basil on her own and got off the phone, eager to be on her way on what was turning into a hot, humid afternoon. *Perfect for making pesto,* she thought as she went back inside.

Not that she'd ever made pesto.

Given the heat, she pinned up her hair and changed into shorts, a sleeveless linen top and flip-flops.

Fifteen minutes later, she parked at Carriage Hill, grabbed her canvas bag of pesto-making ingredients and headed up the stone

159

walk to the kitchen ell. Maggie would have been by early to see to Buster, and Phoebe expected to have to use the extra key Olivia kept hidden behind a gutter. Instead she found the main door to the kitchen open and Buster nosing the screen door.

"Hey, Buster, did Maggie forget to lock up?" Phoebe pulled open the door and stepped past the big, rambunctious dog into the country kitchen. Buster went from nosing the screen to nosing her as she set the bag on the counter. "Easy. You remember me. I'm Phoebe. Olivia's friend."

"I do remember you."

Phoebe jumped, startled at the sound of a man's voice, coming from the adjoining living room.

Noah Kendrick appeared in the doorway. "Phoebe O'Dunn, the slug-hunter," he said with an enigmatic smile. "Hello, Phoebe."

She subtly breathed out in relief. "Noah — hi. I didn't realize anyone was here. I thought Dylan and Olivia were on their way to San Diego."

"They are. I stayed behind."

"But you'll be joining them?"

"Eventually," he said.

He wore a black T-shirt over dark jeans, and as he entered the kitchen Phoebe saw he was barefoot. He didn't make a sound,

160

his movements smooth, controlled. She'd noticed that about him during their brief meeting yesterday. She could see him glued to a computer but at the same time she could see him — what? Doing yoga, maybe. She did yoga herself, at least sort of, and always felt more physically in control, poised, after a session.

Buster followed Noah to the white porcelain sink and plopped down at his feet.

"Buster seems to like you," Phoebe said.

"I'm the man with the food. I think he misses Olivia. Maybe Dylan, too."

"You're taking care of Buster?"

He leaned back against the sink. "You seem surprised."

*No kidding.* "I guess I am. Olivia didn't mention you'd be staying."

"It was a spur-of-the-moment decision."

Phoebe wondered what had prompted it but shook off her questions. "I'm here to make pesto." She pointed toward the mudroom and the back door out to the terrace and gardens. "With the basil. For Olivia."

"Ah. Yes. Before it goes to seed."

"My sister Maggie was supposed to join me but she got called away."

"Anything I can do to help?"

Help? Phoebe didn't know why she was so flustered, then realized she had every

161

reason to be, with a house-sitting, dog-sitting Noah Kendrick a few yards from her. He had to be used to a different lifestyle than what he'd find in Knights Bridge. He also had to be used to having more to do — or at least other things to do — than what Carriage Hill offered.

She unloaded her canvas bag. "I brought pine nuts, garlic, parmesan and olive oil. I think that's all I need." She didn't want him hanging around, watching her, bored, and quickly tried to think of something he could do. "Olivia said she has a mortar and pestle. Do you think you could find them?"

"A mortar and pestle," Noah said, his tone unreadable.

"They should be in a cupboard. You know what they are?"

"Mmm."

He hadn't moved but she was intensely aware of his scrutiny as she set the bottle of virgin olive oil she'd brought on the counter. "I've never actually made pesto but Maggie emailed me a recipe. I assume you've never . . ." She stopped herself, rephrased. "Have you ever made pesto?"

He smiled that smile again. "I haven't."

"It doesn't look hard."

Why was her heart beating so rapidly? Just because he was even richer than Dylan didn't mean she had to get crazy. But it wasn't just that. It was the way he looked at her, his air of self-control and calm. Those eyes. That smile. She hadn't noticed them yesterday the way she did now, perhaps because she'd been preoccupied with getting the transcript of the conversation she'd overheard to Dylan, so that he could get it to her swashbuckler. She'd planned to ask Maggie how that had gone when they were making pesto. She hadn't thought to ask her on the phone.

Phoebe cleared her throat. "How did your first night in Knights Bridge go?"

"Quiet," Noah said. "Just Buster, an owl and me."

The twitch of a smile, that spark of humor in his deep blue eyes — Phoebe felt a rush of heat that she couldn't define or understand. She blamed Friday night. Sneaking past her sister and friends into the masquerade, dancing with a stranger and overhearing an alarming conversation from another stranger had kicked her adrenaline into high gear. Even venturing up to the hidden room in the library attic had taken a toll on her normally calm, sensible nature. If she hadn't found that room, she realized, she'd never have gone to the masquerade.

She turned to Noah with a pleasant smile,

the sort that she often used when she was at a loss at the library. "How long will you be here?"

"I'm not sure. We'll see."

"I don't want to disturb you. I can pick the basil and then make the pesto back at my house." She gestured vaguely with one hand. "I live in the village."

"You won't be disturbing me," he said. "It's not as if I have a lot to do."

A bored high-tech billionaire. Just what she needed. "So you think pesto-making has possibilities?"

He laughed. "I wouldn't go that far, but I'm happy to help."

"Great," Phoebe said, half meaning it, half not. "Why don't you look for that mortar and pestle while I start on the basil?"

"Sounds good."

He seemed genuinely willing to help, but Phoebe wondered how long his interest would last before he got restless. If staying behind at Carriage Hill really was a spur-of-the-moment decision, then he wouldn't have any of his regular amusements and diversions with him. She supposed he could be working on a new business project. Something that required some quiet time to think.

She couldn't get out of the kitchen fast

enough. She didn't even know why. Noah hadn't made any sarcastic remarks. He hadn't been condescending in any way toward her. He just put her on edge. She hated to think it had to do with his financial status. She wasn't the type to judge people by their net worth.

Not that she'd met many billionaires, she thought as she made her way through Olivia's backyard to the garden shed. But it wasn't that. It wasn't money. It was . . .

"I just don't know," she said to herself, grabbing small clippers off a hook. Her swashbuckler Friday night and now Noah Kendrick Sunday afternoon. Maybe *she* was the one who was bored and restless.

She ducked out of the shed and up the path to the basil patch.

Noah and Buster wandered out to the terrace. "I found the mortar and pestle," Noah said.

"Excellent. We're in business."

Given past experience, Phoebe expected Buster to barrel to her and tear into the basil, but he stretched, yawned and lay down in a shady spot by the bench.

"Good dog," Noah said, obviously as surprised as Phoebe was. "It must be Olivia's influence, or perhaps the heat. I haven't had him long enough to have an influence.

How's the basil?"

"It smells wonderful."

He stepped off the terrace into the grass. He was still barefoot. Phoebe noticed the muscles in his bare arms and, under his T-shirt, his shoulders. He was lean but clearly strong, far more fit than she'd have expected. His eyes settled on her and he smiled without saying a word, as if he knew she'd been appraising him.

With a flush that had nothing to do with the summer heat, she snipped a healthy hunk of basil and realized she hadn't brought anything to put it in. As she considered what she could use, Noah leaned over and took the basil from her. "I'll get a colander," he said, then headed back to the terrace and into the kitchen.

Phoebe took a breath, hoping to calm her racing heart. Maybe she should have rescheduled the pesto-making, after all.

Noah returned with a colander. She laid more fresh-picked basil in it and thanked him. If he stayed this close to her, it was going to be a long afternoon. "You don't have to do this," she said. "If you want to take Buster for a walk in the woods, feel free."

"We already hiked up Carriage Hill this morning."

Carriage Hill rose up beyond the open

fields behind the house. "I see." She snipped another basil plant and asked casually, "How was hiking in the White Mountains?"

"We went at hockey-player pace," he said with a wry smile.

"Is that faster or slower than your pace?"

"Faster. Much faster. I prefer to savor each step up a mountain. I tend to be very deliberate about what I do." He reached down and brushed her bare shoulder with his fingertips, then smiled as he stood straight again. "Bumblebee."

Phoebe's mouth had gone dry at his touch. "The bees like the catmint," she said, nodding to the frothy purple-flowered border. "Olivia plans to move it to a less-trafficked area."

"Bumblebees have a natural preference for purple flowers, which tend to have more nectar than flowers of other colors."

"I didn't know that."

He shrugged. "I read it in an article some-where."

As smart as he was, she thought, he probably remembered everything he read. She tackled more basil, leaving enough for regrowth. Noah waited, then carried the overloaded colander to the terrace, Buster stirring enough to follow him inside.

Phoebe returned the clippers to the shed.

After sneaking into the charity ball on Friday and dealing with Maggie's suspicions yesterday, she'd wanted a quiet Sunday. *Needed* a quiet Sunday to get her bearings.

And here she was, picking basil and making pesto with Noah Kendrick.

When she returned to the kitchen, Buster was lapping water out of his bowl in the mudroom and Noah was sipping a glass of water at the table. The basil was in the sink. "I rinsed it," he said. "I didn't see any ants, spiders, worms or slugs. Just dirt."

"That's good. I'll do a second rinse. I always do with anything fresh out of the garden. It's not that I don't trust you."

He picked up his water glass. "Of course not."

As she approached the sink, she noticed that one of the flyers Olivia had designed for the fashion show was on the table. It hadn't been there before. It announced the show and called for donations of pre-1975 vintage clothing in good condition.

Noah tapped one finger on the flyer. "I saw this on Olivia's bulletin board in the mudroom. A vintage fashion show at the local library. Your idea?"

Phoebe nodded. There'd been a change in him since he'd taken the colander inside. She couldn't put her finger on what it was, except that she was feeling caught, trapped — as if he knew something that she didn't know.

She kept her tone even, professional, as she answered him. "It came together fast and the response has been tremendous."

"And you're holding the show at the library?"

"That's right. It has a stage. The founder, George Sanderson, insisted the design for the library include one. He envisioned lectures and concerts."

"Have you received many donations?"

"Far more than I anticipated. It's been fun so far."

Noah drank more of his water, then got to his feet in one smooth movement. "Is that where Olivia and Maggie got their dresses for the other night?" he asked as he walked over to the sink. "Did they come in with a donation?"

Phoebe plunged one hand into the cold water. "It's a bit more complicated than that, but the short answer is yes."

"And the masks?"

"My youngest sisters made those. Ava and Ruby —"

"The theater majors."

"That's right." Phoebe tried to sound casual. "So how did you enjoy the ball?"

He leaned back against the sink and crossed his arms on his chest. "It was quite a night."

*Yes, it was,* Phoebe thought. She hadn't noticed Noah in the ballroom, but she'd been too caught up in avoiding Olivia and Maggie and dancing with her swashbuckler to notice much else. Then there'd been Brandon, and the man she'd overheard. She hadn't even thought about Dylan's best friend, although she knew they'd been hiking in the White Mountains.

Noah turned and got a stainless-steel grater out from a lower cupboard. "I can grate the parmesan," he said.

Phoebe had the feeling his mind wasn't on pesto but she smiled. "That'd be good, thanks."

She laid the basil leaves on paper towels, watching him as he placed the grater and the hunk of parmesan on a wood cutting board. He glanced at her, and this time she paid close attention to the line of his jaw, the color and shape of his eyes. His smile was confident, knowing, but at the same time not at all easy to read, deliberately so, as if the man behind it guarded against letting anyone in.

She remembered her swashbuckler moving through the crowd to get to her, every movement precise, smooth, controlled.

It was all she could do not to gasp.

*It's him.*

*Her swashbuckler was Noah Kendrick.*

If she'd been the one grating parmesan, she'd have cut herself. As it was, her hands shook. She tried to focus on blotting the basil dry but her mind was spinning. She'd danced with a billionaire. With Dylan Mc-Caffrey's best friend. She'd let him kiss her.

And he'd disappeared on her. Had he really meant to come back? Had he lost her? Had she left the ballroom too soon?

*Does he know it was me?*

Why hadn't she recognized him sooner? His voice, his eyes, his lean build — so what if he'd shaved and wasn't wearing a mask and cape?

She hadn't expected that her swashbuckler would be Noah Kendrick. It was just that simple.

She blotted the basil, her heart hammering. Noah continued to grate the cheese for the pesto. It was all she could do not to think up an excuse and get out of there but she knew that would only draw more attention to her discomfort. He was a smart man. He'd figure out she'd asked him about the masquerade ball right before she unraveled.

Maggie had to know it'd been Noah in

the swashbuckler costume. Why hadn't she said so? *Because I told her I didn't want to know.* No doubt Maggie had assumed Noah would never recognize her sister as his princess.

Phoebe didn't understand the intensity of her reaction. Why not just admit she recognized him? That it was her in the Edwardian dress?

Because it hadn't been her. Not really.

She should have just gone to the ball openly, with Maggie and Olivia. Then Noah would have known who she was. Probably he never would have danced with her — or if he had, they wouldn't have gotten so carried away.

She glanced at him. He had a healthy mound of parmesan grated onto a cutting board. He gave no indication he thought of her as anything but the librarian friend of his best friend's fiancée.

Of course, that was what she was.

Phoebe sighed and stood back from the sink. A slight breeze floated through the open window, calming her. Maggie would have given her note to Olivia, who would have given it to Dylan or even directly to Noah. *That* was why Noah had stayed behind in Knights Bridge. He wanted to figure out what the story was with this man in the coatroom. Dancing with a woman at a masquerade ball was probably par for the course for him, fun while it lasted but not particularly memorable.

*Let us both pretend that night never happened.*

As matter-of-factly as she could, Phoebe nodded to the clean, reasonably dry basil. "If you can chop the basil, I'll roast the pine nuts and mince the garlic."

"Then they all get pounded into a paste with the mortar and pestle." Nothing in his smile suggested he knew that she could hardly get a decent breath. "I'm guessing, because I've had pesto."

"We pound the basil and garlic first. Then add the nuts. Then the parmesan and olive oil."

"And what do we do with all this pesto?"

"Freeze it in ice-cube trays. Olivia and Maggie will use it all winter. They might use it at Olivia's wedding in December." Phoebe managed a smile. "It'll remind everyone of summer."

"I'm sure it will."

"Will you be back for the wedding?"

"Yes, absolutely."

Phoebe looked at the parmesan, basil, garlic and pine nuts and thought about the work ahead to turn them into pesto. How would she be able to stand it, knowing what she did? She gathered up the damp paper towels from the basil and tossed them in the trash. She tried to appear casual as she turned back to Noah. "You know, if there's somewhere else you'd rather be —"

"There isn't. I'm exactly where I want to be." He opened a drawer and removed a knife. "I'll chop. You mince and roast."

Once the pesto was in the freezer, Noah saw there was no keeping Phoebe at Carriage Hill. She was out of there, tucking her empty canvas bag under one arm and all but racing out the door. Although he wasn't by nature a patient man, years of martial arts practice and running a successful company had taught him that sometimes the best course of action was just to bide his time.

He followed her to her car. The afternoon sunlight caught the streaks of gold in her dark strawberry hair as she yanked open her car door. She turned to him with a quick smile. "Thank you for your help with the pesto. Enjoy your stay."

"Anytime."

She climbed behind the wheel, and he shut the door for her. With another quick smile, she had the car started and was on her way.

She'd recognized him as her swashbuckler, obviously, but she still believed — or was telling herself she believed — that he hadn't recognized her.

Well, he had.

It was the fashion show flyer on the bulletin board that had finally done the trick. He'd started to suspect when he'd found her in the kitchen. The way she'd licked her lips, smiled, moved. The line of her jaw, the deep turquoise of her eyes, the sound of her voice. The shape of her hips, the curve of her breasts. They'd all come together when he saw the flyer, and he'd known.

Phoebe O'Dunn was his princess.

Noah walked back through the house and liberated Buster from the mudroom. They went out to the quiet terrace, but the big dog looked as restless as he was. "If you run off," Noah told him, "I'll find you and I won't be happy about it. So spare both of us and stay put."

Buster sat, panting, his dark eyes focused on Noah as if he'd gone crazy.

Noah laughed. "I just might have, my friend."

The pesto was in the freezer and the kitchen cleaned up, but even out on the terrace, he could smell the mix of basil, garlic, roasted pine nuts and pure virgin olive oil.

Virgin olive oil. A Freudian slip, there. Dancing with his princess, he'd imagined her a virgin, as bold and as daring as she was when he'd swept her into his arms.

Was Phoebe O'Dunn a virgin?

Noah grimaced. Dylan would kill him dead for even letting such a question cross his mind. Dylan still had to tread carefully in Knights Bridge. Phoebe O'Dunn, her sister Maggie — these were Olivia's people.

Telling Phoebe that he knew she was his princess was out of the question until he'd had a chance to think. He could act quickly, decisively, but not when he didn't have a clue what in blazes to do. As he'd watched her pound the basil and garlic into a thick paste, he didn't know why he hadn't recognized her sooner. He hadn't been thrown off by her dark strawberry hair and freckles as much as the fact that she was from Knights Bridge and Olivia Frost's friend.

The note about his mystery man further complicated the situation.

Buster stirred, and Noah noticed a thickset man hopping over the low stone wall from the field behind the house. "Brandon Sloan," the man said, stepping over knee-high herbs onto a path. "You must be Noah Kendrick. Dylan mentioned you'd be here for a few days. I'm working on his place up the road."

"You're one of the carpenters?"

"Sloan & Sons. I'm one of the sons. There's a sister, too, but she showed up after the company was named. Sore subject." He polished off an energy bar and dusted his hands as he stepped onto the terrace. "What do I smell?"

"Pesto." Noah pointed to the patch of trimmed basil. "Phoebe O'Dunn was here."

"Maggie, too?"

"Not Maggie, no. You two are . . ."

"Married." Brandon pulled out a chair at the table and sat down. "I saw you the other night in Boston. You'd just come from hiking in the White Mountains. One of my favorite things to do."

"It was an experience," Noah said. "You were at the masquerade ball?"

Brandon grimaced. "I decided to go at the last minute. I'd told Dylan I'd rather have burning bamboo shoots shoved up my fingernails than go to a masquerade ball."

"What changed your mind?"

"I found out Maggie was turning up — I have my sources."

The other Sloans of Sloan & Sons, Noah suspected. He wondered if Brandon's presence at the ball explained why Maggie had

177

been so upset. Noah decided his and Dylan's lives in San Diego, running NAK, were simple compared to the lives of the people he'd met so far in Knights Bridge.

"Is Maggie aware you're working on Dylan's place?" Noah asked.

"Not yet, no. Olivia doesn't know, either. I asked Dylan to let me tell Maggie first." Brandon stretched out his thick legs. "I'm camping up there. We start demolition on the house soon. I figure I can use the facilities here if need be. Olivia won't mind."

He seemed confident, even matter-of-fact, not at all presumptuous. He'd probably known Olivia — and Maggie, his wife — most if not all his life. Noah's one near-lifelong friend was Dylan.

"When did you arrive?" he asked.

"This morning. I pitched my tent out of sight of the road. I'm glad Phoebe didn't see me. She's protective of her sisters. They stick together, those four." Brandon settled back in his chair, obviously not concerned about the O'Dunn sisters or anyone else. "How do you like Carriage Hill?"

"It's not as quiet as I thought it would be."

Brandon grinned, then glanced around at the lawn and gardens, the fields, the hills in the distance. "I want to get my two boys out here to help with the work on Dylan's place."

"How old are they?"

"Five and six. Tyler's almost seven, though. Don't worry, I'm not talking about real work on the site. Just get them started on learning how to use a hammer and screwdriver. Maggie's got them baking tarts and peeling artichokes. I don't object, but they need this, too."

Noah would guess that Brandon had learned to say he didn't object to his sons learning to bake tarts and peel artichokes. What he meant instead was that he was afraid his young sons were missing the influence of their rough-and-tumble father. Noah didn't have the particulars on Brandon Sloan's troubled relationship with his wife but could see that he loved his sons.

Brandon stood abruptly, as if he wanted to escape wherever his thoughts had just taken him. "Dylan offered me a ticket to this masquerade ball but I didn't take it. I wanted to pay my own way. I went as a pirate. Maggie made me faster than I thought she would. Maybe I should have gone as a banker instead." He paused, then added wryly, "She'd never have recognized me as a banker."

Noah made no comment but he thought

that Brandon had a point.

Brandon turned, his expression serious as he narrowed his dark eyes. "Don't tell her that I'm camping out up at Dylan's. Leave that to me."

"No problem."

"I don't mind camping. I'm back on my feet financially but I want Maggie to take me as I am. With or without money."

"For better or worse," Noah said.

"That's right."

"Why are you sleeping in a tent?"

"It beats staying with my folks or one of my siblings." Brandon gave a mock shudder. "Trust me."

"Then you don't have your own place?"

"I gave up my apartment in Boston the first of the month. I'm saving every dime I can. I was in and out of work for a while, but I've been working nonstop for the past six months. It's good. No complaints." He paused, looked at Noah. "I won't drag this thing out. I just have to do this in my own time. Understood?"

"Of course," Noah said. "I'll respect your wishes."

He thought that Maggie O'Dunn Sloan — or any woman in her position — would appreciate knowing that her estranged husband was sleeping in a tent a few miles from her, but he wasn't one to offer advice on relationships.

"I can help out with anything you might run into here," Brandon said.

"I just made pesto with the town librarian. What could I run into?"

Brandon grinned. "Snakes in the stone walls. 'Course, where you're from, you have poisonous snakes. A little old garter snake probably won't bother you, right?"

"Probably not," Noah said.

"Bats?"

He hadn't considered bats. He smiled. "The hazards of country life."

Brandon tilted his head back, eyeing Noah with an intensity that other people might find intimidating. "You're not up to anything here, are you? Why didn't you go to San Diego with Dylan and Olivia?"

"I'm dog sitting."

At first Brandon didn't respond. Then he laughed. "Right. Dog sitting. Enjoy your pesto, or did Phoebe take it all back with her?"

"It's in Olivia's freezer."

"I'd never had pesto until I met Maggie. I've known Phoebe since nursery school. We're the same age. She's a special person in Knights Bridge. She looks after all of us." He settled his gaze again on Noah. "And we all look after her."

"Good to know," Noah said mildly.

It was as clear a warning between two men as one could get without Brandon Sloan coming right out and saying that he'd be watching and Noah had best behave himself with Phoebe O'Dunn.

And why would Brandon think that Noah might not behave himself?

Because he knew that his sister-in-law had dressed up as an Edwardian princess the other night and had seen her dancing with her swashbuckler, who was now dog sitting in Knights Bridge.

Noah assumed that Olivia and Maggie, who also had to know about Phoebe, didn't realize that Brandon was in on the secret, too.

Complicated, complicated.

Brandon headed off, back over the stone wall and through the field up to the house — or what was left of it — that Dylan had inherited from his father.

Noah went inside. It was five o'clock in the afternoon. Now what was he supposed to do?

He'd take Buster for another walk, then see what Olivia had in terms of movies.

And tomorrow?

Tomorrow was supposed to be another

hot day.

Perfect for a trip to the Knights Bridge Free Public Library.

# NINE

Loretta Wrentham parked in the driveway at Dylan's stucco house on Coronado. He'd left her three messages while she was sweating through a horrid exercise dance class. She'd finally texted him that she'd be right over, then showered, reapplied her makeup, put on slim jeans, a white shirt and red heels and, feeling energized if not any happier about exercise, headed across the San Diego–Coronado Bay Bridge to the upscale island town where Dylan lived.

He'd told her that Coronado wasn't home for him like Knights Bridge was home for Olivia.

Loretta believed him.

Her cell phone trilled and she assumed it was Dylan again but saw Noah's name on her screen. This couldn't be good. Something clearly was up. She debated answering, but Noah was even worse about pestering her if he wanted a response. "Isn't it the middle of the night on the East Coast?" she asked him, knowing perfectly well what time it was in New England.

"It's midnight. I'm listening to my owl. I have all the windows in the house open. The stars are out. It's nice."

"I like stars. I heard an owl once on vacation in the mountains." Of course, she realized he hadn't called to talk about stars and owls. "What can I do for you, Noah?"

"Julius Hartley, Loretta. Who is he?"

She was silent. Hartley. No wonder she had so many messages from Dylan and now Noah was on the phone with her.

"Loretta?"

"He's your mystery man," she said.

"Is that a question or do you know?"

"I know now that you've said his name. How did it pop up?"

"Dylan checked the guest list at the masquerade ball. He couldn't resist. The name Julius Hartley stood out. He bought a ticket at the last minute, he came alone and he's from Los Angeles. He left his street address blank. Dylan doesn't know him."

Loretta swore under her breath. "I'll take care of this."

"Who is he, Loretta?" Noah asked mildly.

She decided to tell him. "Julius Hartley is a scumbag private investigator who won't return my calls."

"How do you know him?"

"I don't. He showed up in my office a couple of weeks ago. I didn't think about him as a possibility for our mystery man until you told me you'd spotted your stalker in Boston. Something about your description this time finally clicked. I tried reaching Hartley. I only have his cell phone number and he didn't answer." She needed air and got out of her car. A cool evening breeze was blowing onshore off the Pacific. Damn. Had she screwed up this time? "Where is Hartley now?"

"I have no idea," Noah said, no hint of impatience or exasperation.

"All right. I'll see what I can do and call you when I know more."

"What did he want when he came to your office?"

"He asked me about Duncan McCaffrey."

"Dylan's father? Why?"

Loretta had told Noah as well as Dylan about her brief affair with Duncan shortly before his death. At least she wouldn't have to rehash that indiscretion — which was what it was, even if she didn't regret it.

Finally she said, "Hartley told me he was fascinated with treasure hunts and was curious about what would happen to Duncan's

186

unfinished projects. Duncan's been gone for two years, so I figured it was a lame cover story for worming information out of me about Dylan, about you and your work together at NAK, what's next now that it's gone public."

Loretta stood on the sidewalk in front of Dylan's house so that the breeze off the ocean caught her full in the face. She could see Julius Hartley in her office in La Jolla, a good-looking man around her own age, cocky, not really giving a damn that she didn't believe a word he was saying.

She should have pegged him as Noah's stalker from the get-go.

"I'll get to the bottom of this, Noah," she said.

"I know you will," he said, as calm as ever.

"He hasn't turned up in Knights Bridge, has he?"

"Not that I know of."

A stiff gust of wind brought with it the smell of saltwater. She could taste it as she tried to picture Noah alone in the out-of-the-way little New England town and found that she couldn't. Not that she'd ever been to Knights Bridge herself, but she'd never seen Noah outside of Southern California. Well, once at his winery on the Central Coast. He and Dylan had invited her up for a party celebrating NAK's fourth anniversary.

Optimist that she was, when Dylan had told her he'd agreed to work with Noah, she'd figured NAK would go bust within months. But Dylan had been broke, going nowhere after ignoring one piece of good advice after another from her.

A good thing she'd kept her mouth shut about NAK.

Dylan and Noah had done well in their work together, and Loretta had done well by Dylan and got to know and like Noah, even if she'd never understand him.

What the hell did Julius Hartley want with him?

"Got anything more going on than listening to owls and watching the stars?" she asked Noah, hoping she didn't sound as out of sorts as she felt.

"Olivia's dog keeps breaking out of the mudroom and getting up on the couch."

"The legendary Buster," Loretta said, then promised to keep Noah informed and disconnected.

Her attempt at good humor didn't last. Dylan had come out onto his front porch and was waiting for her. She tossed her phone into her handbag and headed up the steps, the wind at her back now. Dylan had his eyes narrowed on her in that distinctly McCaffrey manner. She'd known him since his early days with the NHL. He was more aggressive than Noah. He'd pounce. With Noah, she thought, you could be bleeding on the floor before you knew he'd even come close to you.

"Does Julius Hartley work for you?" Dylan asked.

"No. Never. He works up in L.A. He stopped by my office a couple of weeks ago."

"Why?"

"I thought he was fishing for information on you and Noah. I kicked him out."

"As only you can," Dylan said.

Loretta turned to look out at the darkening ocean and sky. The stars would be out here soon, too. She didn't know about owls.

Dylan stared at the Pacific, white caps visible as waves rolled onto the wide beach. "I can't just step back from this, Loretta. Whatever Hartley is after involves Noah or me, or both of us."

"Could someone in Knights Bridge be a threat to Noah?"

"Like who?"

Loretta waved a hand. "I don't know. I'm just thinking out loud."

"Who was Hartley talking to on Friday?"

She shook her head. "No idea. No idea

who his client is, either. I'll find out. You and Noah don't need to worry about this."

Dylan didn't look convinced but Loretta wasn't surprised. He'd had Noah's back for four years, allowing his friend to focus on his strengths in building NAK into a highly profitable company. It wouldn't be easy for him to give that up.

A fair-haired woman Loretta took to be Olivia Frost, Dylan's fiancée, stepped out of the house. Dylan introduced them, and any misgivings Loretta had about their sudden romance quickly disappeared. Olivia was smart and sophisticated, but also natural, and down-to-earth. She was perfect for Dylan. And Loretta saw that Dylan was perfect for Olivia, too.

"How do you like San Diego so far?" Loretta asked.

Olivia smiled. "I absolutely love it. It's so different from Knights Bridge. That's where I've lived most of my life."

Olivia's eyes lit up when she mentioned her hometown. Then Loretta saw it, too. What Dylan had been trying to tell her. That as much as Olivia might like other places, her town on the edge of the Quabbin Reservoir was home. That meant Dylan would make Knights Bridge his home.

So what were she and Noah supposed to do?

Maybe that was why he was dog sitting, listening to owls and chasing a masked princess. In his own way, he was trying to figure out what he'd do with his best friend and business partner — a man who was like a brother to him — living on the other side of the continent.

And if Noah and Dylan both ended up in Knights Bridge?

Loretta didn't want to think about it.

She'd focus on tracking down Julius Hartley instead.

# Ten

Phoebe dressed for a hot August day but the library was cooler than she expected when she arrived early, well before eight o'clock. Mondays were generally quiet, and she was the only full-time employee. The part-time staff and volunteers wouldn't start arriving until after the library opened at nine-thirty but she appreciated the time to herself.

With a shiver, she grabbed an old sweater off one of the stacks of sorted vintage clothes on the stage. The sweater was several sizes too big and a dingy coral acrylic that didn't go at all with her sunflower-colored sundress but she wouldn't need it for long before the library warmed up.

She'd planned to shelve books and catch up on paperwork but instead went up onto the stage and sorted a box of clothes that had come in over the weekend. For the most part, donors had respected the specifications for the show and weren't just dropping off junk, although not everything could be used — including the awful sweater she'd thrown on.

The front door creaked open at the stroke of nine-thirty. Phoebe looked up from her box, filled with a colorful collection of maxi skirts, fringed vests and headbands from the early 1970s. She expected to see her administrative assistant, but instead it was Noah Kendrick entering the library.

Phoebe stood up, realized she still had on the old sweater. She wished she'd taken it off, then decided it was just as well. She hated the stereotype of the dowdy, introverted librarian and knew it didn't fit her or most professional librarians she knew, even if Noah was thinking exactly that right now. She was practical. She'd been cold and the sweater had been handy. She wasn't a princess.

Not that Noah had recognized her as the woman he'd danced with.

She certainly had no intention of telling him.

He smiled, maintaining a stillness about him as he approached the stage. "I half expected a ghost."

"Lots of people have said they've encountered ghosts in here, going back to when the library first opened in 1872."

"What a surprise," he said mildly.

She went to the edge of the stage. She expected to jump down to him on her own, but he caught her by the waist and lowered her to the hardwood floor with the same ease and sureness with which he'd swept her across the dance floor on Friday night.

Glad for the dim light in the library, Phoebe pushed back strands of hair that had come out of its pins. Her oversize sweater had come off her shoulders. She let it drop to the floor and shoved it aside with one foot, then got control of herself.

"Good morning," she said politely, stepping back from Noah. "What can I do for you?"

It might have been her imagination, but she thought she saw a spark of pure male sexiness in his deep blue eyes, as if to say that she could do a hell of a lot for him. But he simply said, "I was thinking I might borrow a book or two. Is that allowed?"

"Sure. We'll figure it out. Wander around." Phoebe realized she wasn't cold anymore. "Let me know if I can help you find anything."

Noah peered up at the stage. "The fashion show is shaping up well?"

She nodded. "Some of the clothes we've

received are amazing. Others, not so much. The historical society is interested in checking out some of the unique items."

He shifted his gaze back to her. "Are you involved in the historical society, too?"

"Yes, as a matter of fact."

She didn't know why she felt defensive. There was nothing condescending in his tone or manner. His eyes were half closed, almost navy in the dim light by the stage. They lingered on her shoulders, then lifted to meet hers.

*He knows.*

She couldn't pinpoint what had tipped her off, but there was no question in her mind that Noah Kendrick had figured out that she was the woman in the Edwardian gown on Friday.

Had he known yesterday?

She felt the heat of embarrassment but hoped he didn't notice her discomfort. "The fashion show is turning out to be a lot of fun for everyone." Her throat was dry, tight, as she suddenly tingled with the memory of their brief kiss just two nights ago. They'd gotten carried away. No question about it. She added, "Every donated garment has a story behind it."

"What's the story behind Maggie's and Olivia's dresses?"

*"And yours?"* Phoebe could almost hear him ask.

"They're copies from movies," she said. "As I'm sure you know."

*"To Catch a Thief* and *Breakfast at Tiffany's."*

"That's right." She didn't explain further. She had no intention of telling him about the hidden room when she still hadn't told her sisters and Olivia — anyone — about it. "Maggie and Olivia had a great time at the ball."

"So did I." His eyes held hers. "More than I ever imagined."

Phoebe reminded herself that she was a professional, experienced librarian, accustomed to dealing with tricky situations with the public. She would think of Noah as just that. A member of the public. She motioned toward the stacks. "I'll let you get on with your browsing."

"Thanks." He walked over to the fireplace, then glanced back at her. "Ever light a fire in here?"

"Not in years."

"The library's centrally located. Do many people from out of town stop in to ask for information on residents?"

"Some." She knew he was thinking about the note about the phone call she'd overheard. Did Noah realize she'd written the note? Was that why he was here? She pushed back her own questions and focused on what he'd asked her. "We don't give out private information on anyone. That would include Olivia's guests, in case you're wondering."

"So you won't be spreading the word that I'm staying in town?"

Phoebe went behind the curved circulation desk and tried to act as if it was just another Monday morning. "That's right."

Noah glanced up at the oil portrait of an imposing George Sanderson. "Has anyone been asking about Dylan or me?"

"Not that I know of. Do you have anyone specific in mind?"

Noah moved back from the fireplace and scooped up the coral sweater she'd had on. He laid it on the stage. She had a feeling he knew it wasn't hers. "What would you do if someone did ask about us?" he asked.

"I might offer to take down a name, address and phone number and give them to Dylan, or to you if you're still in town." Phoebe shrugged, still containing her reaction to Noah's presence. "Otherwise I stay out of personal business involving anyone in town."

"Smart. If someone does ask about either

Dylan or me while I'm here, you'll let me know?"

She nodded. "Happy to."

"Thanks. I think I'll check out what you have on fencing. It's a hobby of mine. Classical fencing. In fact, Dylan couldn't resist having me dress up as a swashbuckler on Friday." Noah smiled. "He has a sense of humor."

"So I've discovered."

He headed off to the stacks, but Phoebe knew he wasn't serious about checking out what the library had on fencing books or anything else. Once he was safely out of sight, she sat at her computer and let out a long, cathartic breath.

Vera Galeski, Phoebe's part-time assistant, arrived, cheerfully grumbling about the heat. In winter, she grumbled about the cold. She was a high-energy woman in her early sixties, devoted to books, married to a retired teacher, mother of four, grandmother of six and ever hopeful that Phoebe would find a man.

Vera nodded vaguely in the direction Noah had just gone. "Who's that man dressed head-to-toe in black on a hot day like today?"

"One of Dylan McCaffrey's friends," Phoebe said, hitting a few random keys on her keyboard to help herself look nonchalant.

Vera's pale blue eyes widened. "Not Noah Kendrick," she whispered.

Phoebe nodded, then added quickly, "It's not something we're advertising."

"Of course not. I understand perfectly. Oh, my. I read an article in a magazine at the hairdresser's that mentioned him. It was about that actress . . . I can't think of her name. The one on that Sunday-night show that just got canceled. She played a lawyer."

"I should read more gossip magazines," Phoebe said with what she hoped was a credible laugh, then made an excuse to go upstairs.

Without so much as a glance in Noah's direction, she headed to the back stairs and ran all the way up to the attic without stopping. She switched on the dim overhead, then squeezed between the freestanding twin metal closets and entered the hidden sewing room. It was hot, airless. She opened the second door in the corner, letting in daylight from the small window overlooking the common. Children from a nearby daycare were sitting in a circle in the shade in front of the Civil War statue.

Noah Kendrick's arrival notwithstanding, nothing in Knights Bridge had changed.

This Monday was like last Monday.

*And next Monday?*

Phoebe pulled her gaze from the window and unzipped one of the garment bags. Inside were four dresses in various shades of red, as well as accessories carefully draped on hangers — bright red scarves, sequined belts, gaudy costume jewelry.

Who was the woman who'd sewn here, most likely in secret? Had she despaired that she was living in a small, out-of-the-way town? Had she wanted something that Knights Bridge just couldn't give her?

Phoebe ran her fingertips over a scarlet crepe flapper dress. Would Noah have noticed her if she'd worn it the other night, or was there something about the Edwardian dress that had caught his eye, fired his imagination?

She glanced out the window again and saw him crossing South Main to the common. He didn't have any books with him. Had he returned to the circulation desk expecting to find her, or simply seized the moment to get out of there, leave her to her work? His princess, after all, had evaporated. She was a small-town librarian.

And her swashbuckler?

Phoebe watched him walk in the shade. He was one of the wealthiest people in the country, brilliant, successful, a master fencer, an expert in karate. As far as she could see, he was just missing the black cape, mask and sword at his side to be a real swashbuckler.

Had her seamstress looked out at the window at a man crossing the common, yearned for him — for a life other than the one she had, tucked up here with her fabrics and sewing notions?

Phoebe's throat tightened at the thought of the carefully conjugated French verbs. A student doing homework, or a young woman dreaming of a different life?

Noah disappeared from her view. Phoebe shut the corner door, the little children rolling in the grass now, playing some kind of game.

Who was she kidding?

This Monday wasn't like last Monday. Last Monday, she hadn't met Noah Kendrick.

She left the hidden room, ran down the stairs and got back to work.

Phoebe left the library at four, as she did every Monday, and dropped off books at Rivendell, an assisted-living facility on a ridge just outside the village center. As she carried a box of fiction and nonfiction titles to the main entrance, she could see a peek of Quabbin in the distance, its pristine waters barely visible in the steamy haze. A number of the elderly residents remembered the Swift River Valley before it was flooded, and several were from the lost towns, including Grace Webster, Dylan's newly discovered grandmother.

After leaving the books in the reading room, Phoebe went down a wide corridor to the sunroom, its tall windows overlooking the center's beautifully landscaped grounds. Grace was seated next to Audrey Frost, Olivia's grandmother, each with a set of binoculars. Grace, a retired teacher in her nineties, was an avid bird-watcher. Audrey, a former bookkeeper at the high school and a few years younger than Grace, was always up for a new hobby and was getting into the spirit of things.

"Phoebe, so good to see you, dear," Audrey said, lowering her binoculars. She had told Phoebe that she loved assisted living because she didn't have to cook every meal for herself, although she could if she wanted to, and she could still have her car. "Did you bring us some good books? Your friend says he saw you at the library this morning."

Phoebe frowned. "My friend?"

"Noah Kendrick," Grace said. "You know him, don't you? He's Dylan's business associate and friend from San Diego."

"He was here?"

"He still is here," Audrey said. "He stepped outside for a minute to look at the view."

Phoebe sank into a cushioned rocker and looked out at the array of bird feeders just outside the sunroom. They were empty now but would be kept filled over the winter. Bird-watching was a favorite activity for Rivendell residents.

The two older women eyed her. In addition to her work at the school, Audrey Frost had helped her late husband in his business specializing in custom reproduction millwork. Their son, Randy Frost, Olivia's father, now ran the mill with his wife. It was located behind a nineteenth-century sawmill the Frosts had converted into a residence.

Until recently, people in Knights Bridge would have said they knew all there was to know about Grace Webster's life. She'd moved to Knights Bridge as a teenager with her father and grandmother and became an English and Latin teacher. She'd lived out on Carriage Hill Road until two years ago, when she'd sold her house to Duncan Mc-Caffrey and relocated to Rivendell. But

Grace had her secrets. As a teenager, her family facing expulsion from their home ahead of the damming of the Swift River for Quabbin, she'd created a hideaway in a cabin on a small pond and met a British flyer on the run. They'd fallen in love, but he'd gone back to England, promising to return.

With a war on, starting her life over in a new town, Grace had discovered she was pregnant and realized her British flyer wasn't coming back to her. She gave birth to a baby boy in a Boston area hospital, put him up for adoption and went back home to Knights Bridge, only her grandmother and father ever aware of her secret.

Seventy years later, Dylan's treasure-hunting father showed up in Knights Bridge and unearthed the story of his birth mother — met her — just before he died. Only he'd failed to tell his son, leaving Dylan to find out on his own. Even Grace hadn't realized that the handsome daredevil in his early seventies was the baby she'd never even held.

Phoebe felt a rush of emotion, as she did whenever she thought of Grace's story. No one in town had ever guessed. People were still getting used to the idea that the starchy retired teacher was Dylan McCaffrey's grandmother.

Phoebe realized that Audrey Frost was peering at her. "What's on your mind, Phoebe?" the older woman asked.

She collected her thoughts. "I was wondering if you remember anyone from your days at the high school who was especially good at sewing, maybe took French and had an interest in Hollywood. She might have worked at the library, either as an employee or a volunteer."

Grace frowned. "What brought this up?"

"I found some dresses that someone sewed and hid away. I'm not sure how long ago. Forty years, at least, I'd guess. I don't have enough information to talk about the details yet."

Both Grace and Audrey had no immediate memory of anyone who could fit Phoebe's vague description but promised to check their records.

The two elderly women smiled suddenly, pointing as Noah came into view out among the bird feeders. Audrey said, "He's as good-looking in his own way as Dylan, don't you think?"

Grace concurred. "You can tell he's a master fencer. He has the poise of a sword-fighter." She glanced at Phoebe. "He told us he helped you make pesto yesterday."

"We had to do something with Olivia's basil," she said, suppressing any reaction that might alert Grace or Audrey that something was up between her and Noah.

He entered the sunroom through a set of French doors and greeted the two Rivendell residents before turning to Phoebe. "We do keep running into each other, don't we?"

"It's a small town." She got to her feet, noticing that gray clouds were moving in from the west. "I should get going. Grace, Audrey, good to see you."

Phoebe quickly left the sunroom and got almost to her car when Noah caught up with her. "Where's your car?" she asked him.

"I don't have one. Olivia said I could borrow hers, but I walked into town and then out here."

Phoebe stopped abruptly. "You walked?"

He smiled. "It's something to do." He pointed up at the threatening sky. "I didn't think about the fact that it rains more often here than in San Diego. Looks as if we're expecting a downpour."

"You don't worry about getting kidnapped walking around on your own? Not because Knights Bridge is a dangerous place, but given your —" She waved a hand. "You know what I mean."

206

"I do, and I don't worry about kidnappers, no. I take reasonable precautions and I don't advertise my whereabouts. Besides, who would pay the ransom if I was the one snatched?"

His tone was reassuring, not at all dismissive. Phoebe imagined he'd gotten over any surprise or disappointment he'd felt at discovering his Edwardian princess was one of Olivia's friends from Knights Bridge.

Feeling more at ease, she opened her Subaru door. "I can give you a ride back to Carriage Hill if you'd like. I'm done for the day. My assistant, Vera, will lock up the library."

"A ride would be great, thanks," he said.

Phoebe got behind the wheel and waited as he came around to the passenger side. He settled next to her and snapped on his seat belt. She started the car, wondering if she'd flat-out lost her mind.

She tried to think of something innocuous to say. "We're supposed to get scattered thunderstorms this evening. You don't have many thunderstorms in San Diego, do you?"

"We don't."

"Have you heard from Dylan and Olivia? Do you know how she likes it out there?"

"Dylan and I spoke last night. It was early evening in San Diego." Noah's tone was unreadable, as if deliberately so. "He and Olivia had just come back from a walk on the beach."

"That sounds so romantic."

"Yes, it does," Noah said quietly.

Phoebe felt his gaze on her and wished she hadn't mentioned romance. She drove out of the Rivendell parking lot, then turned toward the village. She heard a rumble of thunder in the distance. "A front's moving through," she said. "I won't mind saying goodbye to this heat and humidity."

A fat raindrop splattered on her windshield, then another. Lightning flickered, followed immediately by a clap of thunder. By the time she pulled in front of Olivia's house, they were in the middle of a downpour.

Phoebe looked at Noah next to her. "You don't have an umbrella or raincoat. Anyway, you don't want to get struck by lightning. I don't mind waiting until the storm's passed. It'll probably be just a few minutes. Rain's one thing but lightning . . ."

"Lightning can hurt," Noah finished for her, with a smile.

She switched off the engine and watched the rain stream down the windshield. It made the car feel even smaller. "At least there's not much wind," she said. "I'm glad

you didn't walk back here in this weather."

"I'd have ended up playing Scrabble with Audrey and Grace until the storm passed. They'd have beaten me for sure. I've never had the patience for word games."

"For a lot of other things, though."

"Yes," he said.

She'd meant his patience for his work with NAK but something in his tone made her throat catch, made her think about his patience as a lover. She flashed on him bearing toward her at the masquerade. He'd moved with purpose and intention. Not patience. Patience, she thought, was something different.

He traced a raindrop as it slid down the other side of the passenger window. "The rain's subsiding already," he said, then looked over at her. "Thanks for the ride, Princess Phoebe."

She placed her hands on the steering wheel and stared straight out the windshield. "How long have you known?"

"Not long enough."

"Since yesterday?"

"When I saw the flyer about the fashion show. I was suspicious before then, but not when we met here on Saturday." He paused, then added, with a hint of humor, "The slugs threw me."

"I'm not fond of slugs," Phoebe said, then made herself breathe as she looked at him. "I recognized you yesterday, too. I didn't want to say anything in case you didn't recognize me, or in case you just wanted to forget the masquerade. It's not as if it was that big a deal. We dressed up for a benefit. We danced." She pried her fingers from the steering wheel. "I'm talking too much."

"You're fine," he said. "Olivia and Maggie know?"

"Yes. Well, I know Maggie does, and that means Olivia does."

"Anyone else?"

"No." Phoebe remembered her brother-in-law and gave an inward groan. "Wait. Brandon, Maggie's husband. He saw me and recognized me straight off."

Noah smiled. "I've only met him briefly but I can see that he would. Do you two get along well?"

"We always have, but he knows Maggie's my sister."

"You're on her side."

"Always, but I hope there are no sides. He won't say anything about seeing me at the ball."

"Neither will I. I don't want to disrupt your life, Phoebe. I enjoyed our dance. I'm glad you were there that night."

She realized it was getting steamy in the car; the windows were fogging up. The worst of the brief downpour was over. She pushed open her door, welcoming the rush of air. She heard the water high in the stream across the road, tumbling toward the reservoir. Finally she said, "We were both playing a part."

"What part were you playing?"

"A bold, daring princess who'd let a swashbuckler sweep her off her feet."

"You played your part well, princess."

She jumped out of the car, gulping in a breath as she leaned against the hood, ignoring that it was wet. She was vaguely aware of Noah getting out, shutting his door, walking around the hood to her. This would all be easier, she thought, if he didn't play the role of a daring swashbuckler so well in real life.

He stood next to her but didn't lean against the car and get himself wet. "Are you okay, Phoebe?"

She nodded. "I overheard that man talking about you." She could feel the cool rainwater soaking into the back of her sundress. "I wrote the note Olivia gave you."

"I'm sorry you had to run into him. I'd spotted him. That's why I left you. I went to find him but I lost him. He must have slipped into the coatroom to make the call you overheard."

"You don't know who he is or what he wants?"

Noah hesitated, as if debating what to tell her. "His name is Julius Hartley. He's a private investigator in Los Angeles. He does work for a prominent law firm there but that's not his only client. I saw him on my tail a few times in San Diego. I didn't expect him to show up in Boston."

"He wasn't in the mountains with you?"

"No. Do you recognize his name?"

She shook her head. "It's new to me."

She was aware of Noah watching her as she stood straight, brushed her wet backside with one hand. "Phoebe, tell me the rest. What wasn't in the note?"

She didn't meet his eye. "Hartley — if that's who it was — told whoever was on the other end that you were with, quote, some woman dressed up like she's about to board the *Titanic,* unquote. He said he didn't know who she was but would find out. That it shouldn't be hard."

Noah was silent as she stepped into the middle of the quiet road and picked up a small stone. Everything was wet, dripping. Leaves, flowers, weeds, The Farm at Carriage Hill sign with its hand-painted signature clump of chives.

"It wasn't unnerving." Phoebe tossed the stone into the stream. "I'm not worried or afraid Hartley will find me. He didn't see me, and he has no reason to think I was with Olivia or Maggie, or even that I'm from Knights Bridge. Only Brandon saw me and he was sneaking around himself."

Noah stood with her on the edge of the road, in front of the stream. He brushed off a mosquito that had found him, then picked up another stone and pelted it into the water, the energy of his throw all that suggested he wasn't calm, wasn't unmoved by the prospect of an L.A. private investigator coming to find her. As he turned to her, Phoebe noticed the tension in the muscles in his forearms.

"I left right after I overheard the conversation," she said. "I thought it could be a marital situation. I didn't know . . . I knew he was talking about the swashbuckler I'd danced with but I didn't know the swashbuckler was you. I was avoiding Dylan and Olivia. Maggie, too. Otherwise you and I might have met as —" *As what?* Phoebe smiled. "As ourselves."

"I'm sorry about this, Phoebe."

"It's not your fault. If I remember anything else, I'll let you know, but I'm sure

213

I've told you everything."

He came closer to her. "If you see Hartley or hear from him —"

"I'll tell you right away."

"Call me. You have Olivia's landline, and I'll give you my private cell phone number." He gave a small smile. "I had a new phone delivered. I was angry at myself for having lost you and threw my last one in the sink on Saturday morning. I tend to go through phones."

"You can only take so much intrusion." When he seemed surprised at her observation, she added, "There's a core stillness about you, and you concentrate deeply, even if you have a number of thought threads going on at once. My nephew Tyler is a bit like that. Not Aidan." She paused. "Of course, I don't know you well. I just observe a lot of people in my work."

"I imagine you do," he said. "I want your number, too, Phoebe."

She saw the relentless entrepreneur in him. The drive. The self-possession. The focus on the next step he had to take — on action. "I understand. Noah, if this man is a threat to you —" She broke off, took a moment to collect her thoughts. "A man in your position must have enemies. If Hartley thinks someone in Knights Bridge is involved in whatever bone he has to pick with you, that could be a problem."

Noah winked at her. "You have backbone, Princess Phoebe." He touched the wet bark of a tree. "This is almost the same color as your dress the other night. It was a richer brown."

"Beautiful, wasn't it?"

"Yes."

"I wish —"

When she broke off, he fastened his blue eyes on her, his intensity almost palpable. "You wish what?"

"Nothing. I don't even know what I was going to say." Which was true, and not like her. "Thank you for dancing with me. It was fun."

Noah started to say something but she pulled away from him when she saw her brother-in-law ambling down the road. Thunder rumbled in the distance, to the east, but rays of late-afternoon sun were shining now on puddles and dripping leaves.

"Hey, Phoebe," Brandon said. "Here for more basil?"

She shook her head. "I gave Noah a ride back from Rivendell. What are you doing here?"

"I'm working up the road," he said, a tightness to his expression.

"At Dylan's place?"

He hesitated, then nodded. "That's right."

Phoebe tried to contain her surprise. "Does Maggie know? Where are you staying? Are you working for your family?" The questions tumbled out, and she was aware once more of Noah watching her, tuning in to the dynamics between her and her sister's husband. "Never mind. It's none of my business."

"I need to talk to Maggie first," Brandon said. "She doesn't know I'm in town. I don't want to be a distraction. She's got a lot on her plate."

"You could be a help," Phoebe blurted.

"Maybe I could be, but it's not all up to me, is it? Maggie has a say." He turned to Noah with a wry smile. "That was Phoebe's stern librarian voice you just heard. Can you imagine turning in a book late to her? I once had gum stuck in a book I returned. It wasn't my gum but that's another story. Phoebe was already volunteering at the library then. What were we, thirteen?"

"About that." Still reeling from her conversation with Noah, she pointed a finger at her brother-in-law. "You're putting me in a difficult position, Brandon. I'm not going to get caught between you and Maggie, but I can't not tell her that you're in town."

Brandon was unperturbed. "You don't have to tell her. I will in about five minutes. She's on her way over with the boys." He kept his gaze on Phoebe, the slightest hint of humor in his dark eyes. "I have spies everywhere."

"Your brothers, you mean."

He shrugged, as if she'd stated the obvious, then glanced at Noah. "Was I interrupting anything?"

"Nothing," Phoebe said, answering for Noah. She crossed the road back to her car. "I'll be on my way. Tell Maggie I said hi."

Neither man stopped her as she climbed back behind the wheel of her old Subaru.

As soon as she arrived on Thistle Lane, the skies opened up again, but it was just a passing shower, no thunder and lightning. She parked in her driveway, then ran through the rain onto the porch. Soaked and shivering, she sat on a wicker chair, smelling roses and wet summer grass and thinking about Noah Kendrick's hand on her cheek.

# ELEVEN

Maggie fidgeted, grabbing a canvas bag of who-knew-what out of the back of her catering van just to give herself something to do, fussing at Aidan and Tyler when they jumped out of the back straight into a puddle. She didn't care one way or the other whether they got wet or muddied their shoes, and she wasn't at Carriage Hill to cook. She was just checking on the place.

Checking on why she'd seen Phoebe driving in this direction with Noah Kendrick in the front seat of her car.

Maggie shut the van door. She just needed to stay busy, give herself a chance to think.

Phoebe, Noah.

*Brandon.*

It was too much.

Brandon scooped up his sons, one in each arm as if they weighed nothing. They got mud on his cargo pants but he didn't seem to notice as he set the boys on the grass in

218

the front yard and turned to Noah. "These are my sons, Tyler and Aidan Sloan. Guys, this is Noah Kendrick."

"Pleased to meet you," Noah said as the boys greeted him politely, then promptly went back to their puddle-stomping. He glanced at Brandon, then Maggie. "I'll be out back."

Maggie almost stopped him so that she wouldn't be alone with Brandon, but she kept quiet. She was being ridiculous. She'd known Brandon all her life. Even if he didn't want to live in Knights Bridge, his family was here. Now his sons were here. Whatever her relationship with him had become, he was still a part of her life.

She held her canvas bag against her hip, remembered that it contained different oils she and Olivia wanted to try out in their soap-making. Olive, almond, soy, coconut. "Where's your truck?" she asked Brandon.

"Up at Dylan's."

"I didn't see it there."

"It's out back."

"What did you do, park where I wouldn't see it?"

"I didn't want you to run away or throw a brick through the windshield." When she glared at him, he held up a hand. "It was a joke, Maggie. If you have things you need to do here, I can take the boys up to Dylan's and show them what's going on. Demolition starts this week."

"I'm not staying. I should get Aidan and Tyler home and into the tub."

"Why?"

"Because they're dirty, Brandon."

"I mean why the rush?"

"Schedules. Routine. Summer's winding down. School will be starting soon. Anyway, I don't have time to explain their day-to-day lives to you." She immediately regretted snapping at him. "I'm sorry. I'll give them a few more minutes to get wet and muddy and then go."

Brandon didn't fire back, as he would have six months ago. "They can see Dylan's place another time."

"Another time? Aren't you going back to Boston?"

"No. I'm working here, Maggie."

She was so shocked she gasped. "With your family?"

He nodded without hesitation, without any indication he was embarrassed, bitter, settling, anything.

"But why?" she asked.

"It's a job." He spoke with a finality that shut down further questions.

Maggie took a breath. "Okay, then. Where

are you staying? You're not commuting from Boston —"

"I pitched a tent at Dylan's." He gave her that devil-may-care Sloan smile. "It's rent-free. I promised the boys I'd take them camping. I was thinking we'd just camp out here."

"They'd like that," Maggie said, her throat tight with emotion.

He started for the kitchen door. "I'll head upstairs. I need to take a shower. Helps with the camping out."

"Helps with the smell, too."

He grinned at her. "You never were one to beat around the bush."

"You're sweaty. It's not . . ." *Why* had she brought up something as personal, as intimate, as that? "Olivia and I made a spearmint-olive oil soap. I think there's some in the hall bathroom."

"No goat's milk?"

Maggie didn't know if he was making fun of her and Olivia's goat's milk soaps or if he was genuinely curious. She decided to give him a straight answer. "It's the one soap we've tried so far that doesn't have goat's milk. Spearmint works for guys as well as women. You know. Instead of a lilac scent or something."

He scratched the side of his mouth and

let his gaze linger on her. Maggie knew he was thinking about the two of them in the shower. She didn't know what had gotten into her, bringing up soaps. She wanted to blame him, because it'd be just like him to lead her down a dead-end road and let her figure out how to get out of there on her own.

He swaggered inside. He knew what she was thinking. He always knew. That was half their problem. She wished sometimes she wasn't so damn transparent.

She saw that the boys had settled into making mud pies and checking out worms. "I'll be in the kitchen," she told them. "I can see you from the window."

It was as much a warning to stay out of trouble as reassurance that she was near. They weren't toddlers anymore. She headed into the kitchen and set her bag on the island, then unloaded the oils. She might as well go ahead and leave them in Olivia's pantry.

Why was Brandon back working with his family?

It wouldn't last. He disliked construction on a good day. He did it to make a living. They'd married so young, had the boys so young. They'd both had to juggle dreams and practicalities. He was already restless, frayed at the edges, when his work slowed down in Boston last year and he got laid off. Brandon didn't do well being idle. No Sloan did. One day, Maggie came home to a note telling her he'd taken off on a canoe trip down the Moose River in Maine. He'd be back "whenever."

And that was that. She'd packed up herself and the boys and moved to Knights Bridge. She started her own catering business, and now she was working with Olivia, not just providing food for events but helping to shape The Farm at Carriage Hill.

Maggie loved what she was doing, but her relationship with Brandon remained unresolved, in that no-man's-land between estrangement and divorce.

It wasn't as if there was another man in her life. It'd always been just the two of them.

Noah came in from the mudroom, where Buster was sound asleep. In a combative mood, Maggie decided to confront him about Phoebe. "My sister gave you a ride back here? Why?"

"It was raining and I'd walked into town."

"Phoebe's . . ." Maggie smacked a bottle of coconut oil onto the island with more force than was necessary. "She loves books and history, and she knows everything that goes on in town. She's a good soul."

"She's a little quirky, too," Brandon said, entering the kitchen from the living room. He'd made fast work of his shower, the ends of his dark hair still damp.

Maggie flashed him a look. "Phoebe's reserved."

He shrugged. "Compared to you and the twins, maybe. Ask the boys about her at story hour. She gets into it."

"I'm here every week for story hour. I have asked them." Maggie gritted her teeth, wishing she'd just gone straight home instead of coming out here, then smiled apologetically at Noah. "I should go."

Noah's interest clearly was piqued but he seemed to contain it. "Was there a story hour when you all were Aidan and Tyler's age?"

"There was," Maggie said. "Brandon was disruptive."

He grinned at her. "You remember."

She resisted comment.

"Phoebe and I know we danced with each other at the masquerade the other night," Noah said calmly.

Maggie didn't bother hiding her relief. "I'm glad that secret's out, at least among us. The whole town doesn't need to know." Then she remembered who she was talking

224

looked him up on Facebook last year. He was a lawyer now, married and living in Orlando. She knew Phoebe would never look him up herself but hadn't told her that she had.

Knowing Phoebe, she wished him well.

Maggie didn't.

Her ability to hold a grudge was something Brandon used to appreciate about her. He didn't anymore. *"Let it go, Maggie,"* he'd tell her. *"Just let it go."*

"Mom," Aidan said from the back. "When can we go camping with Daddy?"

"He has a tent," Tyler said, sitting next to his brother.

Maggie's idea of camping was a cabin with heat and indoor plumbing. "We'll work out a date with your dad, okay?"

They thought that'd be great and proceeded to regale her with all that they'd do with their father on their camping trip, even if it was just in Dylan McCaffrey's backyard.

That was Brandon, wasn't it? Always able to fire up their sons, fill them with can-do optimism. Even at his darkest moment, when he'd watched his dreams go up in smoke, when a temporary lay-off had dragged into flat-out unemployment, he hadn't taken his disappointments out on Tyler and Aidan. Maggie wasn't even sure if he'd taken them out on her, but she'd felt them, internalized them, let them make her bleed.

She hadn't wanted him to throw his dreams overboard and yet she'd known they were weighing them down, hurting their chances of creating a stable life for their sons. For themselves.

Now here he was, in their hometown, working for Sloan & Sons.

*"If I ever go back to Knights Bridge, Maggie, you'll know I've failed."*

He'd been seventeen then.

Things changed, she thought. People grew up.

And yet, as she drove along the common and turned onto her own pretty little side street, she couldn't help but feel that Brandon had given up. That he did see himself as a failure . . . and maybe so did she.

After Maggie O'Dunn Sloan whirled out with her two sons, Noah got two beers out of the refrigerator, opened them and took them out to the terrace. He handed one to Brandon, who'd dried off a couple of chairs at Olivia's round table. He took a long drink. "So, Noah. You may be good with a sword, but if I've misplaced my trust and you do anything to upset my wife or her sisters —"

"You'll key my car?"

Brandon grinned. "Right. Key your car. You really are a trip. You don't even have a car here." He drank more of his beer. "Why are you here? Really."

Noah sat down. A cool breeze stirred. He swore he could smell pesto but assumed it was just rain-drenched basil. Finally he looked across the table at Brandon. "A Los Angeles private investigator named Julius Hartley has been on my tail. I don't know why. I saw him several times in San Diego. Then I saw him in Boston."

"At the masquerade?"

"That's right. I can't say for sure that he followed me east."

"But it's a safe bet," Brandon said.

Noah didn't disagree. "I stayed in Knights Bridge in part to make sure he's not hanging around here."

"Do you think he was hired by someone from here or from California?"

Brandon Sloan obviously had grasped the situation immediately. Noah drank some of his beer, appreciating the cooler, drier evening. How frank could he be with this man? "It could be either one," he said finally.

"Explain."

Noah told Brandon what he knew, but he left out his reaction to Phoebe — and her reaction to him. The attraction they'd experienced at the ball hadn't been just a fleeting thing born of their anonymity and the roles they were playing.

Phoebe O'Dunn, his princess.

If anything, he found her even more appealing with her wild red hair, in her element making pesto, working at the Knights Bridge Free Public Library, talking to Audrey Frost and Grace Webster at Rivendell.

Her baggy sweater that morning at the library wasn't in the same league as her elegant Edwardian gown, but Noah didn't care. It'd been chilly in the library and Phoebe had obviously grabbed the sweater from the collection of vintage clothes for the upcoming fashion show. He appreciated her ease with herself and her surroundings.

He'd also noticed the swell of her breasts as the old sweater had slipped off her shoulders, but he blocked that image from his thoughts, in case Brandon Sloan could read minds and decide to throttle him.

These were treacherous waters he was navigating, Noah thought.

"Do you think Maggie and Phoebe have anything to do with this Hartley character?"

Brandon asked. "Because if you do, you're wrong."

Noah appreciated the other man's confidence. "I understand your concern but I don't think anything. I'm trying not to speculate."

"You sound like my cop brother."

Noah thought that was a compliment, or at least a neutral observation, but he couldn't be sure and therefore said nothing.

Buster put his head on Brandon's lap. Brandon scratched behind the big dog's ears as he looked out at Olivia's garden. "How much do you know about Phoebe?"

"She's the director and sole full-time employee of the Knights Bridge library." Noah started to add that she could dance but reconsidered and said instead, "She's the eldest of four sisters. Phoebe, Maggie, Ava and Ruby."

"Their mother is Elly. Elly O'Dunn. She's still around." Brandon patted Buster, then motioned for him to lie down on the terrace, which, miraculously, he did. "Their father died when Phoebe was a junior in college. Maggie had just started her freshman year. The twins were still in school here in town. His death was sudden. An accident. He was trimming branches on a white pine and cut corners with safety. He fell and that was that. Broke his neck."

"I'm sorry to hear that," Noah said. "It must have been a terrible shock."

"Patrick O'Dunn was a good guy but I don't think he ever figured he'd live a long life. He worked in forestry. He knew how to trim a tree. He made a mistake he shouldn't have made. I'm not saying he meant to die that day." Brandon drank more of his beer. "It's all history now, anyway."

"Was Phoebe close to her father?"

"They all were. He left Elly and the girls more or less penniless. Elly's managed to keep things together but I don't know that her daughters always see it that way, Phoebe especially. She likes to think of herself as the sensible O'Dunn."

"You've known them all a long time," Noah said.

Brandon nodded thoughtfully, then grinned. "As far back as I can remember, I've been arguing with one O'Dunn or another. Maggie and I have been together forever." He sighed, serious now. "Were together forever, I guess I should say now."

"What happened between you? Do you mind if I ask?"

He shrugged. "I don't mind. You'll hear different stories around town. I was the dreamer she wanted but all my dreams went to hell. That's the short version." He held up his beer bottle. "Now I'm having a beer with you instead of going home with my wife and sons."

"You're protective of all of them," Noah said, not certain Brandon Sloan would appreciate the observations of an outsider. "Maggie, Phoebe, their twin sisters. Their mother."

"I guess I am. Just don't tell any one of them. I don't have anything against you or Dylan, Noah. In fact, so far, I like you both. Dylan's given my family work and therefore me work, and I'm happy to pitch a tent at his place. I hear talk about both of you — you two are getting into venture capital, he's dabbling in adventure travel, finishing up some of his father's treasure hunts."

"Those things are true."

Brandon shrugged. "Some people thought his interest in Olivia would fizzle once he got used to the idea that his father had come here looking for his birth mother as well as a fortune in missing jewels. I can see that's not going to happen."

"He and Olivia love each other," Noah said simply.

"They do. I saw that for myself Friday night. You and Phoebe . . ." Brandon grimaced as if he were questioning whether he

233

should have begun his next thought that way. "Phoebe's the sweetest person in Knights Bridge. She has a true heart of gold. Everyone here is protective of her."

"Point taken," Noah said. "I gather there's no man in her life?"

Brandon looked straight at Noah and said, "No. There's no man in her life."

Noah wondered at the certainty in Brandon's tone. Also the finality. He wasn't saying anymore. Noah appreciated the history between the people in this little town, and he understood that he wasn't part of it.

He knew when he was the outsider.

Brandon finished his beer and headed back to his tent.

Noah hooked a leash on Buster and let the big dog lead the way down the road, in the opposite direction of Dylan's place — Grace Webster's former home. He tried to picture the road before Quabbin, when it wound into a picturesque valley populated with small New England towns. Now Dana, Greenwich, Enfield and Prescott were gone.

He and Buster came to a yellow-painted gate that marked the border of the Quabbin watershed. The old road continued on the other side of the gate, eventually leading into the water's edge, as if the lost towns still were there.

"Sorry, Buster," Noah said. "No dogs allowed. We have to turn around."

They walked back up the road to Carriage Hill. The dog pulled hard on the leash and Noah noticed a squirrel chattering at them from a pine branch. He could hear birds, but otherwise it was a cool, quiet summer evening, the daylight graying with the approach of dusk.

By the time he and Buster arrived in Olivia's kitchen, Noah was hungry. First, he'd feed Buster, then he'd heat up soup she'd frozen. He could always add some of Phoebe's pesto, or go pick a few herbs in the garden. He'd already learned that Knights Bridge had only one restaurant, so he better save that option. By the standards of the people who lived there, the town wasn't isolated — they were used to driving to stores and restaurants in nearby towns.

By Noah's standards, it was the middle of nowhere.

He found a rag in the mudroom and wiped the dog's muddy paws. "Well, Buster, my friend, there may not be a good Mexican restaurant within thirty miles, but we can consider ourselves lucky they take in strays around here."

While his soup heated, he called Dylan but didn't reach him and hung up without leaving a voice mail.

Two minutes later, Dylan called back. "You're bored," he said.

Noah stirred his simmering soup with a wooden spoon. "How could I be bored? There's always something to do here. If I'm not walking the dog, I'm giving him food and water, and if I'm not doing that, I'm dodging bees in the catmint."

"Catmint, Noah?"

"It's the purple stuff by the terrace."

"I know what it is. Olivia told me. Who told you?"

"Maybe I already knew."

"You didn't already know," Dylan said, confident.

Noah wished he hadn't brought up catmint. "How does Olivia like San Diego?"

"Loves it. Who doesn't? We're out on my porch now looking at the ocean." Dylan paused. "Anything new on Julius Hartley?"

"Not on my end. I haven't talked to Loretta yet today. Why don't you forget about Hartley and enjoy the ocean breeze with Olivia?"

"She got a good dose of what Loretta's like last night. We had martinis and talked about your stalker private investigator while we admired the sunset over the Pacific."

Noah sighed. "I miss the Pacific."

Dylan ignored him. "Any sign of Hartley in Knights Bridge?"

"No. I'm sorry you found out about him. Two years ago, we wouldn't have paid any attention. We'd have been too busy. Now you're busy and I'm . . ." Noah frowned, noticing that Buster had wandered into the living room and jumped up on the couch. "Does Olivia let Buster on the couch?"

"No. Noah?"

"I have to go. Buster and I need to straighten out who's boss."

"Good luck with that," Dylan muttered.

Noah hung up and shooed Buster back onto his spot in front of the fireplace. The soup was bubbling on the kitchen stove. He found a pottery bowl and dumped in a healthy serving. The soup was orange and had a faint, pungent smell he couldn't identify. He checked the handwritten label on the freezer container.

*Carrot soup.*

Not much help. He knew carrots, but that wasn't what he smelled. He debated calling Dylan back to ask him. Or he could call Phoebe, eldest of the O'Dunn sisters. She'd probably know.

Instead he brought his soup into the living room and sat with Buster in front of the cold fireplace. "I'm a lonely man, Buster,"

237

he said with a laugh. "A lonely, lonely man."

And completely insane. All he had to do was dial his assistant, and he could have a car at The Farm at Carriage Hill in an hour and be on a flight somewhere — anywhere — before the sidewalks folded up in Knights Bridge.

He wondered if Brandon Sloan was managing to have a decent dinner up in his tent, but Brandon was a Knights Bridge native as well as a grown man. He could figure out what to eat for dinner.

And Phoebe? What was she up to this quiet summer evening?

Was she regretting that he hadn't kissed her when he'd had the chance during the storm, then again after the storm? Noah pictured her luminous turquoise eyes against the gray rain, and he could see her lick her lips. He squirmed as he felt pressure in his groin. Everyone in Knights Bridge could regard her as untouchable, but he didn't.

All he wanted to do was to touch her.

To make love to her.

He could see her wet skirt as she'd walked away from her car.

He took a long, slow, deep breath, held it, let it out again and tried his soup.

*Ginger.*

That was what he'd smelled. It was carrot-ginger soup, and it wasn't bad on a cool summer night on a dead-end road, with only a big, ugly dog for company.

# TWELVE

After a quiet, uneventful day at the library, Phoebe walked across the common to the Swift River Country Store and made her way back to the wine section. She was debating between two different brands of merlot when she heard a man talking up by the register. His voice sounded familiar but she couldn't quite place it. Abandoning the wine, she edged to the end of the aisle and peered past a display of homemade baked goods.

The man she'd overheard in Boston on Friday — Julius Hartley, the private investigator tailing Noah — was standing at the checkout counter, quizzing Greg Hughes, the teenage son of the owners.

Hartley had on a dark blue shirt, light khakis and light canvas shoes, as if he were about to step out onto a golf course.

He set a large coffee-to-go on the scarred wood counter. "Sleepy Hollow here has one bed-and-breakfast," he said. "I stopped by and guess what? The owners are in Montreal for the week. Doesn't New England have short summers? How can you run a bed-and-breakfast if you disappear for one whole week in August?"

"It's kind of a hobby for them," Greg said from behind the register. He was an avid reader of science fiction and a recent high school graduate, on his way to Bowdoin College in Maine. "They're professors at UMASS. They go to Montreal this time every year."

"Got it. I understand a new place has just opened up on some back road."

"Carriage Hill," Greg said, taking Hartley's money. "It's not really a bed-and-breakfast. It caters to events. Weddings, showers. You know. Anyway, the owner's out of town right now, too."

"I see. Well, luckily I'm not staying. I just need directions to Elly O'Dunn's place. I understand she's selling some of her goats."

Phoebe tensed. How did he know about her mother? What did he want with her?

"You're interested in buying goats?" Greg asked, skeptical.

"Sure, why not? What's the O'Dunn farm like?"

"Simple. A few acres, a couple of sheds, a

241

house that has plumbing and electricity but not much else."

"A stove?"

"Yeah, a stove. I guess."

"You *guess*?"

"You haven't met Mrs. O'Dunn yet, have you?"

"No, I have not," Hartley said. "There are restaurants in town?"

"One right now. Smith's. You can walk to it from here. There are more within easy driving distance. We have a good range of take-out food here at the store."

"Good to know," Hartley said without enthusiasm.

He left with his coffee, and Phoebe darted out of the store, giving Greg a quick wave. When she reached the sidewalk, Noah's mystery private investigator/stalker had already crossed the street to the common and was making his way into the shade of a trio of sugar maples. He sat on a bench. He didn't look to be in a hurry.

Remembering that he didn't know she'd overheard him or even had been in Boston, Phoebe took a breath and slowed down, crossing the street as she would if she had done what she'd planned to do — buy a bottle of wine to go with a quiet dinner at home. No meetings, no family, no friends, no goings-on.

*No Noah.*

She'd dreamed about him. She didn't know what that meant but she'd awakened in a sweat and went out to the garden at dawn, calming herself by dead-heading her flowers. Noah Kendrick was off-limits. They'd gotten caught up in the drama of their night together, the thunderstorm, the moment of recognition that their identities were no longer secret.

His life was in San Diego. Hers was in Knights Bridge.

He was a billionaire with a fancy for Hollywood starlets, and she was a small-town librarian who loved her job and was devoted to her family. No Hollywood rakes for her. No men at all, lately.

And Noah was Dylan McCaffrey's and now Olivia Frost's friend. Phoebe was, too, and she wasn't about to complicate their lives by getting involved with him.

Which was getting way ahead of herself but it'd been an intense dream.

She walked across the lawn, past the Civil War monument, her normal route back to the library, but instead of continuing to the opposite street, she paused in front of Julius Hartley. She couldn't let him drive out to her mother's place on the pretense of buying goats from her. That wasn't going to happen, Phoebe thought. It couldn't happen, and she wasn't waiting to get Noah out here to take care of it.

"Phoebe O'Dunn," Hartley said, looking up at her from the bench. He took a sip of his coffee. "Town librarian and survivor of the *Titanic.* That was quite a dress the other night." He sat back and grinned at her. "You can breathe, Phoebe. Your secret's safe with me."

She gave him what she hoped was a cool look. "How did you know?"

"I've been here in Sleepy Hollow for four hours. I know a lot about you and your little town." He pointed with his coffee. "I even read the plaque on your Union soldier. It's my job to find out things. I'm good at it."

Phoebe plucked a maple leaf off a low-hanging branch. He'd said he'd find out who she was, and he had. "Your name's Julius Hartley. You're a private investigator from Los Angeles."

"So you've been busy, too. Who told you? Noah Kendrick? Dylan McCaffrey? Loretta Wrentham?"

"It doesn't matter." She dropped the leaf into the grass. "I want you to leave my mother alone."

"I can't go look at her goats?"

"No, you can't."

Hartley got to his feet, casually, as if he didn't have a care in the world. "You're tougher than you look, Phoebe O'Dunn." He drank more of his coffee. "It's not apparent at first. You come across like a mild-mannered redhead in a pretty little sundress and sandals, but you're a pit bull when it comes to protecting your mother and your sisters. Who protects you?"

"We all look after each other."

"What about Kendrick? Are you looking after him now, too?"

"I'm not discussing Noah or anything else with you."

"Except for your mother's goats," Hartley said, clearly amused. "Okay. I left my thumbscrews in California." He squinted toward the library, where two young children Phoebe recognized were running down the steps ahead of their very pregnant mother. "I wonder what their favorite books are. I was a creepy little kid, I think. I liked Edgar Allan Poe."

"At four?"

"I was a little older. Eight, maybe." He winked as he turned back to her. "Consider that a telling clue, Phoebe. Are you going to tell Kendrick I'm in town?"

"That assumes I'm in contact with him."

"Yes, it does."

She tilted her head back and eyed him. "What are you doing in Knights Bridge, Mr. Hartley?"

"Right now I'm drinking coffee and enjoying a pleasant summer afternoon."

"Are you here because of me — because I danced with Noah?"

"You two did steal the show the other night. Noah's friend Dylan is marrying a local girl. Olivia Frost. You know that, of course."

Phoebe hadn't expected that response. Was he here because of Olivia? Because she was engaged to Dylan?

"Whoa. Easy there, Phoebe. No fainting."

"I'm not close to fainting." She straightened her spine. "If I even think you're here to cause trouble, I'll notify the authorities."

Hartley laughed. "Trouble? You have a good imagination, don't you? I guess being surrounded by books would fire up the creative juices." He paused, studied her again. "You and Kendrick the other night. There was some kind of connection. Some sizzle between you two."

"We were in the land of make-believe." Phoebe immediately regretted her comment. She couldn't let this man get to her, couldn't engage him — especially about

Noah. "I have to finish up at work. You'll leave my mother alone, right?"

"Sure. No problem. Relax, Phoebe."

She didn't respond and ducked under the low maple branch.

"Does Kendrick know it was you the other night?" Hartley called to her, his voice soft but no less cocky. "A billionaire could solve all your problems."

Phoebe spun around at him. "I don't have any problems I can't solve on my own."

Hartley grinned at her. "Sure you do. We all do. We all have dreams, too. I'll bet even you have dreams, Phoebe O'Dunn."

*Even you.*

He crushed his coffee cup in one hand, kept his eyes on her. "Noah Kendrick could make your dreams come true, don't you think? Then there's your sister the caterer, your twin sisters the theater majors and your eccentric mother. They all have big dreams. What about you, Phoebe? Do you have big dreams or little dreams?"

She knew she should just walk away but didn't. "There's no such thing as a little dream."

"Maybe so. A small-town New England librarian and a California billionaire. Dreams don't get bigger than that, do they?"

He was overstepping, and Phoebe saw that

he knew it. She met his gaze, drew on her experience with the public and her natural reserve to keep her emotions to herself. "Why are you here, Mr. Hartley? Are you making sure we locals don't take advantage of Noah and Dylan? Are you looking for information on them for a client? For some blackmail scheme? Is that what this is about?"

"How would you work your mother's Nigerian Dwarf goats into blackmail?" Harley laughed, then waved a hand at her. "Easy, Phoebe. I'm harmless. Go back to your musty books."

She didn't know if he was trying to be funny or deliberately insulting. She took a breath and watched him walk in the opposite direction across the common, back toward the country store. "You still can't pretend you're interested in buying any of my mother's goats," she called to him.

He held up a hand without turning around, signaling acknowledgment of her statement more than acquiescence.

She headed back to the library, dialing the cell phone number Noah had given her. When he picked up on the second ring, she hardly waited for him to say hello. "He's here," she said. "Your guy. Julius Hartley. He's in Knights Bridge."

"Where are you?"

"At the library. We close early on Tuesday."

"Wait for me there."

Phoebe headed up to the attic and into the hidden room, hot and stuffy even with the cooler, drier air. It'd be another ten minutes before Noah would get there from Carriage Hill. She opened the corner door, light streaming in from the window, no sign of Julius Hartley on the common. Did his reasons for following Noah east have anything to do with Knights Bridge? With Olivia or Dylan, or their upcoming marriage? Phoebe couldn't even guess. Noah and Dylan lived in such a different world than the one she knew.

Whatever he wanted, she hoped Hartley was on his way back to San Diego.

She certainly didn't need him skulking around town ahead of the fashion show.

She would have to decide soon about using any of the dresses created by her mystery seamstress, exposing this room to town scrutiny.

She heard footsteps on the worn attic floor and assumed it was Vera, who was staying late to sort a new box of donated clothing for the fashion show. She'd been happily pulling out silk scarves when Phoebe had ventured up to the attic. "I'll be right out," she called, quickly shutting the corner door by the window. She hadn't told Vera yet about the hidden room.

"It's me, Phoebe. Noah."

*Oh, damn.*

He was just outside the door that the free-standing closets had concealed. She'd pulled them away and left the hidden door — now not-so-hidden door — partly open. He had to have noticed. Not that he realized she was hiding anything. Which she wasn't, not really. She was just taking her time before she revealed her discovery.

She was suddenly sweating, her heart racing, as if the mysteries of her unknown seamstress somehow revealed deep, dark secrets of her own — as if Noah would be able to see through her defenses.

Except she didn't have any deep, dark secrets.

"Phoebe," he said, his voice very near now. "Are you —"

"I'm right here." She opened the door wide, not surprised to find Noah standing there. She smiled, feeling ridiculously nervous, even self-conscious. "You're not a ghost."

"No, I'm not a ghost."

"What did you do, drive a hundred miles

an hour to get here this fast?"

"I was almost to town when you called. The library's closed but your assistant let me in. Can I come in?"

She nodded. "Of course. It's hot in here. I was just about to leave."

Noah stepped into the tiny room. Since she'd closed off the window by shutting the corner door, the room was almost dark. She switched on an old lamp she'd dragged in from another part of the attic. It didn't offer much light as he glanced at the shelves and baskets of fabric and sewing supplies, the trunks and garment bags, the dresses she'd pulled out and left draped on a chair.

"I didn't expect this in a library attic," he said. "The dresses you and Olivia and your sister wore to the masquerade came from here?"

"This room's something of a mystery," Phoebe said, keeping her tone neutral. "I didn't realize it existed until a few weeks ago. I haven't told anyone else about it. I stumbled on it when I was chasing marbles."

"Something for a librarian to do. Chase marbles."

His tone held a hint of humor, but she could see his focus and suspected he was trying to keep himself from pushing too hard, jumping on her for immediate answers about her encounter with Julius Hartley.

She ran a finger along the edge of the old sewing table. "It's as if whoever created this room just stepped out, but I'm guessing it's been decades. I want to know who she was. Is, maybe. Someone in town, someone who left town?"

"Any clues?"

"Not many. She studied French and was clearly fascinated with Hollywood, and she could do anything with a needle and thread. She must have made her own patterns for most of these dresses."

"You found your Edwardian gown here?"

Phoebe stood back from the table. "It's one of the first ones I came across. I had it and the dresses Olivia and Maggie wore cleaned —"

"But you didn't tell them about this room."

"Right. I will, though." She waved a hand. "You're not here about an old sewing room, and it's not why I called you."

"You said Julius Hartley is here in town."

"I saw him at the country store. He took a coffee out to the common and I talked to him there."

Noah steadied his gaze on her, his eyes a deep navy in the dim light. "What did you two talk about?"

His stillness, his control struck her as incredibly sexy, but she kept her reaction to herself and repeated her conversation with Hartley. She left out only his comments about dreams.

When she finished, she picked up a sequined dress she'd draped on a rickety metal chair. "You're sure you don't know Hartley or anything about why he's following you?" she asked, folding the dress, a design of peach silk crepe, sequins and fringe.

"I'm sure," Noah said.

He'd remember, Phoebe thought. That was how his mind worked. "What could he want with my mother? He's not interested in buying goats. I don't want that man in her life at all."

"I'll make sure he stays away from her. Where does she live?"

Phoebe shook her head. "I appreciate the offer, Noah, but I'll see to my mother. She's off work now. She'll be at home. I think she was planning to can tomatoes tonight."

"Hartley's my problem, Phoebe."

"And my mother's mine," Phoebe said with a smile, then set the folded dress on the sewing table.

"Any idea how Hartley knew she keeps goats?"

"Not specifically, no, but it's not a secret. If he asked around town, someone would have told him."

"Olivia and your sister Maggie are getting into goat's milk soaps. That might explain his interest in your mother." Noah touched the fringe on the folded dress. "The workmanship is impressive."

"It is, isn't it? It's so precise. Whoever worked up here paid attention to every detail. Maybe it wasn't right to wear the dresses to the masquerade. I'd assumed we'd use some of the more fun and interesting outfits in here for the fashion show."

"That makes sense."

"When I came up here just now . . ." Phoebe glanced around the small room. "It felt as if I was intruding into someone's private life. Someone's hidden life."

Noah turned from the sewing table. "If no one was supposed to find this room, then why leave everything behind? Why create it in the first place?"

"I should get Olivia up here when she's back home. She collects vintage linens. Maybe she can help. And Ava and Ruby know more about Hollywood-related fashions than I do. I recognized the dresses Maggie and Olivia wore, but who wouldn't?"

"They're in good condition."

"They were stored properly. The fabrics have faded and yellowed over the years, but almost everything's in remarkably decent shape." Phoebe noticed that Noah's eyes were half closed as he watched her, and she forced a small laugh. "Did I lose you at 'vintage'?"

"You haven't lost me at all."

She believed him. She took in a breath. "Who knows, maybe this room's the work of our resident ghost. Some people believe the library really is haunted."

"By a handsome sea captain?"

"You never know."

"I don't see you sneaking up here to talk to ghosts."

"Not even a sea captain?" She angled him a smile, ignored the sudden rush of emotion, of pure awareness at being alone with him in such a confined space, in the heat, the stillness and quiet of the hot summer afternoon. "A swashbuckler, maybe?"

He touched a finger to a long strand of her curls and tucked them behind her ear, where there was no chance they'd stay put. "I'm sorry Hartley showed up in your town, Phoebe. He got under your skin. I won't let him hurt you or your family."

"You're more intuitive than you like to let

on, I think." She realized he hadn't pulled back, hadn't tucked her hair behind her ear just because it was driving him crazy. "You like people to think you're just a math genius who got lucky, but there's more to your success than that. You're always in control, aren't you?"

"Not always," he said, then let his finger drift down to her cheek as if to give added meaning to his words.

Phoebe licked her lips, cleared her throat. "I've read several books and magazine articles on entrepreneurial thinking. You're a natural entrepreneur. You're young — I wouldn't be surprised if you end up as a serial entrepreneur who is energized by starting new businesses, and helping other people start new businesses." She suddenly felt the bodice of her sundress sticking to her breasts. What was she saying? *Just stop. Be quiet.* "Anyway. That's neither here nor there."

He smiled. "I like it that you're trying to figure me out. Most people just give up."

"You're a good listener," she said, realizing she wasn't embarrassed at rattling on about entrepreneurship. "I could talk to you all night." She winced at her own words, embarrassed now. "Sorry. That didn't come out right."

"You can talk to me anytime, Phoebe."

She was used to talking to people in her work and around town, but not like this — not with romantic undertones, with *sexual* undertones, and not to a man like Noah. Not to the best friend of her friend's fiancé. Phoebe couldn't deny she was attracted to him. She couldn't even pretend she wasn't. She just knew it didn't mean anything, and she wouldn't do anything to make things awkward between him and Dylan.

"We should go," she said. "Do you have any idea what Julius Hartley wants with you? I imagine you have your share of troublemakers in your life. Is he one of them?"

"He could be. I don't know. I'll figure it out." Noah traced a fingertip across her jaw, into her hair. "I should have guessed you have red hair."

"Because of my freckles? I used Ava and Ruby's pancake theatrical makeup to cover them, but dancing with you took its toll. You put me through my paces on that dance floor."

He threaded his fingers through her hair. "Not because of your freckles. Because of the color of your eyes."

Phoebe could hardly breathe. It was as if being in the hidden room had returned them to the fantasy of the masquerade, to the intensity of their attraction to each other — as swashbuckler and Edwardian princess.

"Phoebe." His voice was just above a whisper. "I'm sorry Hartley interrupted us on Friday. I'm sorry he's in your town now. That I brought him here. You all don't have to worry about me." He curved his palm over her bare shoulder as he gave her one of his enigmatic smiles. "I can take care of myself."

"You don't have a real sword with you, do you?"

She was kidding, but he was amused. "Only at home in San Diego."

"My guess is you don't do much by half measures."

He smoothed his hand down her upper arm. "Hold that thought."

When Olivia had first told her about Noah, Phoebe hadn't considered that he'd be this sexy, irresistible to the point that she was tingling, even burning. "I think meeting me as an Edwardian princess colored your ideas about me."

"Nope. Meeting you hunting slugs in your scarf and shorts did."

She gave a small laugh. "Are you making fun of me and my hometown, Noah?"

"Never."

"Personally, I think you're just bored."

"Anything but bored, Phoebe."

He slipped his arm around her waist. She didn't protest, didn't pull back. It was as if they were dancing again. Their musty surroundings and the hot, still attic and the Hollywood dresses, the reality of their circumstances, didn't matter. She could almost hear the laughter of Friday night, the clinking of glasses, the music. She leaned into him more than she had then, in front of hundreds of people. He was all taut, lean muscle. That would be a surprise to most people, no doubt.

"I'm glad we danced," she whispered. "It made the night special. Memorable."

He said her name again, then his mouth found hers, his lips grazing hers in the lightest of kisses. Yet it had her reeling, aching. He was so controlled, so deliberate. He knew exactly what he was doing. She put a palm on his arm, felt the hard muscle. In every way, he wasn't a man to underestimate.

"Something happened between us when we danced," he said, kissing her again. "It's not going away."

She nodded. "I know."

He looked into her eyes with an intensity she'd never experienced. "It'll be okay,

Princess Phoebe. I promise."

"You're more of a real swashbuckler than I am a real princess."

"I don't think so." He stood straight, glanced around the small room. "Maybe this room was meant for you to discover."

"A custodian could have dusted and vacuumed in here and not realized no one knew about it. Anyway, I need to get out to my mother's and make sure Hartley didn't stop in, after all. She'd probably talk him into buying a goat. It'd serve him right." Phoebe inhaled, realized she was about to hyperventilate. "I live just down Thistle Lane. I'll run and get my car. Did you walk?"

"I have Olivia's car. Come on. I'll drive you out to your mother's place."

# THIRTEEN

Noah figured he could be Errol Flynn and it wouldn't make a difference to Phoebe O'Dunn.

He could be a real-life Zorro.

A real-life musketeer.

He could be worth a trillion and she wouldn't be intimidated.

He wondered if she knew that about herself.

Elly O'Dunn lived a few miles out of the village center, on a winding dirt road that, according to a sign, led to a state forest. Somehow Noah didn't need Phoebe to point out that the mailbox topped with bluebirds marked her mother's driveway. He turned into it, pulling up behind a dark brown house nestled among shade trees, stone walls, gardens and a large yard that needed mowing. As he got out of the car, he noticed a couple of small, rough-wood outbuildings, a fenced-off pen, open fields and surrounding woods, still and green in the afternoon summer sun.

"My mother's and my sister Ava's cars are here," Phoebe said. "I don't see any other cars. Maybe Hartley changed his mind."

Noah recognized sunflowers standing tall in the late-day sun. *A lot of sunflowers,* he thought as Phoebe joined him on a flagstone walk.

She squinted at the flower and vegetable gardens. "It's quite a bit for Mom to take care of on her own but she loves it."

"Does she have help?"

"Ava and Ruby have been here this summer, and now Maggie lives in town. We all do what we can to help."

He smiled. "I hope you like sunflowers."

"And goats," Phoebe added with a laugh.

"Are the goats much work?"

"A ton, at least by my standards. They have to be milked twice a day, for starters. Mom never cared about having them earn their keep, but the artisan goat's milk soaps Maggie and Olivia are trying out could at least help with expenses."

"Do you have any pets?" Noah asked as he followed Phoebe toward the screened-in back porch.

She shook her head. "Not a one. I get my pet fix here. Mom has two cats and the laziest dog on the planet, too. She's probably lying in the sun somewhere. My mother's dog, not my mother." Phoebe laughed again, visibly more relaxed. "Do you have pets?"

"No pets." He heard wind chimes tinkling on the porch in the slight breeze. "It's a lovely spot, Phoebe."

"My parents built the house together. It's got its quirks but it's warm in winter and the roof doesn't leak."

A young woman with purple-black hair emerged from the six-foot-tall sunflowers. She carried a basket on one arm and waved as she stepped over a low wood-and-chicken-wire fence. "I swear I never want to see another tomato, but I say the same thing at this time every year." She smiled at Noah. "You must be Noah Kendrick. Hi, I'm Ruby O'Dunn, Phoebe's sister."

Noah returned her smile. Her natural hair color, he guessed, was a shade of red. She wore a tank top, a long black skirt and sandals, and her basket was filled with fat, ripe tomatoes. "Nice to meet you, Ruby."

"My sister Ava's in the kitchen. We're canning tomatoes. Mom's convinced we'll finish tonight but not a chance." Ruby set her basket on a porch step and stood up straight, frowning at Phoebe. "You look awfully serious. What's up?"

"Did a man name Julius Hartley show up here?"

"No. Why? Do you know him? Who is he?"

"I ran into him in town," Phoebe said. "We need to talk about him."

"Whenever you're ready." Ruby was obviously intrigued but scooped up her basket again. "I'll be in the kitchen dealing with these babies. They're only the beginning." She grinned at Noah. "A friend of mine from New York was up here earlier this summer and said we reminded her of the Weasleys in *Harry Potter.* Red hair and cozy madhouse."

Phoebe laughed. "If only we were wizards, too."

"No kidding. Then Ava and I could wave our magic wands and these tomatoes would be canned and in the cupboard in a flash. See you guys later. Noah, nice meeting you."

As Phoebe led him across the lawn, past the fenced-in gardens, he thought Ruby's New York friend might have a point. The O'Dunn place was ramshackle and homey, radiating a chaotic warmth and good cheer that he suspected was more accidental than intentional.

They came to a small barn with an attached pen, miniature goats prancing in the grass. "They're Nigerian Dwarf goats," Phoebe said. "Cute, aren't they?"

Noah had never considered goats cute. In fact, he'd never considered goats at all.

A woman came out of the shed, shutting the door behind her. Elly O'Dunn, he assumed. She was younger than he'd expected, barely in her fifties, with wild graying light red hair and warm blue eyes. "Phoebe! I didn't know you were here. I was just tidying up the stalls before we start tackling the tomatoes."

Phoebe introduced Noah to her mother, whose bubbly energy was a sharp contrast to her eldest daughter's quieter nature. "Mom, has a man named Julius Hartley been in touch with you?"

Elly nodded, no hint of alarm or suspicion. "He stopped by the town offices and asked if I was interested in selling any of the goats. You know it's something I've been thinking about, since we have about three or four too many. So I told him, and he said he'd be by after I got out of work. I haven't seen him. I don't think he was really serious about the goats."

"Did he say why he was in town?" Noah asked.

"No, but I was under the impression he knows people here." Elly came through a

265

gate, shutting and latching it behind her as three goats with shiny brown coats nudged the fence. "Don't let the size of my little friends here fool you. They're very adept at getting out of confinement. They'll eat anything. Well, I'll be up in the garden if you need me."

Elly headed up toward the house. Phoebe glanced at Noah. "My mother and her goats and tomatoes and such are a bit different from what you're used to, I'm sure," she said.

He smiled. "They don't allow goats where I live."

"My mother got two goats to keep her company after Dad died. I was commuting to college and Ava and Ruby were still at home, but they had their own things going on."

"Were the goats her idea?"

"Yes, but we all encouraged her to find something just for herself." Phoebe smiled wistfully. "Dad would never have had goats. Chickens, maybe, but he didn't really like having farm animals."

They walked past an old stone wall that marked a field that Phoebe told him the goats had cleared last summer. The tall grass was dotted with wildflowers — yellow, white, deep orange. Noah had no idea what

266

they were but suspected the O'Dunns would, Phoebe especially. She was the sort who soaked up knowledge, loved to learn new things.

She seemed pensive and yet also comfortable at her childhood home. She squinted back at the shed. "My father built the shed when he first moved out here. He lived in it for a few years, before he met my mother. He always planned to convert it into a barn. There's a natural spring just into the woods, and a stream that he loved. There's a lake in the state forest farther down the road."

"This area seems to have a lot of water," Noah said.

"It does. Ponds, lakes, streams, rivers. That's why the Swift River Valley was chosen for a reservoir. *Quabbin* is a Native American word that translates as 'place of many waters.' "

"It's a beautiful spot to have grown up, Phoebe."

"My father was twelve years older than my mother. He worked in forestry jobs. He wanted to make money as a farmer but it never happened." She took a breath. "We still miss him. We always will."

"Brandon told me what happened. He didn't go into detail. Phoebe —"

"I found him," Phoebe said abruptly. "I

had to tell my mother, my sisters. It was a difficult time but we got through it. My mother has a full life but she's never remarried. Some days I don't know how she manages this place, even with our help. She has a live-for-today mentality that sometimes makes tomorrow a little sketchy."

"You worry about her," Noah said.

"It's hard not to sometimes. I can't imagine why Hartley went to the trouble of driving out here. The goats are providing milk for Maggie and Olivia's soaps. Olivia's the fiancée of your best friend." Phoebe slowed her pace. "Could Hartley be interested in Dylan and not you? Worried we're taking advantage of him?"

"No one takes advantage of Dylan."

Phoebe stopped, the sunlight deepening the rich turquoise of her eyes as she studied him a moment. "Do people take advantage of you?" she asked finally.

Noah shrugged. "They didn't when Dylan was working down the hall."

"Are you worried they will now?"

"I'm making the transition from having total control over NAK. It's good for the company and its future. Regardless, I've always been better at creating ideas than watching for snakes in the grass."

"Fencing helps?"

"It helps me focus on the present."

"Otherwise you get stabbed," Phoebe said. "It must be a great motivator."

He leaned in close to her. "In classical fencing, we try to touch without being touched. Any touch with a sharp sword can be deadly. Sport fencing is different. It's based on a point system."

"You get points for touching."

Noah saw her amusement and smiled. "It's a bit more complicated than that, but sports fencing isn't the same as a real fight. It's an athletic competition. Classical fencing isn't a real fight, either, since we're not out to kill each other and take safety seriously, but it simulates a real fight."

"Are you good?" Phoebe asked.

"I'm not competitive in that way. I enjoy fencing and karate because they work with my schedule and personality." He heard the caw of a crow out in the field and suddenly realized how quiet it was. "And you, Phoebe? Do you participate in a competitive sport?"

She shook her head. "Never have. I like to walk and work in the garden. I took a yoga class once. I enjoyed it, but yoga's hardly competitive." A breeze blew strands of red hair into her face as she gave him a sideways glance. "So if you don't want to continue to run NAK or end up as the loose-end founder hanging out in the halls, you have to figure out what to do with the rest of your life."

"I could learn to make goat's milk soap."

"Maybe that's why Julius Hartley is following you," Phoebe said quietly. "Maybe the uncertainty about what's next for you and even Dylan is causing problems in San Diego."

"Maybe it is," Noah said, slowing as they reached the shade of a birch tree, its trunk a bright white against the lush green leaves and grass, the clear blue of the sky. "You're perceptive. Have you always been, or has your work at the library helped?"

"Work at the library's helped me in many ways, but I don't think of myself as perceptive. I get surprised by people all the time."

"Who broke your heart, Phoebe?"

Her eyes widened but she smiled. "See? I was just surprised by you. I didn't expect that."

He stood closer. "Have you given up on love? Falling in love is fine for your sisters, your friends, but for you . . ."

"I know everyone in Knights Bridge." She spoke lightly but the way she averted her eyes told a different story. "I'd have to go looking out of town."

Noah saw that she wasn't going any deeper, not here, not now. He smiled. "You could always wait for a rich, good-looking swashbuckler to turn up."

He noticed her immediate relief at his teasing tone. "My perfect fantasy," she said with a laugh. "What's yours?"

"Maybe it's a redheaded small-town librarian."

As they walked back to the house, Noah received a text message from Brandon Sloan that Julius Hartley had just taken a booth at Knights Bridge's one and only restaurant. Brandon was all set to meet Noah there, but Noah texted him back that he'd go alone.

He debated whether to tell Phoebe about the message from her brother-in-law and finally did.

"You can't move a muscle in Knights Bridge without a Sloan knowing," she said, then nodded up toward the driveway where he'd parked. "Go on. I'll stay and help with the tomatoes. My mother or one of my sisters will give me a ride back to town. Smith's is the name of the restaurant. It's just down the street next to the country store."

"I'll find it."

She hesitated. "Are you sure you want to

meet Hartley on your own?"

"I'm the one who brought him here," Noah said. "I'll deal with him."

Phoebe gave him the slightest of smiles. "Then I recommend the turkey club," she said, heading off to her mother's vegetable garden.

Julius Hartley didn't seem surprised or nervous when Noah sat across from him at a dark-wood booth at Smith's, a small, family restaurant located in a 1920s house around the corner from the country store. Framed color photographs of the Quabbin Reservoir and wilderness hung on the walls. Noah studied a photograph of a bald eagle soaring above blue reservoir waters as he collected his thoughts.

"I'm having the turkey club," Hartley said. "I hear it's an O'Dunn favorite."

Noah knew it was meant as a provocative statement, a way to tell him that he was dealing with a private investigator, a man who was good at his job. Noah shifted his gaze from the eagle. Hartley already had a tall glass of iced tea on the table in front of him

"The meatloaf is supposed to be good, too," Hartley added. "Homemade. Have you ever had meatloaf, Kendrick?"

272

"Not in a while."

"Since the first million or the first billion?"

Noah didn't respond. "What did you want with Elly O'Dunn?"

"What, you don't believe I'm interested in buying goats, either?" Hartley grinned and slung an arm over the back of the booth. "I'm taking that as a positive. I assume you've been out to the O'Dunn place."

"I just came from there."

"With your princess?" Hartley waited a half beat for a response and when he didn't get one, lowered his arm and helped himself to his tea. "How much do you know about these people?"

"That's not why I'm here."

Hartley raised his eyes. "Here to kick my ass? No problem. I get that. Elly O'Dunn works in the town offices. She and your librarian princess are probably putting a dossier together on me."

"Good," Noah said.

"And if they aren't, you and your friend Loretta Wrentham are."

"You showed up in Loretta's office. Why? How do you know her?"

Hartley shrugged, clearly unconcerned. "It's my job. As you well know by now, I'm a private investigator in Los Angeles. I had a few questions, I got them answered and now I'm going home. It's all you need to know."

Noah shook his head. "I'll decide what I need to know."

Hartley was clearly not intimidated. "Knock yourself out."

"Who are you working for?"

"You know better than to ask." Hartley leaned back, glanced around the quiet restaurant. "If you think what comes after NAK is here in Sleepy Hollow, you're kidding yourself."

Noah said nothing. A waitress took his order, and he asked just for iced tea. He wasn't having dinner with Julius Hartley, L.A. private investigator. Noah was aware he could be naive about people and oblivious to obvious rogues and scoundrels, but he wasn't *that* naive and oblivious.

Hartley swirled the tea and ice in his glass. "You like the action, the pressure of the work you do. Solving problems. Building something from scratch. Getting other people involved, like your hockey-player friend."

"Dylan was invaluable in building NAK."

"*Invaluable* is one of those words that sounds like it means the opposite of what it means. It doesn't matter to me what comes

274

next for you. I'm not working for your board of directors, in case that's what you're thinking."

"It's not my board. It's the shareholders' board."

"Right. Things have changed for you."

"Is that why you're on my tail? To find out what I'm up to?"

"I just told you I don't care what you're up to."

Their waitress delivered Hartley's club sandwich and Noah's iced tea.

Hartley helped himself to a golden-brown fry. "I can't remember the last time I had fries and a club. I should have ordered a chocolate shake. What the hell, right?" He reached for a bottle of ketchup on the side of the table. "I'm not a threat, Kendrick. If there's a threat, it's these people and their ideas about you and yours about them."

"And you know what their ideas about me and my ideas about them are?"

"They know you don't belong here. You're trying to pretend you do."

Noah didn't rise to the bait. "You were on my tail in San Diego and then you followed me out here. Why?"

"I didn't 'follow' you. Careful with the language."

"I'm giving you a chance by meeting you

here by myself. I could have called my security team at NAK and had them arrange for people to meet you here."

"That'd get this town talking. You don't want that, do you? You can fool them into thinking that you're normal until you summon a big black SUV filled with private security types."

Noah hadn't tried to fool anyone, and even if he had, he hadn't met anyone in Knights Bridge who gave a damn that he was a billionaire. *Except Phoebe,* and then only because he'd kissed her.

"You don't think like normal people, Kendrick." Hartley dipped a fry into his mound of ketchup. "You're a solo operator when it comes right down to it. Dylan McCaffrey got that about you in first grade. That's why you two get along."

Noah drank some of his tea. He was used to people trying to figure him out. "Does your presence here have anything to do with Dylan?"

Hartley ate his fry in two bites. "He and Olivia Frost are an interesting pair, aren't they? I drove out to the Frost sawmill. Pretty setting. Must be tough, your best friend, maybe your only real friend, falling for a woman on the other side of the country. Think that's making you vulnerable to

Phoebe O'Dunn's charms?"

"You're not answering my questions," Noah said.

"You date beautiful Hollywood actresses who want you to bankroll their chance at the big time. Phoebe's not in their league when it comes to being a good trophy." Hartley picked up a triangle of his club sandwich, then grinned at Noah. "You're doing fencing breathing, slowing your heart rate, so you stay calm and don't go for my throat?"

It wasn't that far from the truth. "Did an actress I dated hire you?" Noah asked calmly.

"You're assuming anyone hired me. Relax. I'm leaving Sleepy Hollow as soon as I finish my dinner. The club really is good. You should try it."

Noah wasn't even close to being hungry. "It's good you're leaving town but I still intend to find out why you're here."

"Go for it. The O'Dunns might grow tomatoes and raise goats and such, but it would be a mistake to think they're pushovers, or that they need you to protect them."

Noah didn't want his presence in their town to harm them. Then why had he stayed? Why did he continue to stay?

277

Hartley wiped his fingers with a cloth napkin. "One of the dessert specials is something called apple brown betty. It's made with local apples. First of the season, apparently. I don't think I can resist. I'll be in Boston tonight and back in sunny Southern California tomorrow."

Noah got to his feet and tossed a few bills on the table for his tea. "Then what?"

"We'll see. Have fun in Sleepy Hollow, Noah. Every town has its secrets." Hartley grinned. "So does every redhead. Ask your mild-mannered librarian how she got the scar on her knee."

"We're not done, Hartley."

"Nothing more dangerous than a bored billionaire," Hartley said, more amused than intimidated.

Noah left the restaurant and walked up to Main Street where he'd parked. It was a pleasant summer evening. He was used to being a fish out of water wherever he was and Knights Bridge was no exception, but it was also different — and not just because it was small. His friend had discovered a grandmother here and fallen in love here, and now he was making a home here.

And there was Phoebe.

She was as intriguing as a small-town librarian as an Edwardian princess.

As he started to get into Olivia's car, he noticed Phoebe across the street on the common. She was with her sister Ruby and another young woman he took to be Ruby's twin, Ava.

Phoebe waved to him. He thought she smiled.

Noah was in no rush to get back to Buster. He crossed the quiet street.

Phoebe broke away from her sisters and intercepted him by an old-fashioned gazebo. "That was a fast dinner," she said. "Was Hartley there?"

"He was." Noah nodded toward her sisters. "What happened to canning tomatoes?"

"We got things rolling and then Mom ran us out so she could finish up in peace. She seemed preoccupied, which isn't like her, so we gave her some space." Phoebe pulled a lightweight shawl up over her bare shoulders. "We're figuring out some of the staging for the fashion show. It's such a beautiful evening, we came out here."

"Sounds perfect." Noah suspected that she'd also recognized Olivia's car and hoped she'd catch him and get details on his meeting with Hartley.

"Then they're coming by my place to watch old movies," Phoebe added. "Maggie might join us."

Phoebe's shawl fell back off her shoulders, and she adjusted it again. Noah resisted an urge to help her. He knew what he wanted was to touch her creamy skin. Would it be cool now, in the evening air?

"Is this the life you always imagined for yourself?" he asked her.

His question obviously caught her by surprise. "It's the one I have."

"What about your sisters?"

"Ava and Ruby are just twenty-three. We'll see what they end up doing after graduate school."

"Maggie?"

"She got married so young. It was right after Dad died. Brandon had such big dreams. I don't know how she'll react to him giving them up."

"What makes you think he has?"

"He's sleeping in a tent in Knights Bridge and working for his family."

Noah shrugged. "He's also two miles instead of seventy-five miles from his sons."

Phoebe nodded, thoughtful. "He's always been a good father. What are your plans for the rest of the evening?"

Noah didn't know what he was doing beyond not inviting himself to a girls' old movie night on Thistle Lane. "I didn't gate

Buster in the mudroom. I expect I'll be picking dog hair off the couch."

His touch of humor seemed to go right past her. She pulled up her shawl. "And Hartley?"

"On his way to Boston and then to California. I'm sorry if he caused you any alarm."

"Are you satisfied with what he told you about his reasons for following you?"

"He didn't give me any reasons."

"So does that mean you're still on the case?"

"It does, yes."

Phoebe glanced back at her sisters, then shifted her gaze to him again. "Ava and Ruby have so many great ideas for the fashion show. I think they're enjoying themselves."

"And you?"

She smiled. "Yes, me, too."

"You're an interesting family," Noah said. "Any idea how Julius Hartley would know about a scar on your knee?"

Her eyes widened, and then she burst into laughter. "Because everyone in town knows. I have no secrets, Noah. When I was twelve, I cut my knee at the Frosts' millpond. Maggie, Olivia and Jess Frost and I were swimming. The water was so cold — not that it ever warms up — but it was still early summer so it was especially frigid. They got out and I stayed in. Next thing I knew, one of Brandon's brothers was pulling me out of the water." Phoebe tilted her head back, the turquoise of her eyes rich and deep in the gray dusk. "I had mild hypothermia, and I'd slipped on a rock. There was blood everywhere."

"Did you get stitches?"

"No. We just bandaged up the cut. It's not that bad a scar. I don't know why people remember that story. It's not as if a cut knee is any big deal."

It wasn't just the cut knee, Noah realized. It was also staying in the cold millpond and ending up with hypothermia, to the point that she'd had to get pulled to safety by a Sloan.

It was a big deal because it was Phoebe O'Dunn.

Everyone remembered her cut knee, hypothermia and rescue because they went against their ideas about her.

He touched a bit of fringe on her shawl and suspected it, too, was from the piles of old clothes donated for the fashion show. "You're supposed to be the sensible O'Dunn."

She smiled at him. "I *am* the sensible

O'Dunn."

Noah let her go and returned to Olivia's car. When he arrived at Carriage Hill, Buster had, in fact, liberated himself from the back room and was camped out on the sofa. Noah settled in next to him. He wasn't impulsive. He'd call Loretta. He'd stay focused.

He knew himself and he had clarity about what he wanted.

And he wanted Phoebe O'Dunn.

# FOURTEEN

Phoebe opened a bottle of merlot and Maggie arrived with a variety of cheeses and crackers. They had fresh vegetables from their mother's garden, although Ava and Ruby insisted they couldn't look at another tomato right now.

They gathered in Phoebe's small living room and put on *To Catch a Thief.* They sighed over the beautiful Cote d'Azur scenery, took a poll about who thought Cary Grant was sexy — all but Ava — and argued about their favorite Alfred Hitchcock movies.

"That's my dress!" Maggie pointed at the television with an olive-oil cracker topped with goat's cheese and cucumber. "Oh, my. I'd forgotten how beautiful Grace Kelly was. I looked like a frump in comparison."

"You looked great," Phoebe said.

"At least I managed to get into the dress and we only had to let out a seam here and there." She popped her cracker into her mouth. "Don't you think Cary Grant's kind of old for Grace?"

"It's a movie," Ruby said with a roll of her eyes.

They settled down, enjoying the movie. Ava had the small sofa to herself, Ruby a chair, Maggie and Phoebe throw pillows on the floor. Phoebe hadn't confessed to Ava and Ruby that she'd ventured to Friday's charity masquerade, but, given their sideways glances at her, she suspected they had an inkling. Maggie slipped up a couple of times, and finally Phoebe just told them.

They loved the idea. "Oh, excellent," Ava said. "Now I wish I'd gone, too."

Ruby glanced at Maggie. "Did Phoebe dance with anyone?"

Phoebe reached for a slice of cucumber. "Why are you asking Maggie and not me?"

"Because Maggie will tell us and you won't," Ruby said without hesitation.

Maggie settled back on her stack of pillows. "Phoebe danced with a dashing swordfighter."

"A swordfighter?" Ruby peered down at Phoebe. "Not Noah Kendrick. Olivia says he's a master fencer. You were out at Mom's with him, and then on the common — *Phoebe.* It *was* Noah?"

"Are you the reason he stayed at Olivia's?" Ava asked.

Phoebe shook her head. "I'm not the reason he stayed."

"But he was your swordfighter," Ruby amended.

"Yes, but it's not . . ." Phoebe jumped to her feet. How could she explain to her sisters what was going on between her and Noah when she didn't understand herself? "I'll get more crackers."

She disappeared into the kitchen. She should have canceled tonight but she'd thought she needed it. A fun night with her sisters would remind her who she was — and who Noah was.

At least now Ava and Ruby knew about Friday. Phoebe had thought about it during the day and decided she didn't like that she, Maggie and Olivia knew but the twins didn't. Of course, that was before she'd run into Julius Hartley at the country store and ended up kissing Noah in the library attic.

Phoebe grabbed another box of crackers and headed back into her living room. Her sisters had turned their attention back to the movie, at least for the moment. She set the crackers on the coffee table and resumed her position on the floor, watching Grace Kelly and Cary Grant on their adventures in the south of France.

When the movie ended, Ruby kicked out her legs and sighed. "That was so much fun." She wiggled her bare toes. "We'll have to watch *Breakfast at Tiffany's* next time."

"You still haven't told us where you got the dresses, Phoebe," Ava said.

Phoebe helped herself to a slice of green pepper from her mother's garden. "At the library," she said.

Ruby took a handful of cultivated blueberries, also courtesy of their mother. "Someone donated them for the show?"

"I found them in the library attic," Phoebe said, then told her sisters about the hidden sewing room.

Ruby sat up straight, tucking her knees under her chin. "A secret room in the library attic? Oh, wow. I love it. You'll let us see it?"

Phoebe nodded. "Maybe you can help figure out which outfits are copies from movies and which are original designs."

Ava was as enthusiastic as Ruby. Maggie was quiet, frowning at Phoebe. "What about the man you overheard on Friday night?"

"His name is Julius Hartley," Phoebe said.

"The guy who was interested in buying a goat?" Ruby asked. "He was at the masquerade ball, too?"

287

Phoebe nodded and brought them all up to speed about Noah and his mystery man from Friday night. "Noah's still trying to figure out what Hartley wants with him," she said finally. "I accidentally got in the middle of it. Hartley's going back to California and I imagine Noah won't be far behind."

Maggie started to say something else but Ava stood up. Her hair was in a long, loose braid that hung down her back. "When we were helping you clean up after you bought this place, I found a box of old books in a corner of that big hall closet upstairs. Novels, books on movies, biographies of stars and directors, a *Vogue* sewing book, a couple of books in French — I remember one was *Le Petit Prince.* I wonder if it has anything to do with your hidden room."

"What did you do with the box?" Phoebe asked.

"I left it where it was," Ava said. "I figured we'd get to it eventually. It's in back of the closet with some old curtain rods and wool blankets. Phoebe, you know what this means, right?"

She nodded as she got to her feet. "It's possible that whoever created that hidden room used to live here."

After her sisters left, Phoebe sat outside on a wicker chair in the cool night air and called Olivia in San Diego. "I'm watching fireflies," she said when her friend answered. "What are you doing?"

"I'm sitting on Dylan's porch looking out at the Pacific. It's quite a view." Olivia sounded content. "How's everything in Knights Bridge?"

"You know the mystery man from the ball is Julius Hartley, a California private investigator, right?"

"Yes. Noah and Dylan have been in touch."

"He was out at my mother's place this afternoon. Hartley. It must be because I danced with Noah at the masquerade."

"Is there anything I can do, Phoebe?"

"I don't know that there's anything to be done," she said, then told Olivia about the hidden room. "Has anyone in your family ever mentioned a woman who loved Hollywood and was also an incredible seamstress?"

"Not that I recall. I can ask."

"Maggie, the twins and I think she might

have lived here — in my house on Thistle Lane."

"Maybe my folks remember her. I can ask. Who else knows?"

"Noah." Before Olivia could respond, Phoebe changed the subject. "How do you like San Diego, Liv?"

"I love it. I'm having a great time. Coronado is beautiful. I love Dylan's house. It's across from the beach." She added with a small laugh, "The interior could use some color."

"It sounds idyllic."

"I don't see Dylan giving up San Diego entirely. I don't know that I want him to. We'll figure it out. It's not exactly a problem, you know?"

Phoebe stood up from her wicker chair and looked out at the dark lane, wondered if her seamstress had once done the same. "Sometimes it's harder to open ourselves up to new possibilities than just to stay put where we are, emotionally, physically. You have so much going for you now. Dylan, too. If you hadn't left Boston when you did, the way you did . . ."

"Phoebe? You don't sound like yourself. Is something wrong?"

"No, nothing. It's good to talk to you. I hope you know I'll support whatever you and Dylan decide to do."

"We'll be flying back soon," Olivia said. "We'll be there for the fashion show, for sure."

"I'm sure Noah will head back to San Diego now that he's found his mystery man. Julius Hartley's heading back to L.A., too." Phoebe tried to ignore a rush of emotion. "Maggie and I can see to Buster and your place."

"Have you met Hartley?"

"Just for a few minutes. He was pretending to be interested in buying goats from my mother. Noah and I went over there."

"What did he think of your mother's place?" Olivia asked.

"He didn't say but it's obviously not what he's used to." Phoebe sat on the top porch step, next to the trellis and its tangle of roses, and smiled into the phone. "Have you seen his place in San Diego?"

"Just the NAK offices. They're incredible. It must be weird for him to go from working night and day to not knowing what's next."

"True." Phoebe wished she hadn't brought up Noah's life in San Diego. "We missed you at movie night tonight. My head's spinning a little from the wine. We watched *To Catch a Thief.*"

"And was Grace Kelly's dress as much like the one Maggie wore as we thought?"

"It's identical. It's amazing."

"I understand Brandon's sleeping in a tent at Dylan's place," Olivia said. "Dylan thinks he's there to get her back. What are the odds he does?"

Phoebe didn't hesitate. "He will. No question. I'm just not telling her that's what I think."

They laughed, Phoebe finally relaxing as she and Olivia chatted for a few more minutes. When they hung up and she went back inside, she realized how quiet the house was, and how alone she was. She'd never felt alone before. How could she, here in the midst of her hometown? So, why did she now?

"It's Noah," she said aloud, knowing that no one was eavesdropping in the roses and hollyhocks outside her windows.

She and her sisters had gone upstairs and found the box in the closet. Phoebe carried it downstairs. They went through the contents for any obvious clues to their seamstress's identity. A name scrawled on the inside of a book, an old letter, an old bank statement. But there was nothing except the books themselves.

Phoebe took a yellowed copy of *The Moon-*

*spinners* from the box and brought it up to bed with her. She'd lose herself in Mary Stewart's descriptions of Crete, and she wouldn't think about kissing Noah Kendrick in the library attic.

Brandon Sloan was a damn pirate at heart.

Maggie held that thought as she watched him come out the front door of her Gothic Revival house. It was just the sort of place the Sloans loved: one in need of carpenters.

He sat next to her on the steps. The night was cool enough that he had on an old gray sweatshirt. She was chilly in her sundress but tried not to shiver. It was all she needed, him thinking he ought to put an arm around her to help keep her warm.

"The boys want hockey sticks," she said. "Did they tell you?"

"Hockey? I thought you had them baking cupcakes."

She resisted elbowing him because touching him in any way would just remind her of touching him in all the ways she had in the past.

It had turned into that kind of night.

They'd made such a damn mess of their marriage. It was all she'd thought about walking home from Thistle Lane. Maggie realized that something about the box of

293

books they'd dragged out of Phoebe's upstairs closet had gotten to her. It was as if the books captured a moment in time of a woman's life, provided a window into her hopes and dreams. Sewing and Hollywood and adventures.

What would the odds and ends of her own day-to-day life say about her, now, at this moment?

Maggie pushed back the thought. "The hockey is probably Dylan's influence," she said.

It was a gibe and Brandon obviously knew it, but he didn't jump up and storm off. He just stretched out his thick legs and shrugged. "Maybe it is."

Maggie regretted her crack. Whatever his faults — whatever her own faults — he'd always been there for the boys. *Just not always for her.* But she didn't need him, right? Wasn't that what she'd been telling herself for months? Telling him?

"I have ice skates in the budget for winter," she said. "The town still does the small outdoor rink on the common." It was just a homemade rink done mostly with hoses and shovels, a Knights Bridge tradition going back at least to when her mother was a child. "The boys and I will be able to walk over there so they can skate to their hearts' content. I think I even have my old skates."

"I remember when you and I would go ice-skating together," Brandon said.

Maggie smiled despite a rush of emotion. "You were a maniac. All that energy. What am I going to do if Tyler and Aidan have as much energy as teenagers as you did?"

"Keep doing what you're doing."

"And watch them like a hawk," she muttered.

Brandon grinned. "Like I said, keep doing what you're doing." He looked out at the street, just one window lit in the saltbox house, one of the oldest houses in the village, opposite hers. "You like living in town. The boys do, too. They like being able to walk to everything."

"You think I'm too soft," Maggie said, crossing her arms on her chest as she sat up straight. "I'm not raising them to be tough Sloan men. I have them doing story hour at the library instead of roping a steer."

"Roping a steer? I guess they could rope goats at your mother's —"

"Goats are soft, too, right? She has a well-equipped toolshed, at least. It's got hammers, nails, drills, saws. No guns and fire hoses, though."

Brandon sighed. "What did I say, Maggie?"

"Nothing. I can tell what you're thinking." She stood up, glaring down at him in the dark, on a roll now, her emotions boiling over. "You and your family have always thought I was too soft, because my father was such a dreamer and then he died in a stupid accident and it's just been my sisters and my mother and me for so long."

"Your father was a good man, Maggie, but he still left you all with nothing."

"We have the land. We've all worked hard to help Mom hang on to it. Tyler and Aidan love it out there."

"I know they do." He stood, the light from the house casting dark shadows on his face. "You're coping with a lot on your own, Maggie. It doesn't have to be that way. I can help."

"Help how?"

"Any way you need."

She hadn't expected him to be so calm, not reacting to any of her barbs, deliberate or otherwise. She blinked back tears. "I never should have had wine with my sisters. I'm sorry if I . . ." *If I what?* She didn't even know. "Never mind. Why are you back here, Brandon?"

"My father needed the help."

"You're giving up on your dream of wandering the world?"

His eyes held hers. "I haven't given up on anything."

"What about Boston? You never wanted to live in a small town."

"If I hadn't gotten laid off, I'd have kept working in Boston." He spoke simply, without any obvious emotion. "I do what I have to do. I always have."

"While wishing you were somewhere else."

"Not always," he said softly.

"Why are you living in a tent? I suppose it helps to have a temporary place, so you can pretend you're not really back in Knights Bridge."

"So I can save money."

"For a trip," she said. "Not for ice skates."

He said nothing.

Maggie regretted her sharp words. "I'm sorry. I know you'd do anything for the boys. It's me . . ." She stopped herself, cleared her throat. "You won't be living in a tent once the snow flies. It's fine for now but . . ." She left it at that. He knew what she was saying. What she was asking. Would he be staying in Knights Bridge?

"Don't worry about me, Maggie."

"I'm not worried about you. I'm trying to figure out what's next for you. For us." She waved a hand. "Never mind. Let's talk about something else."

"All right. If that's what you want." He glanced back at her house with its "ginger-bread" Gothic Revival details. "The place is looking good. Going to paint it shades of pink? It's what you used to say when we walked past this place as kids. That you'd paint it shades of pink if you lived there."

"I'm actually thinking about a neutral color. Did the boys tell you they want to build a tree house out back? I can help but I'm not that great with hammers and nails. Mom's better but she's got her hands full."

"Their dad's a carpenter," Brandon said quietly. "I can help my sons build a tree house, Maggie."

"They'd like that. They look up to you. I . . ." Maggie sighed, her shoulders sagging as all the fight went out of her. "When did it become so awkward between us? We used to be able to talk about anything. Not that you were ever a big talker but I never felt I couldn't speak my mind, that you couldn't speak yours. We were best friends."

He touched her cheek, her hair. "You're tired. You're taking on a lot."

"I love what I'm doing. I love being back here. I wasn't sure I would but everything's turning out better than I anticipated. Don't worry, I still have my dreams."

"A gingerbread house in Knights Bridge village."

"Life could be worse, you know."

He smiled. "You could be living in a tent."

"I remember some good nights with you in tents."

He winked. "Damn straight."

After he left and the boys were in bed, Maggie sat at her kitchen table with a stack of cookbooks. The kitchen was in good shape, with a relatively new gas stove and a decent refrigerator, but it still needed work. Buying the house hadn't felt as impulsive as it probably was. She'd been drawn to it since childhood, and she'd thought it'd be a great place for the boys. But it really was a fixer-upper, and here she was, the estranged wife of a carpenter who was related to all the other carpenters in town.

She pictured laughing with Brandon as they painted the kitchen together, but it wasn't going to happen. She was on her own. He would always be the father of their two young sons, but that was it.

"It can't be. It just can't be." Before she could burst into tears, she called Olivia as a distraction, as well as to check in on her friend. "Am I catching you at a bad time?"

"I'm not sure there is a bad time in San Diego. It's a stunningly beautiful day out here." Olivia sighed, obviously content. "What're you up to?"

From the tone of her friend's voice, Maggie suspected Olivia knew that things were a bit complicated back home. "I think we should try making our own essential oils for our soaps. They're so expensive to buy. You have some great herbs at your place. We'd have to dry them, and we'd need to buy equipment for distilling . . ." She realized she was ready to burst into tears. "What do you think?"

"It's something I've been considering for a while," Olivia said. "Will you have time?"

"I'll make the time. Except for harvesting the herbs, we have flexibility. We can save up everything and make the soap during our down times. It should be quiet after foliage season, before the holidays. It'll be fun."

"Maggie? You sound upset. What's going on?"

Maggie immediately felt guilty for making the call when she was in such a down mood. "Nothing I can't figure out. Tell me about California."

"If you tell me about Phoebe and Noah."

"Wait, what do you know about Phoebe and Noah?"

"Not much except that something is going on between them. Phoebe's being tight-lipped, probably because Noah and Dylan are such close friends."

"Maybe she's afraid of mucking things up between you two."

"Not possible to muck things up between Dylan and me. So, what's going on? What am I missing?"

Maggie smiled through her tears and told her friend what she knew, which she realized wasn't everything, and what she surmised, which probably wasn't everything, either.

# FIFTEEN

Coronado was as beautiful as ever, the offshore night breeze prompting Loretta to grab a sweater out of her car as she and Olivia walked down to the historic Hotel del Coronado. Dylan had told them to go on ahead of him. He'd meet them shortly.

"He's worried about Noah," Olivia said, hugging her own sweater to her.

Loretta shrugged. "So far, Noah's managed just fine on his own in your little town."

"It's not just that." Olivia glanced out at the water, the lights of the sprawling hotel reflecting eerily in the white caps of the incoming tide. "Dylan believes that none of this —" she waved a hand back toward Dylan's expensive house "— would have been possible if Noah hadn't knocked on his window when Dylan was sleeping in his car."

"Synergy," Loretta said. "Noah knows he'd have crashed and burned without

Dylan's help."

"And now what? What's next for both of them?" Olivia took a deep breath. "I don't want Dylan to move to Knights Bridge just for my sake. It's too much to ask, and I wouldn't. It's not that Knights Bridge doesn't measure up to San Diego. It does, at least for me. It's home. But this is home for him."

"You can do both, you know. Knights Bridge and San Diego." Loretta shivered in the gusty breeze, but she welcomed it at the same time, let it clear her head, keep back her own emotions. "It's not like you two will be scrimping to pay for groceries."

Olivia smiled. "You're blunt, aren't you?"

"You can't help either of those two if you're not. When Dylan was playing hockey, he could read the ice, read a defense, without thinking. He just knew. Same with NAK and his role there. Noah's smart, but he doesn't always pick up on what's going on around him. Karate and fencing help him tune in, I think."

"He gives people the benefit of the doubt until they give him reason not to."

"It's not a bad way to be. Dylan's not cynical but let's just say he gives people a shorter rope than Noah does." Loretta walked a few more steps as the tide came in on the wide sandy beach below them. "Tell me about Phoebe O'Dunn."

"What about Phoebe?"

As if Olivia didn't know what Loretta was asking. Loretta had already gathered that not much went on in Knights Bridge that Olivia and her family and friends didn't know about. That Grace Webster had managed to keep her affair with a British flyer and the birth of their son a secret for seventy years was a damn miracle as far as Loretta was concerned. Dylan said she'd understand when she met Grace. The assumption being that Loretta eventually would get to Knights Bridge.

Maybe she would. She wondered if she'd understand the late Duncan McCaffrey any better when she did.

Probably not.

She turned her attention back to the matter at hand. "Phoebe was Noah's princess the other night. She overheard Julius Hartley talking on the phone to someone — probably someone out here."

Olivia seemed more amused than surprised. "You do know everything, don't you?"

Loretta laughed. "Not by half. Not when it comes to Noah and Dylan. So what about your friend Phoebe?"

"We've been friends forever. My younger sister and I grew up with Phoebe and her sisters." Olivia glanced out at the Pacific, as if picturing her hometown in her mind. "Jess and I grew up at an old sawmill and the O'Dunns grew up on a small farm. It was a great childhood."

Loretta prodded her. "And?"

"Phoebe's the eldest. She's always felt responsible for the rest of us — her sisters, and even Jess and me." Olivia hesitated, lowering her arms, letting her sweater flap in the breeze. She seemed to welcome the cooler air. "Phoebe found her father after he died in a fall out of a tree he was trimming. His death was hard on all of them."

"Phoebe tried to fix things?"

"I think she just tried to be there for everyone. Her mother was always a live-for-the-moment type but she became even more so after Patrick's death."

Loretta imagined a woman facing early widowhood with four daughters and a farm. "She can be impractical?"

"That's one way of putting it. Phoebe commuted to college from home, so she's never lived anywhere but Knights Bridge. She loves her job at the library. She's good at it. She's smart and sophisticated, Loretta. Don't think just because she's from a small town that she's not."

"Whoa. Phoebe's not the only one who's protective."

Olivia sighed as they crossed a driveway to the hotel, its distinctive red turrets and white exterior glowing in the night lights. "Sorry," she said.

"Don't be sorry. It's good to have friends who worry about you." Loretta grinned, lightening the mood. "I wish I had a few."

"You're like Phoebe. You do the worrying."

"Am I guessing right that something's going on between her and Noah?"

Olivia tightened her sweater around her again. "I think so." She slowed her pace as they continued along a curving walk to the hotel. "Will Noah hurt her, Loretta?"

"Noah's more likely to get hurt himself than to hurt someone else."

"He dates Hollywood types —"

"Who are more interested in his money and his connections than in him."

"He's a very wealthy man, and he can't have taken his company to where it is without being driven, maybe even a little ruthless. Phoebe's a gentle soul, unless she thinks one of us is in trouble."

"Does she think one of you is in trouble now?" Loretta asked.

Olivia shrugged. "I don't think so. I don't know. I'm not there."

"She can be tough, too, from the sounds of it. She kept her cool when she overheard Hartley in the coatroom. And didn't she show up at that masquerade on her own?"

"You're right. I don't want to underestimate Phoebe. She can hold her own with a California billionaire." Olivia turned, the light from the hotel catching her green eyes as she smiled. "I'd put running a small-town library on a shoestring right there next to running NAK."

Loretta thought she heard a hint of homesickness in Olivia's voice. They found their way down to the waterfront behind the main hotel and sat at an outdoor table overlooking the wide beach and glittering ocean. They ordered piña coladas and watched the crowd. Loretta heard teenagers laughing, noticed a young couple holding hands, two older couples chatting quietly together over drinks.

"Do you come here often?" Olivia asked.

"From time to time. It's a good place to take out-of-town guests."

"It's so romantic. Dylan says you two used to come here for a drink after you talked business."

"Money's never been his favorite topic,"

Loretta said with a smile. "That's how he ended up sleeping in his car. As they say, you can lead a horse to water, but you can't make him drink. He wasn't as broke as he thought he was. I'd tucked some money away."

"But you didn't tell him," Olivia said.

"I told him when I did it. He just didn't pay attention."

Olivia laughed, looking at ease with herself, her relationship with the man she would soon marry. Loretta felt a sudden sense of loss as she gazed out at the water. The wind had died down. She listened to the waves washing on the sand and wondered what her life would be like right now if Duncan McCaffrey had never gone to Knights Bridge, Massachusetts.

"I've known Noah and Dylan for a long time," she said finally. "Dylan had just started with the NHL and Noah was still a student at MIT. I met Noah when he was out here on a break and went to one of Dylan's hockey games."

"They're like sons to you, aren't they?"

Loretta ignored a sudden tightness in her throat. "Now you're making me feel old."

"I hope not." Olivia sat back with her piña colada and looked out at the dark ocean. "What a beautiful spot."

308

"*Some Like It Hot* was filmed here."

Olivia smiled. "I'm glad Phoebe didn't try to put me in a Marilyn Monroe dress. It's so beautiful here, Loretta. Dylan's a very lucky man, and I love having him in my life. I love him. We never would have found each other without you."

Loretta fought back tears that took her by surprise. She wasn't one for tears. As she studied the woman across from her, she was satisfied that Dylan had made the right choice in asking Olivia Frost to marry him — as if choice had anything to do with it. The man was in love, and from what she'd heard in Noah's voice since he'd danced with Phoebe O'Dunn, he wasn't far behind. Loretta just wasn't sure he was in for as happy an ending as Dylan.

She kicked off her shoes and enjoyed her drink, subtly sniffling back any tears so Olivia wouldn't notice. Maybe Olivia had a point. Maybe in a way Dylan and Noah *were* like sons to her. She'd never regretted not having kids of her own.

Noah had always struck her as a man looking for a real soul mate. A woman he loved, and who loved him, without condition. A woman he'd fight for, die for. It was the swordfighter in him, Loretta thought.

She'd never met two more decent men

than Dylan McCaffrey and Noah Kendrick. What was she going to do if they both moved to Knights Bridge?

# SIXTEEN

Noah was in jeans — no shirt, no shoes — when Buster stirred and went to the kitchen door, barking through the screen as the two eldest O'Dunn sisters jumped out of Maggie's catering van. "Company, Buster," Noah said, rising from the table with the last of his second cup of coffee. He figured he'd need a full pot of coffee before noon. It'd been a long night alone on the edge of Quabbin. Even Buster had been restless.

Maggie and Phoebe approached the kitchen ell with an ease that suggested they'd forgotten he was dog sitting, which Noah doubted, or had heard rumors to the contrary. They were dressed in shorts and sport sandals. Maggie had on a Red Sox T-shirt, Phoebe a close-fitting tank top in a deep turquoise blue that matched her eyes.

Noah finished his coffee as they entered the kitchen.

And he'd told Buster it would be a boring

morning.

Phoebe all but gasped at seeing him. "We didn't think anyone would be here." She kept one hand on the screen door, as if ready to bolt for the van. "We thought — we heard you'd left for California."

"Who told you that?" Noah asked.

Phoebe averted her eyes. "It was the talk of the country store this morning."

A vague answer at best but Noah let it go. "I see."

"We're here to harvest mint," Maggie said, setting a basket on the kitchen island.

Noah placed his mug in the sink. "Dare I ask what you want to do with your mint harvest?"

Maggie turned to him. "Olivia and I are having a go at making our own essential oils. She has several herbs that could work. We'll start with the orange mint."

"It'll have to dry first," Phoebe said. "We won't actually be making essential oils to-day."

"You're off today?" Noah asked her.

"Just this morning. I have an evening meeting."

She let the screen door shut behind her. Noah took that as a sign that she intended to stay for the mint-harvesting.

"Phoebe hasn't taken any vacation time

this year," Maggie said. "Right, Phoebe?"

"I took time off in the spring to paint the porch."

"I rest my case," Maggie said, digging a pair of utility scissors out of an island drawer. "If you want to help, Noah, that'd be great, but I suggest putting on a shirt. It'll be buggy in the mint patch."

He smiled. "If you're warning me about insects, it means I should expect the worst."

Maggie laughed and grabbed her empty basket. "You're a riot, Noah," she said, heading for the mudroom and out the back door.

Phoebe had her hair in a long, loose ponytail. She redid a clip that held stray curls off her face. Noah reached for a black shirt he'd brought downstairs with him. As he shrugged it on, he was aware of Phoebe watching him. He appreciated her reaction.

He fastened a few buttons. "Did you sleep well last night?" he asked her softly.

Buster stirred, and she patted him. "I read Mary Stewart until the wee hours. You?"

"I was up late looking for things to do. Wood to chop, wild animals to slay. I did manage to chase Buster off the couch."

She laughed, visibly more relaxed. "Olivia will appreciate that. Dylan won't care. Sorry we disturbed you. You don't have to help with the mint —"

"I don't mind."

Noah had a feeling he'd be learning more about essential oils and soap-making than he ever thought of knowing before the morning was done.

Phoebe followed her sister outside, and he put on shoes, grabbed the bug spray and Buster and joined them. The orange mint was at the end of the garden, almost at the shed where he'd first spotted Phoebe and hadn't even considered she might be his princess. He watched her squat down with a pair of clippers, snipping off the tops of the orange mint. He noticed the shape of her slim, bare legs.

It was definitely turning into a different morning than he'd planned. He was glad he hadn't called for a plane, after all.

He helped harvest the mint and bring it into a small room that shared the center chimney. Apparently Maggie and Olivia had conferred and decided the mint would dry there.

"What's it do for you?" Noah asked as they spread the mint on a table, a flea-market find that Olivia had teased about putting on his painting list.

"Orange mint is supposed to be uplifting," Maggie said, then grinned at him.

"Aren't you uplifted?"

"It'll be highly concentrated as an essential oil," Phoebe said. "It's supposed to blend well with other essential oils."

"You never use essential oils directly on the skin," Maggie added. "They're always diluted somehow."

Making an essential oil was a relatively complicated process that also involved a still, which Maggie said she had on order. Noah found the details surprisingly interesting. As they returned to the garden, she explained saponification, the chemical process that transformed a fat and alkali into soap and glycerin.

"We use only fresh goat's milk, not powdered," Maggie said. "Soap making involves a range of my interests. Cooking, gardening, aromatherapy — and my mother's goats, I guess. They've grown on me, finally. Each batch of our soap is handmade. I like that. We leave in the glycerin. A lot of commercial soap makers remove it because they can sell it."

"It's an ingredient in nitroglycerin," Noah said.

She wasn't that amused. "Glycerin is a natural humectant. Goat's milk is very mild. A lot of people with sensitive skin swear by it because it has a pH level that's close to that of our skin."

"So that explains my baby-soft skin," Brandon Sloan said, climbing over a stone wall into the garden. "I've been using the soap in Olivia's upstairs shower."

Maggie wasn't that amused by her husband, either, but Noah could see Phoebe holding back a smile. He kept his mouth shut.

"Where are the boys?" Brandon asked.

"With a couple of their friends. I'm picking them up for lunch." Maggie stepped onto the terrace, her enthusiasm for talking about mint harvesting and soap making on the wane.

Maggie immediately headed back into the kitchen.

Phoebe turned to Noah. "Just leave the mint in the back room, out of any sunlight. It'll be fine." She smiled. "Or it won't be fine and we'll toss it into the compost bin. Anyway, I should go. I have to be at the library soon."

"Weren't you two planning a picnic lunch?" Brandon asked mildly. "You know Maggie. She's always got food figured out."

Phoebe scowled at him. "Our morning didn't go quite as planned."

He shrugged. "You could always leave the food for your poor starving brother-in-law."

"It's still in the van," Phoebe said, as if that explained everything.

She glanced at Noah, then left without another word.

Noah stepped onto the stone terrace. He didn't know if he should follow Phoebe out to her sister's van and see them off — or if he was supposed to take her retreat as her wish that he stay away. Dylan would know. Noah had no illusions that he was particularly good at figuring out what people were trying to say. Much easier if they just said it.

Brandon picked up stray mint leaves off the terrace table. They heard the van start up out front. "Fast exit," he said.

"Time got away."

"Yeah. That must be it. Did you just spend the morning picking mint?"

"I walked Buster, too."

The big dog opened one eye from his spot under the table, as if he knew that life was rough for his dog sitter.

Brandon grinned. "Time to go back to San Diego?"

Noah didn't answer as he went into the kitchen, grabbed two beers out of the refrigerator and brought them outside. "It's now officially after noon and I have nothing to do, so I can have a beer. If you're on the job —"

"I'm not. I'm taking the afternoon off. Maggie's dropping off Aidan and Tyler after lunch. We're hiking up Carriage Hill, then camping out at Dylan's place." Brandon uncapped his beer. "Maggie's giving them instructions on spotting deer ticks. She's paranoid about Lyme disease. I guess that makes sense."

"I hadn't thought about Lyme disease," Noah said, then grinned. "Now I will."

"Going out of your mind in our little town?"

"It's only been a few days. I can do anything for a few days, but I've discovered that Knights Bridge is more complex than it might seem at first, despite the absence of traffic lights."

"I used to think it's isolated. It's really not. It's just small. It does help to have a driver's license if you're going to live here." Brandon dragged out a chair and sat down heavily, as if suddenly he had the weight of the world on his shoulders. "You and NAK — did you ever expect it to take off, get as big as it did?"

"I worked toward that. It's the outcome I wanted."

"There were setbacks?"

"Inevitably." When Brandon seemed to be looking for more, Noah added, "We took steps each day, assessed, made adjustments, managed risk and learned to cope with uncertainty."

"No crystal ball?"

Noah smiled. "No crystal ball."

"Maggie never used to mind taking a few risks. She jumped into catering with both feet, moved back here without a real plan, but she doesn't see it that way because it's her hometown. Her sisters are here. Her mother." Brandon drank some of his beer. "It's me she wants to be practical."

"I think you can be practical and still take risks. You just want to be careful about not risking more than you can afford to lose, and you have to manage the uncertainties and unpredictability of the future."

Brandon glanced back toward the kitchen, as if he were thinking about his estranged wife and their two young sons. He seemed to give himself a mental shake. "Going public involved uncertainty, didn't it?"

"It still does." Noah sat down, drank some of his beer. "I didn't consider what I'd do after NAK went public as carefully as I could have."

"So that's why you're here dog sitting."

"Maybe so."

"Any paths not taken that you can take now that you can be free of the day-to-day running of your company?" Brandon seemed to want to add something but was silent a moment. Finally he said, "I suppose we all have paths not taken."

Noah hadn't considered his situation in quite that way. "I suppose so. What about Phoebe?"

Brandon narrowed his gaze on Noah. "What about her?"

"Her father died when she was in college and she stayed in Knights Bridge." Noah spoke carefully, aware that Phoebe was Brandon's sister-in-law, a woman he'd known since childhood versus a few days. "Was that always her plan, or is there a path not taken?"

"More like there's a guy who took off to Orlando without her. He wasn't from here," Brandon added quickly, as if that were a significant fact. "They were at UMASS together. He was a senior and she was a junior when her father died. This guy didn't like sharing Phoebe with her mother and sisters on a good day."

"You met him?"

"Yeah. Once. I was with Maggie at her mother's place. Those were tough days, right after their dad died. For a while they

320

just didn't know . . ." Brandon scowled as if irritated with himself. "I'm talking too much. I never used to talk at all but I've been practicing."

Noah hesitated but he knew he had to ask. "Did Patrick O'Dunn commit suicide, Brandon?"

Brandon shook his head but the question clearly hadn't come as a shock. "It crossed everyone's minds, but no, he didn't. It was just a stupid accident. Phoebe's guy — he couldn't take it, having her in the middle of a family crisis. It was all about him. He gave her an ultimatum. Transfer out of UMASS and move with him to Florida or they were through."

"Phoebe's still here," Noah said.

"So she is. She hasn't been serious about a guy since then. Not that she'd tell me." Brandon settled back with his beer, no indication he had any bitterness toward Phoebe given his own troubled situation with her younger sister. "You know sneaking into that ball the other night was a big deal for her, right?"

Noah nodded. "She didn't tell anyone she was going."

"It was a last-minute decision. Phoebe's usually not impulsive. I ran into her. I kept my mouth shut but I guess the cat's out of the bag now." Brandon again narrowed his gaze on Noah. "You two . . ."

"I won't cause problems for her," Noah said quietly.

"As you say, not everything is predictable. It's up to us to respond to the unexpected. You didn't expect Phoebe. She didn't expect you." Brandon got to his feet. "Life does have a say, doesn't it?"

Noah leaned back in his chair and thought he could smell orange mint in the warm air. "You're not telling me all this as a friend. You're warning me."

"I guess you could look at it that way. I'm only telling you what everyone in town already knows."

"You don't want Phoebe hurt again."

"Let's just say I'm doing what I can to assess and manage risks."

*And I'm the risk,* Noah thought. He was the stranger sweeping their Phoebe off her feet. Another man who could break her heart. She was happy with her life. No one wanted him to screw that up.

Noah didn't want to, either.

He decided to shift the subject. "What happened with you and Maggie?"

"I'm in a tent for a reason." Brandon looked up at the sky. "I'm not getting her back, Noah. It's not going to happen."

"Giving up easily, aren't you?"

Brandon sighed. "Looking reality square in the eye. It's not something I always like to do, but I want Maggie to be happy. I know that much."

"Because you love her," Noah said.

"Always have, always will. That doesn't mean we can be together. Ack. I hate this kind of deep talk. I've been practicing, because she wants me to talk. Listening isn't enough. She says she has to hear my voice. I should practice talking to Buster. Hell of a lot easier to talk to a dog than to an O'Dunn."

Despite Brandon's attempt to lighten his mood, Noah felt the other man's pain. "I need to go back to San Diego to check on a few things," he said. "You can see to Buster?"

"Sure. I'll see to him." The big dog sat at Brandon's feet, obviously wanting to be petted. Brandon complied and grinned, his dark mood dissipating rapidly as some of his natural spark returned. "The O'Dunn women are smart and quirky and pretty as hell, but damn, they're not easy."

Noah smiled. "What fun would easy be?"

"Maggie's dress the other night makes me wonder if maybe she just wants a little old-fashioned romance in her life. What do you think?"

"Like what?"

"I don't know. Wooing."

Noah stared at his new friend. "Wooing?"

Brandon laughed. "Yeah. I'll figure out some wooing options that won't break the bank. Meantime, I'll go up and take a shower with the goat's milk soap."

Brandon seemed reenergized as he headed through the mudroom into his friend's house. Noah moved his chair into the sunlight and finished his beer. Bumblebees were again in the catmint.

No one in Knights Bridge had expected a man like him — maybe any man — to float into their librarian's life. It wasn't just his net worth. It was California. His work. His MIT background. His experience.

He was forbidden, he thought with a sigh.

At the same time, he liked the challenge, just as Brandon Sloan liked the challenge of "wooing" his wife back.

But what if Julius Hartley was right? Noah stood up in the sunshine, listened to the bees in the catmint, crows out in the fields. It didn't feel as if he'd seized on Phoebe because he was bored, but what if he had? What if he was drawn to her because she was so different, so out of reach? He wasn't

324

playing games, and he was confident she was as attracted to him as he was to her.

Well. Maybe not *that* confident. But confident that his interest wasn't one-way.

He'd had his share of Hollywood babes disappear on him. More who'd needed a push out of his life. He didn't want Phoebe to disappear and he didn't want to push her or cause her embarrassment, scrutiny or anything she'd live to regret.

After his shower, Brandon walked up the road to Dylan's place instead of cutting through the field. Noah almost went with him, but there wasn't much to see. Dylan had shown him the plans for the new house and a barnlike building for his fledgling adventure travel business. He was also talking about finishing some of his father's treasure hunts. He and Olivia would live in the house, which would allow The Farm at Carriage Hill to function exclusively as a destination getaway. In addition to soap making, she and Maggie were talking about offering herbal lunches, tours and lectures at Carriage Hill.

Unlike Noah, Dylan and Olivia and their friends in Knights Bridge didn't lack for ideas of what to do with themselves.

If Olivia hadn't met Dylan, she would have happily continued to live and work at her center-chimney house, with guests coming and going. Noah didn't see Dylan sharing a bedroom with her down the hall from strangers.

He'd shown Grace Webster the plans for her former property, too. She'd told Noah when he'd visited her that she couldn't wait to see the new house.

*"I expect to live that long, you know,"* she'd said with a twinkle in her aged eyes.

He had no doubt.

He occupied himself with a few NAK-related calls, cleaning Buster's bowl, vacuuming Buster's hair off the couch and picturing Phoebe harvesting orange mint.

Then he arranged for his flight back to San Diego himself. At six, he was scrounging in the freezer for something else to thaw for a quick dinner when Dylan called. Noah didn't bother hiding his relief. "Someone to talk to who's not from Knights Bridge. At least not yet. What's up?"

"You tell me," Dylan said. "Is there anything else I need to know about you and Phoebe O'Dunn?"

His friend might as well have been reading his mind. Noah was used to it. "I won't screw things up for you here, Dylan."

"That's not an answer, is it?"

"Why are you asking?"

"I had a drink last night with Loretta and Olivia at the Hotel Del. We got to talking. It's been on my mind all day. Olivia asked how fencing has influenced you."

Noah frowned as he dug out another container of frozen soup. Tomato-basil. Sounded good, and he didn't need much to eat before his flight. "Influenced me how?"

"In life. How you think, how you look at the world."

"Mostly in fencing I'm trying not to get a blade driven into my heart."

"Exactly Olivia's point. Loretta agrees. You should have seen her. It was as if she'd had this sudden epiphany about you, what makes you tick."

Noah set the container on the counter. "Dylan? Are you still jet lagged? You're not making any sense."

"You're skilled at avoiding the touch of a sword," Dylan said, apparently undeterred. "Any touch, not just one that goes to the heart."

"That's because any touch can be fatal."

"Is that how you're thinking now, about Phoebe?"

Noah made a face. "That she's — what, a fencing partner?"

"That in life as well as in fencing, you seek to avoid the blade."

"That's a tortured metaphor, Dylan."

His friend sighed. "I had to try."

"Phoebe and Maggie were here earlier getting a start with making essential oils. That's all I know."

"Essential oils?"

"For the goat's milk soaps. You know, this soap making is interesting."

Silence on the other end of the phone.

Noah grinned. "You're interested. You're just surprised that I am, too. Never mind. I haven't talked to Loretta today. Anything to add about Julius Hartley?"

"He does a lot of work in Hollywood," Dylan said. "You have both business and personal connections there."

"I did have personal connections. I haven't in a while."

"Maybe that's why Hartley's on your tail. Maybe some pissed-off actress you dated sicced him on you when you didn't bankroll her in a movie."

"Maybe," Noah said. "I need to know."

"I agree."

"I'm having a bowl of soup and then flying to San Diego later tonight."

"Good," Dylan said. "You, Loretta and I need to put our heads together and see if we can figure out what's going on."

"Loretta and I can." Noah felt a light

breeze through the window above the sink. "You and Olivia will be walking on the beach."

"She wants to go to the zoo." Dylan sounded reasonably enthusiastic. "She promised to bring back stuffed giraffes for Maggie's sons."

Noah smiled. "Then the zoo it is."

"Enjoy your soup. What kind?"

"Tomato-basil. I might add some of the pesto Phoebe and I made, although that could be overkill."

"Noah . . ." Dylan broke off. "Never mind."

After they disconnected, Noah peeled the top off the soup container. It was frozen solid. He heard an owl or a wild turkey or something in the woods and fields out back. Then he remembered the Sloan boys were camping with their father.

He left the soup to thaw on the counter and went into the living room. Buster had escaped from the mudroom and was back on the couch. Noah left him in peace and cleared a space in front of the fireplace. He eased into a series of basic fencing moves, then switched to karate and did several katas. He focused on his movements, his technique, his breathing. The positioning of a foot, a hand, a shoulder — even a knuckle

— mattered. Every detail was important, worthy of his attention.

When he finished, he took a shower in the upstairs hall bathroom, using a fresh bar of lemon-scented goat's milk soap. It was mild, soothing, reminded him of the beauty of the Swift River Valley and surrounding hills, of the sensibilities of the smart, kind and deceptively tough women who lived there.

He dried off and wrapped his towel around his waist as he went into one of Olivia's unused guestrooms. He noticed neatly ironed vintage pillowcases stacked at the foot of the queen-size bed. He looked out the window at the field behind the house, quiet in the early-evening light.

The library's fashion show was coming up soon. The Grace Kelly and Audrey Hepburn dresses Maggie and Olivia had worn in Boston weren't the only ones in Phoebe's hidden room copied from Hollywood movies.

Noah turned from the window. Thoughts and possibilities — odd connections — came at him fast and furiously. They might amount to something, or they might amount to nothing, but he definitely had to go back to San Diego and talk to Loretta.

And to Julius Hartley.

He walked down the hall to his bedroom

and pulled on clean clothes, then headed back downstairs. Buster had vacated the couch and was sniffing at the counter.

"That's my soup, my friend," Noah said, getting out a bowl. He glanced at his watch. He had time to eat his soup before he had to be at the small private airport for his flight.

He didn't have time to eat his soup *and* stop to see Phoebe.

Seeing Phoebe won over Olivia's soup, as good as it no doubt was.

"On second thought, Buster," Noah said, "the soup is all yours."

Not that the big dog was seriously interested in tomato-basil soup. Noah filled Buster's bowls with food and water, figuring he'd ask Phoebe to make sure someone looked after their friend's dog. It could be his excuse for stopping to see her, should the O'Dunns, the Frosts, the Sloans and the rest of little Knights Bridge be keeping an eye on Thistle Lane.

# SEVENTEEN

Phoebe had said goodnight to the last of a summer reading group that had met while she and the fashion show committee had gone over the last details of what promised to be a fun night. How profitable it would be was anyone's guess but at least they were managing to keep costs down.

She was tidying up the circulation desk, about ready to lock up and head home, when she heard the front door creak. She was surprised to see Noah enter the library. He moved with his usual smoothness, and he wore jeans and a black button-down shirt, his sleeves rolled up. She smiled to herself. He was even sexier than he'd been in his black cape and mask.

He pointed toward the children's section. "I'll just be in here while you finish up," he said, then stepped into the empty alcove.

Phoebe stifled images of him as a five-year-old — then as a father, taking his children to the library. But would he? Had he ever gone to the library himself as a boy, picked out books, sat with other kids through a story hour? With her evening meeting, she'd had a long day and had spent much of it — even while picking mint with him at Carriage Hill — thinking about how little she really knew about Noah Kendrick.

Being a librarian, she'd searched out more information on him that afternoon, beyond what Vera had read at the hairdresser's or what everyone in town already knew since Dylan's arrival there in the spring. Phoebe had a few more facts at her fingertips. Noah was thirty-three, the only child of a structural engineer and a high-school chemistry teacher, both retired and living at their wealthy son's California Central Coast winery.

In addition to the winery, Noah owned a house in San Diego and a condo in Hawaii, and he collected antique swords.

He'd sailed through MIT. No surprise there.

Phoebe thought of her avocado-colored refrigerator and her flea-market finds.

A different world.

The women in Noah's life tended to be very attractive actresses, with or without talent.

Talent, Phoebe suspected, wasn't that big an issue to him.

She glanced at her watch as if she had somewhere else she needed to be, but she didn't. And as Noah left the children's section and returned to the main room, book in hand, she realized she didn't want to be anywhere else.

"You read *The Tale of Peter Rabbit* to the kids?" he asked her.

She nodded. "They enjoyed it. It's hard not to identify with Peter."

"He drinks chamomile tea at the end." He smiled that enigmatic smile she'd noticed straight off at the masquerade in Boston. "You and Olivia and your sisters must love chamomile tea."

"Especially with lemon," Phoebe said with a laugh.

"That Peter is a risk taker. Not all his risks work out that well, but his life is more exciting because he takes a few chances. At least he ends up with some great stories to tell." Noah set the book on the circulation desk. "Okay if I leave it here? My mind was elsewhere and I don't remember which shelf it was on."

"We'll take care of it."

"I'm loquacious tonight. Must be that

uplifting orange mint I inhaled all morning."

Nothing in her research had indicated that Noah Kendrick, founder and CEO of NAK, Inc., had a wry sense of humor, but Phoebe had discovered he did. He stood back, studied a series of framed photographs of Quabbin —Winsor Dam, Goodnough Dike, the cemetery where graves and monuments from the lost towns were relocated and the beautiful, pristine waters of the reservoir itself.

Phoebe eased in next to Noah and pointed to the steep, grassy hill formed by the dam on the southern end of the reservoir. "My mother used to roll down the hill when she was a kid. Can you imagine? They don't allow that anymore, and they closed the road over the dam after 9/11 for security reasons." She nodded to another photograph of an inundated section of what used to be Enfield, the largest of the towns that were depopulated, disincorporated and razed. "Those islands were once hills in the valley towns."

Noah gave her a sideways glance. "You love this valley."

"It was flooded decades before I was born, but when I see people like Grace Webster, it doesn't feel that long ago. She loves that the protected wilderness has helped with the return of bald eagles to the area." Phoebe smiled. "She's holding out for mountain lions."

"Was your father from around here?"

"He grew up in a mill town just north of here. He came to Knights Bridge after he returned from Vietnam. He was drafted. He said all he ever wanted when he got back was to live in a small town and have a small farm." Phoebe went back behind her desk and grabbed her tote bag. "I don't think he ever imagined meeting my mother and having four daughters."

Noah turned from the photographs. "How did they meet?"

"My mother got lost in the woods by our house. There was just the shed then. Dad was living out there alone. He thought he'd be alone forever. Thought he wanted to be. Then Mom showed up, no idea where she was — and she's lived in Knights Bridge all her life. She was dehydrated, covered in mosquito bites and singing Christmas carols. It was the dead of summer, but she says she could only remember the words to Christmas carols."

"What did your father do?" Noah seemed genuinely interested. "Did he have a phone? I think I'd have called the police, or at least an ambulance."

"No phone. He liked to tell us as kids that he tried to pretend the shed was abandoned, but my mother saw his truck and had heard stories about a Vietnam vet living out there, and she doesn't give up easily." Phoebe switched off her desk lamp, then started to the entrance, aware of Noah watching her, his stillness, his intensity. She glanced back at him. "Coming?"

"I want to hear the end of the story. What did your father do when your mother finally got him to come out of the shed?"

"He gave her water and took her home. She said that was when she knew he was the man for her." Phoebe was silent a moment, picturing the two of them together. "Dad always said Mom saved him from becoming a hermit. He really loved all of us so much."

Noah joined her and they went out together. She locked up, then walked down the stairs with him. It was dark now. She'd noticed it becoming darker earlier, another sign the end of summer was near.

"Did your father retain some of his hermitlike ways?" Noah asked as they descended the stairs.

Phoebe noticed their shadows as they walked out to the street. Across the common, two teenagers were playing Frisbee. She took a breath, regaining control over her emotions. "He never liked to go places," she said. "He was content to stay in Knights Bridge."

"What about you, Phoebe?" Noah asked softly. "Do you want to travel?"

"I'd love to. My mother's always wanted to do a walking tour in England."

"What do you want to do?"

She smiled. "A walking tour in England. Jane Austen country, I think."

"So you'd go with your mother."

"Yes, absolutely," Phoebe said without hesitation. "We travel well together, not that we've ever gone that far. Olivia wants Maggie and me to see San Diego."

He glanced at her. "I think you'd like it."

"There's so much I want to see." She expected him to get into Olivia's car but didn't see it parked on the street. Instead he stayed with her as she turned onto Thistle Lane. "I have a travel savings account and I'm accumulating travel points on my credit card. Every little bit helps. What about you? Do you like to travel?"

"When I have time. I haven't traveled for pleasure as much as you might think. Hiking last week with Dylan and his friends was enjoyable but a hotel room on business

338

isn't the same as walking with you on a quiet summer evening."

She felt a rush of heat and was grateful for the darkness. She could feel Noah's eyes on her as they walked down the lane, close to each other but not quite touching.

"You're happy here, Phoebe."

"I'm happy with what I have. My life might be predictable compared to some people's lives, but that's okay. It's good." She looked up at the sky, a few stars glittering against the darkening sky. "It's warm out tonight but I can feel summer's winding down. Can't you?"

He laughed. "Don't tell me it's going to snow."

"I suppose your idea of snow is a ski slope?"

"More like watching other people ski while I sit by the fire with a good Scotch."

"What about your winery? Do you get up there often?"

He shrugged. "As often as I can. The people who run it are good friends, and my folks live up there now. They love it."

Phoebe didn't tell him she'd read about his parents. "Why did you buy a winery?"

"It seemed like a good idea at the time. It's worked out okay."

"But it's not what's next for you," Phoebe said.

He shook his head. "No."

"I'd love to see that part of the country."

"I'd love to show you."

Phoebe felt a rush of panic that she was getting in too deep with him. Falling in love with him. Not the billionaire, she thought. The man.

But he *was* a billionaire.

They came to her small house, a light on above the front door. "I think my mystery seamstress lived here," she said. "We found a box of books and things that could have belonged to her."

Noah turned to her, his face more angular in the dark shadows. "Would you mind if I took a look?"

Her mouth went dry. His tone, his eyes, the way he stood. All she could think about was their kiss in the library attic. She had no idea what he was thinking about, except he did seem genuinely interested in the box, or was doing a good job faking it.

"It's in the kitchen," she said finally. "Come on. I'll show you."

She led him onto the porch and through the front door, switching on lights as she showed him back to the kitchen. She knew he was taking in her simple furnishing

Since it was just her living there, she didn't have to worry about melding her taste with anyone else's.

She offered him wine but he shook his head. "But don't let me stop you."

It would stop her. Definitely. "I don't like to drink alone," she said, then added, "Not that I drink that much."

He was already lifting up a copy of *Assignment in Brittany.* "Have you ever read Helen MacInnes?" he asked.

"Not yet, no, but I was looking at that book last night and would love to read it." Phoebe leaned against the counter, watching him, really wishing she'd had wine. "Helen MacInnes, Mary Stewart, Victoria Holt, Daphne du Maurier — they're all popular with the women at Rivendell. Younger women are reading them now, too. I started *The Moonspinners* last night."

"My mother's a Mary Stewart fan," Noah said.

Phoebe walked over to the table and ran her fingers along the softened spine of *Rebecca.* "I love a happy ending."

He raised his eyes to her. "Do you believe a happy ending is in store for you?"

She shrugged. "I'm not a character in a novel."

He set the Helen MacInnes novel back in

the box and picked up *This Rough Magic,* another by Mary Stewart. "Do you think in real life we only get one chance at a happy ending, and if it doesn't happen, that's it? We've lost our chance for a happy ending?"

Phoebe stood back from the copy of *Rebecca,* her eyes narrowed on him. "Someone told you about Richard."

If Noah felt guilty at all, he didn't show it. "Richard's the name of the guy who moved to Orlando without you?"

*Orlando.* Noah even knew that much. Phoebe faked a laugh. "You can see I wasn't kidding when I told you I have no secrets. Richard dumped me two days after my father's funeral. I'd thought . . ." She took a breath. "Well, I thought he wouldn't do that. Who told you? Not my sisters." She thought a moment. "Brandon Sloan. Male solidarity at work."

Noah smiled. "Brandon is outnumbered by O'Dunn women."

"Maggie's outnumbered by Sloan men. No one would even remember Richard if I'd had a string of affairs or gotten married, but I haven't. I have no complaints, Noah. I like my life."

"You have a life that you think will never change. In five years, ten years, thirty years, you'll be the director of the Knights Bridge

Free Library, living on Thistle Lane."

Phoebe dug into the box for another book. "And what's wrong with that?"

Noah remained intent on her. "Nothing at all is wrong with that, except that I've found that the future is hard to predict."

"I get that, Noah. I get that anything is possible. I could get fired. The library could get shut down. I could decide to move in with my mother and raise goats. I could go into catering with Maggie. You see? I get it."

"Possible doesn't mean probable."

"Is that an MIT way of talking?" With sudden energy — a burst of defensiveness — she lifted three books out of the box and set them on the table. "The library's always been in excellent hands. People love it. It'll be okay regardless of what I do. I'm a temporary caretaker, whether I'm there for five years or fifty years."

"Phoebe . . . I'm not trying to upset you."

She nodded. "I know." She opened the faded, yellowed paperback copy of *Le Petit Prince*. "Do you speak French?"

"Some."

"What does 'some' mean to you?"

"It means I can get along okay in Paris," he said.

"Do you like Paris?"

"Dylan and I were there on business a few

343

times. It's such a romantic city, and there we were, a couple of straight guys on our own, working twelve-hour days. We both thought it was terribly unfair."

"You regretted not bringing one of your Hollywood babes," Phoebe said, then winced. "I'm sorry. That was rude and uncalled for."

Noah didn't seem to take offense. He tucked a finger under her chin. "I regretted not being there with a woman I cared about. So did Dylan. At the time, though, we didn't have that kind of woman in our lives."

Phoebe resisted an urge to grab his hand, thread her fingers into his. It seemed crazy and at the same time inevitable. "You two worked hard," she said. "You had no guarantees that any of the risks you took — all your hard work — would pay off, especially early on."

"Part of what made it fun did." Noah slid a hand along what was left of her ponytail, down her back. "Phoebe . . ."

She knew he was attracted to her. She could see it in his eyes, in the set of his jaw. She could feel it in the way his hand drifted lower on her back. "My seamstress taught herself French and fashion design, and as I said, I'm guessing she lived here."

"You're starting to identify with her."

"I want to know her story. I wonder if she went to Hollywood. If it was her dream and she seized the moment and went. To act, to be a costume designer — I don't know. If she wanted us to find her — anyone in Knights Bridge, I mean — she'd have been in touch in the past forty years. Maybe she doesn't want to be found."

"She could have changed her name."

"I don't even know her name when she was here."

"But you're on the case," Noah said.

She nodded. "I love a good mystery, too."

"Nero Wolfe always gets his man."

"He never really changes. It's one of the things I enjoy about him. But that's not how life is, is it?" She draped her arms over Noah's shoulders. "I think I'd like you to kiss me again, Noah Kendrick."

He was already lowering his mouth to hers, slipping his arms around her waist. He drew her against him, lifting her off her feet, nothing gentle or tentative about him when his lips touched hers. She felt her dress ride up, her bodice go askew, but didn't care about her exposed skin.

He sat her on the table, old books falling onto the floor as he skimmed his hands up her sides, letting his thumbs ease under her breasts, find her nipples under the fabric.

Awareness, the ache of desire, spread through her. She opened her mouth to his kiss, tasted him. She shut her eyes, gasped when she felt him ease her dress off her shoulders. The bodice fell to her waist.

Hardly aware of what was happening, she suddenly felt her bra come off, the cool night air on her breasts. She couldn't breathe. "Noah," she whispered, kissing him again, holding on to his shoulders.

He trailed light kisses down her throat, slowing when he reached her breasts. She still had a grip on his shoulders as he took a nipple between his lips. When she felt the wet heat of his tongue, it was all she could do to stay upright on the table.

The crack of a heavy tome hitting the floor brought him to his senses.

He stood back, gently easing her dress up over her exposed breasts. His eyes were dusky, a rawness to his movements despite his impressive, never-faltering control. Phoebe tried not to let her gaze drift too low, but she knew he wasn't unaffected by their near lovemaking.

She held her dress to her and smiled. "Well. I'm glad we're in the kitchen and don't have to worry about neighbors peeking in the windows."

"It's a small town."

"And you're leaving."

He didn't contradict her. "I'll be back," he whispered. "I promise."

# EIGHTEEN

Maggie was glad when Phoebe knocked on her door at seven-thirty and dragged her to the library before it opened. That way she couldn't drive over to Carriage Hill too early and Brandon couldn't accuse her of hovering over Aidan and Tyler.

She hated an empty house. She'd never lived alone and she'd lain awake most of the night, hearing every creak and groan, imagining what she'd do if a bat got in, remembering having Brandon asleep next to her.

A long damn night.

She met Phoebe on the library steps. It was a perfect August morning. The boys would be having a blast with their father.

Phoebe frowned. "You okay, Maggie?"

"Cranky. I'll get coffee after we're done." She stood back, appraised her older sister. Phoebe wore a dull green sundress with no jewelry, her hair down, barely combed, as if she'd had a bad night herself. "What about you? You okay?"

"Just a lot to do before the fashion show."

It made sense but Maggie didn't think it was all. Phoebe was used to juggling her professional obligations. The fashion show had become personal, too, with the dresses — with Noah Kendrick.

"Noah left a message that he's gone back to San Diego," Maggie said. "I'll stop by Olivia's after we're done here and walk Buster. Did you see Noah before he left?"

"Just for a minute." Phoebe waved a hand toward the street. "Here are Ava and Ruby now."

The twins joined them, looking curious and sleepy but not as cranky as Maggie felt. Phoebe didn't waste any time and took them straight up to the attic.

Her hidden room was even more amazing than Maggie had expected. She had zero interest in sewing and fashion design, but the dresses, the fabrics — the atmosphere of the tiny, cramped room — affected her. She could feel the talent, skill and obsession of whoever had created it.

How many years ago was it? Thirty? Forty?

"I can see why you didn't say anything right away," Maggie said, looking at the fabrics, the finished dresses, the simple

349

shelves and sewing table. "It feels as if we've walked into someone else's secrets."

"Someone who was vulnerable, maybe," Ava added, rubbing her fingertips over the rose-beige silk of a dress hanging in an open garment bag.

Ruby raised the lid on a cedar-lined trunk. "Phoebe, did you bring Noah up here?"

Phoebe opened a creaky corner door, morning light streaming in from a small window. "Why would I bring Noah up here?" she asked casually. "Actually, he came up here on his own. I was checking it out after I called him about running into Julius Hartley."

Maggie stood back, reading Phoebe's expression. Ava did the same thing and emitted something between a groan and a squeal. "Phoebe!"

Ruby's eyes widened. "Has Noah fallen for you?"

"You've fallen for *him.*" Ava raked a hand through her hair. "Phoebe, you know he's a billionaire, right? He's not a regular guy. Dylan's rich but he's a hockey player at heart. Not that I have anything against Noah, but Phoebe . . ."

"I know," she said. "Don't worry. There's nothing between us. Really. He's gone back to San Diego."

Ava seemed to regret her words. "I just want you to be happy, Phoebe. I don't know Noah. He seems nice."

"It was that dress you wore the other night," Maggie said. "It sucked you into romantic fantasies. They'll bite you in the end. They always do."

Phoebe gave her a knowing look, as if she suspected Maggie's remark had less to do with Noah than it did with one Brandon Sloan.

Maybe it did, Maggie thought.

"What are you going to do now?" Ruby asked.

"I have to work today," Phoebe said. "We have a lot to do to get ready for the fashion show."

Ruby sighed. "I meant about Noah."

Phoebe turned from the open corner door. "My life's here in Knights Bridge." She smiled. "What would you all do without me?"

"Visit you in San Diego in February," Ava said with a laugh.

But Ruby wasn't done yet. "So you're not doing anything," she said, clearly frustrated. "Noah Kendrick is interested in you, and now it's just business as usual?"

"Maybe what's next isn't up to me," Phoebe said quietly.

Ruby groaned. "Then who is it up to?"

Phoebe didn't answer as she ushered her sisters back downstairs. Ruby and Ava stayed behind to work on the fashion show, but Phoebe made them promise not to pester her about Noah.

As she drove out to Carriage Hill, Maggie remembered the look on Phoebe's face when they'd found her billionaire shirtless in Olivia's kitchen. Maggie didn't need confirmation. There was no question in her mind that her sister had fallen for Noah.

If he broke her heart, Maggie would fly to San Diego herself.

*And do what?*

Noah was Dylan's best friend, and Dylan was Olivia's fiancé. That wouldn't stop Maggie from giving Noah a piece of her mind, but it would Phoebe. She'd just keep her pain to herself and carry on.

But what if Noah had fallen for Phoebe, too? What if they were meant to be together, just like Olivia and Dylan?

"Then what?" Maggie asked herself aloud as she climbed out of her catering van.

She ignored a pang of loneliness, loss — she didn't know what it was. She wanted all three of her sisters and all of her friends to be happy and knew they wanted the same for her. Except she wasn't happy, she re-

352

alized. Not romantically, anyway.

"What you are is discombobulated because the father of your sons is living in a damn tent."

Muttering to herself couldn't be a good sign of anything, she thought as she headed into Olivia's kitchen. There was no sign of Buster. She assumed Noah had also let Brandon know he was leaving. She'd run into a couple of Sloans yesterday when she'd stopped at Dylan's place and tried to surreptitiously check out Brandon's tent, telling herself she just wanted to see where the boys would be camping. Sloan & Sons was working hard on carrying out the plans for the property. Brandon's uncle and his eldest brother had caught her peering into the tent and teased her. She'd found their underlying assumption that she and Brandon would get back together both annoying and comforting.

That kind of ambivalence couldn't last, she knew. She needed clarity in her life. Tyler and Aidan needed it, too.

She heard laughter and went into the mudroom, debated a moment before she stepped outside onto the terrace. It was a stunning morning, clear and dry, the sun shining on Olivia's flowers and herbs. Tyler and Aidan were charging up a path, laughing. Brandon ambled behind them with Buster on a leash.

Maggie felt a jolt of awareness as her husband approached the terrace. He hadn't shaved, wore a black flannel shirt over jeans. She noticed the shape of his shoulders, his hips, his legs as he unclipped Buster's leash and warned him to stay out of the gardens. She blamed overwork and her sleepless night for her reaction and quickly looked away, although not before she saw Brandon grin. He'd noticed.

Of course he had. *Bastard.*

She smiled at Tyler and Aidan as they jumped onto the terrace. "Have you guys had breakfast?"

"Cereal," Aidan said. "I wanted pancakes."

"I bet I can find the ingredients for pancakes," Maggie said. "I know Olivia has a griddle and maple syrup."

Tyler obviously liked that. "Can we have blueberry pancakes?"

"I don't know if there are blueberries —"

"We picked some with Dad," Aidan said.

She hadn't noticed the small covered plastic container that Brandon had in one hand. He set it on the table. "Should be enough for pancakes."

It was what they'd done every summer since they were teenagers. Picked wild blueberries together. Made pancakes. Maggie fought back tears and grabbed the container. "Why don't you guys burn off some energy out here and I'll see what I can do?"

"Do you need any help?" Tyler asked.

He was her budding chef, but she shook her head. "You're on vacation today."

She returned to the kitchen. She'd catered a number of events for The Farm at Carriage Hill already and knew her way around the kitchen well. She quickly got out a pottery mixing bowl, measuring cups, measuring spoons and ingredients — stone-ground cornmeal, baking powder, baking soda, salt, canola oil, buttermilk.

Brandon came inside and dug out the electric griddle. Maggie tried not to think about how familiar it felt to have him there, working in the kitchen with her while the boys played outside. Familiarity was an illusion. They had gone their separate ways months ago.

"Noah's gone back to California," Brandon said.

"I know. He left me a message."

"We talked some about Dylan's plans to get into adventure travel. I could almost see the wheels turning in Noah's brain. Guy's smart. Always thinking."

"Does he want to get into adventure travel, too?" Maggie asked, surprised.

Brandon shook his head. "No, but he thinks I should. He figured out I have a touch of wanderlust."

"More than a touch," Maggie said. "You'd be good at adventure travel, Brandon. Do you think you'll talk to Dylan about it?"

"I don't know."

She whisked together the dry ingredients for the pancakes. "It'd be okay with me if you do. I'd like that. I never wanted you to give up your dreams. I just . . ." She set aside the bowl and lifted the strainer of blueberries out of the sink. "I was scared."

Brandon opened his hand an inch above the griddle, testing the heat. "I was in a dark place last year. Took it out on you."

"No, you didn't." Maggie dumped the blueberries onto paper towels. "You took it out on yourself, and I reacted. I let my fear of going broke and all that went with it infect everything. What I did, how I felt, how I thought."

"My lack of faith in my future — our future — affected you. I didn't see that. I was caught up in my own stuff." He pulled his hand from the heat and turned to her, his eyes dark, filled with pain. "I was out of work and I let pride get in the way of mak-

356

ing good decisions. I didn't do right by you, Maggie."

She patted the blueberries dry, grateful that she had something to do. "I don't want you coming back to Knights Bridge and working for your family just for me."

"There's no better reason, is there? Come on. Let's get these boys fed."

Maggie mixed the dry and wet ingredients, and Brandon dropped the pancake batter onto the hot griddle while she sprinkled on a handful of the freshly picked blueberries. While they waited for the bottoms to brown, he leaned against the counter, holding a spatula. "What are you going to do with your best friend marrying a multimillionaire and your sister marrying a billionaire?"

Maggie took a breath. What *would* she do? She scooped up another handful of berries. "You're jumping the gun with Phoebe and Noah."

"Nope."

In spite of her concern for her sister and her emotional state — the risks of getting involved with a man as complicated and intense as Noah — Maggie liked hearing the confidence in Brandon's voice. She watched him flip the pancakes, smelled the sweetness of the heated, softened blueberries.

"What's on your mind, Maggie?" he asked.

"Phoebe and Noah . . . I don't want him to break her heart."

Brandon leveled a steady gaze on her. "What if she breaks his heart?"

Maggie opened a jar of maple syrup that her mother had made in the spring from her own trees. Was he talking about Phoebe and Noah, or about himself and her? She didn't want to read too much into his words. Being physically close to him had her in a mess.

"Noah's the one who left Knights Bridge," she said. "Phoebe's still here."

"Maybe that's part of the problem. Maybe Phoebe's got to give a little, too. See the possibilities."

"They've only known each other a few days."

"Instead of all their lives?"

Before Maggie could respond, he grabbed a platter and flipped the pancakes onto it, then dropped more batter onto the griddle. She added the wild blueberries, wondering if he was right about Phoebe. About her. About them.

He went to the mudroom and called out the back door for the boys to come in for the pancakes. "Get them while they're hot."

Maggie watched him return to the griddle, wink at her as he picked up his spatula, and she realized she was in danger of falling in love with him all over again.

Phoebe worked in her backyard when she got home from the library. Pruning, weeding, checking for insect damage. It was a beautiful evening, and she appreciated having time to herself.

*Needed* time to herself.

After her sisters had left that morning, she'd checked with the library's part-time custodian, a retired machinist and avid reader, but he didn't know a thing about any hidden room. His predecessor hadn't mentioned it. He'd died last year. Phoebe remembered him as a solid, unimaginative man. He could have cleaned the hidden room periodically and not thought twice about it.

She went back inside. She'd stacked up the books that she and Noah had knocked over. Her skin burned when she thought of sitting on the table with her dress half off.

What was he doing now in San Diego?

She grabbed a Diet Coke out of her refrigerator and put the cold bottle against her cheek. She sat at the table. It stood to reason that someone who'd created a hidden room in a library would like to read. Seventy years ago, Grace Webster had buried herself in classic adventure tales while her world disappeared around her, literally scraped, burned, razed and carried off. She'd read *The Three Musketeers, Scaramouche, The Scarlet Pimpernel.*

Phoebe wondered if Mary Stewart, Victoria Holt and Helen MacInnes had fired the imagination of her seamstress, diverted her on a bad day, entertained her on a good day.

Maybe she'd collected the books for someone else or just hadn't gotten around to reading them.

*Who was she?*

As Phoebe fingered one of the sewing books, she couldn't shake the feeling she'd had when she'd first discovered the attic room — that somehow the woman who'd sewn there, dreamed there, had felt trapped by life in Knights Bridge.

Had she abandoned the life — escaped the life — Phoebe was now living?

She gave an inward groan. So what if her mystery seamstress had hated Knights Bridge? Phoebe didn't. She loved her work. She loved her cottage. She loved her family and friends, being close to them, connected to her childhood.

She was just on edge and overthinking everything because of what had happened between her and Noah. She *never* should have let herself get so carried away with him. What had she been thinking?

She hadn't been thinking, obviously.

Once again she opened the yellowed copy of *Le Petit Prince,* its pages brittle with age.

*Lorsque j'avais six ans j'ai vu, une fois, une magnifique image, dans un livre sur la Forêt Vierge qui s'appelait "Histoires Vécues."*

Could her unknown seamstress have taken off to France? Phoebe flipped through the Antoine de Saint-Exupéry novel. She didn't know what she hoped to find. An old letter tucked in the pages? A signature?

She opened her Diet Coke and methodically checked each of the books, looking for anything that could offer answers, even a clue that would point her in the right direction.

There was nothing.

Had her mystery woman sat here, in this spot, listening to the crickets on a pleasant summer evening?

She heard a knock on her front door. "Phoebe?" It was her mother's voice. "Can I come in?"

"Of course," Phoebe said.

She started to get up but her mother was

already through the living room. "I worked late and thought I'd stop by," she said, getting a glass down and filling it with water from the tap. "You don't mind, do you?"

Phoebe shook her head. "It's water, Mom. Do you want anything else?"

"No, this is fine."

She had on her work clothes, a flowered tunic over wide-legged white linen pants with neutral-colored slides. Phoebe had changed into shorts for her gardening. "Mom?"

She drank some of her water, then set her glass on the counter and walked over to the table. She patted the top book on the pile. "The *Vogue Sewing Book*. My mother had a copy. She taught me to sew. I was never any good at it, but she did her best. I was always more interested in gardening and boys. My best subject in school was math. Isn't that funny? It didn't translate into being good with money, obviously."

"You've always managed to get by," Phoebe said.

"Barely." She tapped a finger on the front cover of the sewing book. "Ava and Ruby told me about their visit to the library this morning. They said you gave them permission to tell me about the attic room."

"Did you know about it?"

"No. I've only been in the attic once. A friend and I went up there in search of ghosts. We were in junior high . . ." She sank into a chair, clearing her throat before she continued. "We took French together. My friend was good at it but I just couldn't get the hang of it. There was a young woman who worked at the library who was fluent in French. She offered to tutor me."

Phoebe stared at her mother. "What was her name?"

"Debbie Sanderson."

"Sanderson?"

"She said she was George Sanderson's great-great-granddaughter but none of us ever believed her. She was here such a short time. It's been forty years, Phoebe. I was just a kid myself."

"What was her job at the library?"

"I don't really know. An assistant, I think. She wasn't a librarian. I know that much. There was a bigger staff in those days."

"Four people instead of two," Phoebe said with a smile. "How long was she here, do you know?"

"It couldn't have been more than two years. She tutored me for half the school year. She didn't want any money, but my parents insisted on paying her."

"Did it work? Did you pass French?"

"I most certainly did pass."

As she watched her mother pick up the copy of *Le Petit Prince,* Phoebe envisioned Elly O'Dunn — then Elly Macintosh — at twelve, conjugating French verbs. "What was Debbie Sanderson like?"

"She never wanted to be a librarian, but she had a fantastic imagination and loved to read. She loved to dress up in exotic clothes and speak French to us, and she loved movies, gothic novels and poetry."

"Poetry?" That caught Phoebe by surprise since she hadn't discovered any poetry books in the box.

"That's right. I remember because . . ." Elly set *Le Petit Prince* back on the table. "Oh, Phoebe. I haven't thought about Debbie Sanderson in such a long time."

"Mom, you're about to cry. We don't have to talk about her —"

"It's okay. It's not that. I just tend not to let myself go back too far into the past. I didn't know your father yet when Debbie was tutoring me. He had just moved here. It wasn't long after he got back from Vietnam. He'd put enough money together to buy a few acres and was building his shed. He was a recluse, really."

Phoebe pictured her father roaring with laughter when she and Maggie had told him about getting the better of the Sloan boys at the pond at the Frosts' sawmill. Ava and Ruby had been toddlers at the time, and he'd had them bouncing on his lap.

"He never liked being around a lot of people," Phoebe said. "But he didn't stay a recluse."

Her mother nodded, then said quietly, "Because of Debbie."

"Did they — were they an item, anything like that?"

"It wasn't like that. He stopped at the library for a do-it-yourself book on plumbing, and she was there. She introduced him to poetry. He couldn't concentrate on a novel back then, but he could read a poem. He especially loved Robert Penn Warren's poetry."

"I remember," Phoebe said.

"He went on to reading novels. Robert Parker, Tom Clancy, Ross McDonald. He had so many favorites, but he continued to read poetry, too." She blinked back tears. "He was a wonderful man, Phoebe. I had him — we had him — for the time we did because of Debbie Sanderson and the library. They helped him heal. They saved his life. There's no question in my mind."

Phoebe felt her throat tighten with emotion. "Do you know why Debbie came to

Knights Bridge?"

"She chose it because of her great-great-grandfather, but I think she came here to heal, too. I didn't realize she liked to sew as much as she must have, or that she was so good at it that she could copy Hollywood dresses. I knew very little about her. Just what I've told you."

"Did she say goodbye when she left town?" Phoebe glanced around her small kitchen, wondered if it'd been much the same forty years ago. "Did anyone notice she was gone?"

When her mother looked away, focused on the darkening night out the window by the table, Phoebe could see a glimpse of Elly Macintosh O'Dunn at twelve. "It was summer," her mother said. "I didn't even realize Debbie had left until I started school in September. I should have taken more of an interest. She was invisible, in a way."

"Mom, you were twelve."

"When I think back, I realize how young she was, too. Maybe twenty-one. She was such a dreamer. I could see it when she tutored me. She wanted a life that Knights Bridge couldn't give her."

"And all Dad wanted was Knights Bridge," Phoebe said quietly. "He read poetry to us as kids."

366

"Poetry helped him cope with his experience in combat," her mother said. "He didn't have a long life but he lived longer than many of the young men he served with. He took each day as it came and lived in the moment. Maybe that meant he wasn't as good with money and planning as some."

"But we have the land because of him."

Her mother turned from the window. "I have a good life, Phoebe. I like my job. It gets me out every day. What would I have done with a big insurance policy?" She smiled, a spark coming back into her eyes. "Blown it on horses instead of making do with goats."

Phoebe smiled, too. "Now the goats are coming in handy with Maggie and Olivia's soap making."

"Who'd have ever thought?" Her mother laughed, but her lightheartedness didn't last. She leaned forward, took Phoebe's hand. "Honey, I know you've helped me and I appreciate all you do, but I don't want you to worry about me. I don't want you not to live your life — to feel tied to Knights Bridge — because of me."

"I've never felt tied to Knights Bridge because of you or anyone else," Phoebe said. "I like my life."

Her mother didn't seem to hear her.

"Change is a part of life. Even if I knew deep down it was a delusion, I thought I'd grow old with your father. Instead I became a young widow with four teenage daughters. You have a big heart, Phoebe. Sometimes you ignore it so that you can be quote-unquote sensible. Don't ignore it now, okay? Not because you're worried about me, or your sisters. Open up your world if that's where your heart takes you."

Phoebe shot to her feet, uncomfortable. She and her mother seldom had deep conversations and she didn't know what to make of this one.

"You have things to do," her mother said, rising. "And I have more tomatoes to can tonight. I might turn them into sauce. I'll decide on the way home."

"Thanks, Mom," Phoebe said as she followed her through the living room. "Thanks for stopping by."

"Phoebe . . ."

"I'll be fine. Don't you worry about me, either, okay?"

"I'm your mother. It's my job to worry." She laughed, and became her bouncy self again as she left.

Phoebe returned to the kitchen and threw out the rest of her Diet Coke. She poured the last of a bottle of pinot grigio, took it out to the front porch and sat on the steps. So much for not drinking alone. It was quiet on Thistle Lane, but it always was. She sipped her chilled wine and smelled roses in the night air. A half moon created shadows that stirred in a gentle breeze.

She'd brought her cell phone out with her and stared at it in her palm. She had Noah's number memorized. That was a clue to her feelings, wasn't it? She debated just texting him but instead dialed the number.

He picked up right away. "Phoebe."

His voice was calm, deep and made her heartbeat quicken. "Hi. I hope I'm not catching you at a bad time —"

"Not possible."

She smiled and told him about Debbie Sanderson, her mother's French lessons, her father's poetry. He didn't interrupt. She could feel him listening to every word she said. She told him she'd brought her sisters up to the attic room that morning but didn't mention their questions about him.

He asked about the fashion show and what she was doing, where she was right now.

"It's a beautiful night," she said. "It's nice after the heat."

"Helps since you have no air-conditioning."

"I only wish I had it a few nights a year. I have fans. I put one at the foot of my bed and . . ." Phoebe stopped herself. "I manage."

Noah was silent, and she wondered if he was picturing her lying on her bed in next to nothing, or nothing at all, with a fan on her.

"Tell me about San Diego," she said.

"It's warm, sunny and not humid." He paused, and she could feel his smile. "The same."

"Have you been to your office?"

"Yes. I had pencils to sharpen."

She laughed. "I love a good pencil."

"So do I, techie that I am. I'm meeting Loretta Wrentham tomorrow. She's getting Julius Hartley down here."

"I hope you get to the bottom of what he's up to."

"I'm sure we will," Noah said. "Tell me again about Debbie Sanderson and her time in Knights Bridge."

# NINETEEN

Loretta paced on Dylan's porch while she waited for Julius Hartley to park his BMW and join her. She could smell the ocean and taste it on the breeze, but she didn't care. That told her just how keyed up she was. She loved the ocean, the sand, the rocks, the birds, the colors of sky and water. Watching Navy SEALs run on the beach wasn't bad, either. She lived in La Jolla but she enjoyed coming out to Coronado.

Just not today.

Dylan had disappeared with Olivia, saying something about stuffed giraffes from the zoo for kids back in Knights Bridge. Loretta knew what that meant: she was on her own. She'd helped make this mess with Hartley by trusting him, by not realizing sooner that he was Noah's mystery man.

Now she could clean it up.

Noah was back in San Diego, on his way to Coronado. He and Dylan would have already talked. She didn't know that for sure, but it was how the two of them operated. It was how it had always been and always would be. Friendships like theirs were rare. She'd seen that the first time she'd met them. Dylan and Noah had each other's backs. Dylan had a woman in his life now who understood that. Loretta didn't know if Noah ever would.

She watched Hartley mount the steps to the porch. He had on an expensive pale blue polo shirt and dark tan trousers, and he looked more like a country-club type than a scumbag private investigator. She'd dressed in a crisp black suit with her red heels and hoped she looked like she not only wanted to kick him down the stairs but could do it.

He smiled at her, no sign he knew how mad she was. "Hi, Loretta. Nice day, isn't it?"

"It's Southern California. It's always nice." She let him get onto the porch before she glared at him. "You took it upon yourself to snoop on Dylan McCaffrey and especially Noah Kendrick. You snooped on a little rural town in New England."

"Yeah. Sure. It's what I do."

She pointed a red-nailed finger at him. "You're a son of a bitch, Hartley."

He shrugged. "Okay."

"Who were you on the phone with on Friday when Phoebe O'Dunn overheard you?"

"It doesn't matter."

"It does matter." She paused to catch her breath. He was as roguishly good-looking up close, out of the sunlight. She reminded herself to stay focused. The man couldn't be trusted. "Was it your client? Are you working for an attorney, or is this one of your private clients?"

He turned and faced the water. "This is nice. McCaffrey's giving up this place for Knights Bridge, huh?"

"For Olivia Frost, and I don't know that he's giving it up. He hasn't asked me to look into putting it onto the market. Not that he will." Loretta gritted her teeth. "I'll probably be banished from Noah's and Dylan's sight before cocktail hour tonight, thanks to you."

"That's some drama going there." Hartley gave her a sideways glance. "Am I supposed to — what? Feel guilty?"

"You're supposed to tell the truth. I can't believe I didn't see through you sooner, but I just didn't take you for a snake."

"That's because I'm not a snake." He grinned, his eyes crinkling at the corners. "Well, I'm not always a snake. I can be when the situation calls for some slithering. I tried to be discreet with my scrutiny of Dylan and Noah, if that helps any."

Loretta shook her head. "It doesn't."

"It was easier in Boston. Any stranger would stand out in Sleepy Hollow, but I really did. I had this thing in my head that I was looking into rich guys and should therefore try to blend in with them."

"Should have left the Rolex at home, huh?"

"I'm just saying that I can see how people thought I was sneaking around."

"You *were* sneaking around," Loretta said.

"If I'd been sneaking around, no one would have ever known." His dark eyes narrowed on her. No smile or hint of humor now. "Trust me on that, Loretta."

"Am I supposed to be intimidated?"

He surprised her by laughing. "Damn, you're a pain in the ass. I wanted to know what was going on with your two pals and this Sleepy Hollow little town in Massachusetts. That's all."

"That's not all, and Dylan and Noah can take care of themselves." Loretta squinted out at the ocean, added without looking at him, "Are you providing intel to NAK corporate enemies?"

"Let's not play twenty questions, Loretta."

She ignored him. "The NAK board? Do Noah and Dylan have personal enemies I don't know about?"

A breeze off the water lifted the ends of Hartley's gray-streaked dark hair but he didn't seem to notice. "Noah needs to decide what's next for him. It's driving the NAK board crazy not to know if he's going to try to run things there or open a fencing studio. But he knows that. You know that."

Loretta tightened her hands into fists at her sides. "You spied on my friends and you used me to do it."

"No one uses you, Loretta. I outwitted you. There's a difference."

She raised her chin at him. Not all men were taller than she was. "I'm going to find out what you're really up to."

He didn't seem that threatened. "You understand I have to respect attorney-client privilege."

"You're not an attorney. You're a sleazy private investigator."

"Part right. I'm a private investigator. I'm not sleazy. Which you know. You're just irritated because you're not in control of what's going on. You haven't been since Duncan McCaffrey left Dylan that house in Knights Bridge and you didn't know the whole story." Hartley had some sympathy in his expression now. "You didn't know Dylan would go out there and fall for Olivia Frost."

"I'm glad he did," Loretta said stubbornly.

"You're glad he has someone in his life. You wish it was a woman from La Jolla instead of an out-of-the-way little town on the other side of the country. Now Noah's falling for this redheaded librarian." Hartley's sympathy turned to a knowing grin. "I can just see you at the Knights Bridge Free Public Library. It's haunted, you know."

Of course it was haunted. Loretta forced her palms open, tried to release some of her pent-up tension as Hartley pivoted and walked back down the steps without another word.

She inhaled deeply. She'd never been good with men.

She called to him. "Do you like Mexican food?"

He glanced up at her. "I hate it."

"I love it." She followed him down to the sidewalk. "There's a great place down the street. You can have a salad. Let's go. We can walk."

"You're the most difficult woman I've ever met. I think that's why I like you." He angled her a knowing look. "Is Kendrick meeting us at this restaurant?"

Loretta didn't bother hiding her surprise.

"This one wasn't even hard to figure out," Hartley said with a bark of a laugh. "You'd have had me meet you in La Jolla at your office if you weren't involving Dylan and Noah."

"Mr. McCaffrey and Mr. Kendrick to you," she said, sounding petty even to herself.

"Sure thing, Loretta. I have a son their age. He probably wants me to call him Mister, too."

"A son?"

He grinned at her. "Relax. I'm divorced."

She didn't relax but she didn't want to kill him as much as she had twenty minutes ago. They walked to a cluster of shops and restaurants, and for seconds — or maybe only one second — she pictured them as one of the honeymooning couples at the Hotel del Coronado. She'd never been married. Never had kids. Dylan's engagement had her thinking about what might have been, even if she had a good life, even if she had no regrets.

No serious regrets, anyway.

They got a table in the courtyard of the bustling restaurant. Loretta ordered a margarita and guacamole made fresh at the table. Hartley ordered a beer.

She dipped a warm tortilla chip into chunky, spicy salsa. "You're going to tell Noah and me everything."

"No, I'm not. You know better than to ask."

"Then you are working for an attorney."

"I'm not saying."

"Why did you come if you're going to stonewall?"

His beer arrived. "Because you asked nicely."

She hadn't, but whatever. "What did you think of Knights Bridge?"

"I suffered. Goats, Loretta." He drank some of his beer, helped himself to a chip and salsa. "Olivia Frost and the O'Dunn sisters are making soap out of the goat's milk."

"Goat's milk soap is nice."

"I'm sure it is."

"Hartley . . ."

"Julius, okay?"

Loretta helped herself to another chip. "Julius, did you check out the goats?"

"Almost. I pretended I was going to buy one."

"And they bought that?"

"No." His tone was matter-of-fact. "The O'Dunns and their allies were about to get out the hot tar and pitchforks, so I made my exit. They're little goats, by the way. Nigerian Dwarf goats."

Loretta felt laughter bubbling up despite how mad she was. "Have you ever seen a goat in real life?"

"The zoo." He sat back, looking at ease, comfortable in his own skin. "Then there are the herbs for the soaps. The nineteenth-century library. The town common with its Civil War statue. The country store."

"It sounds idyllic."

"It's pretty," Hartley said, making it sound like a concession.

"Dylan says not to be fooled," Loretta said. "Despite any evidence to the contrary, time hasn't stopped in Knights Bridge."

"Time never stops, does it?"

Loretta heard a note of wistfulness in Julius's voice, or thought she did. Maybe she was projecting. Maybe that was why she hadn't figured out what was going on with him to begin with. She'd wanted him to be someone he wasn't because she herself was coming to terms with the changes in her life. She'd been Dylan's attorney and business manager for a long time. She'd loved his father, even if for a short time.

"I'll have to see Knights Bridge myself soon," she said, digging into the fresh salsa. "Dylan and Olivia have invited me to their wedding."

"It's at Christmas, you know."

She nodded. "So I get to go there when it's freezing. I'll have to find myself a cute country inn with a fireplace, flowered wallpaper and a decent liquor cabinet."

Their waiter whipped together their guacamole and set it on the table with fresh, warm chips. Julius helped himself. Their table was pleasant, shaded by potted trees. Deep pink bougainvillea cascaded over a wall.

Finally he said, "Dylan and Noah are decent guys."

"Yes, I know."

"They're independent. Defiant, even. They do things their own way."

"What's Phoebe O'Dunn like?" Loretta asked.

"From what I saw and heard, she's smart, positive, encouraging and genuinely nice."

"And?"

"And protective of her family. She looks out for them."

"Who looks out for her?"

"She'd say they look out for each other. Maybe they do, but she's stuck there."

"Maybe your idea of 'stuck' is her idea of fulfilling herself."

"That was before Noah Kendrick spotted

her at that masquerade ball. Getting involved with a billionaire . . ." Julius shrugged. "Easier to fall for one of the local firefighters but she hasn't. She'll sacrifice herself if she thinks her family needs her. She's done it before."

Before Loretta could ask more questions, Noah arrived and joined them at their table. He was centered, focused and clearly on a mission. He was a man, she knew, who did best when he had a purpose, a result he was going after. Aimlessness didn't suit him.

Julius picked up his beer, took another deliberate sip. "How's Sleepy Hollow and your librarian? Same as ever?"

Noah leveled a cool gaze on him. "Phoebe is getting ready for the vintage fashion show at the library. You know about that, right, Julius?"

"I saw something about it when I was in Knights Bridge."

"You knew about the fashion show before you arrived there. It's what prompted you to check me out in the first place."

Loretta frowned and noticed that Julius had gone silent. She glanced at Noah, but his gaze was fixed on the older man across from him.

Noah reached for his water glass. "It was logical to assume that I was the one who brought you to Knights Bridge, but it's not that simple." He sat back, as in control as Loretta had ever seen him. "You knew that Dylan and his work with NAK, his friendship with me, could bring scrutiny to Knights Bridge. Could change things there. You figured out Phoebe must have discovered the hidden room where your client sewed and designed dresses as a young woman."

Loretta held on tight to her margarita. Olivia and Dylan had told her about the hidden sewing room in the Knights Bridge library attic. She'd figured that sort of thing happened in small-town New England. She'd liked the idea of the Hollywood-inspired dresses. She hadn't considered — not even for a split-second — that they had anything to do with Julius Hartley.

"That hidden room," Noah said, "is why you checked me out here in San Diego and why you followed me to Boston. It's why you went to Knights Bridge. You weren't just checking on me there. You were checking on the O'Dunns. Specifically, on Phoebe."

"It didn't take long. She's what we call an open book." Hartley smiled, added, "No pun intended."

"Debbie Sanderson is the given name of

the woman who created the hidden room." Noah kept his eyes on the man across the table. "She lived in Knights Bridge for a year. Then she took off for Hollywood and reinvented herself."

"Are you speculating, or do you have facts to back up this claim?" Julius asked.

Noah pointed his water at him. "You're protecting Debbie Sanderson's new identity."

Julius sighed. "You MIT types are just so damn smart, aren't you?"

Loretta let all the pieces fall into place in her own mind. She set her margarita on the table and looked at Julius. "What did she have you do, watch for Knights Bridge in the news?"

"She does that herself," he said. "She saw a gossip piece saying that Dylan was engaged to a graphic designer from Knights Bridge. She read about his hockey years, his treasure-hunter father, his best friend the billionaire founder of NAK."

"Did she have you investigate, or did you volunteer?" Loretta asked.

"She's a very special lady."

Meaning he'd volunteered, Loretta thought.

"I'm the one who told her about the fashion show," Julius said. "She knew it meant her room had been discovered. With you and Dylan in the picture, I had to investigate."

"What's her name now?" Noah asked quietly.

Hartley didn't answer.

Noah leaned forward. "It's Daphne Stewart, isn't it?"

Julius looked uncomfortable but said nothing, and Loretta decided to give up on her margarita. She frowned at the two men. "Who's Daphne Stewart?"

"She's a highly respected independent costume designer in Hollywood," Noah said, his eyes still on Julius. "She's worked on any number of movies. Daphne Stewart is the name she gave herself after she left Knights Bridge forty years ago and headed west."

"She guards her privacy." Julius suddenly wasn't as cocky. "You of all people can understand that."

Noah's expression softened. "I won't intrude on her privacy. Neither will Dylan. Is she a friend?"

"She's become one, yes. She's a client with a law firm I do a lot of work for. She's got a keen sense of drama. She likes knowing a private investigator." Julius seemed slightly less shaken by Noah's knowledge.

"What about Olivia and Phoebe O'Dunn and her family?"

"What do you think?" Noah asked, his tone as steady and controlled as ever. "Do you think they want to intrude on Miss Stewart's privacy?"

Julius sighed. "I've already told her that it's my judgment that they don't and her privacy and anonymity are safe if that's what she wants. Is Phoebe using any of Daphne's dresses in the show?"

"I spoke to her a little while ago," Noah said. "The library will only use the dresses with Miss Stewart's permission, now that she knows her identity. Even if the library can claim the contents of the sewing room she created, they won't. Miss Stewart is free to reclaim anything she left behind."

Loretta shifted her attention from Julius to Noah. "Have you seen this secret sewing room?" she asked.

Noah nodded. "It's just as Miss Stewart left it at twenty-one." He steadied his gaze again on Julius. "Please let her know that the people of Knights Bridge would welcome her anytime she'd like to return."

Julius raised an eyebrow. "Phoebe told you that?"

Noah didn't hesitate. "Yes."

Loretta sat forward. "Is she here in San

385

Diego?"

"Not now, no," Noah said, his tone unreadable.

"Phoebe figured out that Debbie Sanderson and Daphne Stewart are one and the same?" Julius asked.

"With the help of her sisters." Noah drank more of his water before he continued. "Miss Stewart left a number of books behind in the house she rented while she lived in Knights Bridge."

"Phoebe's house now," Julius added.

"That's right. *Rebecca, The Moonspinners.*"

"Daphne du Maurier and Mary Stewart," Loretta said. "Daphne Stewart."

Noah smiled for the first time. "Exactly. Phoebe and her sisters figured out that the Debbie Sanderson who worked at the Knights Bridge library forty years ago and sewed dresses secretly in the attic had to be Daphne Stewart of Hollywood."

"I'll be damned." Loretta grinned. "I read Daphne du Maurier and Mary Stewart as a kid. I love their books."

Noah looked out at the San Diego skyline from his corner office suite at NAK, the company he'd founded, built and taken public. He'd had the kernel of the idea for

386

it at twelve. It had grown from there, so that now NAK was a leader in the convergence of technology and entertainment. It was an exciting company, with people clamoring to work there.

"We did a good job," he said, knowing that Dylan had entered the office.

"You did." Dylan joined Noah at the windows. "I just helped you so that you could put your skills to their best use."

"You had my back. Who has yours, Dylan?"

He shrugged. "You do. You tapped on my car window four years ago. Where would I be if you hadn't?"

"You'd have figured something out. You could have gotten into adventure travel with your father, or gone on treasure hunts with him, instead of keeping the jerks at bay so that I could do my thing. Now your father's gone —"

Dylan interrupted him. "Noah, my father and I had our chances to do things together. I have a chance now to fulfill some of his dreams, the dreams we shared. Think I'd have that if I hadn't thrown in with you and made all this money?"

Noah smiled. "That is one way of putting it."

Dylan looked out at the city they both

loved. "Olivia's family and friends in Knights Bridge watch out for her. She didn't know that at first. When her friend in Boston betrayed her and she moved back home, she let her pride get in her way. Now she knows."

"She'll do anything for her family and friends, and they'll do anything for her."

Dylan glanced sideways at Noah. "It's that way with the O'Dunn sisters, too."

Noah watched a U.S. Navy ship far out on the Pacific, just a gray blip on the blue water. "Phoebe doesn't realize that it's not just her protecting her family and friends. They're protecting her, too."

"Maybe too much so," Dylan said.

"They think what she wants is to live alone in her little house on Thistle Lane for the rest of her life."

"What if it is what she wants?"

Noah didn't take his eyes off the ship. "They don't want to see her heart broken again, so they tell themselves she's given up on love."

Dylan was silent a moment. Then he blew out a breath. "Noah, you and Phoebe —"

He turned sharply away from the view and smiled at his friend. "Never mind. I'm talking out of my hat. I'm no good at figuring out people. I'm just glad we figured out that

Julius Hartley was protecting Daphne Stewart and had no particular bone to pick with either of us."

Dylan seemed unwilling to change the subject, but finally he sighed. "He and Loretta are going to L.A. to talk to Miss Stewart. You're going with them, aren't you?"

Noah shook his head. "Loretta and Julius are already in L.A. You and I, Dylan my friend, are meeting them at Daphne's house in Hollywood Hills."

Dylan scratched the side of his mouth. "We are, huh?"

"And Olivia, too. I've already talked to her. She wants to be back home in time for the fashion show. I've arranged for a flight from L.A., after our visit."

"You never fail to surprise me."

"Likewise," Noah said. "How long have you known it was Phoebe in that Edwardian dress at the charity masquerade?"

"Olivia didn't recognize her —"

"Olivia doesn't have your objectivity or experience with people. Design and colors, yes." Noah followed Dylan out of the office. "When, Dylan?"

"When you danced with her," he said when they reached the hall. "I didn't tell Olivia because she didn't ask. She didn't tell me when she found out because I didn't ask. Worked out just fine."

"You two have a great life together."

"I like how you put that. We have a great life together now. It's not just in the future." But Dylan's eyes were serious as he and Noah stopped at the elevators. "Noah, I don't want you worrying about Olivia and me if you and Phoebe . . . if you two . . ." He grimaced. "Hell."

Noah grinned. "Not going to have my back with this one, are you?"

"I don't need to. You're a smart guy. You know what you're getting into."

As the elevator dinged, Noah could see Phoebe's turquoise eyes, her smile, her dark strawberry hair against her creamy skin. Yes, indeed. He did know what he was getting into, but what was going on between Phoebe and him was for them to sort out on their own — without Dylan McCaffrey, Olivia Frost, Phoebe's three younger sisters, her eccentric mother, her brother-in-law, the rest of the Frosts, the rest of the Sloans or the rest of Knights Bridge.

The elevator doors opened and he and Dylan got in. "Sometimes we hold on to an image of ourselves because we're convinced it's what we're supposed to be. It's what we want, what other people want from us." He was hardly aware that he was speaking to

Dylan. "I was supposed to be the techie rich guy with a babe on each arm."

"Maybe Phoebe is just who she is, Noah."

"She has a great life and a great job. I don't intend to mess that up for her."

"From what I saw in Boston . . ." Dylan paused, glanced at Noah with a smile. "I'm not sure Phoebe O'Dunn's given up on having a man in her life as much as she wants everyone else to think."

"Come on. Let's go to Hollywood."

# TWENTY

Phoebe had been involved in countless library and other town events since she was a kid, but tonight she was nervous. The vintage fashion show was special. Different. Not just because it was a first for Knights Bridge but because of the hidden attic room and the woman who'd created it, and why. The lasting impact of Debbie Sanderson's brief time in Knights Bridge, on herself, on the people she'd encountered here.

On Phoebe's own family. Her mother, her father.

She slipped into the rich brown sequined Edwardian gown. She'd debated whether to wear it to host the fashion show or just to model it. Wearing it to host had won out. She'd walk to the library and meet her mother and sisters there. No word from Olivia yet, but she and Dylan had planned to be back from California in time for the show.

And no word from Noah . . .

Phoebe adjusted the dress. She'd skip the matching hat tonight. She wasn't trying to conceal her identity from anyone, as she had at the masquerade ball. Now that Noah was back on his home turf, did his short stay in Knights Bridge seem completely unreal to him?

It almost did to her, she realized. Tonight would help get her refocused. Then she planned to take a week off. She'd stay home, work on her garden, help Olivia and Maggie with Carriage Hill, her mother with the goats and her freezing and canning. After that, she'd be into her fall routines at the library. She couldn't wait, really.

*So why do I feel out of sorts?*

She made herself smile in her bedroom mirror. As host tonight, she had to be happy and cheerful.

*Vivacious.* That was the word she was looking for.

She didn't feel vivacious.

She carried her sandals by the straps in one hand and headed downstairs barefoot. No black wig, mask or heavy makeup tonight, either. She'd found instructions for an updo on the internet and managed to follow them, if imperfectly. A few wisps of hair were already out of the pins. The do just had to last a couple of hours. Maggie was catering the post-show wine and cheese party, but then she, the twins and Phoebe would meet back on Thistle Lane and celebrate with a couple of bottles of white wine already chilling in the refrigerator. Phoebe didn't know if Olivia and Dylan would join them.

How much had Noah told his best friend about his stay in Knights Bridge? How much had Dylan guessed?

Phoebe shook off the question. She couldn't change what had gone on between her and Noah. She knew now that she wouldn't even if she could. Any self-consciousness, embarrassment or awkwardness she might feel had to be endured.

Was worth it, she thought as she stepped out onto the porch. She didn't know what was next in their relationship but she had no regrets so far.

She set her sandals on the porch floor. The evening was warm and clear, perfect for the fashion show. She couldn't have ordered up one better. They'd have a good turnout. She looked forward to telling people how Daphne Stewart had gotten her start as a Hollywood costume designer in their town.

A sleek black sedan eased to a stop on

Thistle Lane. A uniformed driver stepped out, went around and opened the back door. Noah got out, and the driver returned to his position behind the wheel.

As the car turned around in Phoebe's driveway and headed back up Thistle Lane, Noah crossed the yard, his movements as smooth and purposeful as she remembered from the first time she'd seen him. He wore an obviously expensive black suit this time. No cape, no mask, no sword.

Phoebe watched him, her heart hammering. Her attraction to him wasn't going away. If anything, it had deepened, becoming not just physical, not just a fleeting connection to liven up a quiet summer. She loved hearing his voice, loved talking to him, listening to him. It didn't matter that she'd known him such a short time. She'd never felt like this about anyone. Her sisters, her parents, her nephews. She loved them with all her heart, but this was different.

*It's too fast. Too crazy.*

Maybe so, but she couldn't deny the rush of emotion as he mounted the porch steps.

"Olivia and Dylan are right behind me," he said. "I wanted to see you first."

Phoebe steadied herself. "My sisters are at the library already. Ava and Ruby are helping Maggie set up for the party after the fashion show. I'm meeting them there." She realized Noah couldn't possibly care about these details but she couldn't stop herself. "Maggie's serving a merlot from your winery. She thought that was fitting. She says it's excellent. She knows more about wine than I do."

"Probably more than I do, too. I bought the winery for the view."

"And to help a struggling friend," Phoebe added, then smiled. "I read about it in an article."

He stepped up onto the porch and gave her one of his slight, enigmatic smiles. "I also liked the idea of wine."

"That's how you operate, isn't it?" She felt his gaze on her and remembered she was in her Edwardian dress. She ignored a tingle of awareness and continued. "You get an idea. Then you take action."

"It's hard to get anything done if you just think about it." He touched an errant curl that had flopped from her updo onto her cheek. "You look beautiful tonight, Phoebe. I like the dress even better with your natural hair."

"I'm hosting the fashion show tonight. It seemed fitting to wear this dress."

"It's perfect. Tonight's special in a number of ways."

"Yes, it is." She felt calmer, steadier, even as she recognized that her head was spinning at having him back in Knights Bridge. "Thank you for being here. I haven't talked to Olivia, so I didn't know you were coming."

"I asked her not to say anything. Things have been happening fast." He glanced back at Thistle Lane, then turned to her again. "I appreciate all you and your sisters did to help figure out what Julius Hartley wanted."

"You're the one who put us in touch with Daphne Stewart."

"Through Hartley."

Phoebe nodded. "It's really exciting. I knew the hidden sewing room was special but I had no idea the woman who created it ended up in Hollywood. I haven't told anyone. I've just said it's okay to use the dresses — that won't give Miss Stewart away, if she wants to stay anonymous."

"I don't know that she does," Noah said quietly. "Olivia and Dylan will be here soon. They have Loretta Wrentham and Julius Hartley with them, and a guest."

Phoebe stood straight. "Noah?"

His eyes seemed so blue in the evening light. "We met Daphne Stewart in Los Angeles. Hartley had told her about the fashion show, and how you'd discovered her old sewing room. She said she wanted to be here tonight, if it's all right with you."

"She's here in Knights Bridge? Noah . . ."

"I'll let her explain everything."

"She really is George Sanderson's great-great-granddaughter, you know."

Noah smiled, visibly more relaxed. "George Sanderson, the intrepid founder of the Knights Bridge Free Public Library."

"I wonder if being here inspired her."

"Or maybe his ghost did."

Noah tucked another curl back into Phoebe's pins, then stood back as Dylan's car pulled in front of her house. He and Olivia got out. She gave Phoebe a quick wave, as if to say everything would be all right. Then the sleek black sedan returned, parked behind Dylan's car.

Julius Hartley emerged from the backseat while a tall, slender woman in tight black pants, a belted white top and red heels stepped out from the front passenger seat. Julius helped another woman out of the back. She was petite and elegant, with copper hair in a pixie cut. She wore a simple rust-colored dress with a teal-and-rust scarf and sparkly gold flats.

The tall woman glided up the walk to the front porch. "I'm Loretta Wrentham," she said, coming up the steps. "Phoebe, right?"

Phoebe nodded, aware of Noah standing even closer to her. "It's nice to meet you," she said. "I've heard a lot about you."

"I'll bet," Loretta said. "Cute place. I like wicker."

"Me, too," Phoebe said with a smile.

Noah frowned at Loretta. She shrugged. "Well, I do."

He said nothing.

The copper-haired woman crossed the lawn with Julius Hartley at her side. Phoebe started down the porch steps. Noah took her hand and walked with her. Loretta followed them. Phoebe thought she heard the older woman sigh.

The copper-haired woman left Julius's side and went to the trellis, tears glistening in her deep green eyes as she touched a pink rose. She lowered her hand and turned to Phoebe and Noah. "I never thought I'd ever see this place again."

Julius cleared his throat. "Daphne, this is Phoebe O'Dunn, director of the library here in Knights Bridge. Phoebe, this is Daphne Stewart, or, as she was known when she was living here, Debbie Sanderson."

"It's a pleasure to meet you, Miss Stewart," Phoebe said, aware of Noah, silent, still, next to her.

"Likewise, Phoebe, and you must call me

Daphne — although standing here, seeing this place . . ." She smiled through unshed tears. "I feel like Debbie Sanderson again."

Phoebe returned her smile. "I can imagine. I'm glad you're here."

Daphne stood back, eyeing Phoebe with obvious emotion, then pointed. "Your dress . . ."

Phoebe glanced down at the beautiful gown. "I couldn't resist."

Daphne laughed unexpectedly. "That's good. Excellent, in fact. My heavens, that dress does look stunning on you."

"I agree," Noah said softly.

Phoebe noticed Loretta all but roll her eyes, but Daphne continued, "You're Patrick's daughter. I can see him in you." She breathed in deeply, looking at the rose trellis and the small house where she used to live. "I have roses at my home in Hollywood Hills. It's a cute little bungalow not that different from this place. Oh, I had such big dreams when I was here."

"Looks as if some of them came true," Loretta said, her directness breaking through the nostalgic mood.

"A lot of them did," Daphne said.

Olivia touched Dylan's arm. "Let's take Loretta and Julius to the library and get settled. Noah, Phoebe and Daphne can

400

meet us there."

Hartley looked reluctant but made no comment as he followed Olivia, Dylan and Loretta out to Thistle Lane. Daphne smiled, watching them. "Julius is someone you want to have on your side," she said quietly.

"You're welcome to come inside and have a look around," Phoebe said.

"Thank you but you have a show to put on." Daphne brushed back a few tears. "I wasn't sure I'd even get out of the car. I'm glad I did. I'd like to walk to the library, if you don't mind."

"That was my plan, too."

"I thought it might be." She looked out at the shaded yard, a breeze stirring in the trees. "I assumed someone had discovered my old sewing room years ago and given everything to Goodwill. It never occurred to me that it was still intact. I feel a little like Sleeping Beauty."

"It's a big attic," Phoebe said with a smile.

"I was surprised when Julius told me about the dresses Olivia, her friend Maggie and Noah's mysterious dance partner wore." Daphne brushed back a few tears. "It's funny how things work out sometimes, isn't it? I see an article about Dylan Mc-Caffrey and Knights Bridge, and you discover my secret sewing room. Meant to be, maybe."

"Maybe so."

Daphne fingered another rose, as if re-membering herself at twenty-one. "I came to Knights Bridge because of my family's roots in the Swift River Valley. I thought it would help me to be close to my great-great-grandfather's energy, his can-do spirit. And it did, just not in all the ways I imagined. Well. Shall we go? Can you walk all right in that long skirt?"

"Not a problem. I even danced in it."

Daphne gave her a knowing smile. "So I hear."

With a sudden burst of energy, she headed down the front walk. Phoebe glanced at Noah. "Go," he said. "I'll be right behind you."

She crossed the lawn and met up with Daphne Stewart. Noah stayed a few feet behind them as they started down Thistle Lane toward the library.

Daphne hooked Phoebe's arm into hers. "My father was a troubled man and as a result I had a troubled childhood. I knew I had to make a clean break. I saved up and moved to Knights Bridge."

"And you got a job at the library your great-great-grandfather founded," Phoebe said.

"I always knew it wasn't permanent. I loved it, and I loved the little house I rented, that you now own." Daphne tightened her hold on Phoebe, as if she needed to steady herself. "I knew that to save myself, I had to totally reinvent who I was — even who I thought I was. I was invisible here, but that's what I wanted."

"Invisible, maybe, but not unappreciated."

Daphne cut her a sideways look. "Thank you for that."

"How did you end up creating your sewing room?" Phoebe asked.

"I volunteered to tidy up the attic." Daphne's grip eased, and she sounded more at ease, more the confident, successful woman she'd become. "I thought it'd be a good opportunity to think, perhaps to encounter a ghost or two. I cleaned out a storage room and decided to make it my own. I enjoyed sewing. I knew what I was doing with a needle and thread. My grandmother taught me the basics. Then I got books out of the library and learned more."

"Did you know you wanted to be a designer?"

"I knew I didn't want to be me," Daphne said quietly. "Having a secret room allowed me to take risks I otherwise might not have. Not all risks involve jumping out of airplanes and climbing tall mountains. Some involve daring to strip away the limiting beliefs about yourself and seeing what's left."

Phoebe glanced back at Noah, knew he could hear them, but he just gave her a slight wink.

Daphne lowered her arm from Phoebe's and inhaled the night air. "I never imagined at twenty that I'd fly back here in a private jet, that much I can tell you." There was no hint of tears in her eyes now. "I used to walk to the library with fabric tucked under my coat. I spent every dime I had on fabric, thread, notions. I'd haunt thrift stores for old clothes that came in that I could tear apart and use in my sewing. I followed patterns at first. Then I found myself adapting them, adding this or that. I had such a good time."

"You taught yourself dress design, then."

"I did. I loved old movies. Of course, some of them weren't so old back then. I learned and practiced by copying dresses I took a fancy to in the movies. Then I pretended I was in charge of costumes for various movies and created my own designs."

"The dress I'm wearing is one of your original designs, isn't it?" Phoebe asked. "It's lovely. It caught my eye right away."

"You're very kind, Phoebe. Yes, I pretended I was designing costumes for a movie about the Titanic. It's not all that different from one of the dresses Kate Winslet wore many years later." Daphne sighed heavily, but with none of the earlier raw emotion. "There was something about being up in the library attic . . ." She trailed off, then smiled as she glanced again at Phoebe. "Maybe it was my great-great-grandfather's presence."

For all Phoebe knew, it was.

Daphne took Phoebe's arm again as the library came into view. "He's quite a man, your Noah."

"We're not . . . He isn't . . ." Phoebe took a breath. "Sorry. I'm not usually tongue-tied. I just don't want to give the wrong impression."

"But you aren't, are you? You don't have to answer. You remind me so much of your father. He was new to town, too. We helped each other. Knights Bridge was exactly where he wanted to be."

"He was such a dreamer," Phoebe said with affection.

"The war took its toll on his natural spirit and optimism, but he finally decided that the best way for him to honor the friends he lost was to live each day."

"He did that. No question."

Daphne squeezed Phoebe's hand, then let go as the library came into view. "One night, he walked me home from the library. It was January, absolutely frigid." She gave a mock shiver. "Believe me, I've never missed below-zero temperatures living in Southern California. That night was so clear. I've never seen stars glittering in a night sky like that. Patrick said it was a combination of the cold air and Quabbin, the absence of ambient light. Now that I do miss."

"I love the night sky," Phoebe said.

"That night . . ." Daphne looked up at the early-evening sky, gray with dusk. "It felt as if the stars were talking to me. I knew I had to leave. I got home and packed up and left Knights Bridge that night."

"My father —"

"He knew I wasn't meant to stay here. He was so comfortable that night, as cold as it was. It was as if he were back in his own skin again. He was like a brother to me, you know. I'd have done anything for him."

"Did you stay in touch?"

"I didn't even say goodbye," Daphne said softly, almost to herself. "It was so, so cold that night. So cold, Phoebe. I knew it was Patrick's destiny to stay here and be himself just as it was mine to leave and become myself. I don't know if that makes sense to you but it does to me."

"It makes perfect sense," Phoebe said, meaning it.

"My attic room tells my story in a way, doesn't it?"

Phoebe smiled. "It certainly does. How did you get to Hollywood?"

"I took buses across the country. I was flat broke by the time I hit Wilshire Boulevard, but I got a job waitressing, found a roommate. I started working on sets, doing whatever work someone would hire me to do, and eventually I got into costume design." She grinned suddenly at Phoebe. "That's the short version."

"Did you ever marry, have kids?"

"Marry, yes. More than once. Have kids, no. Patrick O'Dunn, though . . ." She shook her head in obvious amazement. "Four daughters."

"With your former French student," Phoebe added.

"Will Elly be here tonight?"

"She wouldn't miss it."

They walked under a sugar maple and across the library's side yard to the front entrance. Phoebe saw Ava and Ruby on the steps, in their flapper dresses from Daphne's hidden room.

"I'm honored, Phoebe," Daphne said in a hoarse whisper. "I thought I needed to pretend my past here never existed. I didn't want any reminders, anyone else to know about Debbie Sanderson and her abusive, alcoholic childhood."

"No one needs to know who you are," Phoebe said. "If it's what you want, you can attend the fashion show as one of Dylan's friends from California."

Daphne paused as they came to the main entrance. "Loretta says you should introduce me."

"That sounds like Loretta," Noah said, joining them, easing in next to Phoebe. "We'll do whatever you want."

Daphne didn't respond, and Noah took her by the arm and escorted her up the library steps. Phoebe saw Ava and Ruby staring at her and gave them a quick smile as she followed Noah and Daphne.

Dylan and Julius were waiting at the top of the steps as people gathered for the show. Olivia would be with Maggie, changing into their Audrey Hepburn and Grace Kelly dresses.

Daphne stopped at the open front door. "I don't know what I'm getting worked up about. No one will remember me or give a hoot about meeting a Hollywood costume designer." She peered inside at the rows of chairs, filling up with people from the town where she'd lived for such a short time. Her great-great-grandfather stared down at the audience from his portrait above the fireplace. "I used to talk to old George's ghost."

"Did he talk back to you?" Dylan asked, taking her other arm. Julius, obviously protective of Daphne, scowled, but Dylan just shrugged. "Fair question."

Daphne laughed, visibly more at ease. "In his own way, he definitely talked back to me. My father wasn't like him at all. That much I know." She left it at that and pointed into the library at Grace Webster and Audrey Frost, sitting next to each other up front. "They encouraged me when I started tutoring a few kids in French. I could speak the language, but I was no teacher."

Phoebe said, "I thought at first whoever created the room had gone to Paris."

"I love Paris but Southern California is home." More tears shone in Daphne's deep green eyes. "And for a while, so was Knights Bridge. Now go, Phoebe. Do your thing and enjoy every minute."

As she excused herself and headed backstage, Noah and Dylan, with Julius right behind them, escorted Daphne into the library. Noah caught Phoebe's eye and she mouthed, "Thank you." She looked around for Loretta Wrentham but didn't see her . . . until she arrived backstage. The California lawyer — Dylan McCaffrey and Noah Kendrick's friend — had on a tie-dyed shirt, a fringed vest and wide-legged turquoise pants.

"I think I wore this outfit in sixth grade," she said with a grin. "It's those twin sisters of yours. They could talk a frog into camping out under a cactus."

Phoebe burst into laughter, and then Loretta did, too. Daphne Stewart, aka Debbie Sanderson, was living the life she always wanted. Phoebe realized that her father had, too — that his untimely death didn't change the fact that his life in Knights Bridge with his wife and four daughters was exactly what he'd wanted.

She was living the life she wanted, too.

Except everything had changed when Noah Kendrick swept her onto the dance floor in the Edwardian dress that Daphne Stewart had sewn in her attic room forty years ago.

Daphne Stewart/Debbie Sanderson was greeted like the celebrity she was, on the stage her great-great-grandfather had insisted be included in the small-town library

410

he founded. Noah thought Phoebe was even more beautiful in her princess dress without the mask, the heavy makeup, the black wig — the pretending to be someone else. With her dark strawberry curls falling out of their pins, framing her face, she smiled and laughed among people she knew and loved.

He sat with Julius, Dylan and Daphne in the row behind Grace Webster. Grace would glance back at Dylan as if he she'd dreamed of having a grandson just like him.

Maggie and Olivia wowed the crowd with their Grace Kelly and Audrey Hepburn dresses, and Ava and Ruby O'Dunn had everyone laughing when they did a short skit in their flapper dresses. Their mother modeled a simple, elegant dress that Grace Webster's mother — Dylan's great-grandmother — had worn long before the people of the Swift River Valley had realized their towns were doomed.

Loretta obviously had a grand time showing off her hippie outfit.

Julius leaned toward Noah and whispered, "That Loretta's a stitch."

Dylan overheard him and just shook his head. Noah didn't try to hide his amusement. Brandon Sloan was across the aisle with his sons. He looked more comfortable in his own skin, if also more interested in the women in the dresses than the dresses themselves. They were his friends, and one was his wife. Even if he packed up his tent and moved to California, Brandon would still be a part of Knights Bridge.

It was a warm evening. Noah found himself alone as the after-show party spilled outside onto the lawn and across South Main onto the town common. Daphne had grabbed a glass of wine and was chatting comfortably with Elly O'Dunn.

He spotted Phoebe under a tall, graceful elm and grabbed two glasses of wine and joined her. She'd slipped off her sandals and was barefoot in the grass. She thanked him as he handed her a glass, but her mind was clearly elsewhere.

She sipped the wine, her gaze on her mother and her former French tutor. "My mother stayed in Knights Bridge and Daphne took off for Hollywood — changed her name, became someone else."

"Or thought she became someone else," Noah said.

"It's what she needed to believe at the time. She wasn't running from her life here. She was running from her past and its hold on her." Phoebe turned to him, her eyes almost emerald in the shadows. "Knights Bridge was a stop on the way to becoming who she is now. I'm glad it worked out for her, and I'm glad she's here tonight. Thank you for making that happen."

"You did far more than I did."

He saw spots of color in her cheeks as she smiled. "Ava and Ruby are beside themselves. They're trying not to get too crazy but they're so excited to have Daphne here."

"I think Daphne's excited, too."

"People seemed to have a good time tonight. I hope you and Dylan and Julius weren't too bored."

"Not bored at all," Noah said, letting his gaze settle just for a moment on the swell of her breasts in her elegant gown. The spots of color in her cheeks deepened. He smiled. "You did well, Princess Phoebe, and you look beautiful."

He saw she hadn't expected his comment. "Thank you," she said, then quickly drank more wine.

Several people approached Phoebe to comment on the evening. Noah stood back, observing her as she interacted with her family and friends. Elly O'Dunn broke off from Daphne to chase her grandsons, who'd clearly had enough of vintage fashion and partying. Daphne met up with Dylan and Olivia. They got wine and approached him under the elm.

He sipped his wine, knowing that he stood apart from the people around him. Forty years ago Debbie Sanderson had come to Knights Bridge as an outsider. She'd appreciated the welcome she'd received, but ultimately she'd decided she didn't belong.

Phoebe did, Noah realized. She always would.

In her mind, belonging in Knights Bridge meant living there, being the director of the library, fixing up her little house on Thistle Lane. Any change would seem to her like the drastic break that Daphne had made.

As Phoebe glanced at him with a smile, Noah also saw that she'd convinced herself that he would never want to stay in Knights Bridge and make a place for himself there.

Maybe she was right.

He felt himself go very still as he watched her, and he thought . . . no. She wasn't right.

But he couldn't tell her.

She needed to see it for herself.

"This could have all gone wrong but it didn't," Loretta told Julius as she helped herself to a third glass of wine. They were small glasses. Knights Bridge–size glasses, she thought with a grin. She'd changed back into her regular clothes but kind of missed her hippie outfit. "I had a great time. Were you ever a hippie?"

Julius looked at her as if she'd turned green. "No."

"Always a button-down type?"

"Always."

"Now you're a high-priced private investigator for a high-priced Los Angeles law firm. You went to law school yourself?"

"UCLA. Never took the bar."

"You went into the military," Loretta said, because it was what immediately made sense to her.

He nodded. "I lost an uncle in Vietnam. My mother's brother. Great guy. He was twenty. The baby of the family. It affects you forever, that kind of loss."

Julius was pensive, no wine for him. They'd promised to take Daphne to Boston tonight and then fly back to L.A. in the morning. She had things to do, she'd said, but Loretta knew she'd needed an exit strategy before she could commit to returning to Knights Bridge. Now the Hollywood designer was mingling with people she'd known forty years ago and hadn't seen since.

Knights Bridge was a pretty town, small and off the beaten track, but Loretta could see that Dylan was right. Time hadn't stopped here.

Finally Julius said, "Daphne's time here in Knights Bridge meant something. It wasn't just about hiding and then running away. It wasn't just about her. I hope she sees that now."

"You're thinking about Patrick O'Dunn," Loretta said.

"Yeah." Julius's gaze was fixed on Daphne as she approached Phoebe under a big shade tree. His expression tightened. "She wanted me to do it. I told her I couldn't."

"Do what?"

"Watch. It's not easy to tell Daphne no, but this was for her to do."

He was silent as they watched Daphne hand Phoebe an envelope.

"What is it?" Loretta asked.

"It's the letter she wrote to Patrick O'Dunn when she got to California. She never mailed it."

Phoebe opened the envelope and unfolded the note inside. Loretta bit back her impatience. "What's it say? You read it, right?"

Julius scowled. "You're such a know-it-all, Loretta. Yeah, I read it."

"Well?"

He hesitated, obviously debating how much to say. "Daphne tells him she made it to Hollywood and while she doesn't know what the future will bring, she knows she made the right decision. 'Thanks to you, Patrick, I've finally found my home.' " Julius cleared his throat. "She tells him she'd never have made it to California without him. He helped her find the courage to take the plunge, go after her dream, just because he got up every day and lived his life, did the best he could."

Loretta choked back tears. "Damn. I think I'm going to cry."

"Don't do that," Julius said with a sudden grin. "The world as we know it really will come to an end."

Dylan and Olivia chatted with Noah, whose gaze was on Phoebe O'Dunn and only Phoebe O'Dunn. Loretta sighed. "It already has, but it's okay."

Julius slung an arm over her shoulders. "It's more than okay. It's damn good."

# TWENTY-ONE

Maggie slammed the door behind her as she entered Olivia's kitchen. After last night's perfect weather for the fashion show, the temperature had spiked today. It was midafternoon now and over ninety. The humidity level and dew point made it feel even hotter. Because The Farm at Carriage Hill was a getaway, Olivia was installing air-conditioning, but it wasn't up and running just yet.

Olivia glanced at her from the sink. "You're all red, Maggie. What have you been doing in this heat?"

"I'm broiling hot and broiling mad." She raked a hand through her hair, determined not to take her mood out on her friend. "I need to cool off."

"Why don't you take the boys up to the mill and jump in the pond? The water's always cold there."

Maggie grunted. "I could just dump a tray

of ice cubes on Brandon's head. That'd cool me off."

Olivia stepped back from the sink, drying her hands with a white dish towel. "I had a feeling your red face had something to do with him. Do you want to talk about it?"

"No."

Olivia raised her eyebrows.

"I don't," Maggie said, adamant. "You deserve a quiet day. Did you see the orange mint Phoebe, Noah and I harvested?"

"It's drying nicely," Olivia said, setting the towel on the island. "I also saw the pesto in the freezer."

"And the dog hair on your couch?" Maggie tried to smile. "Noah's a pushover when it comes to Buster. You've got him back on the straight and narrow?"

"Noah or Buster?"

Maggie saw the smile in Olivia's eyes but couldn't relax, couldn't let go of how mad she was — how upset. She sighed. "Yes. Yes, I want to talk. Or tell you, anyway. Maybe not talk, because there's nothing to talk about. It is what it is."

"Do you want to go outside and sit?"

Maggie shook her head and started to pace in the kitchen. It was such an ideal kitchen, in an ell by itself, with great light and lots of cabinets and counters and a warm, country feel. She loved working there.

"Maggie . . ."

"I'm sorry. I was thinking about how much I love it here. I love what you're doing with Carriage Hill."

"What we're doing," Olivia said.

"We do make a good team. This place has such possibilities. I've started to dream again, Olivia. I've started to have hope in the future. I don't dwell on the past so much." She stopped abruptly, stared out the window over the sink and noticed the haze, felt the oppressive heat. "Brandon's been working nonstop for the past six months. He didn't tell me."

"Working for his family?" Olivia asked.

"Mostly. Exclusively now."

"Is that good or bad?"

Maggie leaned back against the island. "Good, I guess. Good that he's working. He's cut expenses to the bone. He's not living in that damn tent because he's broke. He's living there because he's saving every dime he makes."

"For what?"

"To prove himself to me."

"He told you this?"

Maggie snorted. "Are you kidding? He never tells me anything. I had to ferret it out on my own."

"Meaning you got one of his brothers to tell you," Olivia said.

"Christopher." He was the youngest of the six Sloan siblings, one of two full-time firefighters in town. "It didn't take much doing. He says I need to prove myself to Brandon, too. Me. Like I did something wrong."

"What are you supposed to prove?"

"That I still want to be with him, regardless of money."

Olivia picked up her towel again and polished the butcher-block counter. "Christopher said that, huh?"

"Not in those exact words but I got the message." Maggie suddenly wished she had something to cook. She held up a hand before her friend could interrupt. "I'm not asking you to take a side. I know you have to live in this town and it's crawling with Sloans. Whatever made me think I could come back here?"

"There are a few O'Dunns here, too," Olivia said, her tone neutral.

"For how long? Ava and Ruby are going back to school. They'll end up in Hollywood or New York. And Phoebe. I don't know where Phoebe will end up. I used to think she'd always be here in Knights Bridge."

Maggie hesitated, glanced toward the mudroom and back door. "Where are Noah and Dylan?"

"They're up the road talking demolition."

With Brandon, no doubt. Maggie gritted her teeth. "I don't know. Maybe I'm crazy and Phoebe's not going anywhere. She and Noah seemed so good together last night at the fashion show, but she was in that Edwardian dress again. Maybe that makes all the difference."

"Or getting her out of her Edwardian dress," Olivia said half under her breath.

"Olivia!"

"Well. Come on. You saw the sparks between those two."

"Yes, but —" Maggie stopped herself. "I can't talk about my sister that way. And this is Phoebe. It's not Ava or Ruby. You know what I mean?"

Olivia nodded. "I do, and maybe that's part of the problem."

Maggie suddenly wished she'd brought something to do. Her mother had invited the boys up to the house to make pickles and would drop them off at the library later. Maggie would pick them up there. She hadn't planned on a project with Olivia, figured it was too soon after her return from San Diego. Too complicated with Noah

Kendrick as a houseguest.

And she was too mad at Brandon.

She made herself smile as she changed the subject. "Daphne Stewart is something, isn't she?"

"She wants to come back to Knights Bridge for a proper stay," Olivia said. "She only stayed last night because it was all so last-minute and she had to get back to L.A. I also think she wasn't sure she could handle being back here."

"It was emotional for her. You could tell. She lived in town for such a short time but it had an impact, on her and on the people she met. She needed a brother, a man she could trust — who wouldn't beat her up."

"Your father," Olivia said.

Maggie nodded, emotional herself. "Daphne helped him but he helped her. He was such a good guy, Liv."

"I remember."

"We all lost out when he died, but Phoebe most of all, although I don't think she and that rat bastard from Orlando were meant for each other. But she's never really had anyone since then."

"Maybe that's because she was waiting for a swashbuckler to sweep her off her feet," Olivia said with a smile.

Maggie felt her own mood lighten. Sweat

trickled down the nape of her neck. "Phoebe's used to having people need her. Noah doesn't need her. What does she have to offer a billionaire? She's not a starlet. She's . . . Phoebe."

"Maybe Noah's wondering what he has to offer her."

"A winery, for starters," Maggie said, partly serious, partly facetious.

Olivia went to the refrigerator and helped herself to a handful of crushed ice. She offered some to Maggie, rubbed her arms with hers. "Maybe Phoebe doesn't want a winery. Maybe she just wants what she has."

"That would be my sister," Maggie said with a sigh. "She's stubborn, you know. She'll tell herself she doesn't want anything but what she already has."

"Noah took her by surprise, didn't he?"

"They took each other by surprise. It's not like Brandon and me. No surprises. I've known him my whole life. I know how he thinks. Wouldn't you think he'd know how I think?"

Olivia watched the ice chips melt on her arm and didn't answer.

"He can be such an idiot," Maggie said, back on that train of thought. "What went on between us was never about money."

"If Brandon wasn't so thickheaded sometimes, Maggie, you wouldn't love him so much." Olivia took her towel, blotted her arm dry. "Maybe you two got into a pattern of thinking that you knew what was going on with the other person — like two halves of one whole instead of two individuals."

Maggie wasn't willing to go that far. "I talk."

"Maybe you both should talk." Then Olivia added, "To each other."

"I'm too hot to talk, and when did you get so wise, my friend?" Maggie smiled. "Why don't we let the guys talk demolition while we go swimming in the millpond?"

Olivia grinned. "I'll grab my suit."

"I've got one in the van."

They drove out to the nineteenth-century sawmill the Frosts owned on a tributary to the Swift River. The small millpond and wood-sided mill, now converted into an apartment, were still intact. Maggie shivered just looking at the clear, clean, copper-tinted water. Tyler and Aidan hated swimming here. They preferred the warmer water of their friends' pools. Maggie thought they might change their minds when they were older, although she didn't want them to get the cuts and bruises that she, Phoebe and Olivia had swimming out here growing up. Like their nephews, Ava and Ruby had never been big on plunging themselves into ice-cold water.

Maggie sat on a sun-warmed boulder and dipped her feet into the water, then pulled them right out. "It didn't seem this cold when we were kids."

Olivia laughed. "It did, too. We were just oblivious."

They eased into the water, each finding a rock to stand on as they got used to the chilly temperature. Maggie shut her eyes, appreciating the contrast between the waist-down cold and the waist-up heat. She remembered sneaking out here on a moonlit night with Brandon, back in the days when it felt like anything was possible.

She opened her eyes and realized Olivia was looking at her with concern. "I'm okay." She smiled before she could burst into tears. "It's a perfect day to be out here, isn't it?"

"Perfect."

The pond was only five feet at its deepest. As she lowered herself into the water, getting wet up to her neck, Maggie listened to the flow of the brook over the stone dam. Olivia splashed her, and Maggie splashed her back. They shrieked with laughter as if they were twelve again.

Maggie ducked her head underwater but popped up almost immediately. "Whoa, that's refreshing," she said. "I think I have goose bumps."

Olivia eased back up onto their sunny boulder. "Don't get hypothermia," she said.

Maggie splashed her. "Just like you to bring up hypothermia."

Olivia pointed at her. "Purple lips, shivering, goose bumps. You tell me."

"All right, all right." Maggie climbed up onto another boulder and stretched out her legs. She had purple-blue knees, too. She reached for a towel on the stone wall — of course Olivia had remembered towels — and draped one over her legs. "It's still hot as blazes."

"It won't be for long." Olivia nodded up at dark clouds looming above the trees to the west. "Looks like a storm's headed our way."

"That does look nasty," Maggie said. "I guess we're done playing hooky for the afternoon."

She dried off as best she could and slipped back into her shorts and T-shirt. Olivia did the same. Thunder rumbled in the distance, the kind of low, deep, rolling thunder that suggested a strong storm was bearing down on them.

They headed to the parking lot by the much newer Frost Millworks building.

Dylan was there, getting out of his car. "We're not going anywhere right now. Knights Bridge is under a severe thunder-storm warning."

Maggie shook her head. "I have to pick up the boys at the library. I've driven in loads of storms —"

"Not like this one. I've seen the radar."

"We can duck into the mill," Olivia said. "Where's Noah?"

"And Brandon," Maggie added. "He's not in that stupid tent, is he?"

"They're at Carriage Hill," Dylan said.

They hurried up to the mill. No one else was there late on a Sunday afternoon. Maggie used the phone in the small front office and tried calling the library but no one picked up. Her mother would have dropped off the boys by now but Maggie called her just to be sure.

"I dropped them off twenty minutes ago," her mother said. "Phoebe's there alone. We get thunderstorm warnings all the time, Maggie. It'll be okay."

But Maggie heard the note of worry in her mother's voice. They promised to keep each other updated.

"Stay at the mill," her mother said. "Prom-ise me, Maggie."

The phone went dead.

428

Maggie cradled the receiver and went into the outer room. She could see wind whipping through the trees on the other side of the pond. Small limbs fell into the water. The ground was quickly littered with leaves and twigs.

Then came the hail.

Olivia and Dylan held hands. Maggie wrapped her arms around her middle and watched the pebble-size hail hit the walk and the rock walls. It pelted into the brook and collected on the grass.

She jumped at a simultaneous flash of lightning and crack of thunder.

"It's just the edge of the storm," Dylan said.

Maggie insisted he hand her his iPhone. The local weather radar was still up on the screen. Reds, yellows, purples. It was a dangerous, severe thunderstorm, and if it stayed on course, Knights Bridge center was taking a direct hit.

Maggie's stomach lurched. She bolted for the door but Dylan grabbed her. "I have to get to the library," she said. "The boys — Phoebe."

"Phoebe knows what to do in a storm," Olivia said, white-faced.

"If she knows it's this bad . . ."

"We wait this out," Dylan said. "Then we

go."

"Aunt Phoebe! Aunt Phoebe!"

"I'm here," she said, sitting up, wincing in pain. It was Aidan screaming her name. She tried to keep from moaning and further scaring her nephews. "It's okay . . ."

"Listen," Tyler told his younger brother, his tone reassuring. "You hear the sirens? Uncle Chris will get us out."

They were alone in the library attic. They'd lost power but that was the least of their troubles. Despite the heat, Tyler and Aidan had wanted to see the attic and Phoebe's secret room. They didn't care about sewing, but someone had mentioned there were ghosts in the attic. Phoebe told them about the antique marbles she'd found, and they'd charged up the stairs ahead of her.

What harm was there in a spooky little adventure on a hot summer afternoon?

She'd been right behind them on the back stairs when she noticed the threatening sky, the greenish light in the window on the second-floor landing. She'd grabbed the boys and started downstairs to get to an interior room, but the storm hit suddenly. A fierce wind gust uprooted a sugar maple and sent it into the library. Branches broke the window on the landing below them, just missing them and blocking their route back downstairs.

She all but threw the boys up to the attic. They took cover in Daphne Stewart's windowless sewing room. Hail pounded on the roof. Wind howled and whistled. The tiny room seemed to rattle with the booming thunder.

Phoebe had held on to her nephews, shielding them in case part of the roof blew off.

The storm finally passed, and now it was quiet except for the sirens.

"I need to let someone know where we are," she said, keeping her voice calm. "That we're safe."

"We're not safe," Tyler said, the pragmatic Sloan.

Aidan sucked in a breath and pointed at her. "Aunt Phoebe . . . you're bleeding."

She saw that she was, in fact, bleeding from a cut on her left arm. She didn't remember being hurt, hadn't felt any pain until now. She took in a shallow breath. "It's not bad. Are you boys okay? Let me look at you."

"We're fine." Tyler stood up. "I'm going to yell out a window."

"You won't be able to open any of the

431

windows up here," Phoebe said.

"We can throw a brick and break the glass," Aidan said.

Tyler rolled his eyes. "Where are we going to get a brick?"

"Then use something else," his brother said, impatient, scared.

Phoebe struggled to her feet. "I'll do it," she said. "You two stay right there where I can see you and don't move. Understood? Don't move."

As she crept to the corner door, she heard a creaking sound in the tiny room. A ghost after all, maybe. She opened the door, felt blood drip into her eyes. A cut on her scalp, too? At least the blood hadn't reached her face and the boys hadn't seen it.

She saw Christopher Sloan down on South Main, yelling past two uprooted trees to someone out of view. Olivia was there with her father, a volunteer firefighter, and Dylan. No Noah. Then she saw Maggie, looking stricken as she approached her brother-in-law, picking her way through fallen limbs and scattered leaves.

Phoebe tried to open the window, but she couldn't get it to budge. What was wrong with her? Her head was spinning, aching. Her arm stung from the cut.

She glanced back at her nephews with a

quick smile. "Everything's fine. We just have to give your Uncle Chris time to get up here."

"Because of the broken glass," Aidan said.

"And the tree in the way," Tyler added sarcastically. Phoebe saw that his toughness was a pretense, his own eyes wide with fear.

"Aidan! Tyler!"

Brandon. Of course. He was close, probably by the freestanding closets.

"We're in here," Phoebe called. "We're okay."

"Aunt Phoebe's not okay," Tyler yelled.

Brandon burst into the sewing room. "Aunt Phoebe saved us," Aidan said, sobbing as his father scooped him up.

Her brother-in-law looked straight at her. "Sit, Phoebe."

"I'm fine —"

"You're not fine. Sit."

Then Noah swept in behind him. "Phoebe." He seemed hardly able to speak. "I know a bit about cuts."

"From your fencing," Phoebe said, then clutched his arm, steadying herself. "Oh, hell, Noah. Damn. I think I'm going to faint."

"Then you're right where you need to be."

And she knew she was, even as she passed out in his arms.

# TWENTY-TWO

Noah stood on Thistle Lane thirty yards from an ambulance as Phoebe reassured the crew that she was just fine. He'd hated to leave her but all eyes were on her. She'd regained consciousness almost immediately after she'd passed out, probably as much from heat and dehydration as anything else. She'd refused to wait for a stretcher. After firefighters had cleared the tree out of the way, she'd walked down from the attic on her own, Noah at her side.

"Phoebe's right," Dylan said, approaching Noah. "She will be fine. Her cuts are superficial. She doesn't even need stitches."

"You should know. You got cut in hockey all the time."

"Regularly. Not all the time."

They both grinned, but Noah could still feel the after-effects of the adrenaline rush. He and Brandon Sloan had arrived in the village center minutes after high winds had

434

blown down trees and wires, ripped off parts of roofs. Brandon managed to park his truck on South Main, and he and Noah jumped into action, charging into the damaged library.

For a terrifying minute, they'd thought Phoebe and the Sloan boys were under the debris on the stairs.

Noah shook off the memory. Olivia was with Phoebe. Police and firefighters had cordoned off the library's side yard where two trees had come down in what they believed was a microburst.

Maggie paced on the narrow lane as Tyler and Aidan told their story to their firefighter uncle.

"She's blazing," Dylan said.

She certainly was, Noah thought. "She's had a fright."

"She needs to vent," Brandon said as he joined them. "She can cater a dinner for seventy-five people without breaking a sweat, but this is different. It's her kids. The boys are good, though. All's well that ends well."

Noah had entered the library with Brandon and knew how terrified he'd been for his sons, and for his sister-in-law.

Maggie stalked over to him, hands on her hips, some color returning to her cheeks.

"Why didn't you wait for the firefighters?" she asked as if in midthought.

"Noah and I were right there, Maggie," Brandon said. "What were we supposed to do, twiddle our thumbs?"

She ignored him and glared at Noah. "You, too. You both had to go tearing into the library on your own." She didn't give him a chance to respond and spun back to her husband. "What if that tree had dislodged and fallen on you? Phoebe and the boys were safe."

"We wouldn't have gone up if it wasn't safe," Brandon said.

"You would have."

"I've worked construction since I could pick up a hammer. I knew it was safe. I didn't know Phoebe and the boys were okay." His tone was patient, unwavering. "We had a good angle. We got through. Coming back down with Phoebe and the boys was risky, so we waited for the firefighters."

"Phoebe had everything under control." Maggie blinked back tears. "But if she and Tyler and Aidan had gone up those stairs thirty seconds later, and that tree, the window . . ."

"They'd have been in a world of hurt," Brandon said bluntly. "Lucky that didn't

436

happen. Don't think about what could have happened, Maggie. Think about what did happen."

She nodded, calmer. Her sons edged toward their parents. Brandon slung an arm over Aidan's small shoulders. "Aunt Phoebe protected us," the boy said.

Tyler nodded. "It was a scary storm."

"We don't get many storms like that," Maggie said, reassuring them despite her own lingering fear.

Tyler kicked a small stone in the lane, then looked up at the adults, his eyes still wide. "Aunt Phoebe said we just had to wait for someone to come get us. We were trapped, weren't we?"

Brandon pointed at the fallen tree. "The storm took down that tree. It was blocking the stairs. It wasn't even close to you guys in the attic. You can see that from here, can't you, Tyler?"

"Yeah," the boy said.

Next to him, his younger brother took his father's hand. "I wasn't scared, Dad."

"It's okay to be scared. We all get scared." Brandon looked straight at his wife. "It's what we do when we're scared that matters."

"Aunt Phoebe is brave," Aidan said.

437

Brandon nodded. "She did the right thing today."

Maggie looked at Noah. "That's Phoebe. It's who she is. She always tries to do the right thing, for all of us."

It would be like that, Noah knew. The O'Dunn sisters would stick together. An attack on one — even a perceived attack — was an attack on all four. Most of the time, their solidarity was probably a positive for all of them. He glanced at the ambulance. Phoebe was back on her feet, her arm bandaged as she stood next to Olivia. She looked steady, her hair shining in what was now a clear, cool afternoon. He wondered how much freedom she had to do what she wanted and not just what her family wanted, or what she thought they wanted.

Elly O'Dunn arrived with Ava and Ruby, and Brandon and Maggie and their sons joined them at the ambulance. Phoebe smiled at her family. Noah knew that it'd be her instinct to reassure them.

Dylan sighed. "Damn. That was too close for comfort."

"As Brandon says, all's well that ends well," Noah said. "Phoebe and the Sloan boys are in good shape. The damage to the library is repairable."

"What about you, Noah?" his friend asked

438

him. "You got to be a swashbuckler without having to stab anyone. Feeling pretty good?"

"You were annoying in kindergarten, too, Dylan," Noah said with a grin. "I don't know how we've stayed friends."

"We didn't do the same things. You're a swordfighter and I'm a hockey player. You're good at math and I'm not." Dylan paused, his gaze on Phoebe and Olivia. "You and Phoebe do different things, too."

"No kidding," Noah muttered.

"It's good. You get bored easily. In fact, you're a pain in the ass when you're bored." Dylan looked more relaxed than when he'd arrived at the library. "Brandon Sloan's a natural to work in adventure travel. He could do it on the side and still keep up with his construction work."

Noah nodded. "You could use the help."

"I thought this adventure travel initiative might burn out fast, but it's not going to. It's already taking off and we're not even fully set up yet."

Noah wasn't surprised. With Duncan McCaffrey's treasure hunting background and Dylan's interests and contacts, adventure travel was a perfect next step for him. But it wouldn't be the only one. After four years of hyperfocusing on NAK, he was as ready to explore multiple interests as Noah was.

"Maggie and Olivia are on their way to becoming full business partners," Dylan added. "Maggie's taking over more of the day-to-day running of Carriage Hill. She loves it and she's good at it. Olivia loves the design work, planning, coming up with new ideas."

"Finding old pillowcases," Noah added with a smile.

"And soap making. They're having a great time."

Noah could get used to mosquitoes, and he could learn to love small-town life and hiking in the woods, but he wasn't going to get into making soap. He suspected Dylan was of a like mind.

"NAK's a success," Noah said. "It's in good hands, but we're not done."

Across South Main, people were gathering to check out the damage from the storm. The Civil War monument was intact, the stone Union soldier standing tall amid several downed trees. Several of the buildings on South Main had sustained damage. Across the common, the Knights Bridge Country Store was untouched.

Except for Phoebe's cuts, there'd been no injuries. Noah watched her kneel down at eye level with her young nephews as she spoke to them. After their scare, they'd need reassurance.

"We're friends, Noah," Dylan said next to him. "That's not changing, whatever comes next."

He meant Phoebe, Noah knew.

She stood, Tyler and Aidan laughing now. Everyone looked more at ease. Noah felt his throat tighten. "I'm as sure about Phoebe as I've ever been about anything."

"I know," Dylan said.

"That obvious?"

"It is to me."

"Phoebe and I need time together, but it won't change how sure I am." Noah went very still, a cool, gentle breeze blowing now. "I know it won't."

Dylan didn't argue with him.

Olivia broke off from the Sloans and O'Dunns and Dylan met her on the corner of South Main and Thistle Lane. He put his arm around her as if he'd known her forever. Noah glanced at the library. Brandon had said he thought it would reopen quickly, within a few days, although the damage would take longer to repair. Would Phoebe lead that effort as library director?

She hugged her mother, then left her family and walked toward him. He wanted to go to her but waited for her to reach him.

"Thank you, Noah," she said, stopping

441

next to a small downed tree limb. "I've never passed out before."

"You're sure you don't need to get checked out at the hospital?"

"I'm sure. I've been cleared to go home. My mother wants us all to come out to her place for hamburgers and hot dogs." Phoebe smiled, added, "And tomatoes, of course."

"Fresh from the garden," Noah said.

"Absolutely."

"Phoebe . . ." Then as he let his fingertips graze hers, out of view of her family and friends, he heard himself tell her that he was going back to San Diego. "I'm not a guy from Knights Bridge. I never will be. That's a statement of fact, Phoebe. It's not an apology."

Her turquoise eyes widened but she didn't speak.

"When we saw each other that night in Boston, it was like having a flash grenade go off in our lives. It changed everything. I had it happen when NAK took off and turned me into a very wealthy man." He resisted an urge to touch her hair, her lips. "You need time, Phoebe. I'm giving it to you."

If she said anything as he left, he didn't hear it. He waved a hand at Dylan, who immediately joined him on South Main.

442

"Noah, what's going on?"

"I need a ride to the airport."

"You're going back to San Diego?"

"Tonight."

"For how long?"

Noah glanced back at Phoebe, walking alone down Thistle Lane. "For as long as it takes."

Word got out that Noah Kendrick had left Knights Bridge for the second time in less than a week. Phoebe was pouring wine when Maggie, Ava, Ruby and Olivia descended on Thistle Lane to take her to her mother's house. Brandon was already there with Tyler and Aidan.

Maggie, looking emotionally ragged, took the wine bottle out of Phoebe's hands. "Are you out of your ever-loving mind, Phoebe? It's bad enough I've screwed up everything with Brandon, but you can't screw up things with Noah because you're afraid of not being there for us, for Mom, for Knights Bridge. You just can't. I won't let you."

Ava glanced at her watch. "Noah doesn't have that much of a head start. You have time to get to the airport before his plane takes off."

"You're assuming I was invited," Phoebe said.

Her sisters groaned in unison. "Who cares? Go!"

"I'll drive you," Olivia said. "If we're wrong and he doesn't want you on his plane, I'll drive you back here —"

"And we'll drink a case of his wine," Maggie said.

"It's a risk but not a crazy risk," Ruby said. "He wants you to take it. He wants to prove he's not too much for you. Too rich, too California, too smart, too — you know. Too everything."

"And he needs to know you're falling in love with him," Maggie added quietly. "He needs to know he has something to offer you."

Phoebe took a breath. "Something to offer me?"

"You have everything you need right here in Knights Bridge," Olivia said. "Your family, your job, your friends."

But not Noah, Phoebe thought. She didn't tell her sisters and friend that even before the storm — fainting into Noah's arms — she'd drafted her letter of resignation from the library, just to get a feel for what it might be like to try something new. She could volunteer. She could get into adventure travel, work on Carriage Hill soaps, learn about venture capital and serial entrepreneurs. She could read books and chase toddlers.

There was so much she could do.

She saw possibilities where before she had only seen the path she was on.

Before Noah.

"It'll take me two seconds to pack," she said, already heading out of the kitchen.

She didn't know what she threw in her suitcase. If she forgot anything, there were stores in San Diego. *And maybe I won't need clothes,* she thought with a jolt. She blamed her scare with the storm, her mad dash up to the attic with her nephews. She still ached from her cuts, but at least she hadn't required stitches and didn't have a concussion.

In other words, she could fly. She could see the sights in San Diego.

Make love to Noah.

She let out a breath. *Don't get ahead of yourself.*

On the drive to the small airport barely twenty miles from Knights Bridge, Olivia gripped the steering wheel, her eyes on the road as she spoke. "If things don't work out with you and Noah, you and I will still be friends. You know that, right, Phoebe? It won't change anything between us."

"But Dylan —"

"It's the same for him and Noah. They've been friends for almost as long as we have. We're all grownups now, Phoebe. You know? We'll figure it out. You and Noah need the space to be whatever you're meant to be to each other."

"I appreciate that, Olivia," Phoebe said. "You and Noah seem to get along well."

"Noah is — he's just Noah. Not everyone gets him."

"Women?"

"I don't know much about his past relationships." Olivia smiled. "Except that they're past."

"I've never been to San Diego," Phoebe said half under her breath.

"You won't be intimidated by Noah's life there. You're not the type. Just because you're quiet and kind doesn't mean you're a pushover. You'd never have managed Knights Bridge Free Public Library if you were a pushover."

Phoebe laughed. "That's for sure."

Olivia slowed for a curve. "That's what Noah sees, you know. He believes in you."

They arrived at the airport.

Noah's plane hadn't taken off yet.

Phoebe had a strong suspicion that Dylan had given his friend advance warning. The pilot greeted her by name and escorted her to the private jet himself.

Noah was there, fresh out of the shower, in a clean black shirt and dark jeans. He looked every inch the billionaire he was. He had champagne waiting, and when she sat next to him on a leather seat, Phoebe knew there was nowhere else on the planet she'd rather be.

Brandon slept on the couch at Maggie's "gingerbread" house off Knights Bridge common. It hadn't sustained any damage, but he said he wanted to be close to the boys their first night after their scare. Maggie didn't mind. It made sense, she told herself. Tyler and Aidan needed both parents.

Brandon had an early start at work. He hadn't even stayed for coffee.

It was almost as if he hadn't been there.

The second night, however, was a different story.

His folks took the boys for the night. Christopher had promised he'd show his nephews some basic search-and-rescue techniques. Tyler and Aidan were so excited, Maggie couldn't say no, although she was reluctant to be apart from them. Never in her life had she had such a scare as when she'd arrived at the library after the storm.

She still wasn't over it, she thought as she crossed the yard to Grace Webster's old house — the one Dylan's father had bought and then left to him, a simple act that, ultimately, had changed all their lives.

The heat of two days ago eased with the storm; it was downright chilly. Maggie had promised her in-laws that she'd drop off a jug of corn chowder for Brandon. She and her mother and younger sisters had made up tons with fresh corn from the garden.

He stood by an open fire in front of his tent. "It's still warm," she said, handing the chowder to him.

"Thanks, Maggie."

She heard something in his voice but couldn't figure out what it was. He had a blanket spread out on the grass between his tent and the crackling fire. She appreciated the warmth of the flames.

"Sit with me a minute?" he asked her.

She shrugged. "Sure, why not?"

She sat cross-legged on the blanket. He sat next to her, his legs stretched out, the light from the flames flickering on his face. He smiled at her. "Nice night. I don't miss the heat."

"Me, either, although I'll probably regret saying that in January." She fidgeted, uncrossed her legs. "I shouldn't stay long. I have things to do at home."

"At least stay until the stars are out."

She went still, narrowed her eyes on him. That was it, she thought. That knowing tone. That Sloan smugness. "I've been set up, haven't I?"

He leaned toward her. "You didn't stand a chance. All of us Sloans united to get you out here tonight."

"My sisters weren't involved, were they?"

"Do you see them here with pitchforks?" Brandon asked wryly.

"It's not that they're against you. They're just with me."

His gaze softened. "So am I, Maggie."

She looked away from him and saw a star twinkling brightly in the darkening night sky. "Brandon . . ." She didn't go on. What else was there to say?

"If you want to leave, Maggie —"

"I don't."

The words were out before she'd realized she'd said them and that it really was what she wanted. Brandon edged closer to her, and she sank against him, felt his arm settle around her. It was so quiet, just an owl hooting across the field toward Carriage Hill and Quabbin.

"Ah, Maggie," Brandon said. "Maggie, Maggie."

"We're not kids anymore, are we?"

"Maybe not, but we have years of fun left in us." He kissed her on the top of her head. "Decades."

As they watched the stars come out, he talked to her about the work he was doing with his family, and he asked her about her catering business and what was up with her and Olivia at Carriage Hill. They talked about adventure travel and treasure hunts left over from Dylan's father.

The night turned dark, stars glittering overhead. Maggie watched the fire die down, just glowing coals now. At least she'd had the sense to wear jeans and a sweatshirt given the cool temperature. The mosquitoes left them alone.

Finally she said, "I was so afraid of wanting to be back in Knights Bridge — wanting to raise Aidan and Tyler here — that I ended up blaming you. I had to come home because we were on the skids. It was an excuse." She picked at a loose thread on the blanket, then looked up at him. "It was a bad excuse, and it hurt you and the boys. And me."

"I'd talked you into thinking it'd be a sign of failure to come back here, and that I didn't want to."

She grunted. "You didn't want to, Brandon. I've been listening to you say you couldn't wait to get out of Knights Bridge and then that you never wanted to go back for years."

"Yeah. I know." He shrugged. "But things change."

Maggie sat up straight, shocked. "You want to be here?"

"Pretty much." He grinned that easy Sloan grin. "My family's been waiting to hear me say that since I was just out of diapers. Maggie, I don't care if you needed someone to blame for wanting to come back here for the boys — for yourself. I can take it."

"I was so afraid of being impractical and impulsive. Starting my own business, buying a fixer-upper." She pushed hair out of her face. "Oh, Brandon. I've been such an idiot."

"No, you haven't. I shut down. I told myself you and the boys would be better off on your own."

"You were wrong," she said, more forcefully than she'd intended. "I know you've been through a rough period and you're being responsible, but I don't want you to give up your dreams. Not for my sake."

"When I lost my job, I felt like my dreams were what got us into trouble, and I dug a hole deeper for you and the boys." He touched a finger to her chin. "There's a lot of history between us, Maggie. When I lost my job, I felt like a failure. I felt like everything I'd told you for years about what I was going to do, how we were going to live, was just a lot of BS."

"We were teenagers, Brandon. I wasn't going to hold you to what you said when you were seventeen."

"Or twenty-five? Thirty? And there you were, still filled with such dreams yourself. I felt like mine had only caused trouble for you and the boys, dug us a deeper hole. I put myself and my pride before you."

"You put words in my mouth, especially about money."

"They were what I was telling myself."

"I didn't know what to do. You've always been there for me, Brandon. Then you weren't. Or you were, but you didn't believe that you were. I never saw you as a screwup. You always had such hope and optimism. I didn't realize how much that meant to me until they weren't there."

"We went through a hard year."

"Maybe, but I'm stronger because of it. I'd never lived on my own. I'm not saying I needed to, but it worked out."

"I know it did. I can see it in you. The

confidence." He shifted, his eyes lost in the shadows. "I never wanted you to trim your dreams to make me look good. I'm not that kind of guy. In fact, I think that kind of guy's a jerk."

She smiled, even as she wanted to cry. "I don't want you to give up on your dreams. I couldn't stand it."

"I haven't. This adventure travel gig's right up my alley." He leaned back on his out-stretched arms. "We'll see what happens. I know now that the only dream that matters is being with you and the boys."

"I know," Maggie said, up on her knees now, at eye level with him as she touched his dark hair. "Deep down, I've always known."

He flicked a mosquito off her shoulder. "The bugs have found us."

"What do you say we could go into your tent now?"

"I thought you hated camping."

"It's not the camping part I'm thinking about."

"We worry about Phoebe," he said, "but it's Noah we should worry about. The guy has no idea what he's in for getting involved with an O'Dunn."

# TWENTY-THREE

Phoebe was alone in a room dedicated to Noah's collection of antique swords. The lighting and climate controls were set to protect the contents of the room. It was at the back of the house, on the second floor above the pool. She'd already dipped her feet into its warm, silky water. Noah had watched her from the patio. She'd smiled at him, mumbled something about the Southern California sun and her freckles. He'd smiled back and said nothing.

He was letting her get acquainted with his world, she thought as she leaned in close and studied the ornate handle — or whatever it was called — of another sword, an eighteenth-century French rapier.

"Note the shape of the blade," he said, coming into the small room. "It's specifically designed for thrusting."

She stood straight. "Thrusting as in . . ."

"Just what it sounds like." He pointed at

another sword next to it. "This blade has a double edge. It's a bit longer. It can be used for thrusting but it can also slash."

"It's a fascinating subject."

"There are a lot of technical terms but it's not as complicated as it might seem," He nodded to the sharp tip of the first rapier. "One touch in the right place is all it takes to kill one's opponent."

"Are you a thruster or a slasher, or is that too simplistic?" She smiled. "I'm sure I have a lot to learn."

His eyes held hers. "I'd like to teach you."

Phoebe tried to ignore a flutter in the pit of her stomach as she moved to another display. "You have quite a collection here. One antique sword led to another antique sword?"

"It was something to do on quiet nights after work," he said. "What do you do?"

"Lately I've been fixing up my house."

"You have your family and friends, too."

"Don't you?"

"I have a small family and a few good friends. I know and like a lot of people, mostly from work, fencing, karate."

"Hollywood," Phoebe added.

He shrugged. "Some." He walked over to her. "This one is nineteenth-century Persian. Eventually I'll donate most of this collection to charity, to help young martial art athletes."

"You'll still fence and do karate."

It wasn't really a question but he nodded. "And NAK?"

"We'll see."

Phoebe pretended to study the ornate sword but was intensely aware of his presence. They were alone, unlikely to be interrupted. They'd flown overnight. Now . . . she had to consider where she'd sleep.

She cleared her throat. "Olivia and I were talking on the way to the airport. I mentioned that I've been reading about intensive seminars in entrepreneurship. New entrepreneurs spend a long weekend or even two or three months immersed in how to set up their own company. She said you and Dylan would be naturals. You could use the adventure travel barn for classes. People could stay at Carriage Hill. It's a thought, anyway."

Noah was so close now she could almost feel his breath. "It's a good thought," he said. "It would give me another reason to be in Knights Bridge."

She shifted her attention back to the sword but couldn't focus on the details. She saw Noah in Knights Bridge. Saw him in winter, skating with her on the little homemade outdoor rink on the common. Saw him careening down a snow-covered hill in a toboggan with her and her nephews.

It all felt so right when just a short time ago she couldn't have pictured him in her small town at all.

Or herself in San Diego, with him, and yet here she was.

"Phoebe." He stood next to her and took her hands, kissed her lightly on the lips. "Come on. I'll show you the rest of the upstairs."

He explained that the house was new. He'd only moved in six months ago. It wasn't massive, certainly not as massive as he could afford. He'd hired a decorator because he hadn't had the time or the inclination to figure out what to do with each room, never mind what furnishings to use. He'd been satisfied with the results, but Phoebe realized that he didn't care that much about the specifics — things like whether a refrigerator was stainless-steel or avocado-green. He'd wanted comfort, soothing colors, space where he could move, relax, think and entertain.

"Not that I entertain that much," he said as they came to the master bedroom. "You're the first person I've had in here except for the decorators. I gave Olivia the grand tour when she was here with Dylan but we skipped this room."

"It's beautiful," Phoebe said, trying to ignore the catch in her throat. The room was all grayed neutrals and sleek lines. She walked to the windows that looked out at the bay. "The view is breathtaking."

"That's San Diego for you."

He sat on the king-size bed. It was simply made up, the sheets pulled back, white-cased pillows piled at the headboard. Phoebe felt a tingle of awareness as she looked at him. He leaned back on one arm, his eyes a deeper blue than the sky and ocean outside the windows. A nighttime blue. A blue as intense and enigmatic as he was.

There were several guestrooms. She had only to pick one. He'd told her so in that steady manner he had. But as he watched her from his bed, she knew what his preference was.

She walked over to him and sat next to him, not quite touching. "Noah, there's something you need to know about me."

"I want to know everything about you."

She turned to him, placing one knee on the bed. "Everyone thinks I've given up on love and romance. I thought I had, too." She realized she felt comfortable talking to

458

him, and the tension went out of her. She smiled. "Then I found Daphne Stewart's sewing room in the library attic, and I started to see that I hadn't given up. I argued with myself."

"You didn't want to expose yourself to being hurt again," he said. "Or expose your family to your pain."

"And I didn't want things to change. I liked my life." She put her hand on his upper arm. "I've been torn ever since I saw those dresses, felt the presence — the dreams and hopes — of the woman who created them. They connected with me on the deepest level. I didn't see that at first."

"Sneaking into the ball in your Edwardian gown was part of the war with yourself," he said, brushing a curl off her face. "I think I saw that. It's part of why I noticed you." He smiled, letting his hand drift along the line of her jaw. "Also because you were so damn beautiful."

She laughed. "It was the black wig."

His eyes sparked with amusement, and something else. Awareness, she thought. Desire. He leaned closer to her. "It wasn't the black wig," he said softly. "Trust me."

"I do trust you. The moment you swept me onto that ballroom dance floor, I knew I could trust you."

"Sure that's not just jet lag talking?"

She smiled. "Very sure."

"I love you, Phoebe. I don't know if I've ever known what love could be until I spotted you in your princess dress. It got even better when I ran into you hunting slugs, making pesto, warding off a chilly morning in an old sweater at the library."

"I'm not what you're used to —"

"I love you, Phoebe. Not some idea of you."

His hand eased over her shoulder. She had on a sleeveless top, could feel the warmth of his skin on hers.

"Daphne has invited us to lunch at her home in Hollywood Hills," Noah said. "Julius Hartley and Loretta will join us. That's on Thursday. Then I thought we could drive up the coast to my winery. When do you have to be back at work?"

"Whenever I want." She placed her hand on his, on her shoulder. "If I want to go back. My future's wide open, too."

They were lost then. She could see it in his eyes, feel it as he withdrew his hand from hers and skimmed it down her bare arm. He was so close to her. So impossibly sexy. She reeled with a desire that was scarily intense and unrelenting. It made her feel vulnerable and open, as if she couldn't hide anything from Noah even if she wanted to — even if she tried.

He was deliberate, as smooth and centered as he had been when he'd taken her into his arms in Boston, when he'd helped her pick basil and mint and she'd watched him chase after Buster.

When he'd pushed his way through the debris from the storm and found her and her nephews in the library attic.

He was careful of her cuts, asked her if she was okay. She knew what he meant. Her heart skipped as she looked at him in the milky light. Their clothes were already scattered. She took in the ripples of lean muscle on his chest and arms. Damn, she thought. She could have stitches and she still wouldn't want to stop now.

She nodded. "Don't worry." She draped her arms over his shoulders, heard the raggedness in her voice. How was she supposed to talk when she could hardly breathe? When her body was tingling, quaking for him to touch her. She managed a smile. "No holding back."

He responded immediately, lowering her onto the bed, easing on top of her. Every touch, every caress, every kiss made her ache with wanting him. He left no inch of her, no part of her, untouched. As tender as

461

he was, he was hard all over. She touched him everywhere, explored his body, touching, tasting. He was so controlled, so focused . . . until he wasn't.

When he sank into her, she cried out, felt him try to ease up, to slow down, but it didn't work — and she didn't want it to. She grabbed hold of his hips and gave herself up to him and the sensations taking over her.

"Phoebe," he breathed. "Phoebe . . ."

She heard the concern in his voice even as he didn't slacken his pace, didn't stop. "I'm okay." She clutched him. "I love you, Noah."

She barely got the words out before they both lost control. She'd never experienced anything like it before. Time seemed suspended. It was as if they were the only two people in the universe. She cried out with abandon, wrapped her legs around him as he drove into her one last time.

They collapsed together. She could feel his heart racing, his skin warm under her palms. She'd dreamed of mind-blowing sex with a man she loved but had convinced herself it would never happen.

And yet here she was, with Noah.

He turned onto his side and locked his eyes with hers. After a moment, he touched the curve of one finger to her cheek. "Why didn't you tell me that you'd never —"

"Because it doesn't matter." She caught her breath. "Didn't matter."

He kissed her softly. "I'll be more careful next time."

She took his hand into hers and smiled. "I hope not."

Noah enjoyed showing Phoebe the NAK offices. She wanted to see everything and talk to everyone, and she was interested in every detail of NAK's work. He'd already met with his executive team and set up a formal meeting to redefine his role with the company.

Things were changing, because — well, things always changed.

And because of Phoebe. He loved talking to her. He loved listening to her, and making love to her. After two days together, he was as certain as ever that they belonged together. She was kind, intelligent, courageous and so damn beautiful.

She was also still at least a little afraid of what the changes loving him meant for her.

"I thought I could predict my future," she said as she looked out at the view from his office windows. "But then you decided to dog sit Buster."

"I knew Olivia had an idea of who my

princess was."

"If you hadn't stayed in Knights Bridge, my swashbuckler would have remained a mirage." She smiled at him. "But you're no mirage."

He expected he'd proved that over the past two days. He winked at her. "You've got that right, princess." He stood next to her, slipping an arm around her waist. "My best friend is marrying one of your best friends. We'd have found each other."

Phoebe leaned against his arm. "I can't wait for Olivia and Dylan's wedding. I love a happy ending."

Noah kissed her on the top of her head. They'd showered together that morning, and he could still smell the shampoo she'd used on her hair. "Phoebe . . ." For the first time since she'd arrived in San Diego, he found himself struggling for the right words. He'd had an engagement ring delivered to his house at the winery. The timing didn't feel too soon. It felt just right. Perfect, even. Finally smiled at her. "We'll write our own happy ending."

Her smile reached her eyes. "We already are."

They headed down to the lobby together. They didn't want to keep Daphne Stewart waiting. They'd take their time driving up the coast to his winery and enjoying their stay there.

Then they'd go back to Knights Bridge.

Dear Reader,

Thank you for reading *That Night on Thistle Lane.* I hope you enjoyed the story! Since I grew up in a small town on the western edge of the Quabbin Reservoir, I'm having the best time writing books set in the Swift River Valley and surrounding hills. You can find scenes and even a video on my website depicting this beautiful part of rural New England.

I've appreciated hearing from people with ties to the "lost" towns of Dana, Enfield, Greenwich and Prescott, all depopulated and razed to create the massive reservoir. Old roads and trails lace the protected wilderness, much of it open to the public. When I walk there, I look for cellar holes and other remnants of the people who used to live in this beautiful valley, but most of all I just enjoy the incredible scenery.

If you haven't read Dylan and Olivia's story yet, it's called *Secrets of the Lost Summer.* It actually starts in early spring, when those of us in northern climates are eager for March to turn into a lamb.

I'm looking forward to whatever's next for fictional Knights Bridge and the Frosts, Sloans, O'Dunns . . . and, of course, our guys from San Diego, Dylan McCaffrey and

Noah Kendrick. It's a lot of fun for me, and I'm so glad to have you join me!

Please visit www.carlaneggers.com for updates, links, goodies and photos, and join me on Facebook, Twitter and Pinterest. And write to me anytime at Carla@Carla Neggers.com. I'd love to hear from you.

Happy reading,
Carla

# ABOUT THE AUTHOR

**Carla Neggers** is the *New York Times* bestselling author of many novels, including *Heron's Cove, Secrets of the Lost Summer, Saint's Gate, The Whisper, The Mist, The Angel, The Widow,* and *Cold Pursuit.* She lives with her family in New England.

The employees of Thorndike Press hope you have enjoyed this Large Print book. All our Thorndike, Wheeler, and Kennebec Large Print titles are designed for easy reading, and all our books are made to last. Other Thorndike Press Large Print books are available at your library, through selected bookstores, or directly from us.

For information about titles, please call:
 (800) 223-1244

or visit our Web site at:
 http://gale.cengage.com/thorndike

To share your comments, please write:
 Publisher
 Thorndike Press
 10 Water St., Suite 310
 Waterville, ME 04901